A Miracle on Charles Street

PASCO A. VERDUCCI

Bloomington, IN Milton Keynes, UK

AuthorHouse™
1663 Liberty Drive, Suite 200
Bloomington, IN 47403
www.authorhouse.com
Phone: 1-800-839-8640

AuthorHouse™ *UK Ltd.*
500 Avebury Boulevard
Central Milton Keynes, MK9 2BE
www.authorhouse.co.uk
Phone: 08001974150

©2006 Pasco A. Verducci. All rights reserved.

No part of this book may be reproduced, stored in a retrieval system, or transmitted by any means without the written permission of the author.

First published by AuthorHouse 12/28/2006

ISBN: 978-1-4259-1673-2 (sc)
ISBN: 978-1-4259-1672-5 (hc)

Library of Congress Control Number: 2006921296

Printed in the United States of America
Bloomington, Indiana

This book is printed on acid-free paper.

This book is dedicated to my mother and father,
Anthony and Della Verducci

CONTENTS

Prologue   *ix*

1	The Family	*1*
2	The New Kid on the Block	*4*
3	Crazy Ray DeStefanis	*9*
4	The Birthday Party	*16*
5	Patty Turns His Back	*34*
6	Team Work	*65*
7	Dick "El Toro" Di Meo	*86*
8	In the Ring	*153*
9	Patty Becomes a Marine	*161*
10	Mei Feng	*174*
11	Patty Comes Home	*206*
12	Patty Gets Married	*226*
13	Henry Reads the Riot Act	*252*
14	New York	*259*
15	Alabama	*309*
16	Alaska	*339*

PROLOGUE

For generations, the DiMarco family lived in the village of Cassino, nestled at the foot of Monte Cassino 50 kilometers south of Rome. They maintained a modest plot of land with a small orchard of citrus trees and a vineyard from which they produced table wine. Their villa was positioned just below the Abby of St. Benedict in a grove of umbrella pines that allowed for mild winters so that they could sustain a lifestyle of unhurried pleasure.

In the early twentieth century, the family's circumstances began to change. With the combination of ever-rising taxes, and stiff competition from the semi-tropical lands of California and Florida, which were now exporting traditionally Italian crops, it became increasingly difficult for the DiMarcos' to support themselves. Finally, the head of the family, Papa Pasquale DiMarco, made the decision to seek a better fortune in America. In 1926 he took his three daughters and two youngest sons with him across the Atlantic ocean to settle in the Charles Street section of Providence, Rhode Island.

Pasquale's eldest son, Frank, remained behind in Italy with his wife to care for the family's land and to pursue a promising career in professional boxing. Two years passed, and although the checks being sent from America were getting larger, and his victories in the ring were becoming more numerous, the burden of the farm was too great. Frank's wife was growing wary of his fighting lifestyle and desperately wanted a child. Together, they came to the conclusion that they would have to sell their land and join the rest of the family in America, leaving their beloved Italy behind if only to build a better future for a son.

I THE FAMILY

"Tomorrow, we bury Papa and you will assume leadership of this family". Vito DiMarco tried to hide his emotion as he spoke. "Frank, we ask that you come live with us, here in Papa's house. We could run the brick laying business from right here on Luna Street, and the family would be together again."

The three DiMarco brothers stood in the wine cellar, their faces somber and shadowed in the dim light of a single, bare bulb. Vito and Alfred looked at one another tentatively, neither one knowing how their older brother would respond. Frank, taller than both by a good four inches, remained silent. His head was bowed forward to keep from hitting the low ceiling, and they could not see his eyes. Above them, the floorboards creaked with the shuffling of women in the kitchen, and the warm aromas of garlic and butter wafted into the room. They were preparing food for the guests who would return to the house after the funeral the following afternoon.

After what seemed to the younger brothers like ages, Frank finally stuck out his hand. Vito and Alfred broke into smiles, and the three brothers shook on the decision. "I only want to say one thing," Frank said after the hugging and hand shaking had subsided, "And that is we will continue to follow Papa's rules: when the brother's meet no women will be present and no liquor will be served."

September 23, 1939
Mariani Funeral Home in the Charles Street
Neighborhood of Providence, Rhode Island:

Frank DiMarco, known to everyone as Big Frank, calmly maneuvered his broad shoulders through the crowded funeral parlor as he detached from his wife's side and approached the caretaker, Vincent Mariani. He whispered a brief request into Mariani's ear then made his way to the front of the room where he stood waiting for the caretaker to hush the chatty group of mourners. All eyes were soon upon Big Frank, a heavyweight fighter, a man built like Mr. America, as he stood in front of his father's casket, the coffin of Pasquale DiMarco.

"This is a sad day for the DiMarcos," Big Frank began, "and I appreciate very much you all coming to pay your last respects to my papa." He was firm and to the point. "I realize that many of you have not seen each other for some time, but this is a wake, not a wedding, and if you want to laugh and greet each other, please do it outside. Thank you."

Big Frank gave a slight nod to the gathering and stepped down to resume his position alongside his wife and siblings. The implications of his statement silently spread across the room. In keeping with the Italian tradition, Big Frank, the eldest of six children, had just made his first authoritative gesture as senior advisor to the DiMarco family. The role of the Italian grandfather was always the leader and decision maker for the family: this role had previously belonged to the now deceased Pasquale DiMarco, and it would be a responsibility which in turn Frank's eldest, Patty, would one day bare.

Big Frank's wife Anna looked over to their son. His almond eyes, though dry, imparted a sincere grief as Patty waited to approach his grandfather's casket. Though only twelve years old, Patty was already six feet tall. His build was full and strong, and the boy could easily pass for sixteen. In spite of herself, a small smile broke out on Anna's lips. *"How handsome he's becoming,"* she thought to herself, *"the spitting image of his father."* She gave her husband's hand a quick squeeze, perhaps in reminiscence of the popular young man whose heart she won all those years ago, but also not without forgetting her desperate prayers during labor to her patron saint, St. Ann, *"Please, please don't take my baby. Take me instead."*

2 THE NEW KID ON THE BLOCK

The DiMarco men had laid down every single brick in the two tenement houses on Luna Street. Pasquale DiMarco had built the tenements himself once his brick laying business had started to turn a profit, and between those eight walls and six floors he was able to house almost the entire DiMarco family. Sixty-one Luna Street held the families of the three sisters, Evelyn, Josephine, and Marie. Next door in number 63, the families of Vito and Alfred lived over Pasquale's own airy apartment with its high ceilings on the first floor. The day of the move onto Luna Street, Anna, now called Mama Anna was overwhelmed with the amount of unpacking she had to do. All three of her sisters-in-law had come over to lend her a hand, though in truth they gossiped more than they helped. Amidst all the boxes, Anna caught site of Patty's dark hair. "Patty could you do me a favor and run to the store for me?" she called out. Patty appeared in front of her with a scowl.

"Going to the store is women's work," he replied.

"Patty," she said, "Can't you see I'm too busy to go myself right now? Your father will be coming home soon and we have nothing to eat in this house. Besides, all the kids are at the playground, no one's going to see you."

Realizing he had no choice, Patty gave in. "All right, I'll go. But I swear it's just this once."

Half an hour later Patty turned onto Luna Street whistling a Frank Sinatra tune, effortlessly carrying two heaping bags of groceries in his long arms. A group of about 40 kids were playing in the street directly in front of his house. Patty abruptly stopped. His back tensed, and for a moment he froze in the hopes that he would somehow go unnoticed. His hopes, though, were in vain.

"Oh how sweet, the new kid's carrying groceries home to his mommy," Steve, the leader of the neighborhood gang, chanted loud enough for everyone on the block to hear.

"Mama's boy!" his right hand man, Johnny Petrarca chided in.

Patty tried to ignore the boys and started walking again, but they jumped in front of his path, blocking the way. "Where are you going so fast, Patty-boy? Mama going to be worried if you're late?" Patty looked up, his dark eyes burning, but said nothing. In the crowd three of his cousins watched, unable to help.

Meanwhile, Patty's younger brother, Henry, had been looking out the bottom floor window of 61 Luna Street watching the scene unfold. "Come quick, Mama," he called out, "the boys aren't letting Patty through!" Anna ran to the window, and after realizing what a tight spot her son was in, she instinctively began to rush to his aid. Her sisters-in-law stopped her at the door.

"This is something he needs to handle alone," Marie said, arms crossed in a firm stance. "If you help him now, they'll only call him a sissy, and he'll never be able to carry the leadership as his father and grandfather did." At this, Mama Anna started to sob and prayed to St. Anne to protect her child from what seemed like certain harm. Frank, who had recently returned home and was still in his work clothes, stood behind her without a word. This was the code of the children and it was not their place to interfere.

"If you're outnumbered, try to protect yourself as much as possible." The words from his father's lessons raced through Patty's head and he waited to make a move.

"Always try to spot the weakest link – if you take at least one down, they will not escape without a casualty." Patty was on his toes. *"And never, never turn your back where you can't see what's going on."* Big Frank had ingrained these fighting techniques into Patty's head ever since he was four years old.

The hisses and shouts of the gang grew louder as the kids closed in on Patty. Many neighbors opened their windows to get a better view of what was going on; among them was Grandpa Rossi. The old man sighed and shook his head saying, "It's a shame such a nice, good looking boy is going to get hurt." Though fights between gangs and their leaders were common in this neighborhood, never before had one been on such a public display.

The gang tightened around Patty. Steve Cardossa ripped the grocery bags from Patty's hands and threw them to the ground. There was the sound of breaking glass. "What are you going to do now, mama's boy"?" Steve laughed. "We don't have no place for a sissy like you on our street." Patty remained poised. He clenched his fists, his burning eyes reading Steve's every move. From the porch, Big Frank silently pushed his son on.

In a sudden change of events, Steve Cardossa abruptly turned and grabbed Patty's cousin Vito into a bear hug. "I'll take care of the DiMarco family," he declared, and made as if he would strike little Vito first. Before anyone had time to react, Patty responded with a left hook to Steve's throat. The rest of the gang stood in shock as their leader fell to his knees gasping for air. Little Vito scampered off. *"Always throw the first punch at whoever is trying to hurt you,"* thought Patty, and he picked up a broken bottle from the spilled groceries at his feet. Before Steve had time to recover his breath, Patty grabbed him by the hair and held the broken bottle to his face. Steve's lips trembled.

Inside, Anna gasped and covered her mouth. Tears streamed down her face. "Stop him Frank!" She pleaded to her husband, "Stop this right now before our son murders that boy right in front of our eyes!"

"Quiet Anna," said Big Frank. Out in the street Frank saw the mirror image of himself, and he knew Patty was strong enough and intelligent enough to do the right thing. For a brief moment Patty looked up, seeing his father on the porch. Frank spoke to him with his eyes. He would wait until the last possible minute before stepping in.

Meanwhile, across the street the Rossi family was in a panic. They couldn't bear to watch Steve, or anyone else for that matter, get seriously hurt. "Why doesn't Big Frank step in and declare a draw so both boys could save face?" Papa Rossi demanded, his eyes glued to the scene, but barely were those words out of his mouth when Patty spoke to the gang.

"I didn't move to Luna Street to do any harm to any one of you," he shouted, still holding Steve by the hair. "My intentions are to be one of you."

With Patty's words the entire street let out a sigh of relief. Steve Cardossa stared at Patty in disbelief, still out of breath, shocked at the rapid change of events. Johnny Petrarca boldly stepped out from the crowd and extended a grimy hand. "You have just defeated our leader," he said, "and under the code of our gang, you Patty, are now our new leader."

Steve Cardossa got to his feet and composed himself as best he could. He rubbed his neck, grimacing in pain. "Johnny's right, you're the leader now, Patty," Steve said and humbly stuck out a hand. The rest of the gang broke into a cheer, "Patty! Patty!" they chanted and everyone, including Patty's cousins, took their turn shaking Patty's hand. "Patty! Patty!" This chant would follow Patty for a good part of his life.

In a matter of minutes, Patty had gone from the new kid on the block to the leader of Luna Street. His family was overjoyed. Big Frank could proudly be heard saying, "I knew that Patty has my blood and would never harm anyone." Frank had taught his son to think things through before he made a move in any situation. "Never turn your back on an enemy, son," Big Frank said to Patty as he walked back inside, the father's eyes sparkling with triumph.

"Sorry about the groceries, Mama," was all Patty said.

3 CRAZY RAY DESTEFANIS

News traveled fast in the neighborhood, and soon everyone knew the story of how Patty DiMarco became the new leader of Luna Street. It didn't take long, though, before Patty had to prove that his leadership was well deserved. The challenge came from Metcalf Street, only two streets over from Luna Street. The leader of the Metcalf Street gang was Ray DeStefanis known to everyone as Crazy Ray. Crazy Ray did not like anyone thinking they were tougher than he was, and he made it known that he was ready to take Patty on.

Three weeks had gone by since Patty had fought with Steve Cardossa, but since then Patty, Steve, and Johnny had become the best of friends. Everywhere Patty went, Steve and Johnny were at his side. "Set up the fight for Saturday down at the playground," Patty told Steve after hearing about the challenge from Crazy Ray. It was the rule that in a declared challenge only the two leaders fought it out. The rest of the gang could attend, but not participate. The winner of the fight would then become the leader of both gangs.

Crazy Ray DeStefanis had a reputation for being a dirty fighter who would try to catch you off guard. To compensate for his smaller stature he would try to get a bear hug around you then bite as hard as he could. Crazy Ray often drew blood.

"How are you going to plan your attack?" Steve asked Patty.

"I'm not sure yet," said Patty, but there was a stirring in his eyes that said more. Patty was often meager with his words, but his eyes always spoke loudly – eyes identical to his father's.

Back in Italy, the fire in Big Frank's eyes was legendary. He had been a favored contender for the Italian heavyweight championship, and rumor had it that his stare was stronger than his punch. Although moving to America had terminated Big Frank's plans, the dream to be a champion fighter lived on in Patty.

Excitement was running high in the neighborhood when the news broke out that Patty had accepted a challenge from Crazy Ray. Steve reported back to Patty and Johnny that he had arranged the fight for this coming Saturday. Patty responded, telling Steve, "I want you and Johnny to get to Ray's people and let them know that I'm concerned about his cheap way of fighting, and that I'm worried about the outcome of the fight."

"You're not afraid of him, are you?" asked Steve.

Patty's eyes burned. "Don't ask questions!" he shouted. "Do what I tell you to do. I'm still the leader." Both Johnny and Steve put their heads down to show respect and Patty shook both their hands to show there were no hard feelings. The two boys ran off to deliver their message. "Oh, and one other thing," Patty called after them, "Find out if Crazy Ray's right handed or left."

Later that day, Johnny and Steve discussed Patty's situation. They knew that their message to Crazy Ray would hurt Patty's reputation and show fear. Though it was the Italian custom not to discuss an issue further after shaking hands on it, Johnny and

Steve could not help but speak of their concern. However, this was not a desertion from Patty, for the boys were still young and no one was teaching them any better. They did not have fathers like Big Frank who pounded it into Patty's head that if he kept his eyes closed, his nose clean, and his mouth shut, he might just live to be a hundred years old.

Johnny and Steve had given the message of Patty's uncertainty to Crazy Ray's people who in turn reported it to Crazy Ray. When Ray heard of Patty's concerns, he started laughing hysterically. He was sure that Patty was afraid of him, and his confidence began to grow. Word of Patty's fear was also spreading fast throughout the school. Even the girls chattering in the cafeteria were heard saying, "I guess Patty's not as tough as we thought." Soon the rumor reached the number one gang, which was lead by the Salerno brothers, Fat Salerno and his brother Mike. The Salerno brothers controlled the whole school and the entire Charles Street neighborhood. It was their cousin, Skinny Weasel who gave them the news. Wherever they went, the Weasel was nearby reporting back to his cousins everything he heard. The Salerno brothers had been keeping a particularly close eye on Patty.

Word that Patty was shying away from Crazy Ray also reached another gang leader, Danny Boyle. Boyle was the leader of the Irish neighborhood bordering Charles Street. He had heard about Patty's fight on Luna Street and had also been keeping close tabs on him ever since. Being new in the neighborhood, Patty didn't know many of the guys, but people were starting to take notice of him, and Johnny and Steve were bringing him up to date fast.

Patty's first encounter with the Salerno brothers came in the schoolyard one day after lunch. It was early November and the ground was covered with brownish leaves. From across the yard, Patty could see the Salerno brothers, like two hefty bowling balls in their black coats, heated in conversation with a tall, black boy.

"The black kid's Butterball," Johnny whispered in Patty's ear. "He controls all of the black gangs in the school." Fat Salerno could be heard shouting that all the blacks should stay at the far end of the schoolyard. They were ganging up on Butterball who was only with two of his people at that moment.

The scene sparked a fury inside of Patty. Immediately, he grabbed Johnny and Steve and some of his gang members and shouted, "Let's go! Follow me." Patty crossed the schoolyard, pounding through the leaves and stepped right up in between Butterball and the Salerno gang. Such a gesture was unprecedented! Fat Salerno went into a rage, "What you trying to do, side in with the blacks? Who do you think you are? Step aside, this is not your place!" Patty did not say a word in response. Instead he just stood his ground next to Butterball, his intentions clear in fixed expanse of his thick shoulders.

Other Salerno gang members heard the commotion and started to move in on Patty and Butterball. Patty's gang stepped in close behind to support Patty. On the sidelines watching all of this stood Crazy Ray and his gang. Danny Boyle and his gang also stopped to watch the action. This competition was not a challenge and therefore rules did not pertain. Someone threw a punch.

Just then, the bell rang signaling lunchtime was over. A teacher appeared from around the corner shouting at the boys, "Break it up! Break it up!"

Fat Selerno, with his cheeks scarlet in rage yelled out to Patty, "This isn't over yet you black lover!"

Patty didn't say a word. He just stared back at Fat Salerno in silence.

As the boys dispersed and headed back to their classroom, Butterball came up to Patty. The two boys were nearly the same height, though Butterball was much thinner. He stuck out his hand and said, "You've made a friend for life Patty DiMarco, and

I won't forget it." They smiled at each other with their eyes. Butterball exchanged hands with Steve and Johnny, and then turning to Patty he said, "I want to join your gang and I want you to be the leader of my gang without a challenge. What do you say?"

Patty smiled and extended his hand to Butterball, "Welcome aboard," he said.

Patty was moving up fast – he now controlled two gangs. News of how Patty DiMarco took over another gang without exchanging fists, raced throughout the school. In the cafeteria, in the classroom, even in the teacher's conference room, Patty was being discussed. The principal of the school, Steve Mendozzi, turned to his vice principal and said, "Can you believe how popular this DiMarco boy has gotten?"

"He'll just wind up like the rest of them," the vice-principal, Johnny Bishop, remarked offhand.

"I don't know," replied Mendozzi, "He seems different from the rest. Look at what he's got going for himself, he's big for his age and I'm told he is a powerhouse; and He's quite a looker. You know, I spoke to him and his father the first day of school. His father's built as solid as a brick chimney, have you ever seen the guy?" Mendozzi didn't wait for the reply. "Also, when I shook hands with Patty, I noticed something about his eyes. He stared at me with a grin, and his eyes lit up as if they were talking. I don't know how to describe it."

"All I know is I don't like him," said Bishop. "He better stay in line as long as I'm around."

Meanwhile Johnny and Steve arranged the details of the challenge with Crazy Ray. They placed the fight at the Corliss Park Ballfield at two o'clock for the upcoming Saturday afternoon. Patty gathered his gang together and told everyone to arrive thirty minutes late. Johnny and Steve were furious at this. They were afraid that Patty was showing too much fear and they did not want to build up Crazy Ray's ego, possibly giving him an advantage. However, they said nothing of this to Patty.

At exactly two-thirty that afternoon, Patty and his gang arrived at Corliss Park. A member of Crazy Ray's gang could be heard saying, "Look how late he is, he's terrified of you Ray," and Ray chuckled to himself. Upon seeing Patty enter the field, Crazy Ray removed his shirt. Two wiry hairs protruded from his chest, and he puffed them proudly, confident that Patty was afraid. After the handshake, which was customary, Ray planned to give Patty a bear hug and *let him feel his teeth*! That surely would send Patty home running, and Crazy Ray would be the new leader of Luna Street. *"I'll be the talk of the school,"* thought Ray arrogantly.

As Patty advanced toward Ray, he also removed his shirt, and threw it to Steve. Instantly, Crazy Ray went pale. Patty's arms and chest were solid as concrete and he towered at least five inches over the now recoiling Ray. Steve and Johnny looked at one another knowingly, buoyant anticipation in their eyes. Now they understood what Patty was doing. He had tricked Crazy Ray into being unprepared. "Patty's no dope" whispered

Johnny, barely able to contain himself, "His father's been teaching him to fight since he was four!"

Patty stared Crazy Ray down with blazing eyes, prompting a flash of fear to pass through Ray's brain. Patty had unnerved his enemy just long enough to get the advantage. "Now shake hands and come out fighting," shouted Steve, and with that the fight began.

Crazy Ray DeStefanis extended his left hand for the shake. Immediately, Patty knocked his hand down with his right hand and hit him in the stomach with his left. Crazy Ray doubled over in pain. Patty hit him in the jaw with his right hand, and down went Ray! Out cold! End of fight! No one could believe how quickly it had happened and both sides started to chant, "Patty! Patty!" In a matter of minutes, Patty had just become the leader of Metcalf Street. Crazy Ray got up, still a little dazed and shook Patty's hand in respect. This time Ray shook with his right.

On the way home Steve and Johnny asked Patty, "What was that all about? Using the left hand and then the right hand?" Patty explained to them, "You know when I asked you to set up the fight?"

"Yeah."

"Remember, I also asked you to find out whether he was left-handed or right? You came back and told me right handed. Well my father told me that anyone right-handed who shakes hands with his left is going to hold your right hand down and hit you with *their* right – so I beat him to the punch."

Steve and Johnny laughed, "You taught us a lesson Patty, and we will never doubt you again." They praised Patty for being a tough leader and a shrewd person.

4 THE BIRTHDAY PARTY

The winter was now here and Patty would turn thirteen on February 21st. It wouldn't be long and then spring was coming. The winters in New England were cold with plenty of ice and snow. It sure would be a blessing to see the snow starting to melt. Anna brought it to Big Frank's attention that Patty's birthday was coming up and she wanted throw a party for him. Her son would become a teenager. She was very excited and wanted to invite everyone from the family and all of Patty's friends.

"Now wait a minute Anna," Frank said, "where are you going to put everyone? The house wasn't big enough." Anna tried to reason with Frank saying, "Frank, it's the first time one of our children's going to be a teenager."

Frank was firm, "The house is too small."

"You think of something," said Anna, "You always have a solution. You're the one in charge to bring our problems to, and I'm bringing this to you to solve the situation." Anna was trying to use psychology on Frank, for after all, being his wife she learned a lot from him. But she had to be very careful, for Frank was no fool, and would let her know about it in a second—and not in pleasant words either. Frank answered back that seeing she felt that way, he would request a meeting with his brothers Alfred and Vito. But Anna was quick to answer that it didn't have to go that way. She was afraid that Alfred and Vito would side with Frank. She knew that the brothers were like glue.

Now it was Anna's turn to reason. Patty's our son, and if we keep it between you and me, I know you will come up with the smartest solution." Anna was throwing everything at Frank in a round about way, yet she showed Frank the utmost respect. In Italian families the husband was the boss, and Anna was telling him in her own way, that she refused to see Frank's eyes telling her to shut up.

When Frank took their wedding vows and said, "until death do us part" Frank understood it to mean, "I'll be the boss 'til we die." To the Italian's, being the boss doesn't mean telling your wife what to do, rather it means you want respect from your wife, and Anna did respect him—not out of fear, but out of love.

Frank was thinking to himself while Anna was speaking, and said to her, "Why don't we have the party the first Sunday in April? We could have it outside in our big backyard. We could invite everyone and the children could play under the grapevines.

"You just want everyone to see your grapevines Frank." And Anna did not agree with that. Patty's birthday is on February 21, and that's when we will celebrate."

"Okay," answered Frank, "If you're going to be so stubborn, why don't you just think of a solution."

Anna was ready with an answer, "We could have it at St. Anne's Auditorium where we could invite everyone. We could even invite Monsignor Di Mayo, all of Patty's friends, all of our family, and we could throw Patty the best birthday party he ever had. Please Frank, it would be next to St. Anne's Church, and you know where my heart is. You know Frank, I almost died giving birth to Patty, and I prayed so hard to St. Anne, and if we had it next to the church I would feel as if St. Anne herself were invited. Please Frank," she pleaded, "It would make me happy," But she was also quick to add, "Whatever decision you make, I still love you and respect you."

Frank's magic eyes stared into hers. "Anna, come here," he said and embraced her, "I love you too." Over her husband's shoulder, Anna looked at the statue of St. Anne with the lit candle. She winked to St. Anne and whispered, "Thank you."

Frank and Anna did not waste any time in planning the birthday party. Anna asked Evelyn, Marie, Josephine, Marline and Jenny to help organize the party. For sure it would be one of the biggest events of the year. Anna told Patty about the party, and Patty didn't say anything at all, but his eyes lit up. Meanwhile, Big Frank asked the Monsignor if they could use the hall. He said they could as long as they kept it orderly, did not serve any liquor, and cleaned up afterwards. Big Frank offered the Monsignor a hundred dollars for the use of the hall but Monsignor DiMayo refused. So Frank said he would put a hundred-dollar bill in the basket when he went to church on Sunday, and the Father would know that the hundred-dollar bill had come from him. Mama Anna told Patty that he could invite any of his friends including all of his school friends and his homeroom teacher, Miss Cox.

Preparations were being made. The aunts would do all the cooking; it was looking more like a wedding than a birthday party. Mama asked Uncle Vito to bring his accordion. She was so excited. She said to Patty, "Bring your guitar and I want to hear you sing a song for Mama. Patty, you have a beautiful voice. You'll have all the girls chasing you." If she had known the future, she never would have said that.

Frank went to the school and asked the principal, Mr. Mendozzi, if he would like to come to the birthday party, but Mr. Mendozzi declined the invitation, claiming he had another commitment. Frank said to Mr. Mendozzi, "I would like to invite Patty's homeroom teacher."

"Just hang on and I'll call her for you," Mr. Mendozzi responded. He rang her room and said, "Miss Cox, did you know that your pupil Patty DiMarco is having a birthday party?"

Miss Cox was quick to respond, "No, I did not."

"Well, Patty's father is here with me and he has a personal invitation for you. What do you say?"

Miss Cox answered, "I feel honored and I would be thrilled to go. Tell Patty's father thank you and that I will be looking forward to meeting him at the party."

Mr. Mendozzi extended a hand to Big Frank, "It's been a pleasure to meet you Mr. DiMarco, and I can see who your son takes after – he's the spitting image of you. He must be all of you, six feet and still growing. He looks more like 17 than 13 though, and he's a very handsome boy too. How tall are you Frank?"

"Six feet four and a half."

"I think Patty's going to be as tall as you. By the way Frank, were you always a brick layer?"

Frank answered, "No. Back in Italy, I was a heavyweight fighter, but moving to America, I gave it up. My wife Anna didn't like me being a fighter, so I went to work for my father, with my two brothers – we all worked together in the brick laying business. And now with the passing of my father, my brothers and myself run the business."

Just then, they were interrupted by a knock on the office door. In walked Johnny Bishop, the assistant principal. Mr. Mendozzi introduced Frank to them and Mr. Bishop was surprised at Frank's size. When Frank extended his hand to him, Mr. Bishop could not believe the strength of his grasp. It felt like his hand was in a vice.

Mr. Bishop excused himself, and said that he would see Mr. Mendozzi later. Mr. Mendozzi was thinking to himself that he knew Mr. Bishop didn't like Patty very much.

"Frank, it's a pleasure to meet you, and I see who Patty takes after," said Mr. Bishop.

Upon walking home, Frank was satisfied that he met with the principal and would soon be meeting Patty's homeroom teacher. Frank wanted his son to have a good education, and knowing the teachers wouldn't hurt one bit. He also figured if Patty had done anything wrong, he knew the principal and that he could always get in touch with him.

Mama DiMarco asked Patty's two best friends, Steve and Johnny, to invite everyone that Patty knew. She wanted this to be a party her son would never forget. So Steve and Johnny invited everyone. Patty was still getting to know people. After all, he was still considered the new kid on the block, but his popularity was growing rapidly. He invited his whole classroom, and everyone accepted his personal invitation gladly. He even asked Miss Cox if she would like to come. She answered, "Thanks, but I've already been invited by Mr. DiMarco. Of course I'll be there."

Even Crazy Ray was invited. He answered, "You know I'll be there. I wouldn't miss Patty's birthday for all the tea in China." He also was bringing all the guys from Metcalf Street. Crazy Ray said to Steve, "I have no hard feelings with Patty. He beat me fair and square and now he's my leader."

As soon as Steve met up with Butterball, he invited him and all of his friends. Butterball asked, "You sure it's all right if I come?"

Steve answered, "Of course. As a matter of fact, I'm in charge of the seating arrangements and I'm seating you next to Patty."

Butterball said, "Can I ask you a question?"

"Sure."

"Are you inviting the Salerno brothers?"

Steve's answer was, "Heaven forbid. You see Butterball; you don't invite the Hatfields and the McCoys to the same event. It wouldn't look right with Patty's mother and father there. You know the Weasel might make wise remarks. It's not that Patty's afraid of them, but that's not the place to let that happen. That day will come and I promise you that, Butterball. And I predict the outcome on that match."

Butterball was quick to ask, "When will that happen?"

"That's all up to Patty," Steve answered.

In the meantime, the guest list was growing larger and larger. Word was getting around that Patty was having a birthday party, and of all places, in a hall. Boys and girls were approaching Steve and Johnny, asking if they could come. They said, "Sure." The list was getting bigger and bigger. Johnny said, "We better count heads and see how many we got."

Steve said, "Yeah, I think we better do that too." After the head count, they had 250. Steve said, "I didn't think it was that many. I think we better stop and get in touch with Mama DiMarco. I don't think she'll go along with this."

So the two boys went to see Mama DiMarco. They asked if they could come into speak to her about the kids they invited to the party. Mama was thrilled to see them, and told them so. She offered them some homemade cookies that she had baked. Both boys agreed to have some. "Now, boys," Mama asked, "What about the kids you invited?" Johnny and Steve stared at each other and Anna immediately asked, "What's wrong. Tell me, how many are coming?"

Steve replied that they had invited two hundred and fifty, and even more wanted to come. "Oh my God!" Anna answered, "That's too many. It's not that I don't want that many and it's not that the hall won't hold that many, but we are making all the food, and we just couldn't make that amount." Mama tried to explain to the boys that including the family, there would be a little over 300 people. "Boys, don't feel bad. I did ask you to invite his friends, but I didn't know that Patty was so popular in such a short time."

Steve said, "We'll just have to tell most of them that they can't come."

"Now wait a minute," Anna answered. "We don't want to do that just yet. It might make matters worse. Just give me time to think … How about we invite his homeroom, you two boys and a couple of his other close friends to the birthday party at one o'clock and the rest of his friends to the reception at three o'clock. What do you think guys?"

They thought it was a good idea, and celebrated with a handful of cookies. Anna said, "The kids will love it. I asked Patty to bring his guitar and he is going to sing."

"You know," Steve said, "I play the drums, Johnny plays the sax, and Ray plays the piano, we could have one hell of a time. I'll call Patty and tell him we should get together and practice some songs."

Mama said, "Boys, I want you to keep it a secret. Frank and I were thinking about buying Patty a birthday gift that would fit right in with his singing. Be sure to tell everyone that you two and Patty will be performing live music at the birthday party and that Patty will sing.

Although February 21st was a Friday, the birthday party would be held on Sunday.

Just then Patty arrived home and everyone greeted him. Steve and Johnny said that they wanted to talk to him. Mama said, "Take your friends down to the cellar and show them your guitar."

Patty said, "Let's go."

Steve and Johnny said that they hadn't known that he played the guitar. Steve told Patty that he played the drums, Johnny played the saxophone, and Ray played the piano. He was just as surprised as they were. "Look guys," he said, "why don't you go get your instruments and we'll see how we sound together."

The two ran out hurriedly, and Mama asked, "Where are your friends going Patty?"

He explained that they were going home to get their instruments, and would she mind if they practiced some? Mama said of course she wouldn't mind, "that's what a finished cellar is for." Mama beamed from ear to ear. She was so happy that she would be able to hear her son play and sing. She immediately called her sisters-in-law Evelyn and Marie. Josephine was not at home. She told them the news that Patty and his best friends were going to practice as a band.

Evelyn and Marie came over from next door right away, because they wanted to hear the boys play, and more important, to hear their nephew sing. The aunts had never heard Patty sing before. Anna told them that when they lived in Eagle Park, Patty had sung in a minstrel at Veazie Street Elementary School. Mama was so happy explaining this to her sisters-in-law that tears were coming from her eyes. She was so emotional, proud and happy, telling them about how the audience stood up and clapped, hollering, "More! More!" Frank and Anna were hugging each other with joy. Anna again was crying with much happiness. Frank immediately asked Anna, "Why isn't he back on the stage singing?"

Anna replied, "Let's go find out." Anna immediately started hugging her son saying, "What a wonderful voice you have Patty! I'm so proud of you!"

Frank extended his left hand to his son to congratulate him. Patty did not shake his father's hand but asked, "Papa, why 'your left hand? Are you mad at me?"

Frank answered, "No Patty, I'm so excited and proud of you, I wasn't thinking." He hugged Patty and shook his hand with his right. Just then, Patty's eyes met his father's eyes and he could tell what his father was thinking. Patty said, "I love you Pop."

Frank said to Patty, "I'm going to buy you a brand new guitar."

As Mama recounted this story to Evelyn and Marie, the boys were getting their act together downstairs. They could hear the boys playing. Just then Patty's brothers Tommy and Henry, and sisters, Ann Marie and Carol ran inside saying they heard music all the way outside and why was the radio so loud? Mama explained that it was their brother, Steve, Ray and Johnny practicing downstairs. And Patty would also be singing.

The children asked, "Mama, could we go downstairs to listen?"

Mama said, "You could, but I don't want you to interfere with your brother practicing."

"Okay, Mama," the children said.

As they went downstairs, Patty saw them coming. Anna Marie asked Patty if they could listen. They promised that they would be very quiet.

Patty replied, "Of course, and hugged Anna and Carol, for he really loved his sisters. Patty always played a game with them asking, "Who do you love?"

The girls answered, "Patty."

Meanwhile, upstairs Evelyn asked Anna to finish the story. "Why didn't Patty come back out on the stage to sing again?" To her it seemed pretty funny.

"When we asked Patty why, he said he didn't know any other songs. He just knew *Night and Day* that Frank Sinatra sang. Patty loved Frank Sinatra. Patty's teacher Ms. Johnson said it was unbelievable, the reception Patty had received, but she said she understood the situation that Patty came unprepared. She said she would explain it to the audience and see what they had to say about it.

"So she made her appearance on stage and quieted them down," said Anna. "The teacher explained that Patty didn't know any other songs, but he would sing the same song again. At this, the crowd went wild chanting 'More! More!' Frank and I just couldn't believe it. We felt like we were at Carnegie Hall. Then Patty went right on stage and sang again. You could tell he was not ashamed one bit."

"What happened next?" Evelyn asked.

Anna looked down. "Something happened that was so upsetting that I'm too embarrassed to talk about."

But Evelyn and Marie insisted that she tell them. "We promise that we will never repeat it. After all, Anna, he's our nephew and we wouldn't do anything to hurt him. Please tell us Anna."

"Oh, alright, but you promised." They both nodded in anticipation. "You see, there were a lot of young girls in the audience, and when Patty sung again, Frank and I could hear the girls chanting 'Patty! Patty!' They were going crazy. Some were even crying. Frank and I were watching from the stage and all of a sudden we see girls taken their panties off and throwing them on the stage. The teacher closed the curtains and told Patty to stop singing, though she did say to him that it wasn't his fault. She didn't think it would turn into that."

"Oh my God," Evelyn said, "what did Frank say about it?"

"He didn't say a word," Anna said. "But the principal, Mrs. Applegate ran to the back of the stage and told Frank, me and Patty that he did nothing wrong. She extended her hand out to Patty and said, 'You got one heck of a voice, and you got one great future ahead of you. Lots of luck.' I was so embarrassed."

Just then, Anna Marie ran upstairs saying, "Mama, Patty's getting ready to sing!" The aunts followed Anna Marie downstairs, giddy to hear Patty sing. Anna said, "I'll be right down. The baby just woke up and I need to change him, then we'll both come down."

Patty asked, "Where is my mother?"

"She's getting Anthony, she'll be right down."

Aunt Evelyn asked Patty if he would sing a song for them. He said, "Sure what do you want to hear?"

"How about *Night and Day*?"

Anna walked in and said, "Patty, why don't you sing them that song."

"Okay, Mama. But we're practicing, so just that song, and then we're going to play different ones."

Patty sang *Night and Day* for everyone. It was unbelievable how well Patty could sing. The aunts were very much surprised, and told Mama that Patty sang beautifully and that they were quite impressed. Mama was so proud she just smiled. When Patty was done singing, everyone applauded including Steve, Ray, and Johnny. Aunt Evelyn said to Patty, "You're tremendous! I didn't know you could sing like that. It was just beautiful! What I want from you is your autograph, because I know you're going places with that voice."

"What do you think, Mama?" Patty turned to his mother.

"Whatever you want to be Patty, it's up to you," she replied, beaming. "But whatever you're going to be, I want you to be the best."

Mama told the boys that they were welcome to use the cellar to practice any time they wanted. And they started practicing almost every day.

The weeks were going by fast and February 21st was only two weeks away. The boys had their act together and were now playing all kinds of music. During practice, Johnny stopped and said, "Patty, I never thought you could sing like that! You know, you've really got a great voice."

Steve asked, "Tell me Patty, do you want to be a singer or are you afraid of it?"

Patty thought for a moment and replied, "I think I want to be where it matters."

"What are we feeding, a king?" Frank remarked. "Anna, you got a lot of food here."

"No, "Anna said, "I just want my son to have the best birthday party he ever had. Be careful of the cake, I want that to be delivered in the car, not in any of the trucks."

Patty, Johnny and Steve were packing their instruments in one of the trucks. Anna called out, "Don't forget your music sheets. I want you to play real nice."

"Yes Ma'am, Mrs. DiMarco," they replied. But they turned to Patty and asked, "Do we really need the music?"

"No we don't," he replied, "But out of respect for my mother, let's take them along anyway. My mother's proud that I can read music."

Johnny said, "We'll put them on the music stand, and no one will know we're not reading them."

"Come on guys," Patty said, "No cheating."

When they arrived at the hall, Anna was surprised at how perfectly the men decorated and set up the tables – just right. The table in front was for Patty, Steve, Johnny Petrarca, Ray, Butterball, Frank and Anna. "Is this how you want your table to be, Patty"?" she asked.

"Yes," he replied.

Around twelve-thirty almost all of the family had arrived. They were congratulating Patty on his birthday, and commenting on how beautiful the hall looked. Monsignor Di Mayo; arrived, and he was seated at the front table. All the boys greeted Monsignor Di Mayo; he was the coach of the baseball team and knew them all well. The boys joked with him in a friendly way. He was carrying a baseball bat, which he planned to give to Patty for his birthday. "Patty DiMarco" was engraved in the wood.

Pretty soon, Steve started joking with Father asking, "What are you going to do with that bat, Father?"

Father replied, "Any of you guys step out of line and I'm going to tap you on the rump."

Just then, Miss Cox came in. She easily spotted Patty among all his classmates, and immediately went up and wished him a happy birthday, kissing him on the cheek. She said, "What did you do, grow another inch since yesterday?" Patty's mother and father were wondering who this beautiful woman was. When Patty brought her over to introduce her to Frank and Anna, they were thrilled to meet his homeroom teacher. Anna told her that she would be sitting at the front table. Anna was striking up a conversation with her. She was delighted that she now knew Patty's teacher. Miss Cox was telling her what a wonderful son she had, and what a good student he was. "You know Anna," Miss Cox said, "Patty's getting very popular with his classmates, and his marks are very good. He also tells me that he has a paper route."

"He has to help his father in the brick laying business, also," replied Anna.

"Does he earn anything from the business?"

"No, he does not."

"How many days a week does he work with his father?"

"Everyday if he has to."

"And you're telling me Frank doesn't feel he has to pay his own son?"

"You have to understand Miss Fox…"

"It's Miss Cox."

"I'm sorry," said Anna and she started thinking, why the concern? Why was she asking so many questions? "You see Miss Cox, Frank teaches the children responsibility. Patty is not just some kid we hired off the street, he is one of family and someday, the business will belong to him and his brothers and sisters."

"Well, at least Patty can keep the money from his paper route," said Miss Cox.

"No," replied Anna. He must put that money in the bank. Frank teaches the children to save their money so that they will have it when they really need it. Patty doesn't need any money right now. Frank and I take care of anything that he might need." All these explanations were making Anna upset, and she smartly added, "After all, Miss Cox, Patty doesn't mind one bit because he has respect for his parents. Now if you'll excuse me, I have to get back to the party."

Anna called to Frank and her sisters-in-law that it was time to get started with the cake because the other 200 kids would be arriving soon. And what a magnificent cake it was, complete with fourteen candles (the extra one for good luck).

Patty was over talking with Johnny, Ray and Steve, and they were teasing him about how Miss Cox kissed him. Patty replied, "I think she's just trying to be friendly," but his cheeks were bright red.

Anna lit the cake and called Patty over to blow out the candles.

"Mama," he said, "Do I really have to?"

"Yes," she said. "All your friends are here waiting for you."

The entire hall broke out singing *Happy Birthday*. To everyone's surprise, Miss Cox sat down at the piano that had been left in the room, and started playing along. Patty blew out the candles, and his mother gave him a big hug. Over his mother's shoulder Patty noticed that on the stage, someone had left an entire amplifier system, complete with microphone.

"Look!" Patty exclaimed, "Someone left a microphone here. Maybe we could use it!"

Frank smiled at his son, and then proceeded to walk up to the stage. He turned on the microphone and with his eyes aglow, made an announcement. "Happy Birthday Patty," he said. "This amplifier system is our birthday present to you."

Patty could barely contain himself. "Thank you, thank you, thank you!" he beamed. "I love you Mom and Dad!"

Miss Cox upon witnessing the scene walked over to Frank and Anna and said, "I'm absolutely amazed at how much your children respect you."

"We try. That's all we can do," replied Frank.

Everyone at the party had brought a gift for Patty, and after getting the okay from his mother, Patty sat down and opened them one by one. The kids from the street had all pitched in and bought Patty a warmup suit as well as a trophy engraved with the words, "Patty DiMarco Number One." Miss Cox and his classmates had gotten him a jogging suit. The list went on and on. There were so many gifts that they would have to take them home in one of the pick-up trucks.

Three o'clock was now approaching, and the rest of the party started to arrive, filling the hall. One group of about 30 kids came through the door with an enormous sign that read, "HAPPY BIRTHDAY PATTY!" Frank and his brothers immediately started to move all of the chairs and tables out from the middle of the hall to make room for a dance floor. The Monsignor commented to Miss Cox, "I didn't know Patty had so many friends!"

"I had no idea either," replied Miss Cox, "But I will say he is getting more and more popular. You know, there's something special about Patty. I just can't put my finger on it."

Meanwhile, Miss Cox conversed with Patty's Aunt Evelyn. Evelyn mentioned that Patty, Johnny, Ray, and Steve had formed a band and were going to perform. "I hope this doesn't turn out like it did at Veazie Street School; I would just die!" Anna interrupted, and the women looked at each other knowingly.

Evelyn was quick to respond, "We should remind Frank and the rest of the men to make sure nothing like that happens here!" Miss Cox was intrigued, but knew that Evelyn would not tell her what happened if she asked about it straight out.

"Yeah, I hope it doesn't happen again," said Miss Cox.

"Anna just wouldn't be able to take it if the girls took off their underclothes and threw them at Patty, here at his own Party! Especially in front of Monsignor Di Mayo!"

Miss Cox could not believe what she was hearing. Her head was spinning.

Oblivious to her shock, Anna broke in and said, "Now Miss Cox, will you please announce to everyone that we will now have live music supplied by Patty and his friends."

"I would love to," Miss. Cox replied.

Miss Cox got on the stage and asked for everyone's attention. "Okay," she said, "on the count of three let's all wish Patty a happy birthday! One, two, three!" And the crowd screamed in unison.

"Happy Birthday Patty!" The noise was unbelievable.

When everyone had quieted down, Miss Cox announced there would be dancing and later on Patty would sing. The crowd started clapping in excitement. Anna was incredibly uneasy, not wanting the past events to be repeated and she immediately instructed Frank to try to keep order.

The band started playing, and everyone started to dance. Frank and his brothers mingled in with the crowd, and everyone seemed to be having a wonderful time. It was not long before the kids started shouting up to Patty.

"When you going to sing Patty?"

"Yeah, come on! We want to hear you sing!"

With a nod from Patty, Steve, Ray, and Johnny began to play Frank Sinatra's *Night and Day*. As soon as Patty started singing, his deep, clear voice beautiful in the warm acoustics of the hall, the girls started to scream. "Patty! Patty!" They called out, and some of them even started to cry. Frank, the rest of the men, and even Miss Cox were madly scurrying around to make sure that the excitement would not get out of control. One girl started to scream that two girls had passed out and were lying on the floor. It seemed as if something was ready to break loose, and the adults in the place could not believe what they were witnessing. Miss Cox could not believe the girls' reactions right in front of her eyes, but at the same time she could not believe how beautifully Patty sang.

Monsignor Di Mayo was standing to the side of the stage with Anna and Frank, commenting on what a beautiful party it was, and how popular Patty had already become, when they heard the shouts about the girls who had passed out. All of the adults were rushing to the girls who had passed out, and Monsignor Di Mayo shouted to Frank, "Tell Patty to stop singing before we have a riot!"

"No more Patty, that's enough!" shouted Frank above the screams. Immediately, Patty stopped singing, a look of disappointment on his face.

"We were just starting to warm up," he said to Steve, Ray and Johnny.

"Maybe you should have sung *Ave Maria* instead," joked Steve.

While Anna and her sisters-in-law were attending to the girls who had fainted, Frank jumped up on stage and announced that the birthday party was over! He thanked everyone, but said it would be best if everyone went home. Frank knew he had to act fast, and he made the decision immediately without consulting his brothers. All of the adults were surprised to hear everyone screaming "Patty! Patty!"

Miss Cox just shook her head in disbelief and what she had just seen. "This kid's going places," she thought to herself.

5 PATTY TURNS HIS BACK

Miss Cox did not waste any time explaining what had happened at Patty's party, as she ate lunch with her fellow teachers. "Patty started to sing *Night and Day* just the way Frank Sinatra sings it. Two girls fainted and before anything else could happen Patty's father got up on stage and stopped it all."

"I've met Patty's father," Mr. Mendozzi replied, "And as far as I'm concerned he's a wonderful person, who has put a real priority on his son's education."

Miss Hazard, who was Patty's English teacher, commented that Patty was one of her brightest pupils. She said he was a good leader, and was someone who did not start trouble. "When he found out that I had lived in China for 12 years, he even asked me if I would teach him how to speak Chinese," she said, obviously thrilled with the idea.

"I see that he not only gets support from his school mates, but the teachers are in love with him too," replied Mr. Mendozzi. He stared at Miss Cox as he spoke, and she smiled back.

"Miss Hazard, when will you have the time to teach Patty Chinese, when you don't teach it in class?" asked Mr. Mendozzi.

"Patty suggested that he could come to school an hour early every day, and I could teach him then. Of course, I was going to ask your permission," Miss Hazard quickly added.

"Permission granted," laughed Mr. Mendozzi.

In the cafeteria that afternoon, everyone was discussing what had happened at the party, and Patty's incredible voice. The girls flocked around Patty, flirting with him, saying he was going to be famous someday. Crazy Ray, Steve, Johnny, and Butterball all watched on enviously. Across the cafeteria, the Salerno brothers and their cousin the Weasel stood watching the scene. Danny Boyle and his gang were also watching.

"Who does he think he is, the President?" spat Fat Selerno. "You know Stretch, when I get through with Patty he isn't going to be so pretty anymore."

"I'll bet on that," answered Stretch.

Meanwhile, the girls congratulated Patty on what an amazing singer he was. Those who had not been at the party, batted their eyelashes and said they could not wait to hear his voice. The assistant Principal Mr. Bishop and Patty's math teacher Mr. Sullivan looked on. "There's something about Patty that I just don't like," said Mr. Bishop. "I'll watch that kid like a hawk and if he steps out of line, I'm going to bring him down hard!"

"He's just big for his age, that's all," said Mr. Sullivan. "He doesn't do anything wrong. And besides he's very popular with the kids and all of his teachers. If I were you, I'd be careful about picking on him for no reason. That boy has a lot of friends and if anyone goes down it's liable to be you."

Mr. Bishop just chuckled and walked away.

Patty's eyes followed a group of girls as they strutted past him. Suddenly, a beautiful redhead turned and walked straight up to him. "I'm Stacey Boyle," she said, extending her hand. "I've heard a lot about you."

"Glad to meet you," replied Patty nonchalantly, though his heart was pounding in his chest.

"I noticed some of the other girls introducing themselves to you," Stacey went on, "and I thought I would do likewise."

Patty smiled and looked right in her eyes as he grasped her hand. She felt something go through her and trembled slightly. "What's wrong?" Patty asked, seeing her shudder.

"Oh, nothing," she answered, but she felt as if something strange yet exciting was happening to her.

"How about I walk you home after school," said Patty.

"Of course," replied Stacey.

"I'll meet you at the front door at 2:30."

Stacey nodded and turned to go, but Patty called after her. "Wait a minute Stacey. Your last name sounds familiar. Are you related to anyone I know?"

"Well, Danny Boyle is my brother," said Stacey. "I'll see you at 2:30," and she returned to her table where her girlfriends were waiting to hear what had happened and if anything was going on between her and Patty. Stacey could hardly speak, "What a guy! I can't explain. Look at me, I'm still shaking!" The girls wouldn't let her off that easy and they pressed her for more. "There's something about his eyes as he stared into mine," explained Stacey. "It's as if they were talking."

"What do you mean?" asked her best friend Jane. "Is he a devil or something?"

"Oh, no!" said Stacey. "It was a wonderful look. And he has a beautiful smile to go with it. He's just gorgeous, and…I mean…when he shook my hand he was so strong…he's just something…"

"Sounds like you're in love," interrupted Jane.

"Why do you say that?" asked Stacey innocently.

"Just look at you!" replied Jane, "You're trembling all over!"

"You know he asked to walk me home," Stacey said.

"Oh, Oh. He definitely likes you," giggled Jane.

Stacey smiled bashfully, and just then the lunch bell rang signaling it was time to go back to class. "*Saved by the bell!*" she thought to herself.

As Patty was walking back to his class with Steve, Steve asked him if Danny Boyle was going to like the fact that Patty was walking his sister home after school.

"I'm not doing anything wrong," said Patty. "It's just walking."

Finally, 2:30 came and Patty met Stacey at the front door. Stacey greeted him with "Hi Patty," and he felt as if they were old friends. Stacey had the same feeling when she first met Patty in the lunchroom.

"Will you carry my books for me?" was the first thing Stacey said.

"I don't carry books," said Patty. Stacey was utterly surprised. There were plenty of boys in the school that would be honored to carry her books anytime. She then realized that Patty was different from all the others.

"How far do you live from school," Patty asked.

"Not far at all. Just a little ways…about a mile."

As they were walking, they passed by Jack's Ice Cream Shop. Patty suggested that they go get a soda. "I would, but my father wants me home right away," explained Stacey.

"Maybe some other time, then," said Patty.

"Never mind, let's do it now," said Stacey. "We just have to make it fast or my dad will kill me!"

As Patty and Stacey walked into the shop, the other kids stared at them in awe, and greeted them as if they were King and Queen. They made their way to the corner booth and sat down, both ordering Cokes.

"How come you don't carry my books," asked Stacey tentatively.

"Look, I just don't carry books, that's all," said Patty, "and don't ask again."

Stacey could not believe how Patty was speaking to her. No one ever dared speak to her like that. Maybe it's the Italian in him, she thought to herself, for she had heard that Italian men were very stubborn, and liked being the boss. She did not mind it too much, though. She liked a boy with some masculinity and Patty sure had it. She knew she was not going to be able to make him budge, and for some reason that made her feel good. She was starting to realize how much she really liked Patty.

"What are you thinking about?" asked Patty.

"Nothing," Stacey replied.

"Where'd you get that red hair and blue eyes," asked Patty, his eyes sparkling at her.

"I take after my mother," blushed Stacey.

"Is your mother Irish too?"

"One hundred percent!"

"How many brothers and sisters do you have?" asked Patty.

"Four. Three are girls and one boy. Danny is the oldest. It's like having two dads, he's so strict, but I love him. How many in your family?"

"Six. Four are boys and two are girls. I'm the oldest, but my mother and father give us the orders. I don't boss my brothers and sisters around, but if anyone laid a hand on any one of them, I would knock their teeth out."

"Oh, I don't think anyone would do that Patty," said Stacey.

"You're probably right," he replied.

"How tall are you, Patty?"

"Six feet and still growing. I take after my father and he's six foot four."

"Were your parents born in Italy?" Patty nodded that they were. "My parents were born in Ireland," said Stacey. "They're awfully strict. My father won't let me wear lipstick until I'm 16.

The two went on like this, asking one another question after question, eager to get to know one another, unaware of the time. Stacey asked Patty if his parents gave him spending money, and Patty told her how he helped his father and uncles in their brick laying business after school in addition to his paper route. ""I put all the money I make from pedaling papers into my bank account. That's how my father wants it," explained Patty.

"But how do you buy things that you want?" protested Stacey.

"My parents get it for me."

"You know, Patty, my brother Danny also has a paper route."

"I've seen him," said Patty. "He picks up his papers at the same place that I do."

Meanwhile, with every passing minute that Stacey's light blue eyes gazed across the table into Patty's expressive dark ones, Stacey's mother waited at home growing more and more worried about what could be keeping her daughter. Stacey was already an hour late getting home from school despite the firm instructions from her father to come straight home, and so Danny was sent out to find her.

Danny jumped on his bike, and immediately headed for the soda shop. He imagined that his sister most likely had gone there to gossip with her girlfriends over a Coke. To his surprise, however, he walked in to find Stacey sitting with Patty – the two gazing at one another like lovesick puppies. Danny's blood went to his head.

Stacey's girlfriend, Jane, who was sitting at the counter, saw Danny rush into the shop and whispered to the girl on her right, "something is going to happen!" All the kids in the place started to scramble around, anxious to see what was going to happen. They all knew about Danny and most of them had heard about Patty; both the leaders of their gangs. Even the clerk behind the counter was aware of the impending scuffle, and he called back to his boss, Jack, in the kitchen that a fight was sure to break out.

Danny's freckled face was bright red. He went straight up to the corner booth where his sister sat, and yelled at Stacey that she better get herself home that instant. Stacey, utterly mortified at the scene her brother was making in the front of the entire shop, looked down at her hands. Patty jumped up.

"Look here, buddy," Patty said, his eyes locked into Danny's. "We're only talking. What is she in prison for?"

Just at that moment, Jack stepped in between the two boys. "You're not going to start anything in my place. You two boys better take your differences somewhere else!" The authority in Jack's voice made everyone silent. Stacey started to cry, and Jane rushed to comfort her. Patty glared at Danny, unafraid, the tension between them still thick in the air.

"The cops are coming!" someone shouted. Jack had called the cops from the kitchen, afraid that trouble was brewing.

"Okay guys, break it up! Break it up!" Fred Calibri, the policeman on duty, stormed heavily into the shop. Fred knew most of the kids in the neighborhood by name, including the two who stood facing one another now, their muscles taut. "Come on Danny, come on Patty, let's not have any trouble here. Break it up and both of you get home. Patty, I want to see you go your way, and Danny you go yours.

The boys had no choice. Jack followed them outside, and thanked them for not starting anything. "Next time you come in boys, I'll give you a free banana split," he called after them. After all, Jack did not want any future problems in his shop.

On the way home, Danny let his sister have it. He told her that Patty was no good for her, that she should stay clear of him.

"We didn't do anything wrong," pleaded Stacey. "We were just talking."

"That's how it all starts," Danny broke in, now shouting."

"You just don't like him. That's why you're behaving like this," said Stacey. Tears were still in her eyes, "And you're not going to tell me what to do!"

"I'm not? Well we'll see about that! I'm your older brother and you'll listen to me," Danny answered. "When Pa's not around, I'm your father."

"Well, we'll see about that," mocked Stacey.

"I'm telling Pa about you and Patty at supper tonight."

When Danny and Stacey arrived home, their mother was waiting for them at the door. She wanted some answers immediately. Where had Stacey been? Why was she so late? Stacey explained that a boy had walked her home, and they stopped to have a soda and nothing more.

"Danny's making a big thing about it," said Stacey.

"He's not making a big thing about it," her mother replied. "He was worried where you were and so was I. What's the name of this boy you had" 'just a soda with' and who made you late?"

"His name is Patty, Ma."

"Well, at least he's Irish," said her mother.

"He's not Irish, he's Italian," said Danny eager to make Patty look bad.

"What's an Italian doing with a name like Patty?"

"I think his name is Pasquale, and he's just called Patty for short," replied Stacey.

"Well, whatever he is, your father will have to know about this. After supper tonight, we'll tell him. Now get up to your room, do your homework and then come down to set the table for dinner."

"Yes Ma," and Stacey started to walk away. At the bottom of the stairs she turned and stuck her tongue out at her brother.

It was not more than an hour before Mr. Boyle came home from work. Everyone but Stacey greeted him as he walked in the house. "Where's Stacey"?" he immediately asked. Ma explained that Stacey was in her bedroom doing her homework, and after dinner they would discuss what had happened to Stacey that day.

Throughout the entire supper Stacey did not say a word. As soon as the meal was finished, Mr. Boyle excused his two other daughters from the table, and turned to Stacey. "All right, Stacey," he said. "What's wrong? Tell me what happened today."

"Nothing," replied Stacey.

Ma Boyle spoke for her. "Stacey was one and a half hours late coming home from school. I sent Danny out looking for her, and he found her at the ice cream parlor."

"Now what were you doing there, that made you so late, Stacey"?" asked Mr. Boyle.

Danny was quick to jump in. "She was talking to a boy. He was going to walk her home from school."

Mr. Boyle thought this over, and then gently asked his daughter, "Did you ever have a boy walk you home before?"

"No, I never…"

"Is this boy different?"

Stacey looked up. "I don't know. I just met him today."

"Do you like him?"

"Well, he is nice…"

"He's Italian, Pa." Interrupted Danny.

"Is that why you don't like him Danny," replied his father, "because he's Italian?"

"No," said Danny sheepishly.

"Let me tell you something Danny. Your Uncle Johnny married an Italian girl. They have two beautiful children that you play with. Do you see anything wrong with them?"

"No, Pa."

"Then I don't think being Italian or any other nationality means anything. It's the person that counts. You know, son, down at the steer mill where I work there are lots of Italians, and most them are my friends. We have a wonderful time together. We're all human beings, Danny." Then the father turned to Stacey. "What's this boy's name, Stacey?"

"Patty. Patty DiMarco."

"Well, he's got an Irish first name," her father replied. "Was he born in this country?"

"Yes, Pa."

"And what about his parents?"

"They were born in Italy, Pa."

"So you see, Danny," their father continued his lesson, "his parents were born in Italy, and I was born in Ireland. We all come from another country; that makes all of us no different from each other. We may descent from another country, but we are all Americans, and I want you to look at it that way. That goes for any nationality." Pa Boyle was trying to teach his children not to have any animosity towards anyone.

"Now getting back to you Stacey," he went on, "that doesn't give you permission to be late from school and have your mother worried like that. I am going to ground you for the next two weeks, which means you come home from school, do your chores, do your homework, and stay in your room. I don't want to discuss this any longer, you understand?"

"Yes, Pa." Stacey sighed in relief. She imagined it would be a much harsher punishment.

The next day in school, Patty sought Stacey out in the lunchroom, and asked her what had happened. She explained that she was grounded for two weeks.

"Does that mean I can't walk you home," Patty asked.

"Well, he didn't say that," replied Stacey. "So I guess you can."

After school Patty walked Stacey home, right to her front door. Ma Boyle later whispered to Stacey in the kitchen, "He *does seem* like a nice boy."

From that day on, Patty walked Stacey home from school every day. They would talk and laugh the whole way, always arriving at Stacey's front steps far too soon. One day as they were just about to pass Canada Pond, Stacey said, "Let's go over to the pond, I want to put my feet in the water."

"But you'll be late," said Patty.

"Oh, it will only take a minute," argued Stacey and she turned off the path.

As the two started to walk into the woods, they noticed a boy walking from the opposite direction. The boy glanced at Patty, and Patty fiercely stared back at him.

"Well, what was that all about?" Stacey asked after the boy was out of sight.

"Do you know who that was?" Patty didn't wait for her to answer. "He's called The Weasel. He's Fat Salerno's cousin, and that's just what he is – a weasel."

I heard Fat Salerno's a tough guy," replied Stacey, trying to sound off-handed.

"And someday we'll find out how tough he is," said Patty. It was almost as if he was talking to himself.

"What do you mean by that?"

"Oh, never mind," said Patty, and he changed the subject. "I think we better head back. I don't want you to be late getting home."

"It's only been five minutes."

"And that's five minutes too much," he said.

As they reached Stacey's house, her mother was standing in the yard. Patty waved at her, and she returned it with a wave and a big smile. As Stacey passed her to go into the house, her mother put a hand on her shoulder. "Stacey, are you sure he's only 13 years old?"

"Yes Ma."

"Well he looks more like 18, if you ask me. And he's a nice looking boy at that. You sure know how to pick em."

The weeks were flying by and Patty continued to walk Stacey home from school. Her punishment was over, and although Mr. Boyle knew about Patty walking with his daughter everyday, he never said a thing about it to Stacey.

One day at school, Patty told Stacey that he would not be walking her home that day because his father had some work for him to do. He had to deliver the evening papers.

"You pick up your papers where Danny picks up his, right?" asked Stacey.

"That's right," said Patty. "I see him there every afternoon."

At 3:30 Patty finished helping his father, and went to call his friends, Johnny and Steve, to see if they wanted to help him with the papers. When he got to Johnny's house, Johnny told him he was feeling sick. "You take care of yourself," said Patty, and he went across the street to see if Steve was coming with him as he always did. Steve told him that he had to do some work for his mother, but to call him when he got back and they could hang out later. As Patty turned to leave, Steve asked, "By the way, what's going on between you and Stacey?"

"We're getting friendlier," said Patty. "I think she's a good kid. I met her mother with a wave.

"Did her mom have anything to say?"

"No, she just waved back."

"Well, that's good," said Steve. "Don't forget to call me when you get back."

When Patty arrived a little late to pick up his papers he noticed that the only kids there were Danny and five of his friends. Usually, Danny only brought one friend, and this change struck Patty as more than a little strange. Patty assumed things were resolved between him and Danny because he had been walking Stacey home every day and she had never mentioned anything about Danny objecting.

"Hi Danny," Patty said casually.

"Hi Patty," Danny replied.

Patty bent down to pick up a stack of papers; his back was to Danny and his friends. All of a sudden, Patty felt a terrible pain on his shoulders. Someone had hit him with a bat. He was stuck again, and Patty fell to the ground. Danny and three other boys held wooden baseball bats in their hands, another had a chain, and the last boy had a knife.

Patty was on his knees with his back to the boys, and he could not see what was going on. They were hitting him repeatedly, and all Patty could do was attempt to cover his head, and his body rolled around on the ground, writhing in pain. Just then Mr. DeCesare from DeCesare's market across the street came rushing out. "Stop! Stop!" he shouted. "You're going to kill him! I'm going to call the police!" At DeCesare's threat, the six boys scampered off.

Patty lay on the ground, helpless. The words of his father, "Never, never turn your back," echoed through his head.

"Patty! Patty! Can you hear me? Speak to me!" Mr. DeCesare rushed to his side. His wife Maria was right behind him.

"Say something Patty," she cried.

Patty faintly whispered, "Don't call the police. Call my mother."

"You hear him," shouted Mr. DeCesare. "Go into the house and call his mother. Tell her Patty's hurt real bad. Get one of the boys to bring me ice and some towels."

Not one second after she had answered the phone, Anna was screaming. "My son! God help me!" Immediately Anna rushed next door. "Evelyn, Marie! Come quick, Patty's hurt real bad. He's laying on the ground at the old school." Together the three women started to run in the direction of "The old school". As they passed Steve's house, Anna called out to Steve to come quick. She was speaking so fast that it took a moment for Steve to take in what she said. He called out to Johnny across the street that Patty was hurt and soon all five of them were running down the street.

The neighbors, who heard the shouts, also came out and started to follow the pack. Anna tried to explain to Steve what had happened, all the while saying, "Oh, dear God, oh, St. Anne, please help my boy." Steve took off with a burst of speed, and was the first to reach Patty. He could not believe what he was seeing: Patty bleeding on the ground, Mr. DeCesare, Mr Zinno and other neighbors desperately trying to give him first aid.

"Oh, Patty it's my fault. I couldn't come with you today," cried Steve. "If I did, this never would have happened. Who did this to you? Tell me, Patty! Who did this? I'll go after them, I swear…"

Patty did not answer. He stared blankly at Steve.

As soon as Anna saw Patty lying on the ground encircled by people, she feared the worst and started screaming again. "My son! My son! What did they do to you?" She kneeled beside Patty, his head in her arms, crying uncontrollably. Evelyn and Marie were also weeping. Their nephew looked as if he were dead.

Evelyn started interrogating Mr. DeCesare. "Who did this to Patty?" she demanded.

Mr. DeCesare just shook his head, "I don't know." Then he started to shout. "Listen, let's not sit around discussing what happened. Quick, someone run down the block to Doctor Angelone's office. And tell the doctor to hurry, that Patty's hurt real bad, and his mother's losing it."

Anna held Patty in her arms, trying to ask him questions through her sobs. Patty did not answer. "Patty, don't leave me," she cried. Patty I love you very much!" Then looking up to the sky, "Please St. Anne, help me! Oh, Patty…"

Patty did not answer. Someone shouted, Call the police! Patty squeezed his mother's hand.

"No police," he whispered, barely audible.

"No police!" Anna hollered. "We have to get Patty back home. Johnny, go get a wheelbarrow and a blanket. We won't be able to carry him."

Just then, Doctor Angelone arrived, Evelyn running behind him out of breath. The doctor instructed to everyone to get out of the way, to let him through. "It's okay Anna," he said. "I'll take over now." He knelt down next to Patty and said in a calm, soothing voice, "Hello Patty, It's me, Dr. Angelone. Tell me what happened to you. I know…don't tell me you tripped and fell." Patty would not answer. He just stared at the doctor, his eyes as cold as the ground.

The doctor analyzed Patty's condition. It was clear that Patty had been struck repeatedly from behind with blunt objects. He felt Patty's ankle. Patty winced. "Looks like it's fractured," the doctor said. "And he's been punctured – not serious, but he needs stitches." Johnny came running up the street with the wheelbarrow, and the doctor instructed Johnny and Steve to help him lift Patty into it.

When they got to the doctor's office, they put Patty on a table, doctor Angelone cleaned off his wounds, and stitched up the gash from the knife. Anna kept trying to ask Patty who had done this to him, but Patty still would not say a word. "Anna," said the doctor. "I am going to give you some pain killers for Patty to take every four hours. Here Patty, take one now." Patty shook his head no.

"Come on, Patty," his mother pleaded. "Won't you take them?" Patty again shook his head no.

The doctor put a cast on Patty's ankle and told Anna to let Patty rest. "No school for him until he feels he's able," said the doctor. "And call me in a few days to let me know how he's doing. He took a terrible beating, but he's going to be all right."

Okay, okay," said Anna, finally starting to calm down. "Patty, let's get you home."

The boys put Patty back into the wheelbarrow and took him back to his house. They carried him inside, and put him into his bed. Patty's brothers, Tom and Henry, and sisters, Ann Marie, and Carol rushed into Patty's room and surrounded the bed. The girls kissed Patty's cheeks and forehead, asking him if he was going to be all right. Patty nodded yes, and gave a wave to his brothers to say he was okay.

"Alright children," said Anna, "Let your brother rest."

"Mama," little Anna asked, "Why doesn't Patty speak?"

"He's just tired, dear. Now come on, everybody out."

When Frank got home from work, Anna ran out and met him on the sidewalk, and told him what had happened. "Where is he?" Frank asked.

"In his bedroom," Anna replied, and along with Frank's brothers, they all rushed into the house.

Anna followed the men into the bedroom. "He won't speak," she said, "I don't know why."

Frank nodded hi to Steve and Johnny as he walked in the room, and pulled up a chair next to the bed. "Hey Patty," he said, "How are you doing." Patty looked into his father's eyes.

"Patty, what happened?" Frank asked.

No answer came from Patty. Frank did not want to press him, not now anyway, and he ordered everyone out of the room. "Come on," he said, "Let's go to the kitchen. Patty needs to rest." He squeezed Patty's hand, then left, shutting the door behind him.

Once they were out of Patty's earshot, Frank's tone changed. "I want some answers, and I want them fast." He said to Anna, his eyes growing angry. "Where was he?"

"He was at the old school, where he picks up his papers."

"Were you boys with him?" Frank asked, turning to Steve and Johnny.

"No, Mr. DiMarco. We weren't able to go today."

"Did anyone see what happened? Was anyone there that we know?"

"Mr. DeCesare was there and his wife was the one who called here telling us that Patty was hurt," replied Anna; the tears began to flow again at the thought of that phone call.

"That's all I need to know," said Frank. He turned to his brothers, "Alfred, Vito, come on, let's go!"

"Go where?" asked Anna, afraid that she only knew too well.

"Nowhere."

"What do you mean nowhere?"

"Just cook supper and shut up. I'll be right back," and the three brothers left the house, slamming the front door behind them.

Frank and his brothers went straight over to Mr. DeCesare's 'store. Mr. DeCesare had expected them. It was terrible, Frank," he said. "Just horrible."

Dominic, I want to ask you some questions, and I want answers. Who has done this to Patty?" Frank's eyes pierced the storekeeper like knife blades.

"I don't know."

"Don't lie to me!" shouted Frank. "You don't want to get me angry. It's my son we're talking about. He could've been killed."

"Frank, you know I love you like a brother, but I'm afraid if they find out they're liable to do harm to me or my family."

"Dominic, you've known me for a long time. If they ever…I swear, I'll hang them from the nearest tree on Charles Street. Now tell me who they were!"

"It was that Irish boy, Danny Boyle and his gang. If I hadn't stopped it, they might have killed him."

"Thank you, thank you," said Frank and he gave Mr. DeCesare a hug. Frank was now trembling, thinking about what could have happened to Patty. Frank knew Dominic had saved his son from a far worse beating and perhaps even death. "I shall always be indebted to you. Now come on guys, we're going home."

"Should we make a hit on them Frank?" asked Vito. "Come on, why don't we go into one of their bars and take out a few of them."

"No," said Frank, "Let's go see Patty."

Anna was looking out the window when the men returned home. Two of her sisters-in-law, Marie and Evelyn, were behind her in the kitchen silently preparing supper. "Do you want to eat, Frank?" Anna timidly asked. Her eyes were still swollen from tears.

"Not now, I'm busy. Just feed the kids," replied Frank. Anna knew not to ask anymore. Frank was really taking things hard.

Without even looking at his wife, Frank went straight for Patty's room. He asked his brother Vito to get him a chair, and he placed it beside Patty's bed. Frank sat down, and quietly asked, "How you feeling, Patty?"

Patty turned and faced his father, but did not answer. Frank turned to Steve and Johnny and asked them if Patty was speaking to anyone yet.

"He hasn't said a word. He just stares at us," answered Steve.

"Patty," said Frank, "Why aren't you talking?" And as he asked that question, he looked into Patty's eyes. His son looked right back into his. Frank was so hurt to see Patty in that condition. He was holding himself back as he could explode at any moment. Frank controlled himself, though, because he wanted to see how Patty would handle the situation.

"Do you want me to do something Patty?" Frank's question was simple.

Patty lowered his eyes.

"What? You think he's going to say something?" Alfred blurted out.

"He already did. You don't have to hear anything. He answered me with his eyes." Frank turned back to his son, "I can't believe it. I just can't...are you hurting?" Patty looked at this father and made a gesture with his hand side to side, meaning half and half.

"Will you tell me who did this to you, Patty," Frank prodded.

Patty's eyes closed, meaning no.

"Can you speak if you had to?"

Patty looked up, meaning yes.

"Alright," said Frank, "I'm going to ask you a question and if you don't answer, your uncles and I am going to make a strike. Do you understand me?"

Patty answered with his eyes.

"You don't have to talk loud, you can whisper to me." Frank leaned his head down closer to Patty's. "Now, why aren't you speaking Patty?"

"Because I let you down Papa."

"How did you let me down? Because you got a beating?"

"No, Papa."

"Then how? How?"

"You taught me never turn your back on anyone, even your friends. Always face people. I didn't think I was in trouble, and by not seeing what was happening I couldn't take anyone down like you taught me to do. I didn't have a chance to throw a punch even if I was out numbered."

Frank put his arms around Patty saying to him, "You did not let me down. You're here to tell me about it so in a sense you're a winner. You did not let me down. You're here to tell me about what happened. I'm proud of you and I love you very much. And I'm happy now that you spoke to me."

Frank did not realize that Anna was at the bedroom door listening in on the conversation. Tears were streaking down her cheeks.

"I'm going to let you sleep now," said Frank, getting up from his chair. "I'll check on you later."

Anna quickly scurried away, and called from the dining room to come and eat, inviting Steve and Johnny to join the family as well. She had already called their mothers to tell them that the boys would be eating at her place. On Frank's way into the dining room, his brothers stopped him.

"So, what are we going to do?" asked Alfred.

"Nothing," replied Frank.

" Are you serious? Why?"

"Because Patty is going to handle it."

"How do you know? asked Vito, "I didn't hear him tell you that."

"He told me with his eyes he wanted to handle it in his way, so let him. Let's eat."

And with that, Frank directed his brothers towards the table.

Johnny and Steve were getting ready to leave Patty so he could get some rest when they asked him if he wanted them to get some guys together to go after Danny and his boys. Patty gave them the worst look you could imagine. "Alright, alright," both boys answered. Then Johnny went on, "You're still our leader, and we'll do whatever you tell us. Right now just get some sleep Patty," and the two shut the door to his room.

As soon as they stepped into the hall, Anna grabbed the boys and told them to get in there and have something to eat. The boys did not refuse. They went into the dining room and Anna tiptoed into Patty's room to check on him one last time. Patty was asleep. She leaned over and kissed him on the forehead. "I know you're hurting," she whispered, "Mama will take care of you. Good night. I love you very much."

Anna joined everyone in the dining room, and instructed her children that when they got through eating to get ready for bed. She then asked Johnny and Steve if they would ask Miss Cox for Patty's homework. "And I don't want you to discuss anything about what happened to him or to anyone else. If she wants, tell Miss Cox that she can call me, okay boys?"

"Yes Mrs. DiMarco."

"And boys," said Anna, "Thank you so much for your help today. I don't know what I would have done without you. You two really are Patty's best friends. Why don't you come over tomorrow after school and visit Patty? I know he'll want to see you."

After Johnny and Steve had left, and all the children had gone to bed, Anna and Frank sat around the table with Alfred, Evelyn and Marie. "I want to have a meeting with all of you," Anna began, but Frank interrupted her.

"This is not a meeting, we have meetings in the wine cellar and the women are not allowed. This is a discussion."

"Oh Frank," Evelyn said, "Regardless of what it is, I think we should all listen to Anna."

Just then, Josephine, Frank's youngest sister, arrived home from work. Seeing all the lights on she came over and wanted to know what was going on. They told her that something had happened to Patty that afternoon, and he was not feeling well.

"Well what happened to him? Where is he? I want to see him."

"He's sleeping right now," said Evelyn.

"I don't care," Josephine replied, and walked into Patty's bedroom.

"Let her go," Anna said. "She'll have to know everything eventually anyway."

Josephine went right in and looked at Patty. Even in the dark she could see that his face was bruised and swollen, and that his leg was bandaged. She could not imagine what had happened. Anna was at her side and the other sisters were close behind at the bedroom door. Josephine got on her knees to talk to Patty. Her eyes swelled with tears and she whispered so as not to wake him up, "What happened to you Patty?"

Anna put her hand on Josephine's shoulder. "Come on Josephine, let's not wake him up. I want Patty to rest. He's been through so much today."

Still crying, Josephine followed Anna into the dining room to join the rest of the family. Anna asked her to please eat something. "No, I don't want to," replied Josephine, "I want to know what happened to my nephew."

Frank and his brothers just listened, and let the women do the talking. Josephine insisted that they explain immediately what happened to Patty. She turned her question to her brother, "Frankie," she pleaded, "Please, tell me what happened." Frank stood up and walked over to Josephine, calling her baby sister and embracing her.

"You never called me Frankie before, how come now?"

"I don't know why. I just want to know what really happened. Because I'm the youngest, is that why you're treating me like a baby Frank? You're the boss like Grandpa was, and I love and respect you, and I'm still a member of this family, you know. I have a right to know what happened."

"Of course you're a member of this family. I was going to tell you if you just gave me a chance," and Frank started to explain the events of the day. "I just want to say one thing," he said. "Our family is all here, and there is no need to discuss this with anyone else." Frank went on to say that as far as they could tell a group of boys ganged up on Patty and that was all they knew.

"Did Patty fight back," she asked.

"He didn't have a chance, his back was turned to them. It was a friend of ours who threatened to call the police if the boys didn't stop."

"But who were they," Josephine could not believe what she was hearing.

"We don't know yet"---"

"And they hurt my nephew like that? Them dirty bastards, I want them punished. What's being done about it Frank?"

"Slow down, slow down." Frank steadied his sister with his eyes. "We want Patty to get better, and then we'll see how he'll handle it. I want to make it clear to all of you that Patty wants to handle this himself, so let's see what happens."

Anna broke in, "Now wait a minute. It's my son that's involved and I don't want him getting beat up any more."

Frank turned to his wife, "What do you want me to do, go with Vito and John and start punching people around and then have other people do the same to us?" Frank was trying not to name any names, though he had an idea of who they were. "Anyone can start a fight, but it takes a better person to avoid one. As the oldest brother, I'm going to say it once and for all." Big Frank's shoulders suddenly filled with the room, "we're just going to have to wait and see what Patty does. I have faith in him. You know he's not stupid. I think we should all say good night, and let's get some rest."

The next day at school Johnny informed Miss Cox that Patty injured himself playing football and his parents would like him to bring home Patty's homework. The lunch bell rang, and Johnny and Steve asked Crazy Ray, and Butterball to join them with some of their boys, just in case something might happen in the cafeteria. The boys put two and two together and guessed at who was responsible for Patty's absence. They also realized that Patty did not want them discussing what happened to anyone.

Just then, Danny and some of his gang started to approach them at their table.

Johnny whispered to Steve, "Don't let on anything," and quickly said to Butterball and Ray, "if anything happens, just follow us, whatever we do." But Danny, knowing that Johnny and Steve hadn't mentioned anything, walked right past the table.

"Let's go in the school yard 'til the bell rings," suggested Steve.

In the schoolyard, kids hung around Johnny and Steve asking them where Patty was. Their answer was he took the day off. Stacey came over and asked Johnny what was wrong with Patty. "He's not feeling well, Stacey, that's all."

"Well, what's wrong?"

"He doesn't feel good, that's all," and Johnny turned away from her. "Come on Steve, let's get out of here before they all start asking about Patty." Across the schoolyard they could see Danny talking with the Salerno brothers.

Steve kicked at the dirt angrily, "I bet he's filling them in on what happened."

"I bet he is, and you know they'll spread it all over school," Johnny's eyes narrowed in Danny's direction.

Immediately after school, the boys headed for Patty's. They were anxious to see how he was doing. Anna saw them coming up the walk and greeted them whole-heartedly. "Did you remember to get his homework? She asked.

"We sure did, Mama DiMarco."

"'Well, go on in and see Patty. He feels much better. He'll be so happy to see you boys."

Patty was sitting up in his bed and greeted his friends with a casual "hi guys" as if he were out on the street.

"You look a lot better today, Patty," Steve said a little sheepishly, obviously very concerned about his friend.

"I feel better too," replied Patty. "Now fill me in on what happened today." The boys were relieved that Patty was his old talkative self again, and they eagerly sat down on the edge of his bed. "We did it like you wanted us to, and told whoever asked that you weren't feeling good," relayed Johnny. At that moment Anna poked her head into the room and told Patty that Stacey was on the phone asking to speak with him.

"Not now, Mama. Tell her I'm not feeling well." Patty quickly turned to his friends, "Anything else to report guys?"

"Well, we saw Danny talking to the Salerno brothers. We think he was filling them in."

"I bet he was. Let him say what he wants. I'm not worried right now," said Patty, much calmer at the news that the boys expected. "I just want to get better and I'll take care of that matter later. I want you guys to act like nothing's wrong, and again, don't talk about it to anyone."

"We won't Patty."

And Patty leaned a little closer to them with a spark in his eye, "Here's what I want you guys to do. You know the rules, if we go after an outside neighborhood, the Salerno brothers have to go along with us. Forget what Danny told them; they know the rules, and they have to join us or they will lose respect from everyone else."

"Do you really think they'll join us?" There was a good amount of doubt in Steve's voice.

"They will, and I'll bet on that because, here's why: I want you two to get in touch with Bobby DiCristafaro, the head of the Eagle Park gang, John Natale from Silver Lake, and Vinny Lurgio from Federal Hill."

The boys were surprised, "Why so many people?"

"Because this time I'm not going in unprepared ." There'll be plenty of guys watching my back. Danny's no dope. He'll have extra people going with him to peddle his papers."

Steve asked, "How do we get around to see these guys? Do we take the bus?"

"No," Patty answered. Today, my Aunt Josephine stopped in to see me. She said if I needed any help whatsoever, she would help out. She's boiling mad. I asked her if she would drive you guys around to the other neighborhoods, and she said that she definitely would. She said she'd do anything. I even think if I asked my mother to help me get Danny, she'd say 'yes'. With that they started laughing. "Now don't forget guys," Patty went on, "as soon as I start feeling better, we'll get started. We'll call it Operation Pay Back," and Patty winked.

The boys started laughing and cheering, "Atta boy, Patty!" Anna came in to see what all the commotion was about.

"We're just having some laughs, Mama."

Anna was thrilled to see that Patty's energy was up. "Do you have your homework?" she asked.

"Yes, Mama."

"Well, you better start doing it right now, so you can rest later. Your friends can come back tomorrow to see you."

Soon Frank came home from work. The first thing he asked as he walked in the house was "How's Patty doing?"

"He's doing much better," replied Anna cheerily.

Frank went into Patty's room. "Your mother's cooking supper, are you going to eat?"

"Maybe later, I want to finish my homework."

Later that evening when Josephine returned home from work, she stopped into visit Patty.

"I'm glad you came over Auntie, I wanted to ask if you could take Johnny and Steve to Eagle Park, Silver Lake, and Federal Hill to see some friends of mine." Patty's plans were starting to materialize.

"May I ask what this is all about," Josephine could not help but be curious. She saw the gears spinning in her nephew's head.

"I just want to bring my friends up-to-date on what happened."

Josephine knew Patty was up to something, but she also knew better than to ask any more questions. "I'd be happy to give your friends a ride," she said.

"Thanks. You just have to call them tomorrow when you get home."

The following evening, once again, Johnny and Steve went to see Patty, bringing his homework with them.

"Hi boys," Anna called out.

"We got Patty's homework, Mrs. DiMarco," Steve called out. "Can we go in and see him?"

Upon entering Patty's room, the boys immediately closed the door behind them and informed him that Josephine had kept her end of the deal and had driven them all around the city.

"Does she know anything?" Patty asked. The boys shook their heads, no. "Good. The less she knows the better it will be, but I think she suspects something. Let her think whatever she wants, but don't explain anything."

The boys could not stay long; they had their own chores to do. They said goodbye and promised to come over the next day.

The following day, Anna told Patty that she had called Doctor Angelone and he said Patty could go back to school on Monday, but he had to walk with crutches and promise to take it easy.

Monday came fast and Patty was excited to be back at school. Everyone greeted him and Miss Cox told him next time he plays football to be careful.

"I sure will," said Patty.

Steve and Johnny had instructed Butterball and Crazy Ray to keep their eyes on Patty at lunchtime and in the schoolyard as well. They promised not to let Patty out of their sight. Steve went over to Fat Salerno and informed him of what was going on. "We know the rules. We'll be joined with the rest of the guys, and tell Patty he's on my list."

Everything was falling into place. Patty got the message to his friends that he would be sure to let them know when to expect "Operation Pay Back." As soon as Patty was off his crutches, he started to get in shape. He started jogging and going to the Wanskuck Boy's Club to work out and punch the bag. Patty asked his Aunt Josephine if she would drive him, Johnny and Steve to meet his friends in the other neighborhoods. What he did not tell her was that he needed the ride so he could plan his strategy. But he did not need to explain anything; Josephine agreed to take him anywhere.

Patty met with Natale, DiCristafaro, and Lurgio. They planned to meet at Corliss Park the following Monday after school, and together proceed to Branch Avenue, where the evening papers were dropped off. Danny was sure to be there.

Monday rolled around and everyone met at 2:30 as planned. Butterball arrived with his gang, Fat Salerno came with his people and the other three neighborhoods. Patty explained to everyone what was to happen. His confidence was apparent in his solid eyes. "I know most of you guys don't know each other," he said, "so Steve and Johnny are going to put white adhesive tape on your foreheads, that way if it goes that far, you know who not to touch. Understand? Also, we're going to block all of the side streets, but no one makes a move unless Steve tells you to. Okay, that's it. Let's go. We'll move out in small groups and meet at Branch Ave."

Danny and his friends were at the newspaper drop-off as expected. After making sure all the escape routes were blocked, Patty said that he was going to walk across the street. Steve and Johnny were to follow his last minute instructions. No one was supposed to do anything unless they were told to.

Meanwhile, Mr. DeCesare noticed the commotion outside his shop, and ran out to see what was happening. Jerry Renzi from Hopkins Press, who had been inside buying a cold drink, came running out alongside him. Patty reached Danny and shouted, "This is payback time! You got a choice, Danny. One at time or all at once?"

Danny and his friends looked around, surprised at the number of boys that had suddenly filled the street. Stretch O'Leary, the kid that had punctured Patty with a knife, turned red and charged at Patty. He was met with a punch that dropped him to the ground. Then it was Danny who started swinging at Patty. Danny was a tough fighter, but he was met with a punch from Patty and down he went. Patty's friends started hollering. "Get him Patty!" and "It's payback time!"

Mr. DeCesare explained to Mr. Renzi "My God, I've never seen so many kids!"

Patty and Danny were on the ground. "Why did you do that to me? What you got against me?"

"I heard you made love to my sister," Danny grunted out the words in disgust.

"Where'd you hear that? Who told you that?"

"The Weasel."

"What did he say?"

"He told me he saw you go into the woods with Stacey down at Canada Pond and he followed you in."

"Well he's a liar. I never touched your sister. She's a good girl. When the time comes, I'm going to straighten that Weasel out! I guess you were just protecting your sister's honor."

"Yeah, that's all. It wasn't personal."

"Well then, I respect you for that. Seeing it wasn't personal and all, I'll tell you what I'm going to do. You run your gang, but you answer to me. If you get in any kind of trouble and need help, I'll back you up personally and get my friends to help you too. Is it a deal or no deal?"

"Deal," answered Danny. "Now let me up."

The boys got up and shook hands. They put their arms around each other and Patty raised his arm with Danny's. All the boys in the street started shouting, "Patty! Patty!" Even DeCesare and Renzi were shouting, though they weren't cheering because Patty had won, but because he had settled the fight without any real violence.

"That kid's a real leader, commented Renzi.

Patty had to ask Stretch why he used a knife. "I didn't want to hurt you," Stretch said, "I just wanted to sting you."

Patty turned to Danny, "Well, I think you better tell him to throw that knife away. We don't want any of that anymore."

Everyone came up to Patty and Danny and shook their hands. Patty explained, "We'll all be working together now."

6   TEAM WORK

Back in school, the word got around about what happened between Patty and Danny. Everyone was talking about it. In the lunchroom and schoolyard, Danny and his friends were now hanging and traveling around with Patty, Johnny, Steve, Butterball, Crazy Ray- the whole crew. Patty took Crazy Ray aside and said he wanted to talk.

"What's up?" asked Crazy Ray.

"I'm going to change your name replied Patty.

"What do you mean by that Patty?"

"I'm going to give you another name. No more Crazy Ray, because I think you graduated and made it to the big time."

"Yeah? What's the name?"

The rest of the boys listened intently, not sure if Patty was joking. Patty stopped walking. He was serious. "I'm going to knight you and you are now Sir Ray," he said, "because I don't think you're crazy at all, and I don't know where you got that name."

Ray grinned at that and said, "Thanks a lot Patty, I love it." The rest of the guys cheered him on. They looked like a small army walking around the schoolyard.

Danny nudged Patty and said, "Look across from us and see who's watching us." It was Fat Salerno, his brother, and The Weasel.

"Let them watch. I noticed that not even six months ago there were always a dozen guys around them."

"Yeah," said Danny, "Their group's getting thinner and thinner."

Just then, Fat Salerno gave Patty the finger and his brother gave him the "up yours" gesture with his arm. Patty just waved at them politely, like nothing happened. Danny, with his Irish temper, was immediately on the offensive. "Let's go get 'em, Patty." Danny was with Patty 100 percent.

"No," Patty answered, grabbing Danny by the arm, "That's exactly what he wants, and with everyone around me to see me do it. He'd just love to see me get suspended. I'll get him, don't you worry. I have something personal to settle with the Weasel." Across the yard Patty could see vice principal Bishop. "He'll crucify me. I don't think Mr. Bishop likes me too much."

As Patty and Danny were walking back to class, Patty felt someone tap his shoulder. He spun around. It was Stacey. Stacey looked at Patty timidly and asked him if he would like to go for a soda after school.

"I can't. I've got other things to do," he replied.

"Is that the truth or is it that you don't want to go?"

"It's the truth. I'm busy."

But it wasn't the truth. Patty did not want to go because he did not want to hurt Stacey in any way, and he knew he would not stay with her. Also, Danny was his friend and he wouldn't want to hurt

Danny. Patty would not lie to Stacey to get what he wanted. He felt guys who did that to the girls were snakes. He thought God help any man who dared do anything like that to his sister.

Patty returned to his homeroom, and as usual, he was greeted with a big smile from Miss Cox. Her affection for Patty was obvious; after all he was six feet one and looked all of 18, and she was just 22 and fresh out of college. Miss Cox informed Patty that Miss Hazard wanted to see him after school.

When the school bell rang, Patty went to visit Miss Hazard. He greeted his teacher happily and asked what it was she wanted to talk to him about.

"Well Patty, I wanted to tell you that you're doing very well with your Chinese. You're speaking it almost as well as I am. It is obvious that you study a lot at home."

"Yes, I do. My mother keeps asking me what are the funny letters I'm writing and why in the world would I want to learn Chinese when I should be working on my Italian. She doesn't understand how much I am fascinated with the Chinese people and their culture."

"Even so, Patty, you speak incredibly well. How have you been able to pick it up so fast?"

"Well, you know that Chink that does the laundry?"

"Hold on Patty, it's not right to call him a Chink. It is more polite to call him Chinese or a Chinaman. Remember that. I don't want to hear you call him by anything other than his proper name from now on."

"I'm sorry Miss Hazard. I didn't mean any disrespect. I won't call him a Chink anymore. But anyway, when I bring my father's shirts to the laundry, we talk in Chinese. He loves to hear me speak and he corrects me a lot. I told him that when I get older I am going to go over to China and open up an Italian restaurant. He thinks that is really funny and we both laugh together."

"That's wonderful Patty. You know the best way to learn a language is from a native speaker. Listen, I won't be in the rest of the week and I want you to take home this work I've prepared for you. I will test you on Monday. We only have four more weeks of school before summer, Patty. Have a good time with this, and I'll see you on Monday."

That afternoon, Patty went to pick up his newspapers with Johnny, Steve, Ray and Danny. They talked about how summer was coming up fast and soon the school would be closed. "And then I'm going to straighten out the Salerno brothers once and for all," said Patty. The rest of the boys all smiled at this. They wanted to know how and when they were going to do it, and also why Patty was suddenly so eager.

"You guys don't think I'm going to put up with what they did today? I wasn't going to let him suck me into his trap in front of all those people, but I'll get even. I just got to come up with a good plan. As soon as I do, I'll let you all know."

"Can you do me a favor Patty?" Danny asked.

"What do you need?"

"Can I have the Weasel?"

"Let me think about how we're going to do it, and then we'll see. I don't want a spur of the moment hit. I want to plan it."

"Okay Patty, we'll wait 'til you feel the time is right."

On the way to school the next day, Patty confided in Johnny and Steve that he spent all night lying awake thinking about the Salerno brothers.

"What do you mean?" asked Steve. "Are you worried or something?"

"Oh no, I'm not worried."

"You want Johnny and me to take out Stretch and the Weasel?"

"No, I don't want it done that way. I can take the three of them by myself, piece of cake. I just don't want to get caught."

The three boys were approaching Dominic's Market. Patty noticed a beautiful, long-legged girl going inside.

"Let's go in," said Patty grinning. "I want to check that out."

As soon as the girl saw Patty approaching, she walked up to him. "Hi Patty," she said.

Patty was taken aback. "How do you know who I am," he asked.

"I live upstairs over the store, and I see you walking by on your way to school everyday."

"Are you going to work this early?" Patty was intrigued.

She brushed the hair from her face. "Oh no," she laughed, "I'm coming home from work. I just stopped in to buy cigarettes." She gave Patty a coy smile.

"Well, seeing as you know my name, don't you think you should tell me yours?"

"I'm Rosa."

"Well I'll see you later Rosa. I'm late for school." Then Patty turned to the counter. "Hi Mr. DeCesare. Can I have a pack of gum?"

As soon as the boys left, Johnny explained, "Did you see that! Her tits were sticking out. Boy, she's a knockout, and she was all over you Patty!"

"Yeah, I could see that," said Patty smiling to himself.

"You know Patty, you don't go after none of these girls. They come to you," warned Steve. "You guys know anything about her?"

"What do you mean?" asked Patty.

"She's a prostitute."

"Are you sure about that?"

"I know for a fact. That's why she's coming home now."

The next day, the boys were walking by Dominic's on their way to school when Rosa popped her head out the window and threw down a dollar bill. "Patty, would you buy me a package of Lucky Strike cigarettes?"

"Okay!" he yelled back. "You guys go on ahead and I'll catch up with you." He quickly bought the cigarettes and ran up the stairs to Rosa's apartment. He knocked and then slowly walked in. Rosa still in her nightgown, said, "Thanks for the favor. Can you stay for a while?"

"Not now. I have to get to school, but I'll come back tomorrow," said Patty.

"Are you sure?"

"Yes, I'm sure. See you then."

Patty ran down the street to school to be there before the bell rang.

During recess, his friends wanted to know what happened.

"I told her I would come back tomorrow. She said she'd be waiting for me."

"What are you going to do about school?" the boys asked with a stunned look on their faces.

"I'll leave with you guys. When we reach Dominic's, I'll go up to her apartment. Then when school's over, I'll be up at the end of the street waiting for you."

"What do we tell Miss Cox?"

"Tell her that I'm sick."

The next morning they all walked to school like they did everyday. When they reached Dominic's, Patty quickly ran in through the side door. Rosa heard Patty coming up the stairs. She even left the door slightly open. She said, "Come in Patty. Come in the bedroom."

When he walked in she was laying in bed with just her panties on. "Come on in. I won't bite you." As Patty entered the bedroom and saw Rosa lying there naked, except for her panties, he froze in his tracks. "Haven't you ever seen a woman naked before?"

"No, I never have," Patty said sheepishly.

"Come closer to me. Come sit on the bed beside me."

Patty did.

"Now give me a kiss and stick your tongue out."

"No, I'm not going to kiss that way."

"Why not?"

"I'm not going to swap spit with any woman!"

"Let's just say you're not ready yet."

"Give me time."

"Take off your clothes and get in here with me and I'll give you the first lesson. When I get through, you will be a pro because you're being taught by the best," said Rosa.

Patty answered, "When I get through with you, you're not going to want another man!"

It was soon time for school to let out and Patty got dressed. Rosa asked, "Where are you going?"

"I have to be with my friends when I get home. If my mother sees them without me, she'll start to ask questions. Listen, I'll see you tomorrow."

The first thing his friends asked was what happened.

"It was unbelievable," said Patty.

Steve asked, "Do you think we can go too?"

"I don't know, but I'll ask her."

"Are you going back?"

"You bet I am. I'm going to go tomorrow."

"What about school?"

"Just tell Miss Cox that I'm still sick and if she could give you guys some homework for me."

This went on for two weeks, but one thing Patty did not count on was that Miss Cox informed the principal, Mr. Mendozzi, that Patty was ill and hadn't been in school for two weeks.

"That's too bad," said Mr. Mendozzi. "His father and I are good friends, so I think I'll call him to see how Patty's doing."

When he called Patty's house, Frank couldn't understand what Mr. Mendozzi was talking about. But he didn't want Mr. Mendozzi to let on that he didn't know what he was talking about. He looked in the den and there was Patty, doing his homework. He said to himself, "Something's wrong. I'm sure Mr. Mendozzi knows what he's talking about." Immediately, he called his two brothers to meet him in the wine cellar for an emergency meeting. Mama Anna saw him on the phone calling his brothers to meet him in the wine cellar. She knew that something was going on but she didn't know what.

Frank explained to his brothers that the principal called and said that Patty hasn't been in school for two weeks and I don't know why. So the three brothers positioned themselves at different places along the school route. They saw him leave the house with his friends. They then saw him say goodbye to his friends and go upstairs to Rosa's apartment.

Frank and his brothers went into Dominic's and asked who lived upstairs. He told Frank that a young lady named Rosa lived there.

"Let's go guys!" said Frank as they rushed upstairs and knocked on the door.

Patty heard the commotion, looked out the window and saw his father's car. So he went out the fire escape and ran to school before his father could see him.

Frank said to Rosa, "Where's Patty?"

"Patty? Who?"

Frank raised his hand to strike her when his brothers stopped him and reminded him that he might kill her.

"What are you doing with my boy?"

"He's not a boy. He's a man and I'm in love with him!"

"Well, you better fall out of love." Frank went into the closet and found two suitcases and brought them to Rosa. "Now fill these with your clothes. You've got five minutes to get out of here."

She started to sob, "Where do I go?"

"Where do you come from?"

"Boston," she mumbled through her tears.

"Very well then. My brothers will take you. And you must never come back here. If you do, I'm telling you now that you're going to disappear." Frank turned to his brothers and said, "I'll see you guys when you get home."

Frank went down to tell Dominic that his tenant just left and won't be back. "Until you find a new tenant, I'll pay you the rent that you lose."

"No Frank, you don't have to pay me anything."

Frank went home, but didn't speak a word to Anna. It wasn't long before his brothers came home and they explained to Frank, "Don't be too hard on Patty. What you're seeing is you when you were young."

When Patty came home, Frank told Patty he would be grounded for two weeks that he didn't go to school.

Danny was waiting for the boys as they walked up to Esek Hopkins School.

"What's up Patty? You look tired."

"Hi Danny, I didn't get much sleep last night."

"How come?"

"I'm trying to figure out how and where to get the Salerno brothers."

"Why not whack them in the schoolyard?"

"I don't want any witnesses."

"Well, you're the boss Patty."

"Okay, let's go inside, but listen, I want you guys to watch the Salerno brothers. Let me know what they do and where they go while they're in school. Maybe I'll figure something out."

That afternoon, as usual, there was a table in the lunchroom reserved for Patty, Danny, Johnny, Steve, Sir Ray, Butterball and all of their other friends. Patty asked at the table if anyone had anything to report about the movements of the Salerno brothers. Did they do anything special or unusual that he should know about?"

"I don't care how small you guys think it is, I want to hear about it. Anybody got anything?"

Everyone was shaking their heads no, when Sir Ray suddenly said, "I noticed something."

Patty got excited. "What is it Sir Ray?"

"Well it might not be much…"

"Anything, tell me."

"Well, everyday at 1:30, in between classes, I always see them going downstairs to the boys' room for a smoke. There aren't usually many kids down there."

"Okay, let me think about it and see what I come up with. We'll meet tomorrow at lunch." With that Patty extended his hand to Sir Ray, "Nice going. You guys are the best."

"We love you Patty." He had to get that in. Patty just smiled. He loved them too.

"Okay Sir Ray. Keep on those guys and make sure that's the exact time they go to the boys' room and get back to me as soon as possible. We'll discuss it again after this weekend.

Monday came around fast and Patty had his meeting with his guys.

"What do you got for me Sir Ray?"

"It's exactly as I said. I followed the Salerno brothers three days in a row and they never changed their time."

"Okay then, that's where we'll hit them. Now this is how we're going to do it. Johnny and Steve, I want you two guys to stand at the top of the stairs at exactly one-thirty and after the Salerno brothers pass, block off the stairs to make sure no one else comes down. Butterball, you and Sir Ray stand by the door to the woodshop and make sure nobody comes out of there. I don't want any slip- ups."

"What do I do, Patty"?" Danny asked.

"You stay with me. Just wait and see. I've got something nice for you to do."

"When is this going to happen?"

"Tomorrow. Does everyone understand what their job is?" Everyone nodded yes. "Okay guys, this is it. As soon as the bell rings at 1:30, get downstairs fast."

"Should we try to get out earlier?" asked Steve.

"No. That will pinpoint who gets out early and know something is up."

The next day at 1:30, everyone rushed out to their designated positions. Patty told Danny to stop the Weasel if he tried to run.

"Got it," said Danny.

Patty and Danny got to the basement first and waited for the Salerno brothers.

"Here they come, let's go," whispered Patty.

As they were approaching, Patty walked between them, and before they had a chance to react, Patty punched them both in the stomach at once. He hit with such force that they doubled up. Then Patty punched them both simultaneously right in their jaws, and they fell to the floor – out cold.

Just at that moment, the door to the girls' room flung open, and out stepped a girl. She stared at Patty, seeing everything that had happened. Frightened, she immediately rushed back into the girls' room.

Everything was happening fast. The Weasel started to make a run for it, but Danny grabbed him. "You're mine," he shouted.

"Wait a minute," Patty stepped in.

The Weasel started pleading, "Don't hurt me. Don't hurt me. I'll join your gang."

"You don't have a choice," said Patty. "You belong to us. Your cousins are no longer your leader." Then he turned to Danny, "Here's what we're going to do. Take his clothes off. Every bit, de-pants him." It was no sooner said, than done. They stripped the Weasel down and threw his clothes in the boiler room.

"Screw you Rat," Patty hollered. "Go home bare!"

Danny slapped him on the ass, "Screw you Rat!"

Patty hollered to Steve and Johnny to let the Weasel through. "Hey boys, here comes the latest streaker!" And the skinny Weasel ran through the corridor, out the front door and up Charles Street. He ran all the way home, bare as the day he was born, and thankful that Patty had let him off easy.

Meanwhile Danny, Johnny, Steve, Sir Ray, and Patty walked back to class, their sides sore from laughing at the thought of the Weasel's mother seeing him run up to the house naked. "But what about that girl in the bathroom who had seen everything?" Danny asked once they had calmed down.

"Who is she?"

"Isabella Rampone."

"Do you know her?"

"I see her around. She's kind of pretty too. I know her brother. Do you want me to talk to her Patty?"

"No, I don't want you to say anything to her. We'll just wait and see what happens."

News reached the principal's office that two boys were lying down in the basement and appeared to be hurt. Mr. Mendozzi, Mr. Bishop and the school nurse rushed down to administer first aid. Mr. Bishop's first reaction was to call an ambulance, but the nurse stopped him.

"There's nothing broken," she said. "They just got the wind knocked out of them, that's all. And their jaws are swollen." The two brothers were now sitting up, their heads still spinning. Mr. Bishop started questioning them as to who was responsible for this. The boys clammed up, and muttered that they did not know.

"That's all right boys, you don't have to tell me," remarked Mr. Bishop. "There's only one person who could have done this. It was Patty, wasn't it?"

"No, it wasn't Patty," said Fat Salerno.

The nurse interrupted and said that the boys were in no shape to be questioned, and they should be sent home immediately.

"Okay, then send them home. There's no use asking them any questions, they're not going to answer anyway. Let's go back to the office and discuss this upstairs. Send the boys home as long as they're all right. You know Mr. Mendozzi there's only one person who could do this, and you know who I'm talking about."

"We can't accuse him or anyone else unless we can prove it," replied the principal, not wanting to point any fingers.

"Prove it? I'll prove it! I told you way back that he would stumble and I think today is that day. I'm going to call on all of the teachers to see if anyone asked permission to go to the bathroom at the time of the incident. Somebody's got to know something." Mr. Bishop was burning to catch Patty.

"Go ahead if you want, but I think you're wasting your time," answered Mr. Mendozzi.

After contacting every teacher in the school, Mr. Bishop found that one girl had reported to her teacher that she had not been feeling well and had asked to go to the basement bathroom around 1:30. Mr. Bishop called both her and Patty into his office.

"I called you two here because there was an incident in the basement today after lunch, and it has been reported that you were seen there at that time." Mr. Bishop towered over Patty and Isabella, who were both sitting in the low chairs in front of his desk. Mr. Mendozzi was standing to the side, listening. Isabella's big brown eyes were wide open, and she looked nervously towards Patty. But Patty's expression was calm. He knew Mr. Bishop was lying. No one else had been there.

"Patty, do you know Isabella?" asked Mr. Bishop with a glare.

"No sir, I don't."

"And what about you, Isabella, do you know Patty?"

"Well," she timidly began, "I know who he is, but I've never spoken to him before."

"Well listen up Isabella. Someone saw Patty hurt those two boys, and I know you saw the whole thing, and maybe even had a hand in it." Of course, Patty knew Mr. Bishop was bluffing, but it was impossible for him to say anything to Isabella.

"Now you tell me the truth Isabella, or I'm going to notify your parents that you will be expelled from school."

Isabella started to say that she had not seen anything, but Mr. Bishop's words were too much. "You're trying to put words in my mouth!" she exclaimed, "and you're frightening me!"

Mr. Mendozzi took a step forward to interrupt. "That's enough. That's enough, now," he reasoned. "There is no proof of what happened, and this is no way to go about finding the truth. Mr.

Bishop, I think you should let these two go back to their classes. You've interrupted their lessons." And with that, Mr. Mendozzi walked out of the office.

As Patty stood to leave the office, Mr. Bishop blocked his path. "Don't think this is the end of it Patty. I'll get you yet!"

"It's a free country Mr. Bishop, you can do what you want." Patty stepped around the frenzied vice principal, and gave Isabella a quick wink.

After the office had cleared out, Mr. Mendozzi poked his head back in.

"You know John," he said to Mr. Bishop. "You're just wasting your time. Those Salerno boys aren't going to say a word and neither will Isabella or Patty. We only have two weeks of school before summer vacation. Why don't you just lay off of it unless something comes up?"

"Remember John," Mr. Bishop replied, "I've had my eye on Patty. I won't let him off easy."

That afternoon on their way home from school, Patty filled Steve and Johnny in on what had happened. "Isabella didn't say anything. She kept her mouth shut."

"That was top-notch of her," replied Steve.

"I think so," said Patty. "You know she's okay in my book. I think I'm going to call her tonight and thank her." And Patty did exactly that. Promptly after dinner he shooed his younger siblings away, and sat himself next to the phone. A boy's voice answered the phone.

"Hello?"

"Hello. May I please speak to Isabella?"

"Who's calling?"

"This is Patty DiMarco."

"Hi Patty. This is Isabella's brother, Sam. How are you doing?"

"I'm fine."

"Hang down. I'll get Isabella for you."

Patty heard the muffled shout of Sam calling his sister, and suddenly he felt a little nervous. Momentarily, he heard someone pick up the phone.

"Hello?"

"Hi Isabella, it's Patty."

"Oh, hi Patty, how are you?" Isabella was surprised that he had called.

"Okay. I just wanted to say thanks for today in Mr. Bishop's office."

"Oh, that's all right. I really didn't see anything anyway."

Patty knew that she had. "Well, I really appreciated that. Say, would you like to go to the spring dance with me?" The dance was in two weeks, the last event before summer vacation.

"I would love to go," Isabella was embarrassed by how quickly she responded, but she was quick to recover. "I'll see you in school and we can talk about it then. Are you going to sing?"

"I don't know yet. It all depends on Mr. Mendozzi. He said that before I ever sing at the school he has to give me permission."

"Well I heard that you have a nice voice."

"I get by, that's all," said Patty bashfully.

"That's not what I heard," said Isabella smiling to herself.

"I'll tell you what. If I'm allowed to sing a song, that song will be for you."

Isabella's head was spinning. She could not believe that Patty had asked her to the dance, and now he was going to dedicate a song to her!

"What song would you like, Isabella?"

"I don't know, I'll have to think." Isabella paused for a moment, then replied, "Do you know *Kiss Me Once and Kiss Me Twice*?"

"Sure thing. I can do that one. You're on."

"Look Patty, I have to go now, my sister needs to use the phone. I'll see you tomorrow."

"Okay, see you tomorrow Isabella", And Patty hung up.

The following day in school, Patty asked Mr. Mendozzi if he could sing at the dance.

"Well, I don't know Patty, I don't want any incidents. I'm afraid it might get out of hand." Based on the events of Patty's birthday party, Mr. Mendozzi's concerns were legitimate. "Now what do you plan on singing?"

"*Kiss Me Once and Kiss Me Twice*." Patty's eyes gleamed with enthusiasm.

Mr. Mendozzi couldn't say no. "Well I guess that doesn't sound too bad. You can sing that one song, but that's all."

"Oh, thank you Mr. Mendozzi, thank you."

The next two weeks flew by. Patty was busy studying for all of his final exams, and before he knew it, the night of the dance was upon him. He arrived at Isabella's house and found her waiting for him just inside the door. She looked absolutely beautiful in her long, black dress, the same jet-black as her hair. Her large, brown eyes fluttered at Patty.

She looks like a million dollars, Patty thought to himself, and he couldn't help but notice her attractive shape. Isabella introduced him to her mother and father. Her father firmly shook Patty's hand.

"Nice to meet you Mr. Rampone."

"Now make sure you watch over my daughter and get her home early. How are you getting to the dance?" he asked.

"My Aunt Josephine brought me here, and she'll drive us to the dance and pick us up afterwards." Patty then told Isabella's parents that he enjoyed meeting them, and he assured them that he would have their daughter home on time. Then he linked his arm in Isabella's and walked her to the car.

Isabella's family watched the couple from the porch. Her brother Sam turned to his mother, Antoinette, and said, "He seems like a nice boy. I like him." Antoinette just smiled and nodded her head.

Isabella could not get over the way everyone greeted her and Patty as they walked into the dance. She could see the envy in all the other girl's eyes, and the respect with which the boys regarded Patty. Now she knew how it felt to be with the King of Providence. Miss Cox came over to them from across the room. "Patty, I understand you are going to sing tonight," she said with a smile that Isabella considered a little too friendly.

"That's right, I am," said Patty.

"Well, let's do it then. I'll introduce you," she said and went up on stage to get everyone's attention. Miss Cox informed the audience that Patty would be singing one song, and if the crowd became unruly, the singing would immediately be stopped. Then Patty walked onto the stage. Everyone started to clap and cheer.

Patty leaned into the microphone. "I'm going to dedicate this song to a beautiful person," he looked straight at Isabella, "and the song is *Kiss Me Once and Kiss Me Twice*." Isabella was beside herself, a smile beaming from ear to ear.

Patty's voice resonated throughout the dance hall, clear and deep. Many people in the audience became believers of that voice, and everyone remained very orderly. As Patty sung the last notes, the crowd again broke into cheers. Some were screaming, "Patty! Patty!" There were requests for an encore, but Patty kept his promise and left it at that one song. He stepped down from the stage, and asked Isabella to dance. The band began to play a slow ballad, and as he put his hand in Isabella's, he asked her if she was having a good time.

"Oh, yes. Everything is perfect," she replied.

"You know, now that school is over, how would you like to go to a movie with me sometime?"

"I would love that Patty."

Patty called John and Ed aside and said, "I've got to tell you guys something important."

"What is it?"

"Last night my mother said I had a phone call. Guess who called me?"

"Who?"

"It was Miss Cox." The boys couldn't believe it.

"What did she want?"

"I couldn't say too much because my mother was listening. She wanted to know if I remembered when she asked me how to polish her car. I told her I did. She said she was having a tough time doing it and would it be too much trouble if I came over to show her how to do it right. I told her I would come over tomorrow." The boys couldn't believe it, but they knew Miss Cox always liked Patty. "Oh, she also said not to call her Miss Cox but to call her Jane."

"What else did she say?" the boys asked with their eyes open wide.

"I couldn't talk too much with my mother there so I told my mother that Miss Cox wanted to give me some homework for the summer."

"What are you going to do about work?" they asked.

"I'm not going to work."

"Well, what are you going to tell your father?"

"I'll cross that bridge when I get there."

The following day, Patty did not go to work. He told his father that Miss Cox had some summer homework for him to study. His father just told him to come home when he was through.

When Patty arrived at Miss Cox's house, she was waiting for him.

"Thank you for coming over Patty. It is a very warm day so I made some ice-cold lemonade for you. Come in the kitchen and sit down."

"I can stand, thank you, um – Jane." Patty felt a little funny calling his teacher by her first name.

"Do you like calling me Jane when we're not in school?" asked Miss Cox.

"Sure, it's fine."

As she went to the cupboard to fetch two tall glasses, Patty couldn't help but notice what a beautiful body she had. He saw that she was struggling to reach the top shelf. The next thing she knew, Patty had come from behind to reach for the glasses and at the same time was pressing his body into hers. He was pushing himself even closer to her when it sounded as if she lost her breath. She broke into a sweat as Patty put both arms around her squeezing her tighter. Turning her around, he kissed her and slowly started to unbutton her blouse, moving his hands all over her body. He picked her up and brought her to the bedroom and violently made love to her.

She didn't want Patty to leave, but since he had told his father he would be right back he needed to head home.

"Will you come back again"?" she asked.

"Of course I will. I'll call you. Give me a couple books so I can show my parents the homework you want me to do."

She kissed Patty two times and said, "These represent two "A's" for what you've done today."

When Patty got back, he told John and Steve what happened. They both said, "We told you she liked you."

While Patty was talking to his friends, his father was watching him from the office window. He said "Look at my son – he thinks he's bullshitting me. But he's not going to shit a shitter!"

7 DICK "EL TORO" DI MEO

It was summertime now. The days were hot and humid under the hazy, Providence sky. Patty was now working full-time for his father, and Johnny and Steve had also gotten jobs under Frank DiMarco. Big Frank liked to call the boys the Three Musketeers, and he let them work together more often than not. Patty let his brothers Dominic and Henry, take his paper route. Big Frank expected a lot from everyone who worked for him, and he liked to remind Patty, "A little hard work never killed nobody."

One particularly hot day, the "Three Musketeers" sat together on the back of Frank's pickup truck drinking sodas. Steve asked Patty what he was up to that night, and Patty replied that he might call Isabella and see if she wanted to go for a walk. Patty was quiet for a moment, and then he said, "Hey do you guys remember Ricky Sullivan?"

"Sure do," said Steve. "He used to be a professional fighter."

"But he's retired now, right?" asked Johnny.

"Yeah he's retired," confirmed Patty. "He's building a new house, though, that's where I was working last week. He told me he was going to take over the gym at the Wanskuck Boy's Club, and he wanted to know if I would like to train there. He said he would teach me how to box."

"And you could teach him how to punch," joked John. They all laughed.

"Did you tell your father"?" asked Steve.

"Yeah. He said he's been teaching me since I was four years old, and if anyone is going to train or manage me, it would be him. I don't want anyone else anyway, and I can still use the gym."

The following Saturday, Frank took his son to the gym. Johnny and Steve tagged along to get a chance to meet Ricky Sullivan. Ricky greeted Big Frank with a handshake and welcomed him and Patty to the gym.

"Now I'm going to get right to the point," said Frank looking Ricky in the eyes. "I appreciate very much you helping my son by letting him use the gym, but I train and manage my son."

"That's fine Frank. I wouldn't have it any other way. If you or Patty need my help in any way, just let me know and I'll help you one hundred percent." On that, he shook Frank's hand again.

"Okay Patty," said Frank, turning to his son. "Get your trunks on. We'll let you work out a bit, then you and I can spar in the ring."

The word got around the gym fast that Patty and his father were going to box together in the ring, and while Patty was doing his workouts a crowd started to form. When it was finally time to get in the ring, Frank looked around to see that the gym was packed solid with onlookers, and more were trying to get in.

"Look at that," whispered Sully to Jack Simone, the director of the boy's club. "They look like two giants in the ring. Just look at the build on Big Frank and his son's built the same way."

"If Patty follows in his father's footsteps, he'll be one heck of a fighter," Jack whispered back.

In the ring, Frank gave Patty some last minute instructions. "We're not going to punch at each other. We're going to jab and block. Never will I get in the ring to punch my son or have him punch me."

"I wouldn't be able to Papa," replied Patty. "I love you too much."

Frank explained to Patty that this is what was called shadow boxing. "Keep moving to your left. Now jab with your left. Keep jabbing. Now fake a jab, and come in with your right. Good. That's good Patty." Frank blocked every one of Patty's punches. "Now let's switch and let you do the blocking Patty."

Frank could see that something was missing. Patty was holding something back. Big Frank put his finger on it right away. After all, Patty was his son, and all the while that they were boxing, Frank had been looking into his eyes. He could practically hear Patty's thoughts. Frank stopped in the middle of the ring.

"What's wrong Patty?"

"Nothing Pop."

"Come on Patty, you're talking to your father."

"Nothing. It's nothing Papa." Patty respected his father and would never do or say anything to hurt him. Just the thought of hurting his mother or father made Patty feel sick to his stomach. It was the one thing the Italians valued most – respect – the children were taught that before they learned how to walk. Respect and love for your family.

"Listen Patty," said Frank, "I know what's wrong and don't bullshit me. You want to come out swinging, and you want to punch me full force, but you can't do that with me because I'm your father. I understand. Here's what we're going to do. I'll be your manager and let Ricky Sullivan do the training.

"But Pop…"

"No buts. I'm your manager until you want a different one, and I promise you I'll never stand in your way. I'll always love you Patty." With that, Big Frank gave Patty a tap on the cheek.

Frank called Ricky into the center of the ring and explained the situation. "Here's how it's going to be from now on Sully. Patty wants to spar with someone else because he feels I've already been teaching him for long enough."

"Well, I'll see what I can do," replied Sully. "You've got to understand that I wasn't prepared for this, but I'll see if I can find someone for the kid to fight."

The gym was still crowded with the expectant spectators who want to watch Big Frank and Patty fight it out. Amongst the people, Frank noticed a fit-looking group of boys in matching shorts and tops. He nodded in their direction, "Who are those boys Sully?"

"They're the basketball team from Fall River. They just finished playing our team."

"Are they any good?"

"Well they whipped our boys pretty good."

"Ask one of them if they'd like to challenge Patty."

Sully looked at Frank cynically, "Come on Frank, they're seniors in high school."

"So what?"

"So they're 18 years old, that's what, and Patty's still just 13."

"Well let's see what Patty can do." I'm his manager."

"Why not."

Sully shouted into the crowd of boys. "Any of you want to box Patty here?"

No one spoke up. "We got protective gear so no one will get hurt. Anyone up for it?" Patty, Frank and Sully scanned the crowd. Finally, one of the basketball players, a tall kid with broad shoulders, spoke up. "I'll do it," and he bent under the rope to enter the ring.

Frank whispered into Sully's ear, "Regardless of his age, "Patty's just as big as that kid. Let's see what Patty's got. Let's let him test the water."

"What's your name kid"?" Sully asked the boy once he was in the ring.

"Dick. I'm Dick 'El Toro' DiMeo."

"Where'd you get that name?"

"Just use your imagination."

"Are you from Fall River?"

"Yes sir, I am."

"You ever boxed before Dick?"

"Yes I have." Dick's confidence was obvious.

"Well, then you know what it's all about. Where did you box?"

"I boxed for the Fall River Boy's Club."

"Do you know Manny Cabral, the club director?"

"Sure I do. He knows my father."

"Well good luck kid," and Sully gave him a slap on the shoulder.

"By the way, I'm new around here. Who is this kid that I'm going to fight."

"His name is Patty DiMarco."

Patty was in the corner getting some last minute advice from his father. Both Patty and Big Frank were standing up, Patty with his arms across his chest, and Frank leaning in towards his son's face with purpose.

"I just can't get over the build of both of them," Dick mumbled to himself.

"How old are you Dick?" asked Sully.

"Eighteen. Patty's about 18 too?"

Sully chuckled, "No, Patty's only thirteen and a half."

"I can't believe it! He's almost as big as his father is! How good is he?" Dick's confidence was fading quickly.

"Well, I hear he's real good on the street. We want to see what he can do in the ring. How tall are you Dick?"

"Six two."

"And what do you weigh?"

"Around 220."

"Uh huh, that's about what I thought." In his head, Sully was running the stats. Patty was about six feet tall and weighed in at 200 even. The match up as far as size goes was almost even.

"But Patty's only 13," said Dick. It was as if he had been reading Sully's mind, "Should I go easy on him?"

"Don't let his age fool you," Sully warned. "Now I'll explain what I want you to do. First of all, I just became Patty's trainer today, and I never really seen him or his father fight. Now we don't want anyone getting hurt here, but also, I don't want you selling Patty short. His father was a heavyweight fighter in Italy, and word has it a very good one at that. He's been teaching Patty everything he knows since Patty was four, so like I said, don't let his age fool you. We don't know what that kid can do in the ring, but I'm hoping today we'll be able to find out. I just want to know what direction Patty is heading in."

As Sully explained the purpose of the fight to Dick, Dick couldn't help but be distracted by the number of people surrounding the ring. "Patty must be some sort of celebrity," he exclaimed. "This place is jam packed!" Then Dick got serious, "Am I safe in here if I knock Patty down?"

Sully couldn't help but smile, "Of course you're safe. Nothing like that ever happens here. Patty just has a lot of friends, that's all. This is all in good fun, but enough talking. Let's get you two together. Let's get this thing started."

Sully gestured to Frank, and Dick moved to the center of the ring to face Patty.

"Now Frank," said Sully, "I want you to know that Dick is being a good sport not knowing anyone, and volunteering to spar with Patty like this."

Frank extended his hand to Dick. Patty followed suit.

"Now Dick has some experience in the ring," Sully continued. "He's done some fighting at the Fall River Boy's Club, and says he could defend himself pretty good."

Frank nodded his head in understanding.

"Any of you guys got a question to ask, or shall we start?" Sully was getting anxious.

"I got a question," stepped in Dick. "What is it we'll do? Do I just box with him or do I slug it out with Patty? I don't want to hurt him or nothing."

"It's just like we talked about kid," explained Sully. "We want to see what Patty can do. That's what this fight is all about. Return to your corners and when I signal for you guys to come out I want you to come out fighting. Remember, I'm going to referee this fight, and if I say break, then you break, hear me? If I stop the fight, then the fight's over."

The crowd in the gym could see that the fight was about to begin, and the energy in the room began to buzz. A faceless voice shouted out, "Come on Patty, let him have it!" and the rest of the crowd began to cheer along. Sully made the signal for the boys to come out fighting.

Dick threw a quick jab. Patty blocked it and circled to the left, mimicking his father's shadow boxing techniques. Dick threw another jab. Patty blocked it and counter jabbed with his left. He stunned Dick by catching him square on the left jaw. The crowd exploded. Patty circled to the left. Dick backed off a little from the shock of the hit. Patty threw another jab followed by a right cross to the jaw, and Dick went down on his knees. The crowd went wild. "Patty! Patty!" The familiar cheer bounced off the rafters in a deafening vibration.

Frank and Sully jumped into the ring and announced that the fight was over. Dick was now lying in the ring completely limp. Sully waved smelling salts under his nose. Dick's eyelids fluttered, and he started to come around. Both Frank and Sully were extremely concerned, and they waited until they were absolutely positive that Dick was all right before they helped him onto his feet.

"How you feeling boy?" asked Big Frank as he reached down and slid an arm under Dick.

"All right, I guess," Dick mumbled in a daze.

"Let's get you up here. Come on," and together Sully and Frank lifted him up on his feet. Patty stepped back to give them room. Dick's legs couldn't support him, so they carried him to his corner and let him sit down to rest.

Sully responded to the concern in Frank's eyes by telling him, "He just caught a solid punch in the jaw, that's all. He'll be all right soon."

Meanwhile, the gym was filled with discussion. Everyone was talking about Patty's punch. Guys who had never seen Patty fight before, now believed Patty was for real. John and Steve were right by the ropes hugging each other in excitement, wanting to jump into the ring to congratulate Patty. But Frank and Sully knew better than to let anyone in the ring. They did not want anything breaking out, especially after a volunteered fight like this one.

As Dick rested in the corner, trying to recover what had been knocked out of him, and as the boys around the ring, jumped and jostled in commentary on the fight they had just witnessed, Patty stepped back. He modestly stood in his corner, and took it all in. This fight had not been a real challenge to Patty, but after this day, many good fights would be on their way. To everyone's relief, the intelligence was slowly starting to make its way back into Dick's eyes. Patty walked across the ring and put a hand on his opponent's shoulder.

"How you feeling?" he asked.

"Better now."

Patty locked eyes with Dick, "You sure?"

"I feel like I've been run over by a freight train," and Dick shook Patty's hand. "I know you're just 13 Patty, but you sure can throw a mean right."

"Lots of luck," replied Dick

"No, I really mean it."

Sully walked over and made Dick stand up just to make sure he was okay. After he was satisfied that no serious damage had been done, he told the boy to go hit the showers. Frank and Sully had some talking to do. Sully then shouted out to everyone in the gym that the fight was over, and it was time to close the place up for the night.

"Come on, everybody out!"

"Wait a minute," interjected Patty. "Will you let John, Sir Ray, and Steve wait here for me while I shower? I came with these guys, and I'm going home with them."

"They'll be here when you get out, don't worry," assured Frank.

After Patty was in the locker room, and after moving out of John, Sir Ray, and Steve's earshot, Big Frank and Sully discussed things over.

"What do you think?" asked Frank.

"I think this kid's got it. I'm not going to lie. He's one hell of a puncher. I think he's going places. He sure takes after you Frank, and if you don't mind me saying so, I think he's going to be better than you."

"You know Sully, I haven't really asked Patty if he wants to be a fighter. I always wanted him to be a lawyer or a doctor or something like that. I don't think his mother would approve of any of this."

Sully understood completely. "Why don't we do this, Frank? How about we line Patty up with a couple of fights, see what happens, and let it go in the direction it wants to go. You know what I mean?"

"Yeah, I know what you mean."

"Well, the parish is going to have a smoker…"

"A smoker?"

"It's when one parish challenges another from anywhere in the state, Massachusetts and Connecticut too."

"How does it work?" This was news to Big Frank.

"They have heavyweight and light-heavyweight all the way to lightweight. There's the home parish and the visiting parish, and the home parish charges admission and keeps all proceeds. Father Ferrera makes all the arrangements with the other parishes, and he asked me if I'd like to take over the fighters and train them. What do you say Frank? You want to get Patty's feet wet?"

Frank was hesitant, thinking mostly about what his wife would say. "Let's see what Patty has to say, and his mother…you see Sully, I don't want any problems at home."

"All right, why don't you see what you can do."

Frank went home while Patty was still in the showers knowing Patty would probably prefer to walk with his friends. As Big Frank walked up to his front door, he could hear Anna humming as she always did when she ironed the clothes.

"Where's Patty?" asked Anna as soon as he walked inside.

"He'll be home soon. He's coming home with John and Steve." Frank knew that a long line of questions was coming his way, and he walked away from Anna, heading for the kitchen. She was on his heels.

"Where did you guys go?"

"Nowhere special." Frank grabbed a piece of bread from the table and put it in his mouth.

"Where was nowhere special?" She was not going to let him off that easy.

"We just went to the Boy's Club, that's all," mumbled Frank with his mouth full.

"And why did you go? What did you do, join the Boy's Club?" Anna shifted her weight onto one hip impatiently for an answer.

"No I didn't join the Boy's Club, they said I was too young," chided Frank.

"Now cut out the jokes Frank, and tell me what you were up to at the Boy's Club this afternoon."

To tell you the truth Anna, the teachers were having a swimming meet and I wanted to see if I was missing anything." Frank didn't like to lie to Anna, but he was hoping he could deter her for a while. He didn't want to tell Anna right now, but he knew she would not stop until she got the truth out of him. Anna knew Patty was involved, and she wanted to know what it was all about. If Anna asked Frank directly, Frank would not lie to her.

"Don't give me no baloney about the teachers. Remember what I told you.

Eventually you have to sleep and when I get done with you, there won't be any babies being made by you anymore."

Frank laughed. She was a feisty one. "All right Anna, I was going to tell you why I was really at the Boy's Club, but you didn't give me a chance to."

"I'm waiting."

"I went down to see Patty box in the ring."

"You mean fight, not box. And I suppose he fought in the ring like you used to. Why did you allow him to do it Frank? You know I don't want Patty to be a fighter. Back in Italy, I would worry so much every time you went into the ring to fight. I prayed to St. Anne to take care of you, and I was so happy when you retired. That was when I said, 'I'd marry you Frank,' remember? You have made me very happy, but now I'm going to have to worry all over again about my son." Anna looked desperate; her knees sunk as if it were too much of an effort for her to stand upright. "Why did you allow that to happen Frank? Why didn't you stop him from going to fight, you know how I worry. You know, Frank. Why'd you let him do it? I thought maybe he'd follow you in the brick laying business, or if he didn't want to do that, maybe he could be a lawyer. You know that Frank."

"Oh, baloney," said Frank, he knew his wife too well. "You'd like him to be like father like son. You wouldn't been as proud as a peacock. Now listen Anna, I don't want you speaking to me like that."

"I'm sorry Frank, it's just that I'm so worried of what could happen to Patty. I just can't go through that again. I worried about you, now I have to start worrying all over again. Isn't there anything you can do to change Patty's mind?"

"No. I don't think so Anna. Patty's already made up his mind. There's no need to get all upset about it. I think he's going to be a darn good fighter." Big Frank took his little wife into his arms.

In fifteen minutes, Patty arrived home. He gave his mom a brief hello, and immediately headed for his room.

"Patty." Anna called his named in that guilt-inducing tone only a mother knows how to use. "Patty, I would like to talk to you before you go to bed."

Patty's eyes were big and honest. "Sure Mama, what is it?"

"I understand that you were down at the Boy's Club and you're going to start fighting like your father did." Anna didn't wait for her son to respond. "I want you to know that I'm not happy about it."

"But why Mama?" Patty burst out.

"Because I'm going to be worried sick about you getting hurt. I worried so much about your father, and now I'm going to have to go through it all over again." Instinctively, Anna glanced at the statue of St. Anne over the doorway.

Patty walked over to his mother and put his arms around her. He put his chin on her head. "I won't let you worry Mama. I promise you that. If I feel it's too much for me then I won't fight anymore. How about that?"

"I know I can't stop you Patty. I always wanted you to be a doctor or a lawyer, but seeing as you want to be a fighter…then be the best." She hugged Patty, and stood on her tiptoes to kiss his cheek.

"I love you Mama, and I will never hurt you."

The next day at the job site, Steve and Johnny were anxious to hear if Patty's mother was going to let him fight.

"She doesn't want me to make fighting my career. She would rather I be a doctor or a lawyer, and she doesn't want me getting hurt," explained Patty. "But she did say I could do it, and I don't think I want to make fighting my career anyway. What do you guys think?"

"You should just see what happens," answered Johnny.

"Yeah, I think so too," chimed in Steve.

Within that same week, Sully phoned Frank to see if he could arrange a meeting with him and Patty.

"What about?" asked Frank.

"Well Frank, I'd like to get him started training, and you know the agreement you made with me was that I don't do anything without talking to you first."

It's nice to hear you say that Sully. I think we're getting off on the right foot."

"Great. Now where would you like to meet?"

"We can have it right here at my house. How would you like to come over for dinner and I'll have Anna cook you a homemade Italian meal. And what's your wife's name?"

"Delores."

"Why don't you bring Delores along too? I know Anna would just love to have you two over."

"That sounds great Frank."

"Oh, and I got to tell you one more thing, Sully."

"What is it Frank?"

"Well, it's only fair that you know that Patty has other managers besides myself."

"He does? Who?"

"You know Johnny, and Steve, right?"

"Sure, I met them at the gym."

"Well those two boys are real close with Patty, along with three others, Danny, Butterball, and Sir Ray."

"Sir Ray? Where'd a kid get a name like that?"

"Well, he used to be called Crazy Ray until Patty made him a knight, and now they call him Sir Ray."

Frank could hear Sully's hearty laugh on the other end of the line. "No kiddin'!" he chuckled.

"Well, I'll tell you what I'll do," Frank continued. "I'll invite all the boys over after dinner. I'm sure we'll be able to use them, and we'll be able to instruct them what to do."

"Okay Frank. Sounds like it's going to be quite the evening."

"Let's do it next Sunday. Call me during the week."

"All right, talk to you soon."

Frank hung up the phone, and went into the kitchen to tell Anna that they would be having guests over the following Sunday.

"What's it all about?" she asked.

"Sully and his wife Delores will be coming over to discuss Patty."

"You mean about the fighting."

"Yes," replied Frank, looking directly into his wife's eyes.

Anna realized there was no point in arguing anymore, and besides, she loved having guests. "Anything special you want me to cook?"

"No, just the regular Sunday meal."

"Well I'll be cooking quite a few dishes, plus pastries, and I'll want to clean up for the company. I'm going to need some help."

"Just ask my sisters to help. I'm sure they won't mind, and they'll probably be over here anyway wanting to hear all about Patty's business."

That Sunday, promptly on time, Sully and his wife arrived at the DiMarco house. Rich smells poured out from the kitchen, and Frank welcomed the couple and introduced them to his wife. Then Frank called for Patty to come and meet Delores. Patty appeared in the hallway, with combed hair and his Sunday shirt.

"It's nice to meet you Mrs. Sullivan," he said, offering her his hand.

"You can call me Delores. I've heard a lot about you Patty," she said.

"You did? Good or bad?"

Delores laughed. "Don't worry, all good."

Then the three men went into the den to talk.

"Listen Sully," said Frank warmly. "I got all the drinks you can drink, even homemade wine."

"You make your own wine?" Sully was delighted.

"I make it every year. You know it's only fair that I tell you when I'm involved with a meeting concerning anyone in my family no liquor will be served, just so the liquor don't do the talking, we do. Is that all right with you?"

"It sure is Big Frank, and I respect you for that."

"Good," said Frank. "After the meeting we'll get drunk."

Meanwhile, in the kitchen Delores told Anna that she would like to help Anna set the table and she would not take no for an answer. Delores could not believe what Anna had cooked. "I don't believe this Anna," she exclaimed. "What did you make?"

"I made homemade sauce with sausages, meatballs and beef brasual, homemade raviolis, stuffed veal roast, baked stuffed eggplant, chicken cacciatore, and in case anyone wasn't eating meat, all types of vegetables including stuffed artichokes and a large antipasti and homemade pastries."

Delores had never seen anything like it. "Why all of this food?" she asked. "I hope you didn't do all of this just on account of me and Sully."

Anna laughed, "Oh, it's nothing much. I do this every Sunday."

Delores helped Anna set up the table along with Anna Marie, Patty's little sister. Then Anna called everyone in for dinner. Sully was just as astonished at the amount of food as his wife had been.

"What is this, Thanksgiving/?" he asked. He was obviously very pleased.

"Do you believe she does this every Sunday?" gushed Delores.

Anna and Frank looked at one another, knowingly. They were proud of this aspect of their Italian heritage.

They had barely begun eating, when Patty's friends began to arrive. Anna asked them if they wanted to eat, but they replied that they had already eaten dinner at home. "Well then, you boys wait in the den and amuse yourselves," instructed Anna. "You know what to do. Play the music, watch TV or play pool."

Soon dinner was over and Anna along with little Anna Marie started to clean up. Delores insisted that she wanted to help, but Anna would have none of it. "You're our guest," she said.

"So what," Delores answered. "We're regular people just like you are, and besides, the Irish aren't like that."

"I know," said Anna.

"I just wouldn't feel right letting you do everything," and at that, Delores instructed Anna Marie to get her an apron.

As her daughter fetched the apron, Anna relaxed a little. "Listen," she said, "we're not having a meeting, so how about you and I having a créme di menthe cordial?"

Delores laughed. "I'll drink to that!"

Back in the den, Frank and Sully got the boys together. Frank introduced the boys and explained to them why he and Sully were having the meeting, and why they were all invited. First, Frank explained that he would be Patty's manager and Sully would be his trainer. It was up to Sully how Patty would be trained. Then Frank gave Sully the floor so that he could explain what he wanted the boys to do.

"Listen up boys," Sully began energetically. "I want you all to participate in Patty's training." Everyone nodded, making it clear that they would do anything to help Patty. "Now before I instruct you, I want to ask one question. When Patty fought that kid from Fall River, everyone was hollering "Patty! Patty!" As he mimicked the cheer, Sully jumped up and down and put his fist in the air. The boys laughed. After their laughter subsided, Sully continued.

"Now I was just curious. Where does that cheer come from, and how did it start?"

It was Johnny Petrarca who spoke up. "Maybe I can enlighten you Sully. The first time it started was when Patty's family moved here from Eagle Park, and Patty became the new leader of Luna Street. I was personally involved. You see the chant just started up automatically, nobody planned nothing. I guess everyone just has so much respect for Patty that it just happened on its own."

"Well, I tell you guys, I was impressed. It sounded like we were in the Coliseum in Rome. Okay, now I'll tell you what I want from all of you. First of all, do any of you guys smoke?" Everyone shook their heads no. Ray raised his hand.

"What is it Sir Ray?"

"I used to smoke, but I won't anymore just to be able to work with Patty. I swear I never will touch those things again."

"Is that a promise?"

"Yes."

"Good. Now what about drinking, do any of you drink?"

Again everyone shook their heads no.

"Good. Here's why. Patty, if you want me to train you, I will not tolerate drinking or smoking by you, or any of your friends around you. Is that clear?"

Together everyone replied yes.

"The training won't be easy. I want you guys to help Patty with his equipment; you'll carry it in and make sure nothing is forgotten. I expect you boys to conduct yourselves as gentlemen. What I mean by that is I want you to be good sportsmen whatever the outcome of the fight." As Sully spoke, he looked directly at each one of the boys in turn. "Any irregularities, Frank and I will handle it. Is that understood?" Sully was practically shouting now.

"Yes sir!" they all shouted back.

"And another thing," now Sully was on a roll. "I want Patty to start jogging, and I want each and every one of you to accompany him. Anything Patty does, you will be right there doing it along with him." Then Sully walked over to Frank and whispered, "I think that's all I got for now. Why don't you take over?"

Frank positioned himself in front of the boys. They were all seated on the floor in front of him. "In two weeks we're going to have our first smoker."

"Who's it going to be?" asked Danny.

"It's going to be St. Mary's from Hartford, Connecticut."

Everyone was excited. The boys could barely contain themselves.

"So that's it boys," said Sully, "I want you all to start jogging tomorrow and I'll be in touch for the training in the ring."

"The meeting's over," said Frank. "Let's all join hands together in the air."

The boys grabbed one another and started the familiar chant, "Patty! Patty!" They were getting really riled up now.

Upon hearing all of the commotion in the den, Anna, Delores and all of Patty's brothers and sisters came running into the room.

Delores looked at Anna mischievously and said, "Come on Anna, let's go!" And the two women joined in shouting, "Patty! Patty!"

After a while, things settled down and the boys went home. Frank asked Anna to bring up some of the homemade wine from the cellar, and Frank and Sully toasted to the beginning of a new friendship. Sully took one sip and said, "You know Frank, this wine is worth fighting for!" and they both laughed. When the children went to sleep, Anna and Delores joined their husbands to talk. The four didn't break things up until 2 a.m.

The following day, Patty and his friends got together and planned how and where they were going to jog. Patty decided they would start from Luna Street, and proceed straight up Charles Street, right to Lincoln Woods Park, which was a good eight miles one way, to make it a total of 16 miles there and back. They would start on Tuesday after work, and Aunt Josephine agreed to follow in one of Big Frank's trucks.

Patty's friends were very excited, and they made a huge sign that read, "The next heavyweight fighter of the world." Excitement was running high on Luna and Charles streets, and words started to spread that Patty was starting to train for real, and that he would be jogging the following day. Many of Patty's friends from school wanted to join in on the excitement, and with every mouth that the news passed through, the more the excitement elevated, and the more the jog was glorified. Everyone asked their family and friends to drive them in what they now described as a parade.

Frank heard that everyone was going to send Patty off, and he decided to join in. He asked his two brothers to come along in their trucks as well. Frank also mentioned to Anna that he was going to ask Sully if he would like to join Patty in his first jog. Anna was quick to reply, "Why don't you invite the Pope too"?

Saturday rolled around, and it was decided that everyone should meet on Luna Street at 10 a.m. sharp. Anyone who could provide transportation carried as many people as they could. Frank supplied two pickup trucks and one open truck to make sure that anyone who wanted to come would have a ride. The kids had printed leaflets announcing the parade. In bold letters they had printed, "THE KICKOFF TO PATTY'S FIGHTING DEBUT." The leaflet also mapped out the route that the joggers were going to take.

The girls from Patty's class took on the role of cheerleaders. They had practiced a cheer beforehand, and were successful in getting the whole crowd on Luna Street to join in.

"Patty! Patty! He's our man! Patty! Patty! He sure can!"

Even the children, who had been scurrying about through the crowd, joined in. Luna Street was rumbling with noise and excitement. Everyone began to line up in the streets to begin the procession that would follow the joggers. The street had the energy of a battlefield, with Patty's supporters as the assembling troops. However, the enthusiastic faces of the troops revealed that this battle was a surefire victory. Everyone wanted to take part in Patty's training. This was something the boys had initiated on their own; it wasn't just a jog around the town. It was the beginning of a run to the top. Everyone had faith in Patty; he had the potential to go a long way.

In a borrowed Cadillac convertible, Frank rolled down the street. Ricky Sullivan sat at his side in the passenger seat, and Frank's brothers, Vito and Alfred sat in the back. Behind them were the open trucks, then a long procession of vehicles. Directly in front of them were the cheerleaders, their short skirts swishing back and forth before the Cadillac's glistening grille. Whoever wanted to walk would walk up front with the cheerleaders, and if they got tired they could jump on the trucks or in the cars. In all, the boys counted 22 vehicles, 37 bicycles, and 232 people. And at the head of it all were the joggers: Johnny, Steve, Danny, Butterball, Sir Ray, and Patty.

The leaflet that had been passed throughout the crowd also announced that Patty would be representing St. Anne's parish in a fight against St. Mary's parish of Hartford, Connecticut, which they would pass along the parade route. It was unbelievable what was happening. Johnny and Steve had gotten in touch with the kids who played in the Esek Hopkins band and they came marching around the corner to join the parade. The band had been instructed to start off playing marches from John Philip Sousa, but then upon entering Charles Street, they would switch to *When the Saints Come Marching In*. Over the noise of the trumpets and drums, Frank and Sully shouted to Patty to "stretch first!"

Anna and her sisters-in-law were watching the whole chaotic scene come together, speechless. It was unreal how enormous the event had become. Patty's brother, Dominic and Henry, and his little sisters Anna Marie, and Carol, all jumped in the truck with Aunt Josephine. Patty had finished stretching and was ready to go.

Precisely at that moment, with the cars in the parade revving their engines anxious to take off, four motorcycle policemen parted through the crowd, and Big Frank turned off the engine of the Cadillac and stepped out to greet them.

"Anything wrong officers?" he asked. Enthusiasm radiated from Frank's sparkling eyes, though he asked the question sincerely and with the utmost respect.

One of the officers extended an envelope towards Frank.

"What's this?"

"It's a permit," the officer replied. "You couldn't do this without one."

Frank was taken aback. "Who issued this?"

"The gentleman in that black sedan." The officer pointed to a black sedan with tinted windows coming down the street.

"Who is it?"

"Joe Santoro" Joe Santoro was the district councilman.

"Unbelievable," Frank muttered, shaking his head in disbelief. An enormous smile expanded across the width of his face.

Frank approached the sedan, and Councilman Santoro got out to shake his hand. The councilman was thin and without a summer tan. He wore suit pants and a dress shirt with rolled up sleeves. His jacket and tie had been discarded in the back seat of his car.

"I heard about your little parade here, and I didn't think you were aware that you needed a permit, so I went ahead and got you one myself. I also brought along this escort of four policemen. They'll take you to the North Providence line, and then the State Police will take over from there."

"I can't believe this," said Frank, his hand still firmly gripping Santoros. "What do I owe you for all of this?"

"Nothing. I just want to ride in the parade, up front with you Frank."

"Of course you can. Hell, for what you've done, you can sit on my lap!" They both laughed.

Everything was ready to go. The police went to their designated positions, and Frank instructed the drum major to move out and begin playing. "And don't forget, when you hit Charles Street, it's *When the Saints Go Marching In*!"

The streets were lined with people, and neighbors leaned out of the windows to shout, "Patty! Patty!" Many of Patty's friends were throwing confetti into the air. Even the weather seemed to be on Patty's side. A slight breeze blew down Luna Street, cooling the foreheads of the children, swirling the confetti into little tornadoes, pushing out the humidity that would have put a damper on the jog.

From his position in the lead car, Frank saw a pretty teenager break apart from the crowd and run over to Patty. She shook Patty's hand and wished him lots of luck. Frank hollered out to Steve and Johnny, "Anybody knows who she is?"

"Why Frank?" asked Vito from the back seat.

"She's a very pretty girl, and she seemed awful friendly. What do you say guys, anybody know her?"

Steve answered, "Yeah, we know her."

"Her name's Isabella Rampone," Johnny said, finishing Steve's sentence.

"Anything wrong Mr. DiMarco?"

Frank shook his head. "No. But did you see the look in her eyes."

"I didn't notice nothing."

"Well, I did. I have a feeling we're going to see more of her."

The parade was now moving at a steady pace, approaching Ledge Street. Standing on the corner in front of the Manhattan Social Club, were a few wise guys and a couple of bookies, whom Frank pointed out. They referred to the Manhattan Club as their office. The one who went by the name of Bo Bo ran inside to report what was going on in the street. Out came Stogie Capelli, who was the head of all the gambling in the Charles Street area. He stood right on the edge of the sidewalk as the parade passed. Frank waved to him in greeting and Stogie waved back. One of the bookies asked, "How do you know him?"

"We were brought up together in Italy and we were best of friends. He was one hell of a fighter and I'll tell you this, if his son takes after him, he's going to be dynamite."

"You know the kid's going to be fighting in a smoker in two weeks at St. Anne's auditorium."

"I'll make that fight for sure," replied Stogie.

People watching the parade waved to Patty and wished him luck. The cheerleaders started up again, "Patty! Patty! He's our man! Patty! Patty! You sure can!" The rest of the crowd joined in.

Sully leaned over to Frank, "I don't believe this reception. It's like Patty just won the heavyweight championship of the world. There's one thing I'm afraid of Frank."

"What's that Sully?"

"I don't want Patty to get over confident."

"He won't. He's too strong for that."

"Think so?"

"I know so. I've been watching him."

"What do you see Frank?"

"He has his mind on jogging. He's a strong minded person."

Soon the parade reached the North Providence line, and the State Police were waiting there to escort them to Lincoln Woods State Park. Suddenly Frank stopped the car and jumped out.

"Where are you going Frank?" Sully called after him.

"I want to speak to Patty."

"Wait for me. I want to come too." Big Frank and Sully both ran up to Patty, and began to jog alongside of him.

"How are you doing Patty," asked Frank. "Do you want to stop?"

"No, definitely not. I feel fine," Patty replied.

"You want something to drink?"

"No, I'm alright."

"Okay, but just let us know if you want something."

When they were approaching Lincoln Woods State Park, Sully said to Frank, "You know it's another two and a half miles around the lake. I'm not going to let him do that. This will be enough for the first time." Frank agreed.

"From now on," continued Sully, "I'm just going to let him run around the park. I don't want him getting hit by any of the cars. This is all right for the first time. After all, he has plenty of protection from getting clipped by another vehicle. You got to realize also there's a lot of curiosity seekers."

"You're the trainer Sully. I'm glad you think that way."

As they entered the park, other friends were waiting in the parking lot with gallons of lemonade. One of the servers was Isabella Rampone. Isabella immediately headed directly for Patty and offered him a drink. Patty, sweaty and tired, was walking off his run. He had not known that Isabella had come.

"Hi! Patty. Here, this will cool you off." She handed him the drink, smiling.

"Hi! Isabella. It's nice of you to come."

"I wouldn't miss your first jog for all the money in the world."

"Thanks. How did you get here?"

"My brother Sammy brought me."

"That was real nice of him."

On the other side of the parking lot, Frank was watching. He nudged his brother Vito. "You see. What did I tell you?"

"You're right, Big Frank."

"Look at the sparkle in her eye, and let me tell you, eyes don't lie."

"Are you going to ask to meet her Frank?"

"No. If he wants me to meet her, he'll have to let me know."

Just then, Patty started walking towards where his father, uncles, and Sully were standing. Isabella was at his side.

"See, what did I tell you"? said Frank to no one in particular.

Patty introduced Isabella to the men, all the while looking directly at his father.

"Nice to meet you Isabella." As Frank shook her hand, his shoulders looked even wider than usual next to Isabella's small frame.

"I can see why Patty's so tall. He takes after you and your brother's Mr. DiMarco."

Frank could not help but like the fact that she had respected him by calling him Mr. DiMarco. That was a must in Italian families-respect. Frank was strong on that. "Without respect," he often said, "you got nothing."

Frank, Sully and Joe Santoro went over to thank the State Police.

"That's okay Mr. DiMarco. We're happy we escorted the future heavyweight champion of the world," replied one of the officers.

Frank laughed. "We'll see."

The men decided the festivities had gone on long enough, and it was time for everyone to get back home. Frank and Patty thanked everyone for their support, and Sully made sure to remind Patty that he needed to be down at the gym on Mondays, Wednesdays, and Fridays. The other days of the week he should jog, and Sundays would be for rest.

"Okay Sully, and hey, thanks a lot."

Patty waved goodbye to Sully, then called his father aside.

"Papa, should I ask Isabella if she wants to ride back with us?"

"Is she your girlfriend?"

"Not really."

"Then let her go back the way she came. At least for this time anyway."

"Okay Papa, I won't ask her." Patty would never question his father as to why. He respected his father, and his decisions no matter how trivial they seemed.

When Frank arrived home, Anna and the kids were all waiting for them. The children had wanted supper, but they had to wait for their father. Anna looked out the window and then called back to her children. "Here comes Papa. Now we can start to eat."

Big Frank walked in and kissed his wife hello. "Where's Patty?" she asked.

"He'll be home a little later. He's with his friends."

"Oh, all right then," Anna replied. Frank could tell from the way she downcast her eyes that Anna was still unhappy about what Patty was doing.

"You know Anna, Patty introduced me to a girl today."

"He's got a girl?"

"Now, I didn't say that."

"What is she then, just a friend?"

"He didn't say she was his girlfriend."

"Listen here Frank. Anytime you introduce a girl to your father…he must like her."

"Maybe he does, but he didn't tell me that."

"What's her name?"

"Isabella Rampone."

" They the Rampones from Branch Avenue?"

"Same ones."

"I know them. I never met the girl, but I know her mother and father. They're a nice family, those Rampones."

For the next two weeks Patty trained heavily. He was a good listener, and was paying close attention to everything Sully requested of him. The first night of training, Patty was shadow boxing in the ring, when Sully abruptly stopped him.

"Patty, I want you to listen to me. I noticed while you're working out you keep looking back at your friends. Well I'm going to tell you now, I don't want you to look at anyone but me. I don't want you distracted. If you keep looking at your friends they won't be allowed in here while you're training." Sully never raised his voice, but his tone commanded respect.

"Okay, Sully. I won't look around anymore."

"You know Patty, I don't want any distractions. What would happen to you if you were in a fight and you were turning your head looking for your friends? Your opponent would make mince meat out of you. Do you understand what I'm trying to say? I want your eyes pointing straight into your opponent's face and don't take them off him for one second. Do you think because you knocked out that DiMeo kid last week, that all your fights are going to be that easy? I don't want you to take any fight that easy. I want you to be ready for anything. Remember what I am saying, because if I have to remind you again, you're out of here. I'm not going to waste my time. I'm doing this for your own good."

Patty did not flinch once. He stood there and listened to Sully with open ears. After all, even though he was training to be a fighter, he was brought up with strict discipline and respect.

"I'm going to ask you one question," Sully was riding him hard. "Now what do you want to do?"

"I want to listen to you and pay attention also," was Patty's quick, but earnest reply.

"Atta boy Patty. That's what I wanted to hear. I just want to say one more thing. Don't ever play games with your opponent to entertain your friends. What I meant by that is if you're taking it easy on him because you figure you can beat him; he's liable to go the distance feeling he could beat you. Once he gets that in his head, that's all it takes. One lucky punch and that's the end of you. Do you understand me?"

"Yes I do, Mr. Sullivan."

"I'm not throwing your friends out, because I want them to hear this too." Frank, who had come in to watch the practice, silently approved of Sully's stern words. He felt Sully was training his son right, setting him straight from day one.

"Keep shadow boxing," directed Sully. "I want you to speak to your father," and he headed over towards Frank.

Frank nodded his head as Sully approached, "Training's looking good," he said.

"I didn't mean to go hard on the kid," Sully replied apologetically.

"No, no. You're doing fine. I went through the same type of training when I was a kid. Remember, I'm just the manager. You're the trainer."

"Well, here's what I'd like to do Frank. We only got two more weeks and…"

"Yeah?"

"And I've got someone in mind to spar with Patty."

"Who is it?"

"His name is Johnny Ding. He's about 25, six feet tall…he used to fight heavyweight. You know him?"

"Never heard of him."

"His real name is Johnny Fallone, but people say when you ring a bell he comes out fighting, so everyone calls him Johnny Ding. What do you think Frank?"

"Don't ask me, you're the boss."

"Well, I don't think we'll have any problems with him. In the meantime, I want to work on leading off. Did you bring your trunks with you?"

"Sure did."

"Would you like to work out with Patty? I don't want any punches thrown."

"Sure thing, I'll help out," and Frank went to get changed.

Sully signaled to Patty to stop and work the punching bag. He told him he had someone for Patty to spar with, but he wasn't around that day so Frank said he would help out temporarily. "I want to get you started soon as possible. You're first smoker's just two weeks away, and as I understand it, you got a tough opponent. Soon as your father's ready, I'll call you."

It did not take long for Frank to change.

"How does it feel to get back in the ring Big Frank?" Sully asked.

"It seems like old times. Sure brings back memories. Is Patty ready?"

"I want him to spend ten more minutes on the punching bag."

"Whatever you say, Sully. You're the boss."

Patty finished his time at the punching bag with Big Frank watching on. Patty moved almost exactly like his father had.

"Okay, times up. Patty, jump in the ring with your father."

Patty turned and walked to the ring without missing a beat. The punching bag hung alone, still swinging on its chain. Big Frank was waiting for his son in the ring, and as Patty stepped in, the two found themselves in the same position they had been in only weeks before. Father and son faced each other-"two giants in the ring." However, this time they had a coach.

"Now this is what I want you guys to do," Sully's voice echoed off of the gym floors. "I don't want any punches hitting home. You can jab only into each other's glove. Patty, you do as I say. Your father will block your punches. When you move around your opponent, you always move to the left. Got it?"

"Yes sir," said Patty. "Let's go."

Patty moved to the left and started jabbing with his left. Big Frank blocked his punches and threw some jabs of his own. Big Frank's eyes looked steadily into his son's. It was obvious to Sully why Big Frank had been a contender for the heavyweight fighter of Italy. *"That Frank can really move,"* thought Sully. *"He could be an excellent sparing partner for his son."* However, both Patty and Frank had made it clear that they would never trade punches with one another.

Patty started leading to his right. Sully broke in, "No! No! To your left, Patty." Frank kept his mouth shut. He knew his place and did not want to insult Sully's authority.

The two looked good together in the ring. Their shoulders were back and their eyes were level. Patty kept jabbing, throwing his right into his father's left. Patty's arm had to fully extend in order to reach Frank. Frank would in turn block the punches and jab back, his feet slightly wider than shoulder width apart.

"All right. Very good, Patty. That's enough for now. Jump rope for 15 minutes, and we'll call it a night."

Frank and Sully went off to the side to talk.

"So what do you think?" Frank asked eagerly.

"The kid's good. He's going to be a powerhouse, Frank. It's going to be exciting to see in two weeks."

"I can hardly wait," said Frank, a glimmering pride in his eyes. "Well I got to be going Sully. We'll keep in touch. You want a ride Patty?"

"Thanks Pop, I'm going to walk home with my friends."

On the way home, Patty explained to his buddies. "Don't take it the wrong way with Sully. He wants me to concentrate on the fight not on my friends or any spectators. If he were that mad, he would've thrown you guys out of the gym. He felt it was the first time, so he let it go."

"We understand Patty."

"Good. I knew you guys would."

"Hey Patty, listen to what we're planning' to do."

"What is it?" Patty looked slyly at his friends. He could tell by their excitement that they were cooking up another one of their ideas.

"We're going to have some posters printed and place them in every merchant on Charles Street, Eagle Park and North Providence," said Johnny.

"Now where we going to get the money for something like that?" asked Patty.

"We're all going to pitch in," explained Danny. "We all have a little saved up from our summer jobs."

"See how much it costs. If it's too much I don't think we should bother with it. Listen. Why don't we find out if the church will do it? After all, Sully told me there's going to be 15 different fights that night." Patty was always the practical one.

"How many rounds?" asked Steve.

"Just four rounds. I don't know if they're going to charge admission or not. Next time I see Sully, I'll ask him."

For the next two weeks Patty trained as hard as Sully would let him. He did not want any regrets about his first appearance in front of a crowd. The church said they would take care of the posters, and all was set for the upcoming fight. "You'll train on Wednesday, jog on Thursday and Friday, then I want you to rest for the remainder of Friday before the fight." Those were Sully's last instructions to Patty.

Walking home from the gym on Wednesday, Johnny and Danny could barely contain themselves. "You excited Patty?" they wanted to know.

"Yeah."

"Are you nervous?"

"Not really. Sully has been training me not to take any opponent for granted, so I'm not. He also told me that the priest from St. Mary's informed Father Ferrera that their heavyweight fighter is pretty good, and if we didn't have one they would cancel the heavyweight division because they didn't want any injuries. Sully asked me what I wanted to do."

"And you said, 'no problem,' right Patty?"

"I said, 'send him in.' Sully asked if I was sure, and I said, 'of course. I'm not worried one bit. I got other things to think about.' " The boys all started to laugh.

"Who's coming from your family Patty?"

"Well I know my father's coming, my uncles, and Aunt Josephine. My father's telling everybody about the fight, so I don't know who else."

"Did you invite Isabella?"

"No, I didn't think of it. I don't know if I should."

"I think it would be a good idea," urged Johnny.

"We'll see. I'll give her a ring tonight." The boys were now coming up to Patty's doorstep. Patty waved them off and reminded them that they would be jogging in the morning. "See you guys. Goodnight."

As soon as Patty stepped inside, there was Anna waiting for him.

"Hi Mom." Patty gave her a kiss.

Anna took his face into her hands.

"Why are you looking at me like that?" Patty asked.

"I want to see if you got a black eye."

Patty laughed.

"You're going to fight Friday night? Anna asked, though she already knew the answer.

"Yes I am. Mama, are you going to watch me?"

"No, I'm not."

"Why not Mama?"

"Because I don't want to see you get hurt. But I'll be worrying about you that night."

"Don't worry too much, because I'll make short work of him."

"You're just like your father, you know that?"

"Mama, I've got to make a phone call."

"Who are you going to call, your girlfriend?"

"What girlfriend?"

"That Rampone girl. Or do you have more than one?"

"How do you know about Isabella?"

"Remember, I'm your mother and I know a lot of things. I know you introduced her to your father. Is that so bad?"

"Mama, that I did. No, that's not bad if you like her." Patty looked at his mother sheepishly, "Do you?"

"Maybe. Well then you introduce her to Mama, then it won't be 'maybe' no more." Anna could not stay stern with Patty for too long. "Go ahead. Go call her before it gets too late."

Patty looked around to make sure none of his siblings were eavesdropping, and called Isabella up on the phone. It was her sister, Vanessa, who answered. She wanted to know who was calling.

"It's Patty DiMarco."

"Oh, how are you Patty! This is Vanessa, Isabella's sister. Isabella told me about you."

"Good or bad?"

Vanessa giggled. "Oh, good of course. Just a minute, I'll get Isabella."

"Hi Patty, how are you doing?" Isabella's voice was even more delicate on the phone.

"I'm all right," Patty answered.

"Are you still training?"

"Yes."

"Is that what you want to be, a fighter?"

"I don't know if that's what I want to be, but I like it for now."

"What do your parents think?"

"Well my mother wants me to be either a doctor or a lawyer."

"Is that what your father says too?"

"He says whatever I want to be, he'd like me to be the best."

"Well that's good. What about being a singer?"

"I don't know. I haven't thought of anything serious. Are you coming to the fight on Friday?"

"Well, I was thinking about it." Isabella paused for a second as if she was thinking something over. "Do you want me to come?"

Patty would not give her a direct answer. "Well, if you want to."

"If I do come, I'll have to go with my brother, and I have to ask my father because I won't be able to come alone."

"Well, if you're coming, let me know and I'll have one of the guys save you a seat in the front row."

"That would be nice Patty. Listen, my father and brother are home right now. Why don't I ask right now? Hold on a second, will you?" Isabella asked her father if she could go to the fight. Her father, as expected, said it would be fine just as long as she had a chaperone. Her brother said that he would be happy to go; he would love to see Patty fight.

Isabella excitedly picked up the phone and told Patty the good news.

"Listen Isabella," said Patty. "When you go I'll have some of my friends waiting, and they'll show you where to sit. I'll make sure you're right up front where you can see everything."

Isabella could not believe her luck. Not only had Patty invited her, but also he was going to save her a spot in the front row. Just wait until her friends hear about this! Isabella was genuinely flattered, and she thanked Patty.

"Oh that's nothing, seeing that it's you," said Patty casually. "The fight starts at eight-o'clock, so you should be there at seven-thirty."

"Okay, Patty. I'll see you there."

"See you Friday." and they both hung up smiling.

Patty asked his father if it would be all right for him to come in a little late to work on Thursday and Friday so he could jog.

"That's fine for Thursday," replied Frank, "but on Friday, I want you to jog then take the whole day off to rest. And I mean rest – no fooling around. I want you ready for the fight, okay?"

"Fine Papa. I will."

The rest of the week flew by, and fight-time was approaching. On Frank's instructions, Anna made Patty eat at three-o'clock. She made him a small steak, mashed potatoes, and a large glass of milk. Frank and his brothers returned home from work early to make sure they met with Patty for a last minute talk. It was now four-o'clock. Patty's friends had all come over to his house early, so they could all go over to the fight together. Frank asked Patty why he was leaving so early.

"I called Sully and asked if I could loosen up before the fight. He told me to meet him at five-o'clock at the Boy's Club."

"Do you need a ride?"

"No, we're going to walk."

"All right. We'll meet you at St. Anne's then."

Patty hugged his mother, and she told him to be careful. It looked as if she were about to cry, she was so worried.

When the boys arrived at the Boy's Club, Sully was already waiting for him. He instructed Patty to jump rope, punch the bag and shadow box. Nothing else. "And don't wear yourself out,"

Sully warned. Then almost as an afterthought, he asked, "Are you nervous Patty?"

"Never. I just want to get in there and fight."

"Are you over-confident?"

"No."

"That's a boy."

At 6:30, Sully told Patty that he'd had enough, and he should hit the shower, then they would all walk the one block over to St. Anne's together. As they were walking, Patty told his friends that he wanted them to save seven seats in the front row.

"Johnny and Steve, you stay at the door and when Isabella and her brother arrive escort them to the front row. It will be you five and them two, okay?"

"Sure thing, Patty."

"I'll see you guys later on. I have to go stretch in back with the rest of the fighters."

Soon people started to arrive. Frank stood at the door, ready to greet his family and friends. To Frank's surprise, it was Stogie Capelli and his sidekick Bo Bo walking up to the door. Frank smiled and gave Stogie a big hug.

"I didn't know you were coming here Stogie!"

"When I found out Patty was your son I made sure I would make this fight."

Big Frank told Johnny to take Stogie and his friend to the front row.

Isabella and her brother arrived soon after, and Johnny and Steve escorted them to their reserved seats. Isabella ended up sitting right next to Stogie. It was no secret in the neighborhood what Stogie did for a living, and Isabella shifted uneasily in her chair. Stogie looked over at the young lady, and gave her a casual nod and hello. "Hi," replied Isabella quickly.

Her brother Sam whispered discreetly in her ear, "I can't believe we're sitting next to Stogie Capelli."

Stogie turned to the two kids, and warmly asked, "How come you are sitting here up front?" Who did you come here to watch?" He was simply trying to make conversation.

"We came to see Patty DiMarco."

"Hey!" he chuckled, "what do you know. That's who I came here for. Are you Patty's girlfriend?"

"We're just good friends."

"Who do you think is going to win?"

"I don't know, but I'll be cheering Patty on."

Bo Bo, Stogies right hand man, nudged his boss in the side. "How much action did you take on this fight?"

"Two thousand dollars."

Bo Bo opened his mouth in hesitation, "You know, I think you made a mistake Stogie."

Stogie grinned. "Now why's that?"

"Well, you gave odds at five to one that Patty's opponent won't go more than one round."

"That's right. How much did you bet, Bo Bo?"

"I didn't bet Stogie. I won't go against you even though I think it's a suckers bet."

"Well, let me tell you this Bo Bo. I've known Frank DiMarco ever since I was a kid in Italy."

Isabella leaned in a little closer, eavesdropping on the men's conversation. She pretended that she was trying to get a better view of the ring, so as not to look suspicious.

Stogie continued, "When I was about 12 years old, a bunch of kids in the school yard – there was maybe ten or so of 'em – well they were getting ready to gang up on me. None of my friends were around. You see, I had no protection. Frankie, noticed them mulling around me, and he stepped right in beside me and shouted 'Okay Nicky, now it's the two of us.' We both started swinging like madmen. You should have seen Big Frank in action. He was unbelievable. Those other boys were lying all over the ground. He really messed them up good. Well the point is Bo Bo, without Frankie steppin' in like that, I would have gotten a serious beating. I told Frankie that I would never forget what he had done, and maybe someday I would repay him. From then on we were the best of friends. When we got older, Frankie started to box and I followed him through all of his fights. And now we meet again in America.

"How was he in the ring?" asked Bo Bo, now enthralled.

"He was a powerhouse! Nobody ever went more than five rounds with him. He had 21 fights, and they were all knockouts." Stogie was bouncing in his seat enthusiastically. "He was heading for the heavyweight championship in Italy. You see, I've seen Big Frank in action, and I would say his son's going to be even better than he was. I think it's a safe bet to say that this other guy won't even go two minutes."

Bo Bo nodded in understanding.

"You know another thing Bo Bo?" Stogie grinned slyly, "That Frank, he had every woman in Rome chasing him. Quite the lady's man," Stogie chuckled. "And you know what. I bet Patty's going to be worse!"

Bo Bo laughed, nodding his head all the while. Then his expression became earnest and he asked, "So did you ever repay that favor to Frank?"

"No, I never got the chance, but it's still open."

Isabella did not know what to think of all she had just heard. She had already been both anxious and thrilled to watch Patty fight. Then sitting in the front row next to Stogie Capelli, and listening to those stories – Isabella's mind was going in a million directions.

By this time, St. Anne's hall was packed to the seams. Everyone who knew Patty in the neighborhood, wanted to see the fight. Father Ferrera and Big Frank were explaining to the crowd that there was no more room and they were going to have to close the doors. The people outside pleaded with Father Ferrera to please leave the doors open, so a few of them could watch Patty fight then relay it back to the rest of the crowd.

"Patty doesn't fight until the third fight," Father Fererra replied.

"Come on Father," said Big Frank. "Why don't we leave the doors open just this once, and if they don't behave they'll have to answer to me."

"Okay Frank. You tell them. But remember you're responsible. There're over 200 people out there."

"I'll go and have a talk with them," said Frank confidently.

The crowd promised that there would be no crashing of the doors. Frank promised that he would send Steve and John down to notify them just before Patty was about to fight.

Inside, the hall was hot with anticipation. The Father stepped into the ring and announced that this was the first smoker of the season, and if it proved successful and stayed orderly, there would be plenty more to come. "We originally had scheduled 15 fights, but only ten have arrived from Connecticut. Our first fight will be a four-round middleweight."

Father Fererra introduced the fighters and told them to, "Shake hands and come out fighting!" The fight went all four rounds, and

Connecticut took the win. The next two fighters also went the distance of four rounds, and Connecticut came out on top again. Then it was Patty's turn.

"The next fight out will be our heavyweight fighter, Patty DiMarco." The place went wild. The entire hall was rumbling with energy. "Okay boys. Shake hands, and come out fighting!"

The doors at the back had been opened, and people peered in from outside. Sully put his hands on Patty's shoulders and looked him in the eyes. "Don't forget to lead with your left. If he jabs you, block it. If you see an opening, go in with your right. Understand?" Patty nodded sharply. "Good. Now go ahead."

On the sound of the bell, Patty immediately advanced. His opponent jabbed Patty once. Patty moved to his left, keeping his eyes level. He jabbed again. This time, Patty saw an opening and in a quick flash he sent in a smashing right hand to his opponent's jaw. The boy's head spun laxly; it looked as if he were out on his feet. Patty followed with another right to his jaw, and down he went!

The hall erupted. They knew the kid was not getting up. The referee was counting, and the crowd began to cheer, "Patty! Patty!" and they would not stop.

Stogie shouted to Bo Bo, "What did I tell you! He didn't make a minute! Give me the two thousand!"

Stogie was on his feet cheering. Isabella next to him was jumping up and down. Everyone in the hallway and the street continued to chant Patty's name. Patty might as well have just won the heavyweight championship of the world.

"I told you Bo Bo, this kid is going to be better than his father!"

Father Ferrera lifted Patty's hands into the air in victory. Frank and Sully were both in the ring hugging and congratulating Patty.

Then together, the three of them went over to Patty's opponent to make sure he was all right. He was starting to get up, and Patty gave him a hand. The boy's first words as his brain cleared were, "That was some punch! I didn't even see it coming."

Patty just smiled, and asked him if he was okay.

"I'll be all right. And hey, congratulations and lots of luck in the future."

Patty returned to the locker room with his father and Sully. "You were good," said Sully. "Thanks for following my training instructions."

"I always will," replied Patty.

"Did you see how important it is to keep your eye on your opponent, not on the crowd? I want you to train even harder from now on, and don't let up. Father Ferrera has more fights lined up. You will be using the Boy's Club as your training camp. I cleared it with Mr. Simone. You'll have access anytime you want."

Father Fererra walked into the room. He looked a little stunned and when he approached Patty, he shook his head in disbelief and said, "That was some fight. It sounded like the crowd was in your corner! For a time, there, I thought I was in Madison Square Garden."

"Thank you Father," replied Patty humbly.

"But in the future son, don't hit so hard."

Frank was not happy with that remark. Sully put his palm on Frank's chest to keep him from saying anything. "Let me handle this please, Frank." Then he turned to the Father. "Father, if Patty didn't hit hard that would put him in a dangerous situation. I will not have it that way, because Patty could get hurt and being his trainer it is my responsibility to keep him from becoming somebody else's punching bag. Nor will I allow Patty to be put on display. Not just because we're in a church, but that stands for anywhere that Patty fights."

"Well then, calmly reasoned the Father, "If that's the way it is going to be, then maybe Patty won't be fighting in any of our smokers."

"That's okay Father. If that's the way it's got to be, then that's the way it's got to be. These rules don't apply only to Patty, but they apply to every fighter I train."

"What do you mean by that? You know you trained everyone that fought tonight."

"That's right Father. I'm not going to allow any of my fighters to get hurt. They are not on exhibition."

"Well then, how do we handle it in the future?"

"Explain to the other parishes what we have, and that they should come prepared, or don't arrange any fight with them."

The Father was at a loss. "You have to understand that I'm new at this."

"We understand Father."

Just then, the janitor came in and informed Father Farrera that everyone had left, and he would like to clean the locker room. The Father turned to Sully, "One more thing before we go. You guys have done a good job. Forget about what I said before. Let me think about it, and maybe I'll approach the other parishes differently. Good night now."

"Good night, Father," they all answered together.

When they went to the street, the usual crew of Johnny, Steve, Danny, Butterball, and Sir Ray were all waiting. They hugged Patty, and shook his hand enthusiastically. Frank said, "I don't suppose you want a ride?"

"No, I'm going to walk home with my friends."

"Okay, but are you going right home? I know your mother has been worrying."

"We were going to stop in at Jack's for a quick soda."

"Okay, but your mother will be waiting for you, I'll bet on that."

Jack's was hopping that night with all of the kids who had gone to the smoker. When Patty was spotted walking in through the glass doors, someone yelled, "Here comes the champ!" Everyone cheered. Jack, standing behind the corner in his white apron drying off a soda glass, raised his voice over the excitement. "Patty," he yelled cheerily, "in honor of your victory in the ring, I'm going to make you your favorite – just for you, an extra large banana split. Just the way you like it Patty!"

Patty grinned from ear to ear. "The way I like it, right. That's vanilla, chocolate, and strawberry, with extra nuts and whipped cream." The whole diner burst into another cheer.

"This is on the house, Patty! And every time you win a fight, it will be here waiting for you – free of charge."

"I can't complain about that," laughed Patty.

As Jack prepared his banana split, Patty turned around and leaned his elbows on the counter. He scanned all the faces in the room.

"Who are you looking for?" Steve asked.

"I thought maybe Isabella would be here."

"Yeah," he replied. "I asked her to come, but she said her father wanted her to go straight home."

"Hey Patty," Johnny chimed in, "you want to take a ride to see my cousins in the North End of Boston?"

"What time is it?"

"Ten thirty. I know it's late, but we'll be there in an hour. I've been telling them about you and they're just dying to meet you."

"I'd want to," said Patty, "but I know my mother won't go to sleep 'til I get home, so I don't want to be out too late."

"What about if we go after you stop in and say hi to her?"

"No. I wouldn't want to do that to my mother."

"Okay," said Johnny obviously disappointed. "Maybe some other time."

Patty was quiet for a moment in thought. "Tell you what Johnny. Let's go tomorrow. Then we can spend the whole day in Boston, because it's Saturday."

"It's a deal!" exclaimed Johnny. Johnny had talked nonstop about Patty to his cousins, and they in turn had told many of their friends about Patty, "the fighting legend in the making." Quite a few of the guys in the north end of Boston were just itching to meet the champ.

"All right, let's go guys." Patty spooned up the last bite of vanilla ice cream from his banana split, and wiped his mouth with the back of his hand. "I don't want to keep my mother waiting."

On the walk home, Danny asked Patty if it would be all right for him to join in on the trip to Boston. Butterball tilted his head shyly implying that he wanted to come along as well. "Of course guys," Patty said as he swung an arm over Butterball's shoulder. "You're all my best friends."

Butterball turned to Patty and hesitantly asked, "Patty, would I look out of place with you?"

Patty immediately stopped walking. "What do you mean Butterball?"

Butterball was slow to answer. He looked at his feet and kicked the pavement with his toe. "You know, because I'm black."

"So what?" shouted Patty. "All of you are my best friends, and if anyone doesn't like it…well, we won't start anything, but then we're out of there in a second. You hear me Butterball? What do you think about that?"

Butterball's tight mouth broke into a grin. "Well…I don't want to start nothing either." Butterball shook his head from side to side, smiling at Patty in appreciation.

"Okay guys," directed Patty, "let's put our hands all together in the middle here." The boys shuffled together and lay their hands on top of one another's. "Now are we all together?" Patty asked firmly.

"Yes!" they shouted back.

"Are we all together?" Patty asked a little louder.

"Yes!" they shouted back.

"Are we all together?" Patty was yelling now.

"Yes!" The boys shouted as loud as they could.

"And that's the way it's always going to be!" yelled Patty, and he threw their hands up into the air. Then Patty reluctantly turned to go home. "I'll see you guys in the morning, I really need to get home now."

Anna was waiting for Patty in the kitchen as he walked through the door. The lines in her face seemed deeper than usual, and she flipped her pink rosary beads back and forth in her hand.

"Hi, Mama," said Patty casually, and he kissed his mother on the forehead.

"Open the big light, so I can see you better," Anna replied.

Patty turned on the light.

"Now let me look at you," she said, and pulled Patty's face close to her own to scrutinize his eyes.

"What's wrong, Mama?"

"I want to see if you're all banged up."

"Mama, I'm the same way now as when I left you earlier today."

"Give me a hug Patty, I was worried sick about you."

Patty did give her a hug, and he kissed her on the cheek. "Why the rosary beads Mama?"

"I've been praying to St. Anne since you left."

"Mama, I don't want you to worry so much. I'll be all right, I promise you. Why do you worry so much?" Patty put his hand on her shoulder in an attempt to comfort her.

Anna sighed and let her shoulders drop. "I went through this with your father in Italy, and now it seems I'm going to go through this all over again."

"I won't let you, Mama."

Anna turned her face up and looked earnestly into her son's eyes. 'Is this what you want Patty?"

"I don't know Mama."

"Wouldn't your rather be a lawyer?"

"How about I become the president," replied Patty.

They both laughed.

"It's just that I can feel as you grow older, I'm going to do a lot of worrying about you."

"No you're not, Mama." Patty lifted his arm from his mother's shoulder and turned to leave the room.

"Well I'm exhausted, Patty. I'm glad you're okay. I'm going to go get some sleep now." Anna slowly lifted herself from her chair.

"I'm going to watch some TV."

"Go in the den. Your father is in there. But first go say goodnight to your brothers and sisters. They are all excited about your fight."

Patty first went in to see Tommy and Henry. They were both up, sitting together in one bed. When Patty walked in, they jumped up in excitement.

"Patty! Patty! We heard you knocked that other guy out!"

"I sure did."

"How did you do it Patty! Show us how to fight." And Tommy gave Henry a fake punch in the gut."

"Maybe some other time boys. You've got to get to sleep now, okay?" I'll see you two in the morning."

Patty's younger brothers were disappointed, but they could barely keep their eyes open as it was, and they reluctantly crawled into their beds. As Patty walked out of their bedroom, Mama was standing at the door. She pointed to the girl's bedroom.

"Go see them. They're up too," she said.

The girls were sitting up in their pajamas practicing braids in each other's hair. They had been waiting for Patty all night. Patty came in and gave them both a big hug and a kiss on each of their foreheads.

"What are you girls doing up so late?"

"We wanted to see you. We heard you had a black eye, maybe two, and we wanted to see them."

Patty flicked on the big light. "See my eyes."

"But they're not black and blue!" shrieked the girls in surprise.

"Who told you that I had black eyes?"

"Tommy did. And then Henry said you had two of them."

Patty laughed. "Come on girls. It's past your bedtime." He tucked little Anna Marie in, and kissed her.

"I love you Patty," cooed Anna Marie sleepily.

"I love you too."

Patty then picked up Carol and tucked her; in.

"Good night Carol."

"Good night Patty."

"I love you."

"I love you too. Now, have sweet dreams." Patty turned out the light and began to leave, but Carol's quiet voice stopped him.

"Patty?"

"Yes, what is it?"

"I'm glad you don't have any black eyes."

"Thanks Carol. Go to sleep now," and he shut the door.

Once again Patty met his mother as he went out into the hall.

"Go see your father," she said. "He's waiting for you."

Patty went into the den. He was starting to feel exhausted himself. Only one lamp was on, and Big Frank was sitting in the armchair next to it reading a book.

"How are you feeling Patty?"

"Fine."

"Is your mother mad?"

"I don't think so. She just worries that I'm going to get hurt."

"Let me ask you a question Patty." Frank's deep brown eyes looked intently into his son's. "Would you like to be a fighter?"

Patty hesitated for a moment. "I'll just see what happens Papa. I don't really know yet."

"Well I'm not going to tell you what to do. That's a decision that you're going to have to make yourself."

"I know Papa, but will you stick with me in whatever I decide to do?"

"I'll stick with you to the end, Patty. After all, you are my son." Big Frank's eyes were locked into Patty's. He meant what he said with all of his heart. "Now what are your plans for tomorrow?"

"I'm going to the North End of Boston with Johnny. He has a cousin who lives on Endicot Street that he wants me to meet."

"You know I've got a cousin who I haven't seen in years that lives up there. We came over from Italy together. I used to take you up there to visit him when you were just a little boy. I think I'll give him a call and let him know that you're coming up. Would you go see him for me?"

"Okay Papa. I will. What's his name?"

"Carmine DeCheecho. He has a son that's about your age. His son's name is Carmine too. I'm sure you'll get along with him just fine. Now you should get along to bed. I'll call him in the morning."

"Night, Papa."

"Goodnight Patty."

Just then the phone rang. Big Frank wondered who would be calling at this time of night. It was Sully.

"What's up Sully," Big Frank asked.

"I just got a phone call," said Sully.

"From who?"

"Stogie Capelli."

"What did he want"?"

"He wants to arrange all of Patty's fights and we would not have to arrange any of them at all. What do you think Frank?"

"No, we don't need that," Frank replied. "I'll talk to Stogie tomorrow."

The following day, Big Frank went to see Stogie. A voice behind the door asked, "'who was there?" as if they didn't know.

A deep voice replied, "Frank."

Stogie was notified of Big Frank's arrival. They greeted each other with a hug.

"What can I do for you?" asked Stogie.

"Well, I understand you want to take over arranging my son's fights. Well, do you remember when we were kids? You said to me if I could ever do you a favor, just ask and I'll be there.' Do you remember, Stogie?"

"Yes, of course I remember. What is it?"

"I would like you not to arrange fights for Patty because I take care of that."

"Well Frank, it's once in a thousand years a fighter like Patty comes along. It's because he takes after his father and I knew what you were," Stogie exclaimed. "That's the only reason I wanted to arrange his fights. But if it means that much to you, you have my word. Can I just ask you a favor?"

"What is it?" Frank asked.

"Is it all right if I bet on him?"

Frank just smiled and shook hands.

The next morning, Frank called his cousin in Boston.

"Hi Carmine," he said into the phone. A mischievous and uncontrollable smile broke out on his face.

"Frank! You son of a gun!" the voice on the other end bellowed in laughter. "How the hell are you?"

"I'm good."

"Are you calling about the family outing?"

"I remember you told me you were going to put that together this summer, but we can talk about that later. I'm calling for a different reason."

"What's up Frank?"

"Do you remember my son Patty?"

"Are you kidding? Of course I do."

"Well Patty's going to be in the North End with some of his friends today, and I thought maybe you guys could meet up."

"Frank, that's great! I'm really excited that I'll get to see Patty again." Carmine put the phone to his chest and called to his wife, telling her the news. There was a big muffled reply, and then he got back on the phone. "Listen. Julia is going to prepare a big meal for Patty."

Frank cut in, "Now, wait at minute Carmine, let me explain. Patty is bringing along four of his best friends and they are stopping to see one of his friend's relatives before coming to see you. I don't want Julia to do all that cooking for all those boys. You know what I mean Carmine? When we have the family outing, well that will be a different story."

"Are you sure Frank? She really doesn't mind."

"Yes, I'm sure. Please don't take it the wrong way."

"Wait a minute Frank," exclaimed Carmine. "I just thought of something."

"What is it?"

"Well today and tomorrow our church, St. Bartholomew's, is having a feast. We can take Patty there. I don't care how many of his friends he brings. He could bring everyone in Providence, for all I care. There will be plenty of food. Frank, believe me, I'm really looking forward to seeing Patty. Oh, and by the way, he isn't old enough to drive yet, right? So how's he getting here?"

"Well, he drives my truck, but I won't let him take it to Boston. I think Josephine said she'd drive him up and back. Maybe she'll meet a nice guy up there in Boston, you know!"

Carmine laughed.

"No, I'm only kidding with you, Carmine," Frank continued. "Josephine can go any place she pleases. She has my love and blessing, with or without a man."

"So by the way Frank, what is Patty up to these days? How's he doing? Does he take after you?"

"I don't know."

"How tall is he?"

"He's six feet-two inches, 220 pounds and still growing." Pride radiated from Frank's voice as he spoke. "As a matter of fact, our parish had a smoker last night, and Patty fought his first fight."

"Wait a minute," jumped in Carmine, "let me interrupt you before you tell me the outcome. From what it sounds like Patty does take after you, am I right?"

"Well it looks like he does. We're very close you know."

"I bet you guys are. I say if he's taking after his father then he won that fight."

"He sure did. He knocked his opponent out in the first round."

"What did I tell you, Frank? I knew it! Does he want to be a fighter?"

"He hasn't decided yet if that's what he wants."

"Well the next time he fights, let me know. We'll come down to watch him."

"I will Carmine. Well give Julia my regards, and I'll expect Patty and his friends later this afternoon."

A few minutes after Frank got off the phone, Patty's friends arrived at the house. Big Frank greeted them warmly, and told them to come in. "Patty's getting ready, it will just be a moment."

Patty soon came into the kitchen where the boys were all sitting around the table talking with his father. At that moment, Aunt Josephine came in the front door. "You boys ready?" she asked.

"All set," said Patty.

"Okay, let's go then. But give your mother a kiss before you go."

Patty laughed and gave his mother a kiss. They then all headed out the door.

Frank shouted after them to be careful, and to make sure they called when they got to his cousin's house.

Anna said goodbye to everyone. "Have a good time Butterball," she said.

"I will Mama Anna," he said bashfully.

The boys joked and jostled the entire way to Boston. Everyone was in high spirits, and the hour it took to reach the North End flew by. Johnny directed Josephine to his cousin's house, and before they knew it, the boys found themselves being greeted whole-heartedly by Johnny's relatives. In a confusion of hugs and introductions, they were ushered into a tiny living room, which was much too small for the number of people in it. In addition to Patty, Johnny, Steve, Danny, Butterball, Sir Ray, and Josephine, there was Johnny's cousin, four of his friends, and Johnny's aunt and uncle.

Everyone wanted to hear the details of Patty's fight; questions flying from every corner of the room. Patty and the boys enthusiastically relayed the story, but they were sure to keep one eye on the clock. When an hour had passed Johnny politely explained to his family that they could not stay because Patty's relatives were waiting for them, and they had to visit with them as well before heading back to Providence.

"I'm the driver," said Josephine playfully once they were all back outside. "Come on boys, let's go!"

It only took ten minutes to reach Carmine's house, and as they pulled up Carmine jumped out of his chair on the front porch, where he had been waiting for them, and yelled to his family, "Here they are!" The boys spilled out of the truck as the family came out of the house, and they all greeted one another on the front lawn. Patty introduced his friends to everyone, but not after first giving a kiss to Carmine's wife as was the tradition to show his respect.

"My goodness, Patty I can't believe how tall you've gotten," exclaimed Carmine as he studied Patty. "You're built like a firetruck! You sure you're not 18?"

"Wish I was," Patty replied.

"You know Patty, I feel like I was 14 again back in Italy talking to your father. You are the spitting image of him, do you know that?"

"That's what people tell me."

"Your father was the best fighter in Italy. He tells me he's managing you and that you had your first fight yesterday. Patty I'm not going to give you a lecture, after all I know you didn't come up here to hear that, but I just want to say if you take after your father you'll be the best."

"Thank you, Carmine."

"Okay, that's enough of me reminiscing, let's get going. We can walk to the feast; it's just a few blocks away on Prince Street. They even have a carnival going on there. Oh, I almost forgot to mention, there's a dance tonight. Do you guys want to stay for that?"

"It's up to Josephine. She's our chauffeur."

"That's fine by me," Josephine replied. "If it's too much for you guys you can sleep on the way home."

"Too much for *us*?" Patty teased. "It will probably be the other way around. You'll be sleeping, and I'll be the one driving." They all laughed.

Prince Street was completely blocked off to all motor traffic and was crowded with pedestrians on their way to the feast. In the crowd Carmine Junior spotted one of his friends and called him over. His name was Fred DeCieco and he was the leader of all the gangs in the North End – a status equivalent to Patty's reign over Providence.

"Nice to meet you Fred," said Patty with obvious respect in his eyes.

"Likewise," he replied. "I've heard a lot about you, and congratulations on winning your first fight." Then a mischievous spark flashed in his eyes. "Say, why don't you all come with me over to the carnival where all of the girls are. Maybe we could have some fun!"

The boys could not contain their smiles as they eagerly walked through the carnival. The enticing smells of hotdogs, cotton candy, and kettle corn poured from every direction, and shrieks and laughter spilled down from the Ferris wheel above.

Danny nudged Sir Ray as a curvy girl with a blond pony tail bounced past. Sir Ray watched the girl go off into the sea of people then turned to Patty to share his appreciation. But Patty had his eyes fixed on something else.

In bold red print on a white sign, a side show advertised, "Sampson: The Strongest Fighter on Earth!" In smaller print below it went on to read, "If anyone can go one round with the unbeatable Sampson, he will be awarded a prize of one hundred dollars. An additional hundred will be paid for each round thereafter that challenger is still able to fight." And also have another hundred dollars if he knocked the great Sampson out. Patty ran into the tent and joined the crowd that was gathering around the ring. The rest of the boys were right behind him, excitedly scanning the crowd to see if there would be any takers.

"I would like to take him on," said Patty perhaps not even realizing he spoke out loud.

Carmine overheard. "Don't you dare, Patty! I promised your father that I would take care of you."

Josephine jumped in, "Don't be crazy, Patty! You could get seriously hurt." But Patty did not hear a word they said. The voice of the announcer boomed out, "So who's it going to be? Do we have a taker?"

"Stop this nonsense, you're going to get hurt!" Carmine pleaded, but it was no use.

"How old are you?" asked the announcer.

"Eighteen," Patty replied.

"Okay then, you can try."

The announcer shouted out to the crowd that Patty had accepted the challenge, and the fight would begin in one half hour. People began to pay their admission and soon the house was packed.

Josephine grabbed Patty's hand and looked him in the eyes. "You're just a baby compared to him. You can still change your mind."

Patty shook his head. "I'm not going to change my mind. I need the experience. If he knocks me out, he does. So what." With that Patty stepped in the ring. Steve and Johnny were his seconds.

"You sure you're not going to change your mind?" the referee asked.

"Nope, I'm not going to change my mind."

"Okay then, go to your corner."

"Are you sure that you want to go through with this?" Johnny asked, as he joined Patty, in the corner.

"Positive," he replied.

The tent was bursting at the seams. Everyone wanted to see this kid who is stupid enough to challenge Sampson. Who was this eighteen-year-old who thought he could take on a retired professional prize fighter? Their curiosity was peaked, though they were positive the fight would come to a bloody end in a matter of seconds.

Carmine ran up to the ring. "You can still back out Patty!"

"Never."

"I can't let anything happen to you. If I see Sampson's getting to you, I'm going to call the fight."

"Oh no you won't because I'm going to kick some ass."

"You're just like your father."

Just then the announcer called both fighters into the center of the ring to give them some last minute instructions.

"Sampson's enormous," gasped Josephine, and she made the sign of the cross.

The referee turned his attention to Patty. "Okay, kid. If this fight is a no contest and I feel like you're going to get injured, I'm going to call the fight over. You understand? Any question?"

"Yeah," Patty replied.

"What is it?"

"Well, it's just that you should be telling Sampson that, not me."

Sampson looked as if he wanted to bite Patty's head off.

"And, well, if I last one round I get one hundred dollars..."

"That's right."

"Well what happens if I last the first round, then knock him out in the second? What will you give me then?"

"Well, you'd get an extra two hundred dollars, but that's never going to happen."

"Don't bet on it," Patty replied.

"All right, all right, that's enough. To your corners boys."

Patty went back to his corner, where Johnny and Steve were waiting for him. Patty kneeled down and like his mother, said a short prayer to St. Anne. Just as soon as he stood back up, the bell rang and Sampson came charging out at Patty. He said to Patty "let me slap you in the rump and you can run back to your corner." Patty said "Let me punch you in the jaw then you won't have any teeth and you won't have to go to the dentist." Sampson started throwing everything he had at him in an effort to knock him out. The entire tent was absolutely silent. It was as if everyone was simultaneously holding their breath. They all feared the worst. They were positive Sampson was too much for Patty, and no one wanted to see him get hurt. Carmine looked as if he wanted to puke. All he could think about was how he was going to explain this to Frank.

In the ring Sampson was throwing lefts and rights at Patty. Patty had yet to throw a single punch back, and was simply attempting to block Sampson's fists and keep moving.

"I don't like the looks of this," Carmine said to Steve.

"Don't throw in the towel yet," he confidently replied. "Patty's got a game plan. He didn't tell us what it is, but we're sure he has one."

"And hey, look at it this way," added Johnny. "He's not down yet!"

They all focused back on the ring, and watched Sampson throwing everything he had at Patty.

The announcer called out to Sampson that there was only thirty seconds left in the first round, and he better end it quick because they didn't want to have to pay the hundred dollars.

Patty waited until there was fifteen seconds to go, then out of nowhere he lashed out with a left and a right and stopped Sampson in his tracks. The place went wild. Everyone started screaming and cheering for Patty. Johnny, Steve, Sir Ray, Danny, and Butterball started chanting, "Patty! Patty!" and soon they had the entire tent doing the same.

The bell rang signifying the end of the round. Patty went over to the announcer and said, "You owe me three hundred dollars."

The announcer stared back at Patty without saying a word. No one had ever made a single round with Sampson until today. "*Who is this kid?*" he thought to himself. "*Who is this nobody from Providence, Rhode Island?*"

The bell rang and the second round began. The tables had turned and now Patty took on the role of the aggressor. The crowd sensed a turn around and continued chanting "Patty! Patty!" Sampson tried to keep his distance; Patty had stunned him good in the first round and he did not want to let it happen again. Carmine's nauseous expression had transformed into one of excitement. He was now out of his seat shouting to Johnny and Steve that the crowds in Italy had gone wild for Patty's father exactly the same way.

Fully aware of Sampson's attempts to keep his distance by moving to Patty's right, Patty chose not to go around to his left like he had before. Instead he went to his right, which momentarily confused Sampson who did not expect such a move from an amateur. Patty took advantage of Sampson's split second hesitation and let go with a left hook to Sampson's jaw. Sampson was caught by surprise and the punch landed hard. Patty followed with a second left hook, completely stunning Sampson, then he went in with his right and pounded him repeatedly. The crowd started to cheer even louder. Patty backed Sampson into the ropes hitting him again and again with all of his strength. Patty's eyes were on fire, and this time Sampson went down to the canvas, out cold!

The sound of the referee counting him out was lost in the hurricane of shouts from the crowd. "Patty! Patty!" they all shouted. Patty's friends were cheering so loud they were beginning to go hoarse, and even Carmine joined in on the chant. The boys, Carmine, and Josephine all charged the ring to congratulate Patty. Josephine reached him first giving Patty an enormous hug and a wet kiss on his sweaty cheek.

"I told you, Auntie that I was going to kick ass!"

"You're beautiful Patty!" she exclaimed.

When Carmine reached Patty he bellowed out that he was going to call Patty's father as soon as he got home to tell him what a champ his son was. "I'm really proud of you Patty! You're really taking after your father."

All of Patty's friends were around him. Even the kids from Prince Street and Frank DiCieco hugged and congratulated Patty. He had lived up to the rumors and more!

The announcer made his way over to Patty and handed him the three hundred dollars. Patty thanked him politely.

"For an eighteen-year-old, you've got a great future," remarked the announcer still in shock at the turn of events. "How would you like to work for me in the carnival as the new Sampson?"

"No thanks, I'm still in school. You know, I have to tell you I'm not actually eighteen."

"How old are you?"

"Not quite fourteen."

"I don't believe it! I never would've imagined…"

"It's true," said Carmine. "Unbelievable! But true. I was there the day he was born."

"Well, all I can say is you've got one hell of a future in front of you kid!"

Patty's friends and all of Carmine Junior's friends from the North End were waiting for Patty as he walked out of the tent. Carmine was walking at his side.

"You know, Patty," he said. "Your father was the best, but I think you're even better."

"Thanks Carmine."

"I just want to ask you one question, though. Why didn't you throw many punches in the first round?"

"I wanted to make sure I would win the hundred dollars, then deck him in the second round for two hundred more."

"So that was your game plan from the beginning?"

"Sure was."

Fred then came up to Patty. "I want you to meet my sister, Angelina Marie."

Angelina stepped forward. She had long, black hair that reached nearly to her waist, and porcelain skin. Patty was surprised that 'Fred's sister could look so delicate, because Fred himself was as solid and feisty as they come.

"That's a pretty name, and you're a beautiful girl," said Patty. His confidence was even higher than usual after the fight.

"I saw you fight Sampson, and you're everything that we've heard about you. Are you going to the dance later Patty?"

"Yes, I am. Will you save me a dance?

"I'll save you more than one."

Patty then turned to his friends and announced, "We're all going to the dance and it's my treat!"

They all walked together towards the dance tent in one enormous celebratory group. Even Carmine and his wife were coming along. Josephine walked by her nephew and linked her arm into his. "You know Patty, I sure am proud of you," she said. "Are you going to give me a dance tonight?"

"You know Auntie, you'll always get a dance from me."

"Will you do me just one favor, Patty?"

"What is it Auntie?"

"Don't call me Auntie in front of all of these people. I feel like they think I'm much older than I am."

Patty laughed, "Sure thing. What do you want me to call you instead, Sis?"

"Just Josephine is fine."

"Okay, Just Josephine it is!" and Patty gave her a high five.

News of Patty's performance at the fight had spread fast, and many people turned to see the kid who had taken out the infamous Sampson. The dance hall had been decorated with over a thousand white balloons, and white lights hung from the ceiling casting a magical glow on all of the people underneath. Though their clothes were dirty and wrinkled from their long eventful day, Patty and his friends felt like a million bucks.

Soon after the music had started, Fred pulled Patty aside. "Listen," he said, "I hear you can sing. What do you say, are you going to give us a sample?

"Who told you that?"

"Never mine who, we found out, that's all."

"Well, I don't know if I can, you see I didn't really come prepared."

"Just wing it."

Angelina then walked over to Patty and sealed the deal. "I've seen you fight, now I want to hear you sing."

"I don't know what to sing."

"They have two guitar players," piped in Johnny. "We could ask if we could borrow them, and Steve can play the drums. They also got a saxophone and a piano – let's get them to play something fast.

"How about *Good Golly Miss Molly*?" said Steve.

"Well go on and ask them then," replied Patty, smiling wider than a clown.

Steve ran over to the stage and whispered something into the piano player's ear. The piano player looked over at Patty then said something to the band. A few seconds later, Steve came running back. "They'll do it!" he exclaimed. "They said they've seen you fight, so they might as well see what you can do on the mike."

Carmine overheard the boys' plan and looked at Patty in astonishment. "You sing too?"

"A little."

"I don't believe this."

After the next song had finished, Fred got up on stage to make the announcement:

"Attention please! May we have your attention please! We have here all the way from Providence, Rhode Island, Mr. Patty DiMarco who just defeated the carnival's very own ex-professional fighter The Great Sampson!"

A roar went up from the crowd.

"Now not only does Patty fight, he also does a little singing. And so all you ladies can see his softer side, we've asked him to sing just one song for us tonight. Now come on up here Patty!"

Patty, Johnny, Sir Ray, and Steve all went up on the stage and started to warm up. Steve talked to the saxophone and piano player and told them the plan.

"Okay boys! On the count of three – hit it, like we rehearsed!" Steve counted out the rhythm with his drumsticks and they all hit together, fast and loud. Patty started singing and everyone headed for the dance floor.

Carmine leaned over towards his wife and said, "I don't know what he's better at, fighting or singing!"

The boys kept the pace up, and before they knew it, the song was over. Everyone clapped and many people shouted out for an encore. Patty quieted the crowd down and talked into the mike. "That's all I can do for tonight. I didn't come prepared, but I'll make you a promise. At next year's feast, I'll come back and sing for you again. Thanks a lot and God bless you all!" The crowd applauded some more. Everyone was thoroughly impressed not only by Patty's beautiful voice, but also his composure and modesty.

Patty then thanked the band, and went back to join his friends. They all praised his performance. Then the band started to play a slow song, and Patty turned to his aunt. "Would you like a dance Miss Josephine," he asked.

Josephine gave him a sparkling smile, "You didn't forget."

"I'd never forget you."

"Thank you Patty," and Josephine put her hand in Patty's and they began to dance. "You know your father told me to watch over you, and I think it ended up being the other way around. You know Patty, Angelina keeps staring at you. I think I'm going to give her the next dance. Do you mind?"

"You do what you like Josephine," replied.

Patty looked over at Angelina and caught her looking right back at him. Another boy came up to her and asked her if she would like to dance, but Angelina just shook her head no, and kept her eyes on Patty. When the song finished Patty immediately said, "See you later," to Josephine and made his way over to Angelina.

"How about a dance"?" he asked.

"Of course," she replied.

The two began to dance together. Angelina was tall, and rested her dark head on Patty's shoulder.

"You know, Angelina is a pretty name," Patty commented, "but do you think I could call you Angie?"

"I don't mind," she whispered. "You know you were great tonight, both at the fight and on the stage. I really enjoyed watching you."

"I've enjoyed watching you too."

"When are you going back to Providence?"

"I have to leave right after this dance."

"Why so early?"

"Well my aunt is driving us and she is getting tired."

"Will you call me?"

"Sure, why not"?"

The song ended and it was time for Patty to say goodbye to all of his new friends. They all shook hands, and Carmine told him that he better come back soon. They all left the tent, exhausted and bleary-eyed from their long day. Josephine told Patty that he should sit up front with her, but Patty declined and said he wanted to sit in back with his friends. The entire way back, the boys recounted the events of the day. Everyone had had a great time. John put an arm over Patty's shoulder and said in all honesty,

"Patty, you've made believers of us." Patty smiled and looked at his friends affectionately.

It was Danny who broke the silence. "Hey so what's going on between you and that Angelina – she was quite a looker."

"She wants me to call her, but I don't think I will. I think I'm going to try to see more of Isabella. I guess I kind of like her more."

When they finally reached Luna Street, Patty's mother and father were up waiting for him. Carmine had already called and told Frank all of what had happened at the carnival, and the first thing Frank said to Patty as he walked in the door was, "So I heard you had a fight today." Frank's voice was firm, but his eyes glimmered and Patty knew that he was not mad. "So how did you do, son?"

"I did okay."

"Let me look at you." Frank held Patty's face under the light, but he did not detect any damage. "Now go see your mother. She's putting your brothers and sisters to bed."

When Anna saw Patty walk in she immediately scanned his face for even the littlest swelling or scratch. After determining that he was okay, Anna sighed and gave Patty a big hug. Patty's brothers sat up in their beds and asked, "So did you knock that other guy out?"

"I sure did."

Mama Anna smiled faintly. She looked exhausted. "Patty, that girl Isabella called two times tonight, so you better give her a call."

8 IN THE RING

Four years later Patty finally approached the 18 years that he had wished so badly to be that day of the feast. He was now even larger than his father, exceeding him both in height and weight. He was a fair amount more handsome as well, with honestly intense brown eyes; thick dark hair; a strong Italian jaw, and a small neatly kept mustache. If Big Frank had been described as "Mr. America," Patty had gone on to the next level and would now be a fine contender for "Mr. Universe."

Patty had called Isabella that night after his adventures in Boston, and they had been inseparable ever since. They had gone steady for all four years of high school at Mount Pleasant High. Isabella did everything with Patty; she would jog with him, and even go to work with him and help him lay bricks. Big Frank and his brothers would tease the couple endlessly saying, "look at the little lovebirds," but the couple did not mind one bit, and the smile in Big Frank's eyes revealed that he approved of the match. Mama Anna was also fond of the two together, and Isabella would often be seen walking over to the DiMarco house or helping Anna get groceries at the market.

Patty was training more than ever to be a fighter, but he was still undecided about going professional. He had just graduated from high school, and that fall, he enrolled in Providence College. Patty's brother Henry had been doing the paper route for the past four years, and Tommy was right behind Patty at Mount Pleasant High. Throughout junior high and now in high school, the same familiar words followed Tommy into almost every classroom,: "So you're Patty's brother? He's quite a guy."

Isabella was attending Brown University, which made it easy for her and Patty to still see one another often. Johnny, Steve, Danny, Sir Ray, and Butterball all had girlfriends of their own, but they all still saw one another on a regular basis and had not grown even the slightest hair apart.

One day, towards the end of the first semester just after the grand New England trees had dropped their leaves, Frank and Sully got together with Patty to discuss the possibility of Patty entering the ring to fight professionally.

"Maybe just eight rounders to start off with," decided Sully.

It would be possible for Patty to fight at the Arcade in Providence, allowing him to go professional without taking any time off from school, so there was no real conflict of interest.

"Well, I might as well give it a try," agreed Patty.

That evening when Patty told Isabella about his plans to go professional, she was not exactly happy. Her thin eyebrows furrowed, but she said, "If that's what you want to do, then do it." Patty smiled and kissed her affectionately.

"I thought you'd say that," he replied.

"I remember the first time I met you, you were fighting. I walked out of the bathroom and saw you beating up those Salerno brothers. I should have known then that you'd turn into a fighter."

Isabella was smiling. – That was one of her favorite stories to reminisce about.

Patty's friends on the other hand were thrilled to hear Patty's news. They had been waiting for this moment the day of Patty's first practice when they threw him the parade.

The boys told everyone they knew, and the word began to spread. The news traveled through Charles Street, Providence and beyond, reaching all the way up to the North End of Boston. With the news of the fight, it was also time for Mama Anna to start worrying again.

Frank and Sully scheduled the fight for about a month after Christmas on January 29th. The next couple of months flew by as Patty divided his time between training and studying. He used the time off from school designated for Christmas break to step his training up a notch, and by the time the fight rolled around he was in top form.

January 29th fell on a Friday night, and the fight was to take place at nine-o'clock sharp. The tickets had been put up for sale a week before, and within hours they were sold out. People were coming from all over the state and from Boston to witness Patty's debut.

All of Patty's personal friends, and his brothers Tom and Henry made sure that they were ringside, ready to cheer as the fight was about to commence. Frank and Sully sat with Patty in his corner to give him last minute advice.

"Let him come to you, then counter punch with all you got. You understand?"

Patty nodded his head.

A few moments later the bell rang. The announcer stepped into the ring and introduced the fighters. "From Providence, Rhode Island, we have Patty DiMarco making his professional debut, going up against the reigning champ from New York City, Marcel

Fourmier." Then the bell rang and the referee waved the fighters on.

Patty followed his trainer's instructions to the word. He let his opponent come to him, then hit him with a left to the head followed by a right to the head, and Fourmier hit the canvas out cold. The crowd erupted and the familiar chanting of, "Patty! Patty!" rumbled through the stands.

Fourmier was extremely slow to get up and had to be helped to his corner. Patty went over to see how he was doing, and the site was an ugly one. His trainer was trying to get him to speak, but to no avail. The doctor was quickly summoned and after looking into Fourmier's eyes he called an ambulance to take him to Rhode Island Hospital. Frank and Ricky Sullivan followed the ambulance in a truck. Patty wanted to go along too, but Frank told him to go home and wait until he called or came back.

Patty sat at the kitchen table silently waiting up for his father to return. The idea that his opponent could be seriously injured made his stomach churn in the most terrible way. Mama Anna sat across from him, worried to the bone but keeping her mouth shut in her silent prayers to St. Anne. Finally at 3:00 a.m., Big Frank walked through the door.

Patty jumped out of his seat. Frank put his hand on Patty's shoulder. Patty searched his eyes. He let out a sigh, "So he's okay then?" he asked hopefully.

"He'll be all right. He just got hit pretty hard."

It felt like a whole truckload of bricks had just been lifted off of Patty's shoulders.

"Thank you, God," he said.

A few days later Patty met with his father and Ricky Sullivan to discuss his next fight. Sully said he had a heavyweight fighter in mind, a black kid from Oluca, Alabama whom he heard was pretty good. They decided to arrange for a fight in two months.

"In the meantime," stressed Sully, "I want you to keep up with your training. As a matter of fact, I want you training even harder."

Patty took the words of his coach to heart, and trained hard. The months sped by, and soon Friday, March 24th, the night of Patty's second fight, rolled around. The fight was held in the same Arcade, and the now familiar sign "SOLD OUT" hung on the door. From the front row, Patty's family and friends all watched excitedly as Sully and Frank gave Patty their last minute advice before the bell rang.

The announcer introduced the fighters to the audience. "Bubba Johnson from Alabama and our own Patty DiMarco from Providence, Rhode Island." At the sound of Patty's name the crowd thundered. The announcer raised his voice to be heard, "Go to your corners and come out fighting!"

Bubba sprung out of his corner and went straight for Patty with a left jab followed by a right hook. Patty countered with two jabs and a right to Bubba's head, which stunned him against the ropes. Patty quickly came in with a series of hard lefts and rights to the head. Suddenly the referee jumped in and stopped the fight, fearing serious harm to Bubba. Patty lowered his fists. Bubba slumped down in the ropes, out cold.

The crowd was on their feet cheering "Patty! Patty!" They were oblivious to the fact that Bubba might be critically injured. Bubba was not responding to any medical attention, and he was rushed off to Rhode Island Hospital. Patty, Frank and Sully followed the ambulance there. They all stood in the waiting room, too worried to sit down. Finally, after what seemed like hours, a doctor told the men that Bubba had received a severe concussion, and had not yet regained consciousness.

In the following week, Patty went to the hospital everyday. He felt terrible about Bubba's condition, and wanted to help in any way possible. It was not until the eighth day after the fight that Bubba finally regained consciousness. With the doctor's consent, Patty tentatively went in to talk to Bubba.

Bubba picked his head up off the pillow with a surprised look on his face, but before he could say anything, Patty knelt next to the bed and looked Bubba earnestly in the eyes. "I am so sorry for what happened," whispered Patty, but he need not have said a thing; the remorse in his eyes said it all.

Bubba gave Patty a weak smile to let him know that he had no hard feelings. The two then talked for a while about each other's lives. Patty told Bubba that this had been only his second professional fight. Bubba revealed to Patty that he had a wife and six children back in Alabama.

Immediately, after Patty got home from the hospital that afternoon, he called Bubba's trainer on the phone. He asked why Bubba's wife was not at his side. The trainer explained that she did not have enough money for the trip to Rhode Island.

"Well, you call her and tell her she has the money now," Patty replied. "Let's get her up here to be with her husband."

Patty made the arrangements to get airline tickets to Bubba's wife, Denise Johnson. He then called her personally to tell her that the tickets were on there way, and that he would pick her up at the airport and drive her to the hospital so she could be with her husband. Denise began to cry when she heard the news, thanking Patty profusely.

The next night, Denise had arrived and she and Patty sat next to Bubba as the doctor explained that Bubba was in good enough condition to go to a hospital closer to his home, but he would not be able to fight ever again.

Denise told Patty about their six kids, four boys and two girls, and how worried they were about their father. When Patty asked about their financial situation, she explained that Bubba worked at a grocery store 30 miles from their home and he only came home once a week, on Saturday nights. He boxed in the ring for the extra money, and even then, they could barely make ends meet. Denise looked desperate. "I don't know what we'll do now that he can't fight," she mumbled.

Patty was quiet for a moment, then he said, "When you leave for Alabama, I will fly down to meet you, and I'll see what I can do to help you out."

"Why are you doing all of this for us?" she asked.

Patty looked into Denise's tired eyes. "I never meant for this to happen this way," he said. "Bubba can't fight anymore because of me, and I've decided that I'm not going to fight anymore either."

Patty asked Butterball to accompany him down to Alabama to see what he could do to help the Johnson family. Patty located a grocery store in their hometown that was up for sale, and without hesitation he bid on it. Patty's offer was one the owners could not refuse and they accepted it.

"But we don't have any money," Bubba replied when Patty told him the news.

"Don't worry about that," assured Patty. "I'm going to call my father right now."

Patty got on the phone with Big Frank and explained what he wanted to do. "I've been saving up my money for years like you wanted me too, and now I want to give it to Bubba to open the store. What do you think?"

Frank was quiet for a moment. Then he said, "I'll only go along with it if I can put in half the money for the business."

"Do you really mean that? I sure do love you, Papa."

Patty hung up the phone with a huge smile on his face. He told the Johnsons that it was a done deal. "As far as I'm concerned you guys are the new owners of Johnson's Market. Bubba won't have to go 30 miles to work anymore."

There was a commotion of hugging and thanking. Bubba held out his hand to Patty and said, "Patty DiMarco, you have made a friend for life."

9 PATTY BECOMES A MARINE

Patty was now entering his senior year at Providence College. He had stopped fighting, though he continued to keep in shape. He was still dating Isabella, and all of his close friends had steady girls as well. Every Friday night, the boys would get together and Patty, Johnny, Steve, Ray, Butterball and Danny would sit around at Steve's kitchen table to play cards. In the summertime they would all get together and take their girlfriends to Narragansett Beach to lounge around in the sun and play volleyball. When the sun went down, they would head over to George's at Point Judith and load up on fresh seafood. The nights were spent at Dave Julian's High Tide Lounge.

One night, over a plate of clams, the discussion turned as usual to the war that was starting in Korea. Steve said it was just police action, but Patty told him he thought it was going to go further than that.

Sure enough, just a few months later, the situation in Korea had escalated and the U.S. government announced that they were initiating a new draft. Eventually, all of the boys, except Danny who had already enlisted in the Navy, received the notification to report to Fields Point for their physical examinations because they were being drafted into the U.S. Army.

After the examinations were complete, two officers addressed the group of draftees and announced that they needed four volunteers. No one stepped forward, so the officers picked the four men at random from the lines. Patty was one of the ones chosen. As he was taken off to the side the officers explained that they were short four recruits for the Marine Corps, and Patty was now in the Marines. He was given a date to report to the state airport, and in two weeks would be flown to Parris Island, South Carolina for basic training.

When Patty returned home, his entire family was waiting for him. Isabella was there too, sitting next to Mama Anna. They were all surprised to hear that Patty was going into the Marine Corps. Big Frank looked seriously into his son's eyes as if to give him strength. Anna recited a prayer under her breath, her rosary beads in hand. Patty's uncles asked the specifics of the examination, and what the officers had said about the four volunteers. Isabella did not say a word.

When it was time for Patty to leave for South Carolina, everyone went with him to the airport to see him off. Patty shook hands with his father and brother, and gave his mother and the rest of the women hugs and kisses. He walked over to Isabella to give her a kiss. Tears were streaming down her cheeks. She hugged Patty and said to him, "I'm afraid something bad will happen to you and I won't see you ever again."

"Don't be silly," said Patty trying his best to be convincing, "I'm not going to die, and I *will* see you again."

The first thing Patty heard as he stepped off the bus at the main Marine boot camp on Parris Island was the boom of the Drill Instructor's voice.

"All right, you A-holes, the last one off this bus. I'm going to beat his a-s-s."

Patty knew then that his training for the next twelve weeks was going to be intense. He jumped off the bus and joined the other recruits who were waiting in line to be issued their clothing. The same Drill Instructor that had yelled at them had now moved up to the front of the line and was asking each recruit, "Where you from, Yankee?"

The guy standing next to Patty in line, leaned over and whispered, "I betcha that Sergeant weights over 250 pounds."

When Patty reached the front of the line and was asked where he was from, Patty answered, "South Carolina."

"A wise guy, huh?" shouted the Drill Instructor. "Well you're mine, and I'm going to fix your ass!"

Patty learned quickly the rules of boot camp- avoid eye contact, keep your mouth shut and your ears open, begin and end every sentence with the word "sir", and never, *never* ask your Drill Instructor "why."

As the days wore on, though Patty was obedient and performed everything that was asked of him quickly and efficiently, the Drill Instructor was always on his back. The rumor around the camp was that Patty's Drill Instructor was the heavyweight champion in his division. He was so tough that everyone called him Godzilla, though of course to his face it was always, "Sergeant Wilson, Sir!"

From that very first day the DI had it out for Patty, and he was constantly yelling for Patty to drop to the ground and "Give me ten!" Soon it was up to 100 push ups and when he saw that it was not breaking Patty, he started giving him a 100 two or three times a day. But Patty was like a bull. His years of training as a boxer had toughened him up. No matter what punishment the Sergeant dished out, Patty could take it. More important than his strength, however, was Patty's restraint. No matter what offensive or degrading obscenity the DI obnoxiously screamed into his face, Patty would never talk back. He knew that was just what the DI wanted, and he refused to give him the satisfaction.

The guy who had whispered to him in line that first day was Bobby McGee from Mississippi, and he and Patty became instant friends. Patty also got close to a kid by the name of Alasuaq Inukpuk, called "Inu" for short. Inu was an American Eskimo from Nome, Alaska. He, Bobby, and Patty all had something in common besides the Marine Corps; they were all musicians. Patty could sing and play the guitar. Bobby played the piano, and Inu was good on the drums. They all agreed that they would get together and play after basic training.

One day during the eighth week of training, Patty's squad was out on the firing range practicing with their rifles. They had to shoot at targets as they were being pushed up like a window. When a target was hit, the recruit on that end of the field covered up the bullet hole with a sticker the size of a postage stamp. To get a few laughs, Patty cut one of the stickers in half and placed it on his helmet to give the impression that he was a captain. It was a hit among the other recruits, but as soon as his captain saw what Patty had done, he got a megaphone and barked out, "All temporary officers must immediately remove their bars!"

When Sergeant Wilson got word of Patty's stunt, his face boiled red. "Drop down and give me a hundred for starters, then start running around the track until I tell you to stop!"

Two weeks later, Patty's squadron had to train to advance on a machine gun nest firing blanks. The sergeant stood in the middle of the recruits pointing at those who were dead, telling them to get up and get out. The sergeant was advancing towards Patty, when Patty decided to crawl around the other way. Patty crept up behind the machine gun nest and walked in. "It's over guys," he shouted, "I just killed all of you."

The officers were confused as to why the shooting had stopped, and sent Sergeant Wilson to find out what the problem was. Sergeant Wilson tromped up to the machine gun nest and to his surprise he discovered Patty standing there. He demanded to know what Patty was doing there, and why the shooting had stopped.

"Because I killed them all, Sir," Patty explained.

Sergeant Wilson was fuming. "Well you follow me, the captain wants to see you."

Patty obediently followed the sergeant to where the captain was standing.

"What's happened DiMarco?" the captain demanded.

"Sir," said Patty. "I was instructed to advance on the machine gun nest, Sir. No one said how to do it, and when I saw the other Marines getting killed, I decided that wasn't the right route to go, Sir. So I went around and snuck up on the nest from behind. I probably saved the lives of 50 Marines, Sir."

The captain and the officer next to him looked at one another then they both told Patty to get back to his unit. Once Patty was out of ear shot, the captain said, "You know, he's right, he probably did save about 50 lives. Let's just drop it, but I'll tell you one thing – that kid's going to make one hell of a Marine."

Patty walked back to his squad and was greeted by Sergeant Wilson. "I'm not through with you yet, DiMarco," he threatened. At four o'clock the next morning, as everyone was getting ready to march to the mess hall for breakfast, Sergeant Wilson walked up to Patty and stopped him with his arm. "Not you," he said. Despite what the captain thought, Sergeant Wilson was not going to let Patty get away with anything. "Give me a hundred, and a hundred more when you get back!"

There were only two weeks left of basic training, and Patty was counting the days to when his punishment would end. That same afternoon, as Patty was marching with the Marine band, Sergeant Wilson suddenly yelled out, "Double-time!" Then as Patty came by, the sergeant grabbed him by the shirt and pushed him back hard. That was more than Patty could handle, and he stopped and pushed back.

That evening Patty was told to report to the captain in his office. There, Patty was met in the lobby by Sergeant Wilson and another officer, whom he had never met before, Lieutenant Renzi from Pittsfield, Massachusetts. The two demanded that Patty apologize to Wilson, but Patty replied that he would not.

The three walked together in the cold silence to the captain's office. The office had no door, so Patty simply walked through the doorway and approached the captain's desk.

"Didn't you take military courtesy!" the captain shouted, spit flying from his mouth and onto Patty's forehead.

"Yes Sir, I did, Sir."

"Then you should know you have to knock before you come into my office! Now try it again."

Patty walked out of the office and this time he knocked on the door frame. "Patty DiMarco, reporting as requested Sir."

"Di Marco," said the captain coolly, as he walked up to Patty and stood just inches from his nose. "You are going to be charged with pushing your sergeant, and for that you are facing a Court Martial. What do you have to say for yourself?"

Patty was not intimidated. "Sir, you asked if I had military courtesy, Sir. Well, I also had Military Law and it states that if any non-commissioned officer puts a hand on you in any shape or form, you may defend yourself any way possible. Sergeant Wilson pushed me, so I pushed him back, Sir."

The captain stepped back and looked at Patty in silent approval. "Well that's a different story, then. Do you want to press charges against Sergeant Wilson?"

Sergeant Wilson opened his mouth to object, but Patty spoke first.

"No Sir. With your permission, I would like to settle this in a different way. I know the sergeant was the heavyweight champ for the Marines, and seeing that boot camp is almost over, I would like to settle this in the ring."

The captain smiled and turned to Sergeant Wilson. "What do you say Sarge?"

The Sergeant smirked, "I'll go along with that Sir."

"Good. Start arranging the fight."

As Patty was walking out of the office, Lieutenant Renzi stepped up beside him. "Are you crazy Patty?" He asked with serious concern. "This guy is unbeatable. That's why they call him Godzilla!"

Patty stopped walking and made eye contact with the Lieutenant. "I got one thing to say to you about that. I'll be representing New England and make sure you're there."

When Patty got back to his barracks, his friends were waiting to hear what had happened. Patty told them that upon finishing boot camp he was going to challenge Godzilla in the ring.

"I hear he's really tough," warned Bobby.

"Then it will be a good fight," Patty replied. "The Sarge is going to regret all of those push-ups he made me do."

News traveled throughout the camp, and on the day of the fight, the gym was not big enough to hold all of the Marines that came to see the challenge. All of the commanding officers sat in the front two rows of the bleachers. Many bets had been made as to who would win; everyone knew Patty was tough, but they were not sure he was tough enough to beat Godzilla.

The captain stood up and made an announcement to the men. "After the fight is over, you will all go home on furlough for seven days. You will all be given written instructions and airline tickets to special training camps. Before we start the fight, no matter who wins, I don't want this to get out of hand. Everyone needs to remain as orderly as possible." Then he introduced the fighters as "Sergeant Wilson and Private DiMarco. Sergeant Delaney will referee."

Sergeant Delaney called the two heavyweights together and warned them, "Remember – when I say break, you break. If I order you back to your corner that's what you do. Now shake hands." They shook. "Go to your corners and come out fighting."

The bell rang and the Sarge came out swinging. He figured he could end the fight quickly. Patty blocked his punches and countered with a jab to the jaw and a right to the sergeant's midsection. He quickly followed with a strong left hook to the head, hitting the sergeant squarely in the left eye. The sergeant dropped to one knee; blood gushing out of his eye.

The referee shouted at Patty to go to his corner and waved the medics into the ring. The medics said the sergeant needed to get to the hospital immediately, and took him out of the ring.

The referee announced that the fight was a technical knockout, and Patty was the winner. Patty, though, did not even raise a hand in victory. He was right behind the medics, following them to the hospital.

When the doctors said it was all right for Patty to see Sergeant Wilson, Patty walked quietly into the room and stood by the bed.

"How are you doing, Sir?" he asked.

"They want me to stay overnight."

Patty extended his hand and said, "No hard feelings?"

"No hard feelings," the sergeant replied. "You sure throw a hard punch." Then he wished Patty luck overseas. As a drill instructor, the sergeant would not go with the company; he would stay in South Carolina to train more recruits.

The following day, Patty flew back to Providence for furlough. Isabella, Anna and Frank were waiting for him at the airport. "You've gotten stronger, I can tell," remarked Frank at the sight of Patty's arms.

"I missed you so much," exclaimed Isabella as she ran into his arms.

That night, Mama Anna served up a feast of Patty's favorite foods. "It sure feels great to be back home," said Patty as he finished off his second full plate of food.

However, there was a hint of sadness in Patty's expression. Johnny, Steve, Butterball, Danny and Sir Ray were all stationed at different bases across the country and he did not know when he would see them again.

Patty spent every day of his vacation with Isabella, and the week flew by. When it was time for Patty to return to South Carolina for his three months of special training, Isabella once again accompanied the DiMarco family to the airport to see Patty off. As Patty was hugging her goodbye, Isabella slipped a picture of herself into his pocket, and promised that she would write.

Patty arrived to the muggy heat of South Carolina to discover that out of the 200 recruits in his company, he was one of 12 that had been chosen to train for Special Operations. Over the next three months, he went through intensive specialized training that was even more physically demanding than boot camp. The creed of "kill or be killed," was pounded over and over into every fiber of Patty's body. In Survival, Evasion, Resistance and Escape training (SERE), he learned the skills needed if he were ever separated from his unit in a combat zone. "Never be taken prisoner. Never pick up any prisoners unless there is a specific mission to do so." Those were the policies to survive by.

Though the training was still arduous, the men were now given more freedom. Without wasting any time, Patty, Bobby McGee, and Inu decided to go to the nearest town, which was Fayetteville, and see if they could find a gig for their band. Without too much trouble they found a joint called Jim's Mill. The three strolled into the place on a Friday night and found it packed with Marines. There were plenty of women too, which was the fundamental sign that the establishment was doing well.

After ordering a round of drinks, Patty leaned in towards the bartender and inquired about the owner of the bar. The bartender pointed to a heavyset man with a handlebar mustache and told Patty he went by the name of Slim Jim. Patty confidently walked up to Slim Jim and made an offer.

"How would you like to have my friends sing while your band's on break? It would be no charge, and if the music keeps playing then people will keep drinking and that's more money for you."

Slim Jim was skeptical at first, but he finally agreed to let Patty's band have a try. When the regular band was between sets, Slim Jim shouted, "Okay boys, get up there and sing. But if after the first song the crowd doesn't like you, you're out of here!"

Patty nodded with an animated gleam in his eye. The boys were quick to jump on stage. "Okay guys," Patty called out, "let's pick up the beat and play *Blue Suede Shoes*!"

As soon as Inu started playing the beat, a wave of energy hit the people in the bar. Patty started singing, and the place went wild. Everyone was dancing and the drinks were pouring all over the place. There were four MP's making the rounds, and Slim Jim was all smiles.

When the song finished, the crowd began to shout for more. Patty started to walk off stage.

"Why you walking off the stage?" asked Bobby. "The crowd wants more."

"Let me handle this," said Patty. "The price we charge for our first song has just gone up."

"But we're playing for free."

"That was then, this is now," said Patty grinning slyly. "Trust me."

"Okay, you're the manager."

By then, Slim Jim had made his way up to the front of the dance floor. He was all red in the face and was gesturing for Patty to get back on the stage and sing another song. Patty replied, "We're through for the night. No more free songs."

"How much you want," Slim Jim hastily asked.

"On hundred bucks each."

"That's too much!"

"No it's not," Patty coolly replied, "because we're going to play Friday, Saturday, and Sunday nights."

The MP that was standing next to Slim Jim said, "You better make up your mind, because you're going to have a riot on your hands and we're going to have to call for back up."

"Okay," Slim Jim said. "You've got yourself a deal." He shook Patty's hand.

For the next ten weeks, Patty and his band played every weekend. They began to call themselves *The Wilson Trio*, in honor of their former DI, and were a huge hit among the locals. After the ten weeks were up, though, the boys told Slim Jim they were going to have to pack it up because they were going home. Slim Jim was disappointed to see them leave. "I really liked you guys," he said earnestly, "and you were good for business." Patty thanked him, and said goodbye. After a short furlough, they would be shipping out to Korea.

When Patty returned to Providence, he learned that his brother Tom had also been drafted, and would be receiving his training at Fort Dix, New Jersey. On top of this news, Patty had to break it to his family that he only had a three-day furlough. As Patty was explaining that he would be on his way to Korea within the week, Mama Anna did not say a word. She simply stared at Patty expressionlessly. However, she was devastated inside, and as soon as Patty was finished talking, she went into her bedroom and closed the door. Once out of sight of the family, the tears came. Once Anna started sobbing, she could not stop. She went to her statue of St. Anne and lit a fresh candle.

"Please, St. Anne," she prayed, "please protect my eldest son. Please protect my Patty."

At that moment, Anna felt a hand on her shoulder. She turned around, wide-eyed and saw Patty standing behind her. He had followed her into the room, knowing that she was upset.

"Don't cry Mama," he said. "Tell me, what's wrong."

"I'm just afraid Patty, that's all" she sighed, trying to regain her composure.

"I'll be all right Mama."

"I'll keep a candle burning everyday until you come home."

Patty gave his mother a hug, and kissed her on the cheek. He brushed the hair from her damp face, and intensely looked into her eyes. "I'll be all right Mama," he repeated.

"Don't worry, I'll be fine."

The last night before he was due to leave, Patty took Isabella out for a ride. They drove out to Lincoln Woods State Park, and the darkness seemed to go on forever in the trees. The entire way there Isabella cried silently while pretending to look out her window. Once they parked the car, she turned to Patty with a sudden urgency. Her hand was gripping his tightly. "I just can't shake the feeling that something awful is going to happen," she said.

"Listen Isabella," Patty gently replied, his voice steady and calm. "I'm going to tell you for the second time, *nothing's* going to happen to me. And when I get back we'll get married, so stop your crying." Patty then cupped Isabella's face in his hands, and wiped the tears out from under her eyes. "Come on now, let's get back and I'll see you in the morning."

The following morning at the airport when Patty was checking his luggage, Mama announced to the family that there would be no crying in front of Patty. Everyone would do their crying after he left. She wanted Patty to leave with a memory of happy faces, not miserable ones. They said their good-byes, and Patty walked towards the plane with his shined shoes clicking on the concrete, waving heartily to everyone.

10 MEI FENG

Patty shipped out to Korea with his two friends, Inu and Bobby McGee. Their company was immediately sent to the front lines. They were stationed at the 7th Infantry Division's Main Line of Resistance near a hill listed on maps as "Hill 225." Eventually, the soldiers named it "Pork Chop Hill" because of its shape.

The fighting was an endless back and forth with North Korean Forces. One week they would be on top of the hill only to be at the bottom of it the next. Patty did not have time to write home at first; the battle continued night and day, with both sides receiving reinforcements in a never-ending monsoon of artillery shells. Patty soon realized, though, that writing home gave his mind brief rests from the violence, and he tried to get to his pen and paper whenever he could to tell his family he was all right.

When the first mail came, Patty received a bundle of letters from his family and Isabella. Mama Anna sent a snapshot of the entire family in the front lawn of Luna Street, with Patty right in the middle of his brothers and sisters smiling magnificently. Patty loved that picture, and he kept it in his left breast pocket, so he could look at it whenever he could spare a glance.

In Isabella's letter she told Patty that she loved him, and she would never stop loving him no matter what the wait. She said that she had been going to St. Anne's Church everyday with his mother, and everyday they would ask St. Anne to watch over him. She would continue to go to the church and pray for him everyday until he returned.

After a month of fighting, there was no progress made by either side. Soon, all the carefully constructed bunkers were nothing but rubble. The jungle was a chaotic maze of partially covered trenches, which were so tight inside that the soldiers had to squat shoulder to shoulder to keep from getting shot. Patty's regiment received orders to secure a village that was a front for the North Koreans. The village had been pounded by artillery fire, and it was now their job to clean up the area.

As they approached the village, they started to receive enemy fire from within. It was ordered that they all pull back so they could evaluate the situation. When they retreated to a safer location, it was observed that one Marine had not made it back. Patty scanned the faces, and his heart dropped as he realized that it was Inu who was missing.

Patty pointed out to his fellow Marines the two-story building from which he thought the shooting came. He could see Inu trying to drag himself along. Patty shouted out to Inu, "You just stay right there, Inu. You stay right there and don't move. I'm coming to get you!" Patty then yelled out for the others to cover him, and he took off running in a zigzag pattern out to Inu.

"I'm here buddy. I'm here to get you up and outta here," Patty cried out as he reached the spot where Inu lay on the ground. The Marines were firing everything they had in order to cover Patty, and they kept firing until Patty made it back to the group with

Inu in his arms. Patty laid him down in safety and kneeled by his side to check his condition. Inu was having trouble breathing, and blood was gushing from his thigh. Patty tried to put pressure on the wound to stop the bleeding until it slowed down. "Don't leave me now."

Two medics rushed up to help out. Inu had lost a lot of blood, and they had to administer blood immediately. After examining him closer, they determined that he had been hit three times. After they worked on him for a while, he started breathing easier and the medics told the commanding officer that if Patty had not rescued him, he would have died from the loss of blood.

Patty was in an adrenaline shock, but his anger still raged. "I'm going to get the bastards that done this to Inu!" he shouted to no one in particular.

"That's what we've been trying to do this whole damn time," the commanding officer said cynically.

Bobby had a little more faith. "What are you going to do Patty?" he asked. Well you remember in boot camp when we were training under live machine gun fire? The Sarge was telling us to advance right into the fire and he kept on saying, 'You're dead. You're dead. You're dead.' Well, I snuck around and came up from behind. Then I wasted them all, and that's what I'm going to do now." Patty's mind and body were racing. "Someone give me a radio and give me plenty of fire power with it." Then, like a flash, Patty disappeared into the trees. He stealthily worked his way around the two-story building where he had located the source of the shooting. He made it undetected to a back staircase and went up to the second floor. With all the explosions and gunfire in the surrounding jungle, the North Korean forces did not hear Patty's approach. When he looked out the upstairs window, he was almost right on top of two of them as they stood firing at his buddies. Patty took out a grenade and threw it between them. "Trick or

Treat!" he yelled at the top of his lungs, then he ran to the other side of the building and braced himself for the blast.

From the windows on that side of the floor, Patty then saw a mass of troops beginning to advance on the Marines. He got on the radio and told the men where the enemy was. He asked for artillery fire, and told them to fire 300 yards from where he was. At first they only fired a few rounds to check their accuracy. "You're right on!" Patty then yelled, "Let it rip!"

Shells were traveling right over where Patty was crouched, and he was told to get out of there. Patty carefully made his way back down the stairs, and took an extra wide route through the jungle before safely joining back up with his regiment.

When the boys saw Patty coming out of the bush, they ran over to greet him. They hugged him and congratulated him on his heroic actions that had perhaps saved all of their lives. The captain walked over to Patty to shake his hand, but he stopped short.

"You're bleeding," he said.

Patty looked down at his leg. He was wounded just above the knee by shrapnel.

"Get the medics over here to take a look at this." The captain ordered. Bobby McGee promptly ran off to fetch the medic.

The medic came over to attend to Patty's leg. "How did this happen?" he asked.

Patty said it must have happened when he used the grenade to destroy the machine gun nest.

"Well you're going to have to go back 50 miles to get that wound taken care of," said the captain, "and I'm telling you now, I'm putting you in for the Silver Cross and Purple Heart."

Patty stayed at the medical tent for two weeks. He healed well and was told that he would soon be sent back to his company. When Patty asked where Inu had gone, he was told he had been shipped to a government hospital in Germany. "Is there any way I could call him," Patty asked hopefully. And sure enough it was arranged, and a call was put through to Germany.

When Inu was notified that he had a phone call, he was completely surprised. He was even more shocked to hear that it was Patty on the other end of the line. Inu's spirits were instantly lifted, and he couldn't help but smile as he listened to Patty.

Patty explained to him how he had been slightly wounded, but would be back with the company in a few days.

"Listen Patty," said Inu, suddenly very seriously. "I will never forget for the rest of my life what you did for me out there. My family wants to meet you when you get back to the States. I've told them everything about you, and how you saved my life." That was the end of their conversation because at that moment, their time ran out and the line went dead.

Three days later Patty returned to his company, right up at the front lines again. The fighting was as fierce as ever, and the infantry was trying to capture Pork Chop Hill again, after being on top of it when Patty had left.

Within the week Patty was summoned to report to his captain and colonel, for they wanted to have a very important briefing with Patty. The men were straight to the point:

"Patty, you had Special Operations training, is that correct?" the colonel asked.

"Yes Sir, that's correct."

"Well, we are going to send you off for some more special training. Then, in two weeks, you and 19 other Marines will be taken by submarine up the Korean Bay into North Korean waters. From there, you will proceed by rubber rafts to a radar station in Cholsan. Your mission is to destroy that radar station."

Then the captain stepped forward. "Patty," he said, "you cannot discuss this mission with anyone. You can write to your family, but don't tell them anything about what you are doing and leave your envelopes unsealed so we can check the content."

Patty wrote to his mother and father and told them about the medals his captain was putting him up for. He wrote to Isabella as well, and simply told her that he loved her and thought about her everyday.

When it was time to ship out, Patty and the 19 others were taken out to the coast. They were loaded onto the submarine under the cover of darkness. The sergeant had given each Marine specific instructions about their designated target and to destroy it with heavy explosives. It was a simple mission; they were to plant their explosives then get back to the rafts as quickly as they could. They weren't expecting to run into too many of the enemy, and if all went as planned, it would be a huge, surprise attack.

When the Marines arrived at the radar station, however, it was they who received the surprise. The station was heavily fortified. Before they knew what was happening, they were hemmed in with nowhere to go. The North Koreans got on a loud speaker and in English they declared that the Marines were outnumbered and they were better off to surrender, in which case, they would be treated as prisoners of war under the rules of the Geneva Convention.

Patty crawled over to the sergeant and said, "You're not paying attention to that gook, are you?" "You remember our training, kill or be killed."

"I'm the one in charge here," the sergeant sternly reminded Patty, "not you, and what I say to do, you do." Finally they had to surrender.

Patty still had the markings of the sticker he'd jokingly put on his helmet to imitate an officer, back in Boot Camp. The North Koreans thought that Patty was a real officer, and they wanted to question him further.

Patty was instructed to follow them. His hands were tied behind his back and he was loaded into the back of a truck. They tied him down and gagged his mouth. Behind him, Patty could hear machine gun fire, and he could only imagine what was happening to the other Marines. Patty felt nauseous. He wanted to scream, but the gag in his mouth made it impossible. He could not stop thinking about what they might do to him, and he decided if he had to die, he would rather die alongside his fellow Marines. Patty had no idea why he had been taken aside. He was completely unaware that the faded remains of the fake captain bars were still visible on his helmet.

After six uncomfortable hours of driving along a muddy and rutted road, the truck stopped. A group of Chinese-speaking soldiers met the truck and began to talk with the driver. Patty's years of study paid off and he could understand the Chinese perfectly. The gag was painfully removed from Patty's mouth and he was given some rice and water. Though the last thing on Patty's mind at that moment was food, he forced himself to eat knowing that it might be his last meal for a long time. When he had finished eating, the Chinese soldiers then moved Patty to a different truck.

Patty deduced that they were now in China at a Chinese army base. The Chinese soldiers interrogated him, asking him how many troops he had been with and what their orders had been. All their questions were in English, and Patty did not say a word. The Korean soldiers told the Chinese they recognized Patty as being an American Officer. The Chinese men realized that Patty was not speaking, and they were going to have to force the information out of him.

Two of the stockier soldiers, dragged Patty to the base of the tree. They hung him upside-down from one of the limbs, and placed a large barrel of water below his head. One man would whip Patty across his backside, while the other lowered the ropes and dunked Patty's head into the water. His upper body was completely submerged off and on for dangerously long increments of time, nearly drowning Patty each time his head went under. Despite his pain and fear, though, Patty refused to speak.

Finally, the Chinese interrogators decided that they could not waste any more time, and they summoned two Chinese guards to take Patty across to the other side of the river, to the Korean side, because they did not want to leave his remains on Chinese soil. Patty's ankles were untied, and he was marched two miles to the river. Patty's ankles and wrists were bleeding from where the rope had rubbed into his skin, and with every step, intense pain shot up his back, from where he had been whipped. Patty maintained a good pace though, and was holding himself up strong.

Eventually, they reached the Yalu River, dark and muddy from the monsoons. It represented the border between China and Korea. A thin-spanned walkway stretched across the water, forcing the men to cross in single file. The bridge swung precariously from side to side and the three men crossed one guard in front of Patty, the other behind pointing a bayonet between his shoulder blades.

The two Chinese soldiers joked and laughed with one another about how they were going to kill Patty. They did not realize that he understood every word they spoke. When the guard behind him chuckled at a comment the leading guard made, Patty spun around quick as a flash, grabbed the bayonet, and shoved it into the guard in front of him. The front guard was instantaneously killed, and before the second guard had time to react, Patty struck him in his stomach and knocked him down. Patty put his foot on the guard's chest, the bridge still swinging and the water rushing below, and said to him in Chinese: you said you were going to cut off my balls. Well, screw you. And Patty slit his throat.

Patty then slung the rifle over his shoulder, took the soldier's pistols and binoculars, and jumped off the span bridge. Instead of swimming downstream, Patty swam upstream in case the other soldiers came looking for him, and hid in the high weeds. Feeling sick from the adrenaline, Patty laid down in the grass. His entire uniform was drenched in both his own blood from the beatings, and now the blood of the two soldiers he had killed. Patty rested his head on a rock, and thought about his family, Isabella, and his friends. He wondered if he would ever see them again.

Back in Providence, Rhode Island, the federal government notified Patty's family that Patty had been reported missing in action. In the *Providence Journal's* weekly report, it was printed "P.F.C. Patty DiMarco: Missing in Action."

Patty shivered by the riverbank; his feet still in the water. He refused to step on land for fear that someone could discover his footprints. Patty remembered his survival training, and was able to make a spear out of a bamboo branch, and catch a fish. He was so hungry, that he ate it raw.

For four days, Patty stayed in the river. He was chilled to the bone and he kept feeling that something was biting him. All of a sudden, something struck him from behind. It was a pitch-black and moonless night, and he could not see what it was. Patty felt around in the water behind him and discovered a floating log. Patty felt weaker than ever, and he said a silent prayer to St. Anne to guide him out of there safely. In the darkness, Patty hung onto the log for dear life, and floated down the Yalu River.

Eventually, the jungle became visible in the thin morning light. Patty's stomach writhed in hunger pains and he decided to get onto dry land. He dragged the log out of the water and rested on the bank. Downstream he could see a clearing in the vegetation, so he took out his binoculars and scanned the terrain.

Patty knew he was in China, but he had no idea how far he had floated. From what he could tell, he was in farm country. Through his binoculars he discovered in the distance a coolie tending to his garden. Two small children played in the grass beside him. Patty decided that in the cover of night he would head down to that garden, but for now, he was too weak and decided to sleep until evening.

Once the sun went down and the jungle blackened, Patty made his way down to the garden. Though he had spotted the worker less than a quarter of a mile away, Patty was so weak, that it took him two hours to reach the spot. As he drew nearer to the garden he could smell someone cooking. Then a small hut came into view. Patty's mouth was watering as he snuck up to the hut and peered in. The same man he had seen earlier that day was sitting in front of a fire with his back to Patty.

Patty's legs wobbled, and he knew he would have to act fast or else he would collapse on the spot. He decided to crash into the hut, and if he had to kill the farmer, then so be it. With a sudden renewed energy, which was perhaps all that he had left in him, Patty stormed the door with his bayonet in hand. He leaped on the coolie and cupped a hand over his mouth. The coolie's broad brimmed hat fell to the floor and Patty suddenly froze. The farmer he had attacked was a woman and her eyes locked into his in sheer terror. The two kids were crying on the other side of the small hut.

Patty loosened his grip, but still held the woman. He began to speak to her in Chinese, apologizing and explaining to her that he was an escaped prisoner of war and that he had barely escaped death. "I don't mean to bring any harm to you," Patty told her sincerely. "I have a family too." Then Patty took the picture of his family out of his breast pocket and showed it to the woman. "I haven't eaten in four days," he said. "Please, if you could only give me some food, I will leave."

The woman was shaking, but she nodded her head yes. Patty released the woman, now sure that she would not run for help, and reached over and patted the two kids on the head. He imitated the voice of Donald Duck, and the two kids began to laugh. Patty smiled, and wiped his brow. He was shivering with fever and could barely hold himself up.

The woman helped him to the floor, where he sat and ate the food she gave him greedily, like a dog. The woman stared at him the whole time, never saying a word. After Patty had finished, he got up to say thank you. "What is your name?" he asked.

"Mei Feng," she replied. "What is yours?"

"Patty," he said.

Patty then turned to leave, but it was obvious that he could barely walk. Mei Feng pointed to a bed, and told him to lie down and rest for a while. Patty thanked her again, and lowered himself onto the bed. With his eyes half shut, through his groggy vision, Patty could make out Mei Feng coming towards the bed with Patty's bayonet pointed straight at him. Patty did not have any strength left to fight off an attack and he thought for sure that this was the end of the line. He had barely escaped death before, and now his luck had run out.

Mei Feng reached Patty and down came the bayonet. She cut open his fatigues, and the rest of his clothing gently, without touching his skin. Mei Feng had noticed that Patty's entire body was covered with leeches and cuts, and that he had a high fever. That night, Mei Feng pulled each and every leech off his body. She put cold compresses on his head, ointment on his cuts and made him drink many cups of medicinal tea.

The following morning, she checked in on Patty and made him some tea and fried eggs. She could tell his fever was coming down, and she helped him stand up, and walked him to the bathroom. Then she left him to rest and went off to tend to the garden with her children.

That evening when she returned, Patty was up waiting for her. Mei Feng was surprised, and the first thing she did was check his fever. She told Patty that he was doing much better, and began to make supper. As they were eating supper, Patty asked her the names of her two daughters. "The oldest is Ping Ping and the little one we call Ting Ting," she said.

After dinner, Patty helped her put the two girls to bed then he and Mei Feng sat together and drank tea. He asked her if she was married. Mei Feng said she was. Her husband was in the army, but she had not heard from him in three months. "I think he was killed," she said in a very matter-of-fact tone. "The government keeps sending his pay to me – that's why I think he's dead. They haven't told me yet, but they will." Mei Feng's voice did not waiver, but Patty could see in her eyes that she was mourning.

"*She is a very strong woman*," Patty thought to himself.

Over the next few weeks Patty stayed in the small hut. He was getting better by the day, and every night after supper, Mei Feng would sit with Patty's clothes over her lap, mending what she had cut up.

"Do you want to leave Patty?" she asked one evening when the clothes were almost done.

"No," Patty answered looking into her eyes.

Mei Feng looked to the ground. "Why not?" she asked.

"Because I like it here, and I like you too."

Mei Feng raised her eyes and in them, Patty could see her happiness.

"What is the name of the village we are near?" Patty asked.
"Hunjiang."

The following morning, Mei Feng made breakfast for Patty and served him in bed. She then waved goodbye and left with her daughters to tend to the garden. Patty finished his meal then stood up and got dressed. He was still weak, but he felt much stronger. Patty walked along the little path to the garden to meet Mei Feng. She was surprised to see him there, and told him he should not be up yet, and to go back to bed immediately.

"I feel fine," said Patty smiling, "and besides, I'm going to help you."

Mei Feng shook her head no and tried to stop him, but Patty took the hoe from her and began to till the soil. Mei had made some lunch, which she shared with Patty, and the two worked side-by-side for the rest of the afternoon. Before they knew it, evening came, and it was time to head back to the hut.

"Come on Ting Ting," Patty said, and picked the little girl up and put her on his shoulders. He then asked Mei to hand him Ping Ping and he carried both of them back to the house. The girls giggled in delight and Mei Feng walked behind him, a smile glowing on her lips.

"When the girls go to bed, I will make you a bath," Mei Feng told Patty.

Soon nighttime came, and Mei put the girls to bed. She poured Patty a hot bath, then left the room and told Patty to wash himself. After a few minutes, Patty called out, saying that he had dropped his soap, and would Mei Feng please come and help him get it. Mei Feng walked into the room and leaned over by the tub to fetch Patty's soap. As she was handing it to him, Patty put his arm around her tiny waist and kissed her on the mouth. He pulled her into the tub with him. Mei let out a delightful laugh, as she splashed into the water, and Patty was smiling as well. He delicately took off her blouse and started to bathe her. Patty kissed up and down her smooth back and Mei giggled with pleasure. Patty then picked her up and took her to the bedroom. They spent the whole night making love, falling asleep in each other's arms until the sun woke them up.

From that night on, Patty and Mei slept in the same bed. The months passed and everyday the two fell deeper in love. The children also loved Patty, and he loved them as if they were his own. Patty told Mei that when the war was over he was going to take her and the girls to America.

"I don't care where we live," she said, "just as long as we're all together."

One morning, only minutes after Mei had left to go to work in the field, she came running back to the hut. Patty was inside finishing up his breakfast.

"Quick, Patty!" she called out. "You have to hide in the cellar, and she ran over to the trap door and opened it for him.

"What's wrong?" asked Patty, his stomach knotting in fear.

"I saw two Chinese soldiers approaching from across the field! You just hurry and hide. I'll go see what they want."

Mei Feng then calmed herself and straightened her hat. She walked outside, alone, and greeted the two men.

The soldier told her that they needed her property for an airport and she would have to move further up the river from Hunjiang. They would help her move and build her a new house. They assured her that there was plenty of farmland further up the valley and after the war she would be able to return and reclaim the land. Mei Feng nodded that she understood and the two soldiers left.

When she went back inside to tell Patty the bad news, she could not speak she was crying so much. In between her heavy sobs, she explained to Patty what she had to do. She hugged him tightly, not wanting to let go, for she knew what the future held. She could not bare the thought of being separated from Patty, and she knew that once she left, Patty would have no protection.

"I'll come up there and live with you," he said.

"You can't Patty. There will be other people living there who will tell on you. I could not bear to have anything happen to you, I love you too much. Patty if you are discovered, they will kill you."

Patty realized he had no choice but to leave. "Okay then. I'll go back the same way I came. I'll try to float down the Yalu, and if I'm lucky maybe I'll make it to the Korean Bay and get picked up by friendly forces. If I build a raft, I may just have a chance."

Together, Mei Feng and Patty built a bamboo raft. They finished it quickly and Mei told Patty to hurry because she was afraid that the two soldiers would come back. Patty made two paddles, in case he lost one. He also rigged a rope so he could strap himself to the raft in case he ran into a storm. Patty explained to Mei that he would only travel at night, and make sure the spots he rested at along the river during the day were well hidden. Patty knew he had to leave immediately, but he pulled Mei to him and hugged and kissed her for as long as he could.

Patty finally let go of her and began to leave. "Patty," she said, "I have to tell you something." Patty stopped and turned around. "I'm pregnant," she said.

Patty ran back to her, and put his arms around her again. "I didn't know. I want to stay with you."

Mei told him firmly that he had to go. She pushed the raft into the water, and Patty had to jump on it. "No matter what, I will always love you," she called out after Patty and the current took him away.

Patty was dressed as a Chinese coolie, with a woven straw hat to hide his face. By night, the river carried him towards the Korean Bay and by day he fitfully slept in the reeds. After four days, Patty had completely lost all sense of distance. It was impossible for him to calculate how far he had drifted. On the evening of the fourth day, Patty noticed large storm clouds approaching. It was then, that he also saw a patrol boat in the distance. Patty could not immediately tell if the boat was friendly or not, but as it came closer he could see the South Korean Flag flying high upon the deck. The boat stopped and picked Patty up.

Patty was taken back to their headquarters to be questioned about his capture. Patty explained that he was mistaken for an officer and taken away alone.

"What happened to the rest of the Marines that were with you?" the investigating officer wanted to know.

"From what I could hear, sir, they were all shot. They had me tied up, and they taped my mouth. Then they put me in a truck and took me to China."

"How did you know you were in China?"

"I speak Chinese fluently, sir," he replied.

"Well, we're going to give you a check up and send you to Japan for "R and R" and then you will be able to return to your company."

That Sunday, when he knew his family and Isabella would all be home, Patty made a phone call to the States. Mama Anna answered the phone and when she heard Patty's voice, she burst into tears of joy. She told Patty over and over that St. Anne had answered her prayers. Patty told his family that he was going to

Japan for a rest. Finally, Isabella got on the line. She too could not stop crying and she told Patty that she loves him with all of her heart.

When Patty arrived in Japan, he had the words Mei Feng tattooed on his arm in Chinese. While he was in the hospital, Patty found out that on the following Saturday night there was going to be entertainment for all of the soldiers, with a live band from the States. The event would be at the base, and around two hundred thousand service men were expected to attend. If anyone was interested in performing, they were to get in touch with the entertainment committee, all of whose names were listed on the bulletin board.

Patty met with the bandleader and sang a song for him. The bandleader was really impressed and told Patty he would do just fine. "How much time do you have left in the service?" he asked Patty.

"Why?"

"Well I was wondering if you would be interested in joining up with my band. You got one heck of a voice. What do you say?"

"I don't know what I'm going to do after the war."

"Fair enough. But you think about it, okay, and I'll see you Saturday night."

Patty went back to his bunk and lay down. He could not concentrate on anything. He could not stop thinking of Mei Feng. He was truly in love with her and being apart from her was the worst torture he ever had to bare.

Soon Saturday night came around and Patty was introduced to the GI's and officers as "P.F.C. Patty DiMarco from Providence, Rhode Island." As soon as Patty started singing, the crowd went wild. When he finished his first song, the crowd shouted, "More!

More!" So Patty gave them another one. The applause and shouting he received was unbelievable.

After the show, the bandleader approached Patty and asked if he had thought about being in the band. "I told you, I don't know what I'm going to do."

"Okay, but you take my card and I will meet you anywhere in the States."

"Deal," said Patty.

Patty's week of R and R was soon over and he was transferred back to his company. When he saw Bobby McGee, Patty ran up to him and gave him a huge hug. I thought you were dead," Bobby said.

"Nah, I just got lost for a bit, that's all," Patty replied.

Later, when they had a chance to really talk, Patty brought Bobby up-to-date on all that had happened to him. He told him about how he was mistaken for a captain and how he was taken into China to be questioned. "Luckily, I understood every word they were saying," Patty explained.

"Where did you ever learn Chinese?"

"I learned it in Junior High."

"I don't believe it," Bobby said.

"It saved my life," replied Patty.

Patty did not mention anything about the two soldiers he killed, nor did he mention Mei Feng.

Patty began to write home again every chance he got, and he was receiving plenty of mail back from home. Patty's company was on the front lines again, and the fighting was getting fierce. Marines were getting killed all around him. Once, a concussion grenade was thrown and landed near Patty. Luckily, he reacted quickly and was able to throw it out of the way. It exploded six feet from him, and Patty was shaken, but was all right. The sergeant then gave an order for Patty and Bobby to move over to their left to protect their flank. A heavy battle ensued and when it was over, the Marines were in control of the hill - not, of course, without suffering heavy casualties.

Now that the battle was finally over, it was time to tend to the wounded and to gather the dead. There were body parts all over the area, and when everyone had been identified, two Marines were reported missing: Patty DiMarco and Bobby McGee. Patty's tags were found, but they could not find his body. They figured it would be impossible to pick his body out from all of the scattered remains of the soldiers, so he was once again listed as missing in action.

Weeks went by without the DiMarco family or Isabella hearing any news from Patty. The weeks turned into months, and still no word. Patty had always written, and there was no doubt in anyone's mind that something was terribly wrong. Exactly two months after Patty's letters stopped, Frank and Anna received a notice from Patty's commanding officer. They had been writing to him continuously for news about Patty, and finally, they learned that two Marine Corps personnel would be contacting them in person.

As Anna read the letter out loud to Frank, her hands began to tremble. Anna managed to stay composed long enough to notify the rest of the family when the two officers would be coming, so everyone could be there to receive the news. But as soon as she fulfilled her duty to her family, Anna went to her room and dropped to her knees. "Saint Anne," she pleaded, "please, please bring my son home." Though she feared the worst, she would not give up hope.

Two days later, there was an authoritative knock on the DiMarco's door. The entire extended family and many other members of the community were already at the house waiting for the officers. Anna had prepared an array of foods to distract herself from thinking about the officer's inevitable arrival, but no one had eaten a thing. It was Isabella who answered the door.

She greeted the officers with a grave and removed expression and let them in without a word. The officers could not help but feel that they had arrived at a wake. Everyone was silent as the officers somberly shared the difficult information. One of the officers handed Frank, Patty's dog tags, while the other described what had happened the day of the big battle. "The only thing that could be identified was these dog tags," he explained.

A small cry escaped from Anna's mouth, breaking the silence of the room. Isabella began to sob uncontrollably, and the two women held each other, their shoulders heaving in despair. Big Frank's eyes were wide and desperate, though he managed to keep the rest of his face calm. "Isn't there anything else you can tell us?" he asked.

"Because we could not identify a body, your son will be classified as missing in action. If there is a change, we will inform you immediately."

It was a heartbreaking day, not only for the DiMarco's, but for the entire community. Patty's younger brother, Henry, drove Isabella home, her small frame shaking during the entire ride. As soon as they reached her house, Isabella ran inside. Her sister, Vanessa, met her at the door and Isabella collapsed in her arms. Her mother and father came downstairs and between sobs, Isabella tried to recount the officer's words.

"Because they didn't find his body," she wailed, "I refuse to believe that he's dead!"

Her father just shook his head, certain that Patty was dead.

Isabella ran to her room and collapsed onto her bed. She punched the mattress in anguish, and repeated over and over, "He's not dead. I know he's not dead."

Vanessa followed her into the room and put her arm around her sister. She tried to comfort her, but nothing would calm Isabella down. Isabella stayed in her room and refused to come out until the following day. When she finally did show her face, she would not talk to anyone. She could not eat. She could not think. She would not leave the house. The idea that Patty was gone was just too difficult to take in.

Isabella informed her parents that she was going to take a week off from work. "I just wouldn't be able to concentrate," she explained. "I can't stop thinking about Patty."

Her father did not know what to do. "We all love you," he said, "and we don't want to see anything happen to you. It's a terrible thing, I know, and you have every right to grieve. But Isabella, you must understand that you cannot change what's happened. You can't get sick over something you can't change, and we worry about you. Let your mother make you some homemade soup, and maybe you'll feel better. Come on, you have to eat something."

Isabella just shook her head no. She told her parents that she would not be going to work on Monday, and that was all. When Sunday came around, though, Isabella was still spending most of her day in bed. She had come to a decision. She had been thinking about the day that Patty went on his first jog. She remembered the determination in his eyes, and she knew that he would not give up, no matter what obstacles he had to face. Isabella knew Patty would want her to be strong. She decided to go back to work.

Her family was relieved to hear the news. They thought work might help to get things off her mind, at least during the day. When Isabella returned home after work on Monday, Vanessa was waiting for her. "So how did things go today?" she asked.

"Okay," Isabella mumbled.

"Do you have any plans for tonight?"

"I am going to church to pray."

From that day on, Isabella went to church every evening after work. She would kneel at the altar and ask St. Anne to take care of Patty wherever he was. Regardless of the weather, or how exhausting the day may have been, Isabella never missed a day. There was a park that separated her house from the church and she was often seen walking through the grass in the relentless Providence rain, her head bowed against the wind.

Vanessa's boyfriend was often at the Rampone's house, and his best friend Alex almost always came along. Alex had taken a liking to Isabella, and he spoke to Vanessa about it. "I really like her, but whenever I say hi to her, she just ignores me," he confided. As the two were talking about it, Isabella walked out of her room and headed towards the front door.

"Where are you going?" Vanessa asked.

"To church," Isabella replied.

"But you go to church everyday."

"That's right, I do." And Isabella walked out the door.

"We'll see you when you get back," Alex called hopefully after her.

Isabella went straight to the altar and got on her knees. She started to pray and tears began to form in her eyes. Often, if no one else were in the church, Isabella would talk out loud to St. Anne. She would confide that her heart was still full of love for Patty. "Wherever Patty is, please take care of him," she repeated her prayer again and again.

That evening Isabella did not return home, although Vanessa and Alex were waiting for her. Instead she went to the DiMarco's home, where she was more comfortable. When she spent time with the DiMarco family, she felt it brought her closer to Patty.

"Are you still going to church?" Mama asked that night as they washed dishes together. Anna had traded in her normally bright and festive wardrobe for solemn black dresses.

"I go everyday, Mama."

Mama just nodded her head in understanding.

Isabella hesitated for a moment then told Anna what she had been considering. "I think I am going to start wearing black too."

Mama looked up. Her eyes were suddenly very stern. "You don't have to wear black. Black is too harsh for such a pretty, young girl. You know, maybe you should be thinking of moving on."

"I won't," she said, almost snapping at Anna. "I'm sorry. I will never, never forget Patty."

"I know, dear," Mama said tenderly, patting Isabella's back.

"Mama, do you think I could go to your room to say a prayer to St. Anne?"

"Of course."

The two women walked arm in arm into Anna's bedroom. They looked up at the statue of St. Anne. There were candles lit on either side of the small shrine. The flickering light reflected off of Patty's dog tags, which hung around the statue's neck. They both started to cry. Isabella kissed her hand, then reached up and touched the dog tags. Anna looked at her, then lifted the dog tags from St. Anne's neck and offered them to Isabella.

"I will give you these, but only on one condition. If you find someone to marry, then you must give them back to me."

"Yes Mama. Thank you." And Isabella clutched the tags to her chest. Anna could see the love in her eyes.

Isabella lingered in Anna's room, saying a private prayer and when she went back in the kitchen, she found Henry sitting at the table. Henry had just came home form his job working for a jewelry company. Isabella showed him Patty's dog tags.

"I'll get you a beautiful chain and I can plate the tags in silver," he told her.

This made Isabella very excited. She made a silent vow to wear the tags forever.

Later that evening, when Isabella finally went back home, she was surprised to find Vanessa, her boyfriend Anthony and Alex sitting around in the living room. They had decided not to go out as planned. Isabella said a brief hello as she passed through on her way to her room. Vanessa followed her in, asking her where she had spent her day.

"I was at my mother-in-law's, and she gave me Patty's dog tags to keep. My brother-in-law, Henry, is going to have them silver-plated and I will wear them all the time."

Vanessa tried to be polite, but it was obvious she thought her sister was not completely there. "How do you figure you have a brother-in-law? Henry is Patty's brother, right? You're still holding out that Patty's alive, aren't you?"

"Yes, I definitely am," was Isabella's matter-of-fact reply.

"But Isabella, didn't they say that they didn't find his body?"

"Yes, but they also said that they would have to declare him missing, and that's what I will think 'til I die. He's missing until proven otherwise. Now please, I'm going to sleep."

"Wait. I have something I want to ask you."

"Not tonight, now goodnight."

Vanessa left Isabella's room and rejoined the boys. She told Anthony it was probably best if they went home. She needed to have a talk with her parents. After the boys had left, Vanessa sat her mother and father down at the kitchen table. They could see that something was troubling her.

"I'm very worried about Isabella," she began.

"Why?" her father asked. "She seems to be doing much better."

"Well, maybe she is, but she's been saying some strange things"

"Like what, dear?" her mother looked worried.

"Well, for one, she calls Patty's brother, her brother-in-law, and she told me tonight that she plans to wear Patty's dog tags all the time. I don't know, it just seems a little to much, doesn't it? She goes to church everyday without fail. I'm very worried about her, she's acting crazy."

Vanessa's parents were silent for a moment as they considered their daughter's words. Then her father spoke up, carefully selecting his words. "Well, there's no harm in going to church everyday, and if she wants to wear something around her neck, that's her business."

"I just think Patty's dead, and she won't accept it. I seriously think she's going crazy!"

"You know, Vanessa, time heals everything. Maybe if she met someone else, it would take her mind off of everything."

"What about that boy Alex," her mother chimed in, "he seems like a very nice boy."

"I'm trying, but she's not interested."

"Well, keep trying, she'll come around."

The following Saturday, Vanessa made plans with her boyfriend to go to Scarborough Beach in Narragansett. She invited Isabella and Alex to come along.

"I'll think about it," Isabella told her. "But if I do go, you tell Alex that this is not a date, and you tell him not to put his arm around me because I'll just be going along for the ride. I also won't leave until after I go to church in the morning."

Vanessa was delighted to hear that Isabella was willing to go. At least it would be a start. Alex was even more excited to hear the news. He genuinely liked Isabella, and being around her, no matter what the conditions, always pleased him. It had been six months since Patty had been declared missing and she was sure that a trip to the beach was just what Isabella needed to remind her that she was still young, and to help her forget.

Saturday rolled around and Vanessa, Anthony, and Alex picked Isabella up in front of the church, their beach gear all packed up and ready to go. Isabella was silent for the entire ride. She responded to Alex's attempt at conversation with one-word answers and sat on the other side of the backseat, looking out the window. Still, Alex was very happy to be with her.

At the beach, Isabella did not go with them into the water. While the others splashed and played around in the waves, she preferred to stroll by herself. She wandered off and returned much later. She then sat on the beach, watching everyone having a good time, her mind a million miles away.

Alex came up and sat beside her. He offered to buy her something to eat, but Isabella said she was not feeling very hungry and would just have something to drink. Alex came back with sodas for everyone. Vanessa, Anthony, and Alex chatted away. At their offers for future outing's Isabella merely said she would think about it.

That evening, when the boys dropped the sisters off at their house, Isabella made her feelings very clear. "If you guys think today was an indication of me dating Alex," she said," well then you're wrong." She then went inside. Vanessa lingered behind and reassured Alex that Isabella only needed time. Isabella went out on one more ride with Alex a week later, but ceased going with them completely after that. Alex still came over to the house when Anthony was visiting Vanessa, and he soon became very close with the family. However, no matter how accustomed everyone was to Alex's visits, and no matter how much her mother and father praised him, Isabella did not give him her attention.

The morning after the trip to the beach, Isabella did not go into work. Her mother asked her what was wrong, but Isabella only said that she was not feeling well and shut herself in her room. Her mother tried to give her something to eat, but she refused. At suppertime, Vanessa coaxed her into the kitchen. They all wanted to know what was wrong with her, but Isabella only answered, "Nothing."

Finally after incessant prodding, they got it out of her. "I had a strange dream last night," she said, her eyes wide and desperate, "and I couldn't sleep at all."

"Well what did you dream?" Vanessa asked.

"I'm not going to tell you because I know you'll just make a sarcastic remark about it."

"Well the only way to see if that's going to happen is if you tell it to us first."

"Fine. I'll tell you a little. I dreamt that a miracle is going to happen. I can't shake the feeling that it will."

"You see, Papa! She's going crazy. I told you so. She should be in a loony bin."

Isabella's eyes became hard and she stood up. Her mouth was pulled tight and she turned and walked out of the kitchen. It was not until she was out on the front porch that she allowed the tears to fall. Her mother called after her to come back and join them, but Isabella was already out the door. Mrs. Rampone jumped from the table, her napkin falling to the floor and chased after her daughter. She did not want Isabella out in the street alone when she was this upset. Vanessa was close at her mother's heels.

The two women stopped on the front porch and watched Isabella across the street running into St. Anne's church.

"I'm sorry Mama, it's just that I love my sister very much and I worry about her."

"Be careful what you say to her. Can't you see she's still hurting?"

"After all this time, Mama?"

"Love is strange. It takes a lot of turns."

Isabella ran to the altar, blinded by her own tears, her body shaking. Her sobs echoed off the cold marble and into the ears of the Monsignor just as he was walking in. He quietly approached the Rector and asked who this poor woman was.

"She comes in every night to pray and she usually cries."

"What's her name?"

"Isabella Rampone."

"I know that family," the Monsignor replied. "Wasn't she going with Patty DiMarco who was killed in Korea?"

"Yes Father, I believe so."

"The poor DiMarcos – I know their family well," and the Monsignor shook his head in sympathy. "Such a promising young boy he was."

The Monsignor made his way up the pews and approached Isabella from behind. He placed his hand on her shoulder. Isabella was so caught up in her emotions that she did not hear his footsteps as he approached, and was quite startled at the touch. She jumped slightly, and turned around to see who it was.

"Hi Father," she managed to say after taking a few moments to gather herself.

"What's wrong, my child?" the Monsignor asked quietly.

"I had a dream, Father, and now my family is saying I'm crazy."

"What was the dream, dear?"

"I dreamt that a miracle will happen. I don't know how else to explain it. Just the feeling that something is going to happen."

The Father was silent as if to give her room to sort out her thoughts. Then after a moment, he took Isabella's hand and guided her to a pew. He sat down next to her on the dark wood and looked earnestly into her eyes.

"Can I ask you some questions, Isabella?"

"Of course, Father."

"Do you still love Patty?"

"I never stopped."

"Do you believe Patty's dead?"

"No Father, I don't." Isabella was no longer crying and the words came out clear and determined.

"Do you have faith?"

"Yes, Father. I have faith."

"Remember one thing. Keep your faith, because faith can move mountains. God bless you." With that, the Monsignor patted her hand and stood. He gestured to the Rector to ring the church bells. The Rector complied and the warm ringing reverberated throughout the neighborhood.

Mama Rampone and Vanessa were still standing on the porch and as the bells rang, their conversation came to a halt. They looked over to the church and saw Isabella exited the arched church doors.

Two weeks after the night of Isabella's dream, it was announced that the Korean War had come to an end. Both sides would begin the task of constructing a peace agreement. With the end of the war, a new hope lifted Isabella's spirits. She began telling her family that perhaps this was the miracle she dreamt about. Then it was announced that both sides would exchange prisoners on the following Sunday and that the prisoner exchange would be aired on television that same night.

Isabella came alive with the news. She flitted around the house, trying to get all the chores out of the way so she could start watching television. Mama Rampone had invited the whole family over for Sunday dinner, and although she had prepared all of Isabella's favorite recipes, Isabella would not eat. Instead, she kept her eyes glued to the television. Her mother kept calling her to come eat, but Isabella would not budge. Finally, her father said let her be.

"After today, maybe she'll realize that Patty's no more." Instead, he asked Alex to sit down and have dinner. "And maybe after today, she'll start looking towards you," he said.

Soon the television began to show the truckloads of American Prisoners of War arriving. All the men were asked their rank, name and what state they were from. A newscaster then relayed the information to the public. Isabella had her rosary beads in her hand, and was crying and praying at the same time. Vanessa went in to check on her and placed a shawl around her and told her to try and rest. She then went back into the dining room and left Isabella alone. It was then announced that all the prisoners were exchanged.

Sam was very concerned and asked how she was doing.

"Not too good," Vanessa replied.

Mama Rampone went and stood in the doorway of the den and looked in. Isabella looked as if she was about to fall asleep, just then it was announced that a truck had broken down and would arrive shortly with more American prisoners. When Isabella heard the update, her eyes popped open. She sat up straight and kept repeating, "Please, St. Anne, please!"

Now the prisoners were giving their names. When they got to about the fifth soldier they asked his name and he said "P.F.C. Patty DiMarco from Providence, RI," Isabella let out a scream.

Her family came running into the parlor to see what happened. Isabella was on her knees, facing the television shouting, "Patty's alive! He's alive! Look!" and she pointed at the screen. "That's him!"

"Unbelievable," Mrs. Rampone muttered, too shocked for words.

Isabella picked up the phone and called Mama Anna DiMarco.

"Have you been watching the TV?" she blurted out as soon as Anna picked up.

"Yes, we were, but when they said there were no more prisoners, we shut the TV off."

"Well, Patty's alive! The truck he was on broke down, so he arrived late. Mama, I'm going to church."

"We'll meet you there."

Isabella ran out of the house and across the street. The shawl had fallen off of her shoulders onto the sidewalk, but she did not take notice. Other friends who had heard the good news joined Isabella and her family, running across the park into the church. As they entered the church, the Rector wanted to know what was happening. Isabella shouted with happiness, "Patty's alive!"

The Rector started ringing the church bells. The Monsignor hearing the bells ran into the church and asked what was going on. Isabella ran up to him.

"Patty was found alive! Father, it's a miracle – A Miracle On Charles St.!"

"Faith, my child," he answered and gave her a hug. The Monsignor then got everyone's attention and announced that he would recite Mass to celebrate this happy occasion. "An occasion, which I will always remember as A Miracle On Charles Street."

After Mass, everyone congratulated Isabella and the DiMarco family. Isabella hugged Mama DiMarco, both of them sobbing with happiness. Mama asked Isabella to come over to their house. "As a matter of fact, why doesn't your whole family come over!" Mama Anna was so happy, she did not know what to do with herself. She kept embracing Isabella, not wanting to let her go in fear that she would find out she was dreaming.

It wasn't long before they got a long distance call from P.F.C. Patty DiMarco. Patty's sister Ann Marie answered the phone. "It's Patty!" she shouted, and everyone in the kitchen cheered. She told Patty that she loved him and missed him very much then she passed the phone around so everyone could talk to him.

Mama got on the phone. Patty said hi, and Mama began to cry even louder. "I prayed a lot to St. Anne, Mama said, and she pulled me through."

Then Henry got on the phone. Patty asked his brother, "Did Isabella get married?"

"Are you kidding?" Henry laughed. "She's standing right here next to me waiting to speak to you."

"Put her on," demanded Patty.

There was a pause. Isabella took a deep breath then lifted the phone to her ear. "Hi Patty," she said. "I can hardly wait until you come home. When will you be coming home?"

"I don't know yet, but I'll call my mother's house as soon as they tell me."

11 PATTY COMES HOME

Patty went to see his commanding officer before he was to leave for the States, and told him all about Mei Feng and the circumstances in which they met. He asked his commanding officer if there was a way that he could return to Damdong, China to see if he could locate Mei Feng. His commanding officer said, "No way. Not after what you told me about what them two Chinese were going to do to you. They would probably put you to death. Maybe someday you'll be able to go back, but not now. Just forget about her."

"That's the problem, sir. I just can't forget her and it's driving me nuts."

"Don't worry, I'm sure when you get back home, all of that will change."

Patty called his family again and told them he would land at T.F. Green Airport the following Sunday afternoon. Meanwhile, word spread that Patty would be arriving, and it seemed as if everyone in town was going to be at the airport to greet him. As the plane was coming into Rhode Island, flying low over Narragansett Bay, Patty couldn't help but think of Mei Feng. They were now starting to land and though he should have been happy to be home at last, a certain sadness would not let him go. He just couldn't get her off of his mind.

Patty couldn't get off the plane fast enough to meet his family and friends. So many people had come down to meet him that he was overwhelmed. Patty hugged and kissed everyone in his family. When he reached Isabella he pulled her into his arms and gave her a big, long kiss. All of his best friends were there including Steve, Johnny, Danny, Butterball, and Sir Ray. Danny hugged Patty and said, "I didn't think I would ever see you again. You know, Patty, when we were kids, I wished that you had made love to my sister."

Patty laughed. This was not what he had expected to hear. "Why's that Danny?"

"Because maybe you would have been my brother-in-law, that's how much I love you!"

Big Frank then made an announcement that there would be a party at the DiMarco's house that night, and everyone was invited. When they returned to Luna Street banners were waving everywhere, welcoming Patty home. They had even arranged for a band and as the party got underway, Patty was asked if he would like to sing a song.

"Not today," Patty replied, but he promised to sing sometime soon.

Once all the initial excitement and all of the congratulations died down a little, Isabella finally approached Patty, her eyes lit up like a Christmas tree. She was so happy that Patty was at her side again and thought it was the happiest moment of her life.

"Well, Big Guy," she asked, "Are you happy? I would've waited for you forever."

"Yes Isabella, I am."

Patty did not want to tell Isabella, that in fact inside he was a mess. He wished he could tell her about Mei Feng, but he did not want to hurt her. All the while the party was going on and Mama Anna was keeping a close watch on Patty. She knew something was wrong, but for now she wouldn't mention anything to him.

"What are your plans now Patty"?" Isabella asked.

"What do you mean, plans?"

"Well, all your friends are married. Where do we stand on marriage?"

"You mean you and me?"

"Of course – I mean you and me."

Patty wanted to tell her about Mei Feng but he just could not bear to do it. After all, if she waited for him, she really must love him. He wished he could tell someone what was eating his insides. He couldn't stop thinking about everything he had gone through, especially about his best friend Bobby McGee who died in his arms when he was a prisoner of war. And now Isabella was asking him if they were getting married!

Patty took Isabella's hand and sat her down. "Right now I can't think straight. Just wait a while until I settle down. We'll talk about this later. Come on now, let's get back to the party."

When they got back, Mama approached Patty. She knew something was wrong and was very worried. She went up to Patty, gave him a hug and whispered in his ear, "I want to speak to you later tonight." Patty and Isabella went back where everyone else was celebrating and walked over to where all his friends and their wives were. Someone asked, "So when's the big day going to be?"

Patty answered, "We haven't decided yet. As soon as my head clears up, I'll be able to do some thinking."

It was 2:00 a.m. when everything broke up. Patty took Isabella home and told her he would see her in the morning. When he returned home, Mama was waiting up for him.

"Isn't it kind of late for you to be up Mama?"

"Not for my son, it's not too late. What's wrong with you Patty?"

"Nothing is wrong with me."

"No – tell me, what's wrong with you?"

"What do you mean?"

"Remember, I'm your mother and I can read you."

"Nothing's wrong."

"Well you want me to tell you what I think is wrong?"

"What do you mean Mama?"

"Well, in Italy when something like this happens, it means one thing. And I can see that one thing all over your face."

"What is the one thing?" Patty was starting to feel a little nervous. His mother's ability to see through him was uncanny.

"It means there's another woman," said Anna as confidently as if Patty had already said it was true. "Why don't you tell me, and I promise I won't tell anybody. I will take it to my grave, I swear. Let Mama help you."

Now Patty started to think because if he could talk to someone about what was bothering him, getting it off his chest might make him feel better. Mama asked him again. "Let's talk about what's bothering you. I'll only ask you one question. You don't have to answer. Just shake your head – yes or no. Is it another woman?"

Patty figured he knew he could trust his mother and he didn't want the rest of his family to know about Mei Feng because he wasn't looking for another woman, so he answered his mother.

"Yes, Mama, there is another woman and it's tearing me apart."

"I know, Patty, I could see it in your eyes. Tell me all about her."

"Well, you know I can speak Chinese. During the war, when I was captured, they were going to put me to death. They didn't know that I understood their language and I escaped and had to kill two Chinese guards who would have killed me otherwise. In my escape, I found myself on a very small farm. I was in very bad shape. Because I could speak Chinese, we were able to communicate. This woman, she fed me and brought me back to health and we both fell in love with each other. She saved my life Mama. I spent six months with her, I love her."

"I couldn't stay though. I had to get out of there or I would have been discovered. If they found out I was the one responsible for the death of those two guards…well, she was afraid I would have been put to death. We discussed me going back there after the war, but my commanding officer ruled against that because it would be too dangerous. I can't stop thinking about her and it's killing me."

Patty paused and debated what he was going to say next. "One more thing, Mama, she is carrying my baby."

When Mama heard that she made the sign of the cross, but managed not to get emotional. She wanted to see if she could help her son. Anna asked her son what the name of this woman was.

"Mei Feng and her two daughters are Ping Ping and Ting Ting."

"And what's that funny writing on your arms?" Mama asked, not knowing what else to say.

"I have something written on each arm. My left arm is the U.S. Marine emblem and on my right arm is Mei Feng in Chinese. Now you know everything Mama."

"So, what are your plans with Isabella?"

"I like her. As a matter of fact, I like her a lot. But as it stands my real love is in Dandong, China."

Mama then asked Patty, "Do you feel better now?"

"Somewhat," Patty answered.

"Well, let me tell you this, Patty. You can't go back to China. You have to put that behind you and in time you should be okay. What are your plans, Patty, for the future, especially with Isabella?"

"I don't know, Mama. She would make a good wife and mother, too, I know."

"Will you promise me you will put that Chinese girl behind you?"

"I'll try, Mama."

The following day Patty asked his father when he could start to work. Big Frank replied, "Take some time off and in the meantime, maybe you could start seeing more of Isabella."

"Papa, I have a lot of respect for you, but what is this between you and Mama wanting me to see Isabella? I haven't even had a chance to see what direction she wants to take."

"Well I do know she really loves you. Do you love her?"

"Right now I like her and that's all I'm going to say. Papa, I would like to start working as soon as possible. I think it would do me a lot of good."

"If that's what you want, it's all right with me." Frank knew something was bothering Patty.

"Can I borrow your car Pop?"

"Sure. Where are you going?"

"I want to do some serious thinking."

Patty took the car and headed for Scarborough Beach and his favorite watering hole, The High Tide. He just needed to get away for a while. He sat at the bar by himself and started to drink. A lot of people recognized Patty and went up to him to shake his hand saying, "Welcome home, Patty!" He was enjoying watching his friends dance and have a good time. It's been a while since he and Isabella danced all night. A girl came up to Patty and asked him for a dance. Patty offered to buy her a drink instead.

"Okay," she said. "I know your name is Patty. My name is Nicole Nault."

"That's a pretty name."

"The next slow dance is yours if you want it," she said.

"You'll have to forgive me," Patty replied. "I didn't come here tonight to dance."

"Why did you come here – to drink?"

"Not really. I've got a lot of thinking to do."

"You want me to help? I'm a good listener."

"I'd need a week to tell you everything. Oh what the hell, let's just go dance."

A lot of the crowd knew Patty and as he danced with Nicole she said to him, "You seem to be very popular."

Someone asked Patty, "You going to sing us a song tonight?"

"I'll ask Gary Lucier later."

"We'll be waiting."

Who's Gary Lucier?" Nicole asked.

"He's the band leader."

"You sing, too?"

The song was over a little sooner than both of them would have liked. They went back to the bar. "By the way, Nicole, where are you from?" Patty asked.

"Weymouth, Mass."

"You live with your parents?"

"No, I have an apartment at Mediterranean Woods."

"What do you do for a living?" Patty asked.

"I'm a paralegal for a very large firm in Boston."

"Are you driving back to Weymouth tonight?"

"No, I'm on vacation. I've rented a cottage on the beach for two weeks."

"Do you have a blanket I could borrow just for tonight?"

"Yes, I have one, but what do you want it for?"

"I want to sleep on the beach tonight."

"Why?"

"Like I said, I've got some serious thinking to do."

"Why sleep on the beach? Come over to my place."

"I don't think I could do that."

"Why not?"

"Because I came here to do some thinking. That's all I came here for. I've only been home two days."

Soon, the owner of The High Tide, Dave Julian, came up to Patty to shake hands and welcome him back home. "Listen, Patty, we got a request for you to sing a song. What do you say? If you do, the drinks for you and your friend will be on the house."

"You strike one heck of a bargain, Mr. Julian. How could I refuse that?"

As soon as the band's break was over, Dave Julian went up to the stage to announce that his good friend, Patty DiMarco, will now be singing a song. Patty got together with Gary Lucier the leader of the band and discussed what he was going to sing.

"Let's go with a fast number," Gary said. "It will be like old times. What do you want us to play, Patty?"

"Let's play rock and roll music on three."

Gary was glad to see Patty was back. As soon as Patty started singing, the place went wild. The floor was packed and everyone started to dance in between the tables. Nobody was sitting. Only Nicole was still at the bar. Patty gave Dave Julian a wave to go dance with Nicole. Now everyone was dancing. The whole place was shaking.

When the song was over, the crowd wanted more. Patty complied, but after the second song he needed to take a break. Dave Julian went right up to Patty without pretense and said, "Patty, you got a job here. What do you say?"

"I don't know?" replied Patty. "Name your price, and I'll think about it." Then he turned and went back to the bar to join Nicole. Patty had already made up his mind to sleep on the beach for the night, so they both kept on drinking. Nicole began to talk a little more, or more specifically, she began to ask Patty questions about himself. She wanted to know whether or not he had a sweetheart.

"Does it make a difference?" he asked in return.

"No. It doesn't make a difference," she replied coyly. Then she hesitated, "So do you?"

"Yes, I do." And Patty took another swig of his beer.

"Are you going to marry her?"

"I don't know."

Nicole did not mention that while Patty had been singing, she had been doing her research. She asked the bartender what he knew about Patty and he had informed her that Patty was top-notch. He was a very popular guy and was referred to as "The King of Providence."

Soon closing time came around, and the bartender began to put the stools up.

David Julian approached Patty as he was getting ready to leave and asked him if he had made up his mind about the job offer. Patty told him that he would let him know in a day or two.

"Fair enough," Julian quickly replied. "I'll be waiting to hear from you."

Patty gave him a smile then turned his attention back to Nicole.

"So are you going to let me borrow a blanket?" he asked. The grin was still on his face.

"Of course, but it's in my cabin. Follow me there and I'll get it for you."

The two walked side by side, not exactly in a straight line, to Nicole's cabin. When they got there, she invited him in for one more drink.

"Why not," Patty agreed.

Nicole put on some soft music and Patty said to himself, "To hell with it, I'm staying right here." With that he asked Nicole if she'd like to dance. He pulled her into his arms and they pressed close into one another.

The next morning Nicole woke up to find that Patty was already awake, sitting up in bed with his bare back to her. He heard her movement and turned around. "I'm going to go get some breakfast," he stated coldly.

"Want some company?" Nicole asked hopefully.

"No, I'd prefer to be alone."

"How come you want to be alone?"

"That's my business," Patty snapped. Then he thought better of himself, and in a more tender tone he said, "Look, let's have a talk. I told you I have a girlfriend, and I still haven't decided what I'm going to do. I know I spent the night with you, but that is as far as it will go. I'm not promising anything. I know you will be here for two weeks, and I don't know how long I'll be staying here. I still have to give Julian an answer about singing at The High Tide."

Patty ended up staying with Nicole for three days. Then he decided that it was time to call his parents. It was his sister, Anna Marie, who answered. He only needed to say a meager hello before she started in on him.

"Where are you Patty? Everyone is worried sick. No one's heard from you. Is everything all right?"

"Sure it is," Patty replied. "Where's Mama?"

"Standing right next to me."

There was a pause and brief shuffling. Patty swore he could hear his mother's distressed breathing. Then she was on the phone.

"Patty! Where have you been?"

"Hi! Mama. I went to see a friend that's all."

"Where are you?"

"Nowhere in particular."

"Are you coming home?"

"I sure am."

"When?"

"I'm not sure yet."

"Well your girlfriend's been here everyday to see if we've heard from you. Why don't you give her a call and put her at ease."

"I will," he said, "but not right now. Is Pop there? Let me speak with him."

Anna reluctantly handed the phone over to Frank.

Big Frank did not say anything. He just held the phone to his ear and waited for Patty to speak.

"Hi! Papa. I've got your car and I'll be bringing it back soon."

"That's all right. You can use it as long as you want. Your mother wants to speak to you again." The phone changed hands again.

"Patty, aren't you going to call Isabella? She's been staying here all day hoping you would call. She wants to know what's going on. You know Patty, she's a good girl."

"I know Mama. I just need to do some thinking that's all. I've got to go now Mama. I love you."

Patty made up his mind that he would go over and have a talk with Dave Julian at The High Tide and tell him he'd like to sing there for the Fourth of July weekend. Dave was excited to hear the news, and said that he would begin advertising that day.

"I'll put a big ad in the paper and this place will be packed tighter than a can of sardines," he chuckled. "What do you think about that, Patty?"

"It's up to you Mr. Julian."

Sure enough, the next morning there was an ad in the *Providence Journal*, which was straight and to the point:

> **Fourth of July Gala with entertainment at The High Tide on Scarborough Beach, Featuring the singing sensation Patty DiMarco and the Gary Lucier Band.**

Dave Julian knew this ad was going to be successful and the entire three-day weekend was going to be one of the busiest The High Tide had seen in a long time. His energy was high, and his mind was spinning thinking of all the preparations he needed to do.

Back home, Isabella's sister Vanessa caught sight of the advertisement and could not believe what she read. Her sister was worried sick about where Patty had run off to, and here he was being advertised in the *Providence Journal*! Immediately Vanessa got on the phone and called the DiMarco's house – knowing that Isabella would be over there hoping to hear from her man.

"I've found Patty!" Vanessa blurted out to her sister.

"Where is he?" Isabella sounded a little stunned.

"Just wait and see. You won't believe it! I'm coming over, hold on." Vanessa tucked the paper under her arm and went running over to the DiMarco house. She ran straight up the front porch and into the kitchen without knocking, and found Isabella, Anna and Big Frank standing up anxiously waiting.

Still out of breath, Vanessa shoved the paper into Big Frank's hands. "Here! Look!"

Frank was a little puzzled at first, but then he began to read. A huge smile broke out on his face, and he shook his head in disbelief. Both Isabella and Mama Anna were reading over his shoulder.

Once the excitement had subsided Isabella announced that she was going to go to The High Tide to see Patty. "I'm going with you," said Big Frank.

"I'm coming along too," Mama Anna followed.

Everyone then scattered to get ready and within the hour they were all piled in Vanessa's car, headed for Scarborough. Before they even got to The High Tide, they noticed a line of people over a block long. The parking lot was packed, so Frank told Vanessa that their best bet was to go around to the back and park in front of the dumpster.

Isabella's stomach dropped at the thought that they might not be able to get in, but Frank assured her that they would not give up that easily. "Follow me," he said. "We're going to the front of the line."

Standing just outside of the entrance stood Dave Julian, full of smiles and hanging up a sign that read: SOLD OUT. Frank approached him and Dave began to call out that he was not going to let anyone else in, but then he stopped in mid-sentence.

"Why you're the spitting image of Patty!" he exclaimed.

"You mean he's the spitting image of me," Frank corrected. I'm Frank DiMarco, Patty's father." Frank stuck out his hand. Dave shook it enthusiastically. "We came to hear Patty sing," Frank continued.

"Identical," Dave muttered to himself. Then to Frank, "Of course, of course! That's a different story! I've got room for you. Why don't you go around to the back door and I'll let you in."

Walking in through the back of the bar, the group had to turn a few corners, before the stage came into view. The place was crammed with people, and already the temperature was getting warm. Dave led Frank, Anna, Isabella and Vanessa up to a table in the front. Patty was nowhere in sight.

"The best seats in the house," Dave said formally as he pulled out a chair for Anna.

"Where's Patty?" Frank asked.

"You sit tight, and I'll see if I can find him for you." Then Dave was off into the crowd.

Isabella anxiously scanned the faces, looking for Patty's. Finally she spotted him at the bar. Her heart fluttered at the sight of his face. Then she noticed a very attractive woman standing next to him, or rather leaning towards him. Isabella stood up and pointed. "There he is!" she exclaimed. "I'm going over to see what's going on."

"Wait, I'm coming with you," Frank said, already out of his seat as well.

The two scooted their way through the thick crowd – Isabella slipping between the bodies, Big Frank finding it a little more difficult to maneuver. Finally, they made it up to the bar. Isabella did not hesitate. "Hi Patty," she said, fully expecting the surprised look on his face as he turned around.

"Hi Isabella," he said, not being able to come up with anything else. Then he saw his father standing behind her. "Hi Pop."

Isabella turned to Nicole, her eyes full of fire, yet her voice as sweet sounding as could be. "Excuse me," she said smoothly, "so you mind if I take my boyfriend to meet his mother?"

"'Mama's here?" Now Patty was really surprised.

"She sure is," Isabella replied, and she grabbed Patty's hand and started to pull him towards their table.

Now Patty had a lot of respect for his parents, but his mother was right up front, and it would not be easy to reach her. Isabella saw his hesitation and read it as guilt. She pulled harder on Patty's hand, and they slowly made their way back to the front. Dave Julian's head poked above the crowd. He was watching everything just to make sure Patty was okay.

"Mama!" Patty said, pulling his mother in his arms and giving her a big kiss. Anna could not help the smile that escaped from her lips, but she removed it quickly.

"Patty," she said, "I need to talk to you." Everyone else seated themselves at the table, while Anna pulled Patty off to the side of the stage. "I'm going to ask you just one question Patty. Now are you or aren't you with that girl at the bar?"

"She's just a friend Mama."

"And where does Isabella stand with you?"

"She's okay Mama, I'll be with her."

"Then what are you doing in Scarborough?"

"I just needed to clear my head up, that's all."

"Well, is it cleared?"

"I'm getting there."

"Are you coming home tonight?"

"I'm singing here for the next two nights."

"Well you come home each night, then return."

"I don't want to do that Mama, but after this week I promise I'll come home."

Mama did not want to push her luck, so she gave in. "All right Patty, I believe you."

Soon, Dave Julian was on the stage announcing to the crowd that he had a very special singer to help everyone celebrate the birthday of the nation. "Patty DiMarco and the Gary Lucier Band!" The crowd began to cheer, and Patty jumped up onto the stage. The band was already up there, and they began to play as soon as Patty's hands touched the microphone. Patty had never sung with such enthusiasm. He was all over the stage, the notes just pouring out of him.

The dance floor was hopping with the entire beach crowd, and all the kids who had come in from Connecticut and Massachusetts that had gotten there late, were dancing wherever they could find room. Frank asked Isabella if she wanted to dance.

"Of course," she replied, and they hit the floor. Isabella forgot about the girl at the bar for a while, and was just happy knowing Patty was near. Even Mama Anna could not help but move to the music a little. Listening to her son sing always filled her heart. Everyone was under the spell of Patty's voice. Dave Julian even asked Vanessa to dance, and she did not have to think twice before she was in his arms.

The night was speeding by and soon it was one o'clock and time for everyone to head home. As people were leaving, the general buzz in the air was that most of them would be returning the next night for a second dose of the fun. People bought their tickets before exiting, knowing full well that Saturday night would be the biggest night of the weekend.

Mama got the family together and asked Patty if he was coming along. "Not tonight," he said.

"Where are you going to stay?"

"Dave has a cot in the back. I'll sleep there for the night."

All this time, though Isabella had been standing next to Patty, her eyes were glued to Nicole. Nicole was still seated at the bar, and seemed not to notice a thing.

"Are you ready to leave?" Frank asked, trying to get Nicole out of her head.

"No I'm not," Isabella replied defiantly.

"What's the matter"?" Patty asked.

"I'm not leaving until that young lady leaves," she said nodding her head in the direction of the bar.

"Listen," Patty said, I'll follow you guys in the truck until we get out of the beach area. Isabella, why don't you ride with me"?"

When they were in the car, Patty did not waste any time beating around the bush. "Isabella, there's nothing going on with me and that girl. If you don't believe or trust me, then let's end this relationship right now."

Isabella was quiet for a moment then replied, "I will trust you." She could not bear to say anymore, she was still pretty emotional about the events of the day.

"Then I will see you tomorrow night," Patty said. Patty then blinked his lights, and his father pulled over to the side of the road. Patty kissed Isabella goodnight. "I'm glad you came," he said, "see you tomorrow."

When Isabella got back in the car, Mama asked if everything was all right.

"Yes Mama," Isabella replied quietly, and they drove off towards Providence.

Patty returned to The High Tide to find Nicole still waiting for him at the bar. It was obvious that she had continued to drink as she waited. "So where are you going to stay tonight"?" she bluntly asked. "I'm going to sleep in the back tonight."

"Why not sleep at my place again?"

"No. I'm staying here. I explained to you before that I have a girlfriend."

Nicole had seen this coming. "I understand," she said, "but remember, anytime you want, feel free to call me. You'll always be in my heart Patty DiMarco – you know we can always just talk."

"Thanks, I'll remember that."

Before Isabella was dropped off at her house, she told Mama Anna that Patty had promised to come home right after the weekend was over.

"I'm sure he will," Mama said, and hugged Isabella goodnight.

"Are you coming tomorrow?" Isabella asked.

"You can count on it!"

After such a successful first night, Dave Julian was on top of the world. He knew Saturday was going to be even bigger, and he got the idea to set up a sound system outside and put folding chairs in the parking lot so even more people could dance and enjoy the music. He also set up an outside bar, so he could sell even more drinks. The only thought that was running through his head was that this Fourth of July would be the biggest money making weekend he'd ever had. He even hired a policeman to watch over the place, just to make sure nothing would get out of hand and spoil things.

When Dave asked the mayor and his old-time friend, Lenny LaBush, for permission to use the town parking lot for the extra cars, Lenny replied that he could, only on the condition that he gave him a table up front for him, his wife and his two kids.

"Done deal!" Dave laughed, feeling like he was on top of the world.

The next day seemed unbearably long to Isabella, but finally evening came around. She spent an extra hour doing her hair and make up, she was so excited to see Patty again. Anna gave

Isabella a call to tell her that they would be picking her up. She also reminded Isabella of the importance of trust in a relationship, especially a marriage.

The DiMarco's arrived at the Rampone's at 7-o'clock sharp, hoping that if they left early they would find a better parking spot, and more importantly, get to visit with Patty a little longer. Vanessa decided to come along again too. She had had so much fun the night before. The two girls got into the car bubbling with excitement. Isabella looked absolutely beautiful. Anna smiled at her as she got in and gave her a little wink. Isabella crossed her fingers in return.

Though they were earlier than the night before, when they reached The High Tide, there was not a parking place to be found. However, there was a sign directing them to additional parking in the nearby town lot. Policemen were directing the traffic, and surprisingly everything was very orderly. The line at the entrance to the bar was almost twice as long as it had been the night before, and once again Big Frank went straight to the front. Isabella immediately began scanning the room for Patty. She spotted Nicole at the bar again, but no Patty. They all ordered drinks and soon Dave Julian was on the stage announcing the second evening of the hottest band on the beach, "Patty DiMarco and the Gary Lucier Band!"

It was the same thing all over again. With the introduction of Patty DiMarco, the place went wild. Isabella felt a wave of pride rush through her as she looked at the way the other girls looked at Patty, for she knew that she was the only one lucky enough to be his girl. Inside and outside shouts rose up from the crowd. "We're waiting for you Patty!" one voice boomed out from just outside the doors.

Patty got on the microphone and made a quick announcement. "I would just like to welcome my family and thank them for coming out to The High Tide tonight." Then he gestured to the band to begin. The drummer counted off the beat, the band started to play and Patty began to sing.

Just like the night before, everyone was up and dancing. The loud speakers Dave had put outside were working marvelously. Patty's voice vibrated along the beach like a giant magnet, drawing people to The High Tide. During the break, Patty went to sit with his family and told them that he would only be singing for one more night, then he would be heading home.

Sunday night came, and Patty's family came to watch him one last time. After the show was over and Patty said goodbye to Dave Julian, he drove back into Providence with Isabella. Together, in the aftermath of yet another amazing night, the two discussed their future plans.

12 PATTY GETS MARRIED

Patty began working at the family's brick laying business again. Everything seemed to be going well, and his relationship with Isabella appeared stable if nothing else. At lunchtime, though, every day Patty would leave the job site under the guise that he was getting a sandwich from a nearby deli. However, in truth, Patty would go to the nearest pub, down a few shots of whiskey then hurry back to work. Everyday – the same thing. What Patty did not know, though, was that he was not fooling anyone. His uncles could smell it on him, and they mentioned it to Big Frank. Frank was very concerned, but he did not know what to do about it.

"Maybe Patty just has a lot on his mind," Vito offered. Frank nodded; he had been thinking the same thing.

After this had been going on for about three weeks, Patty began taking longer and longer "lunches." Frank decided that something had to be done, so one afternoon he followed Patty. As he expected, he saw Patty heading straight into the pub from work. The next day Patty took the entire day off and sure enough Frank spotted his car at the same watering hole.

Frank went in and took a seat next to Patty. He could see it in his son's eyes, that Patty was a million miles away. Frank tried to start a conversation with him, asking him how everything was going with Isabella. Patty would just answer "Fine," and shut himself up like a clam. Frank's heart ached to see his son like this, but he did not know how to break the barrier Patty had built around himself.

Mama Anna also noticed the change in Patty. She was hoping that he would forget about the girl in China, but instead he was just drinking more and more. "Perhaps if he gets married, things will change," Anna hoped, and she prayed to St. Anne to reach out to her son. Isabella and Patty seemed to be getting along fine, but Anna noticed that it was Isabella who was doing all of the calling.

One evening, Mama received a call from Isabella, asking if Patty was home. She sounded very concerned.

"What's wrong?" Mama asked.

"Well, Patty was supposed to pick me up tonight and he hasn't shown up yet. You know, this is not the first time this has happened."

"If you want me to, I'll ask him what is going on though I don't promise he will tell me anything."

"No, you better not, Mama. I don't want Patty getting angry."

However, there was no denying that Mama Anna and Isabella were extremely concerned about Patty. Frank was in the kitchen, and he overheard part of the conversation. When Mama got off the phone, Frank asked what had happened. Mama explained that Patty had failed to pick Isabella up, and this was starting to be a normal occurrence.

"I'll be right back," Frank said and he went out to his truck and drove away.

The lights were low in the Rainbow Café, but as soon as he walked through the door, Frank recognized his son's form hunched pathetically at the bar. Frank glanced around to see if there were any women hanging about, but none were to be found. Frank was sure the problem was liquor, not women.

He walked up behind Patty and tapped him on the shoulder.

"Hey, can I buy you a drink?" he asked casually, though his eyes were far from lighthearted.

"Hey Pop," Patty replied lethargically. "Have a seat. What brings you here?"

"Well for starters, you. You've been coming here a lot lately, what's going on?"

"I've got a lot on my mind that's all."

"You want to talk about it."

"Not really."

"Come on Patty. We've always been good buddies," Frank pressed.

"Well Pop, I've got a lot on my mind from the war. You know my best friend died in my arms while we were being held captive."

"That's a tough thing to deal with, son, I understand how that could keep you thinking." It seemed that Patty was finally starting to open up a little and Frank wanted to keep him talking. "Do you mind if I ask you something, Patty?"

"Shoot."

"Well back in Italy, when things like this happened, 95 percent of the time the reason was a woman. How is everything with you and Isabella?"

"Everything is okay."

"Is she the reason you're in here tonight?"

"No Pop, it isn't that."

"Then how come you didn't pick her up tonight?"

"I was going to Pop, I swear I was." Patty paused and took a sip of whiskey. "But memories started milling around in my head and I just couldn't shake 'em."

"And you figured drinking would help you forget?"

"Maybe."

"And what happens when the bottle is empty, and you still got the problem? Did you think about that?"

Patty was silent.

"Well I'll tell you what that means," Frank continued, his voice sounded urgent as if he was having trouble holding back his emotion. "It means that the bottle is the real problem."

"I know Pop."

"I'm going to ask you another question, and it might hit below the belt. You think you're ready for it?"

"Try me," Patty said apathetically.

"It's about Mei Feng."

Patty could not believe his ears. It was as if his father had heard the thoughts in his head. He knew his mother would never divulge his secret, so how could his father know about her?

"Where did you get that name," Patty asked, his voice curt, and his eyes suddenly wide.

"While you were sleeping one night, I went into your room and copied that Chinese writing you have tattooed on your arms. I brought it to a Chinese customer we are building a house for, and he told me it was the name of a woman. Please don't be angry with me Patty, I was just worried about you. Tell me, is she really what's bothering you?"

"I really don't want to talk about it," Patty snapped, and he downed the rest of his drink. "Maybe some other time."

"Okay," Frank replied, knowing that he had pushed it too far. "But if you ever do want to talk about this Mei Feng, you know I'm always here to listen."

"Pop, I know you're really busy, and I don't want to bother you."

"Look at me Patty; and Frank's eyes blazed into his son's. "I'm never too busy for you. Don't you ever forget that."

Patty's eyes began to well with tears and he quickly looked away. Frank went on. "As far as Mei Feng is concerned, my lips are sealed forever." Patty just nodded his head, not trusting himself to open his mouth without all of the emotion spilling out. "Just one more question for you Patty, then I'll leave you alone. What about Isabella? Is she in or out of the picture? If you don't want to tell me it's okay, I understand."

"I'll tell you that I've been giving her a lot of thought," Patty replied, slightly more composed now. "I know she's a good girl, and I'm really trying to take our relationship to another level. I've decided that I will go over to see Mr. Rampone. There's something I'm going to ask him."

"That's good enough for me, Patty." Frank put his arm around his son's shoulder. "What do you say we go home, huh? That would make your mother very happy."

"Okay Pop."

Frank paid the bartender, and helped his son up from the bar.

"Oh, and by the way Patty," Frank said as they were leaving. "Your good friend Mo Morin, and his two sons, David and Brian from Fore Court in Cumberland called you twice. They want to know when you're going to see them and play doubles with them in tennis, "Like you guy's always done. They really miss you Patty, why don't you go and see them."

"I will Pop."

"Hey, and it looks like the workout wouldn't hurt either," Frank joked.

A few weeks later Patty decided to purchase a beautiful engagement ring. As soon as the ring was in his pocket, he called the Rampones and asked Isabella's mother and father if he could come up and see them, because he had something to show them.

"Sure come on up," Mr. Rampone replied, "no one else is home."

When Patty arrived, he was greeted at the door. Mrs. Rampone hooked her arm in his and told him she was very happy to see him. They all went inside, and Patty told them to take a seat. Then he took out the ring.

"With your permission, Mr. Rampone," he began, "I would like to give this to your daughter."

Mrs. Rampone let out a little gasp and looked as if she were about to cry. Mr. Rampone stood up with a smile on his face and extended his hand. "Welcome to the family," he said. "When do you plan on giving the ring to Isabella?"

"Don't mention anything to her yet, I want to take her to dinner Saturday evening, and surprise her then."

"We won't say a thing," Mrs. Rampone giggled.

Patty thanked the Rampones, and headed home to tell his parents that the engagement was in sight. Both Mama Anna and Big Frank were delighted to hear the news, not only because they loved Isabella, but also because they thought the marriage would help Patty forget his past and move into a prosperous future.

The next day, Patty started making phone calls to all of his closest friends, and asked them if they wanted to come to a celebration with their girls because he was planning to surprise Isabella with an engagement ring, and he wanted everyone to be there. The plan was to meet at the Venus Di Milo Restaurant that Saturday at 7-o'clock.

After all of his friends had been notified Patty finally called Isabella. His heart was pounding in excitement, and he had to take a few deep breaths before he dialed her number, just to make sure he would sound calm on the phone and would not ruin the surprise. He told her that all of his friends and their girlfriends would be going out this Saturday, and what time should he pick her up?

Saturday rolled around, and Patty could barely contain himself. He picked Isabella up as planned, and found that everyone else was already at the Venus Di Milo, enjoying their first cocktails, by the time they arrived. Patty ordered three bottles of their best champagne in the house, and then asked Isabella to stand with him to make a toast.

"First," Patty announced, "I have something I would like to give Isabella." Then Patty proceeded to get down on one knee and pulled out the engagement ring. "Isabella, I love you. Will you marry me?"

Words could not describe the rush of joy that went through Isabella. "Of course," she said, and then she started to cry.

Johnny Petrarca stepped in and said, "Let's all drink to our favorite couple. They're getting married at last!" Everyone raised their glasses in the air, "To Patty and Isabella," they said.

The celebration went on well into the night. Isabella told Patty not to drink too much, but he only responded by saying, "This is a night to celebrate. Don't you want to celebrate?"

"Of course I want to celebrate," she replied, "I just don't want to get drunk."

"Well, you don't have to drink, and if you want to go home, I'll call a cab for you."

"No, I don't want to go home without you."

All of the guys were having a wonderful time, and Patty kept ordering more drinks. Isabella was very worried, for she could see that Patty was drinking too much. Danny noticed it also, and as closing time approached he gave Steve a nod that meant they should meet in the men's room. Once they were in the men's room and out of earshot, Danny expressed his concern.

"I think Patty's had too much to drink, and I'm worried about him driving home."

"I was thinking the same thing," replied Steve.

"How about we go out to his car and pull out a wire, so it won't start. Then I'll drive both him and Isabella home."

"Sounds like a plan," said Steve.

The next day Patty called Isabella and said, "How about we pick a date for our wedding?" Isabella was delighted that he wanted to set the date so soon, and said she would be right over. Isabella arrived shortly, and immediately Patty led her into the dining room, where they sat down and started discussing the logistics of their wedding. Patty wanted his five best friends to be in the wedding party, along with his sisters Anna Marie and Carol. Isabella agreed to let Patty's sisters be bride's maids along with two of her friends, and her sister Vanessa as the maid of honor. Patty said he would ask Danny Boyle to be his best man.

Everything was moving smoothly and quickly towards the wedding day. Vanessa threw a bridal shower for Isabella, inviting everyone from their family as well as the entire DiMarco family. Mama Anna and her sisters-in-law cooked the feast of feasts for the shower, and all the women chipped in for gifts for the bride.

Danny Boyle threw a bachelor party at a local strip club for all of the boys. They had a blast, and everyone kept kidding with Patty, telling him that he still had time to change his mind. Patty's brother, Henry, gave Patty a large ball that he painted black, with a chain and a clamp attached to it. "This is what you'll be wearing," he said as he handed it over, getting a big laugh from everyone. Meanwhile Isabella was at home, trying not to worry about Patty drinking too much. The thought that his uncles and father were there with him was some comfort.

After the bachelor party was over, Patty and his friends went to an after-hours club. It was there that Patty made up for the drinks he passed on while his father was around. They were all having a good time, mostly reminiscing about their childhood, and all of the times they had been through together. Patty ordered six shots of Canadian Club. He told everyone to take one and form a circle. Everyone put one hand in the middle, and with there other hand they held their shot glasses ready. "Nothing will ever interfere with our friendship," Patty announced. "Now drink up!"

Soon it was time to leave. Danny decided to follow Patty, because he felt that Patty had had too much to drink. When Patty got into bed, though his head was spinning, he could not sleep. He could not stop thinking about Mei Feng. He was trying very hard to move on and forget about her, but his heart just would not let go. He kept reasoning that after the wedding things would be different.

Patty kept working with his father and still went for his liquid lunch every day. His father knew what he was doing but did not mention anything to him. About a week after the bachelor party, Patty's sister Anna Marie answered the phone and took a message for Patty from a girl named Nicole. Anna told Patty, and he told her not to tell anyone else about the call. Then as soon as Patty got the chance, he called Nicole and asked her what was going on.

"Oh, I just wanted to talk to you Patty. How about I buy you a drink?"

"Why not," Patty replied. "Where do you want to go?"

"How about we meet out at Dave Julian's? I have such wonderful memories of The High Tide. But of course, if you can't make it out there, I can always meet you somewhere else."

"No, The High Tide is fine."

"Great. Let's meet this Friday night."

"Sounds good," said Patty and hung up the phone.

That Friday, Patty headed for The High Tide as planned. He did not tell anyone where he was going. About an hour after he had left, Isabella called looking for him. She asked Mama Anna if she knew where he was, and when she said she didn't, Isabella began to be very worried.

"I don't understand, Mama," she said. "I know something is bothering Patty, but he won't tell me anything. I think maybe a lot happened to him in the war that he can't get out of his head."

"Give him time," Mama reassured, "and I'm sure he'll forget."

As soon as Patty reached The High Tide, Dave Julian was at the door greeting him. "I had a feeling you would be here," Dave said, a warm smile on his face.

"Now why's that?" Patty asked.

"Why there's a beautiful girl sitting at the bar asking for you, that's why," and both Dave and Patty laughed. Then Dave went on hopefully, "So are you going to sing a song for us tonight Patty?"

"Well I didn't come prepared, but I'll think about it."

Patty went over to see Gary Lucier, the bandleader and a good friend for whom a hello was long overdue.

"Boy, when you sang here on the Fourth of July, that was the busiest weekend we've had since the place opened. You're welcome to sing with us again any time you want." The end of Gary's sentence trailed off at the end, as if he suddenly became self-conscious of his affection for Patty.

"Yeah, we had a hell of a time, didn't we?" Patty replied.

Meanwhile over at the bar, Dave informed the bartender not to charge Patty for his drinks. Nicole looked over at the stage from her stool, her thick eyelashes fluttering anxiously.

Finally Patty walked over to Nicole, and nonchalantly asked her how she had been. Nicole stood up and gave Patty a big hug. Her sweet perfume filled Patty's nostrils. He backed up a step.

"So Nicole," he said in that same casual tone, "how did you get my number?"

"Oh, I looked it up in the book," she replied. "I looked up Frank DiMarco, you remember that night your father introduced himself to me?"

Patty did not have time to answer. Dave came over and put one arm around his shoulder, "So what do you say Patty? You want to sing a song?"

"Sure, I'll sing one…for old time's sake. But just one, though."

"That's fine, just fine," Dave beamed. "Follow me."

Patty followed Dave up onto the stage and informed Gary that Patty would be singing one song.

"I thought you'd never ask," Gary laughed and made a nod towards the drummer to start a fast beat. Patty took the microphone and began to sing. It felt wonderful to be singing again, and the crowd was just as receptive to his voice as it had ever been. When Patty was finished, he received a tremendous applause. He thanked everyone and modestly made his way back to the bar.

Nicole gave Patty a kiss on the cheek. "Sounded good," she said. "So how is everything going with you these days?" Nicole paused for a second, then asked, "Are you still going with Isabella?"

"Yes I am."

"Still going to marry her?"

"So far, yes."

"You love her?"

"Now you're getting personal, and I don't answer personal questions," Patty said, and he gestured to the bartender that he wanted another drink. He returned to Nicole, "Where are you trying to get with all these questions anyways?"

"Oh, I'm not trying to get anywhere. It's just that I can see something is bothering you, that's all."

"What are you, a mindreader now?" Patty's voice was becoming a little hostile.

Nicole laughed. "I don't read minds, but I do read tarot cards."

"What's that?"

"Well, I have this special deck and if I shuffle it, and you pick cards out of it, those cards will give you good advice. Have you ever had your cards read before, Patty?" as she spoke, Nicole had been looking Patty in the eye.

"No, as a matter of fact, I haven't because I don't believe in it."

"Do you want me to read yours?"

"Go ahead, I'll try it once, but you remember I don't believe in card reading."

Nicole stood up from the bar and took Patty to a smaller table. She took a deck of silk-wrapped cards from her purse, shuffled them, and asked Patty to pick twelve out from the deck. Her eyes lingered on the faces of the cards for a moment then she held her breath and said, "Each card has its meaning. I can see that something is bothering you. It could be some woman in your past. Do you think about a woman from your past a lot?" She looked up at Patty.

"I don't want to answer that."

Nicole did not speak or push him any further. She simply continued to look at the cards, shaking her head negatively, as she flipped over more and more cards.

Finally, Patty could not stand it any longer, "What is it? Why are you shaking your head like that?" He was slightly annoyed.

"I see something about you, but I don't want to tell you."

"Just tell me. I don't believe in it anyway." Though his voice revealed nothing, Patty was getting a little nervous.

"I don't know how to explain it," Nicole continued, "but I'll try." She then adjusted herself in the chair. "Patty, I see a lot of obstacles and sadness coming into your life. Does that upset you?"

Patty did not blink an eye. "No, I'll just accept it as a challenge. Doesn't worry me one bit."

Nicole looked up at him silently, as if waiting for him to say more or to change his mind. Patty held himself stiff and looked at her. He could not come up with what to say. "Well, thank you for the reading," were the words that finally came out. "You can put your cards away now, I've heard enough." Patty stood up from the table.

Nicole slid the cards back in a single pile and reached for the silk cloth to wrap them. "Can I just ask you a question?" she asked.

"Go ahead, but just one."

"Are you in love with Isabella?"

"Well if I'm marrying her, I must be."

Nicole nodded her head, as if she understood the real meaning of Patty's reply. "Patty, I'm going over to Galilee to rent a room for the night, care to join me?"

"No, I'm going home. Let's just be friends, okay? If I want to get in touch with you, I will call you but don't you ever call me. Is that understood?"

"Patty, you shouldn't drive. You've had too much to drink and you might get into an accident."

"If I can't drive, I'll pull over and go to sleep."

"You promise me that you will."

"I don't make promises. I'm going to leave now Nicole, so goodbye." Patty turned and headed towards the door.

Nicole followed him. "Wait, I'll walk you out."

When they reached Patty's car, Nicole leaned into Patty. "You sure you won't change your mind?" and she sweetly looked into Patty's eyes.

"No, I'm going home."

"Will you kiss me goodnight?"

"Okay," and Patty kissed her forehead. "Now, I'm going." But Nicole would not let go of him. Patty pushed her off. "If anything, I'll call you. Bye Nicole." Patty jumped into his truck and shut the door. He drove off without even a second glance at Nicole, standing alone in the big empty parking lot.

"Goodbye," she said softly.

The weeks rolled by and the wedding inched nearer. Patty was spending more time with Isabella and more time with the bottle as well. Each night after dropping Isabella off at her house, Patty would head straight to the Rainbow Tap. His family was aware of how he was spending his nights, drowning himself in alcohol and they talked amongst themselves about it, not knowing what to do. Anna and Big Frank often talked late into the night about it and they both decided that the reason for Patty's behavior was most likely that girl in China.

"I thought he would forget about her in time," Anna told her husband, "but now, I just don't know."

"Maybe after he gets married, he'll move on," Frank suggested, though it was obvious from his tone that he was having trouble believing his own words.

"You can forgive certain things, but a broken heart never really forgets," Anna replied.

"Well, let's give Patty the wedding of all weddings! I am going to call Mr. Rampone and explain to him that although it is usually the bride's family to pay for the wedding, we would like to pay for it and everything else that goes along."

"You do what you think is best," Anna said.

After quite a bit of convincing, Mr. Rampone finally agreed to let Frank take on the costs of the wedding. "Just as long as you let me give the couple a generous wedding gift, I guess I can go along with it," he said.

The wedding was to take place at the Biltmore Hotel in downtown Providence. Frank was going all out and did not even consider the price of things as he made the plans. Nothing would be spared; Patty was going to have the most magnificent wedding possible.

Finally, the day of the wedding arrived. Isabella Rampone became Isabella DiMarco in St. Anne's Church. Her dress was a beautiful white, and her cheeks were rosy and vibrant. From the church, the wedding party went to Roger William's Park to take pictures. The church bells rang in celebration of the new marriage and Isabella could not help but be reminded of the ringing of the bells on the day a miracle happened on Charles Street.

The reception at the Biltmore was a grand event: it seemed as if every family in Providence had shown up and quite a large group from the North End of Boston as well. As Patty and Isabella made their way through their relatives and friends, greeting everyone and thanking them for coming, Isabella's eyes fell upon a lady who was seated by herself in the corner of the room. Instantly, she recognized her as the girl from The High Tide.

Isabella jerked Patty close to her face and whispered in his ear, "What's she doing here? Who invited that girl?"

Patty looked over at Nicole. "Don't ask me," he said, "I didn't invite her."

"Well I don't like it one bit. She has no business being here."

"Isabella," Patty said, looking deeply into her eyes. "Don't worry about it. You're the one I married." He gave her a big kiss.

Isabella let it go and the rest of the evening went smoothly.

After the reception ended, Patty and Isabella went upstairs to the biggest suite in the hotel. The next morning, as husband and wife, they flew to Hawaii.

The honeymoon went flawlessly, and thoughts of Mei Feng only passed through Patty's mind in brief, fleeting moments. It was not until they were about half an hour from Providence, on the flight back home that Isabella finally turned to Patty. "Do you mind if I ask you something, Patty?" she asked cautiously.

"What is it Isabella?"

"How did that girl from The High Tide find out about our wedding?"

"I told you before, I don't know and I don't think we need to ever bring it up again."

Isabella remembered what Mama Anna had said about trust and she let it go. "Just forget it Patty," Isabella sighed and looked out the window at the city sprawling out below them.

Patty was quiet for the rest of the flight. Mei Feng had entered his mind and he just could not shake the thought of her. He was torn between his past love and thoughts of raising a family.

"Why are you so quiet all of a sudden, Patty?" Isabella asked.

"I'm just thinking. Say what would you think about us building a house?"

"I would love it!"

"I know a beautiful piece of property. It's on a corner lot and there are all new houses in the area."

Isabella was beside herself. This was what she had always wanted. "Patty, I'm so happy right now," she said, tears welling in her eyes.

"Let's have a drink to celebrate," Patty said.

Isabella agreed.

When they arrived home, Isabella was quick to call her family and tell them the good news about building a house. Patty took her to the lot that he had been considering and she absolutely loved it. She envisioned a large white house with a big yard and a porch. She could almost see the little children playing on the lawn, and said a quick and silent prayer to St. Anne thanking her for her good fortune. My father's company can build the house for us, and I will be the foreman," Patty was saying. "My father won't charge us for the labor. This house will be our wedding gift from him."

"It's too good to be true, Patty," Isabella explained.

"My father always told us that he would build a house for each one of his kids when they got married."

Though this was a happy day for Patty and Isabella, there was still a hint of worry in Isabella's mind. One thing was bothering her: it was the constant smell of liquor on Patty's breath.

Three months passed and Isabella began to show signs of pregnancy. Patty was filled with excitement at the thought of becoming a father, and he showered Isabella with affection. Both the DiMarco's and the Rampones were ecstatic. This was going to be their first grandchild.

Patty called up all of his best friends and went out with them to celebrate the good news. Isabella waited up late for Patty, worrying about how and when he would get home. When Patty came stumbling in through the door, Isabella asked him if he would like a cup of black coffee.

"Sure thing," Patty slurred. "Hey, why not put in a double shot of Sambuca while you're at it!"

"We don't have any Sambuca," Isabella said coldly.

"Well, that's the only way I drink my coffee," Patty replied.

"I wish you wouldn't Patty..." then Isabella had to stop because a lump was forming in her throat.

"Don't you tell me what to do!" Patty suddenly yelled.

Isabella thrust a cup of coffee down in front of Patty and turned to go to her room. "If you want liquor in it, you can get it yourself," she cried and stormed off.

Patty made a mocking face as she left, then stood up and went to the cabinet. He pulled out the bottle of Sambuca, poured some into his coffee, then lifted the bottle to his mouth. He finished the rest of it off, straight.

The next morning, Patty could not get up to go to work. Big Frank called to see why Patty had not shown up, and Isabella told him that Patty was ill from some food he ate the night before. She was too embarrassed to tell him the truth. Frank knew better than that, though. He could sense a storm coming, but he remained silent out of respect for their privacy.

Six months later, a baby was born. Isabella gave birth to a beautiful baby girl. They decided to name her Anna, after her grandmother, and they celebrated with a huge baptismal ceremony at St. Anne's Church. "Saint Anne will be your patron saint, too, little one," Grandma Anna whispered into the baby's ear. That evening, a gala was held at Patty and Isabella's new house, with all of their friends and relatives.

As usual, Patty had plenty to drink. Isabella kept on making excuses, saying that Patty was just overly excited about the birth of his daughter, but everyone knew his drunken state was not a rare occasion. Big Frank and Grandma Anna were particularly aware of the escalating problem, but they could not say anything to Patty to make him behave differently.

Patty began missing work more and more frequently. He would spend all day either sleeping off a hangover, or sitting at a bar. Some nights, he did not even make it home. Isabella did not know what to do. She was desperate, and expressed her concern to Anna. Frank and Anna had a hard time accepting the fact what they knew only too well to be true: Patty was drinking because he could not forget about Mei Feng in China, and his best friend, Bobby McGee, who died in his arms in the prisoner of war camp.

Frank and Anna were the only ones who knew about Mei Feng and though they discussed it openly between themselves, they never let on to Isabella. Soon Isabella was pregnant again, and thoughts about Patty's problems were shifted onto the back burner for a while. Isabella concentrated on her pregnancy, and as she entered her third trimester, she convinced herself that Patty was letting up a little on the booze.

Isabella gave birth to a baby boy, and they named him Patty junior. At the baptism and celebration, it was clear to everyone in the family that Patty was drinking more than ever. He had gained a lot of weight, and his face was flushed and swollen.

One day, about two weeks after the birth of their second child, Grandma Anna made a visit to Patty's house. She said she wanted to speak to Patty in private, and asked him if he would come over to her house on Luna Street the next day. Patty would never refuse his mother, for he still had the utmost respect for her, so he agreed.

The following day, two hours later than he said he would be there, Patty arrived on the front porch of his youth. He let himself in, and to his surprise Mama Anna was not in the kitchen. He called out to her and he heard Frank reply from the bedroom. "We're in here Patty."

Patty opened the door to his parents' bedroom and found his mother sitting up in bed. His father was at her side grasping her hand. Patty went to her bedside and knelt down. "What's wrong Mama?"

"Maybe I should come back some other day?" Patty asked.

"No, no. I want to talk to you now."

"What is it Mama?"

"Patty," she said, "your drinking is breaking my heart. I want you to stop."

"Oh, Mama, I don't drink that much."

"Yes you do, Patty." Anna coughed and turned her face away for a moment. When she turned back, her eyes were watery and red. "I want you to do something for me, Patty."

"What is it Mama?"

"I want you to pray to St. Anne and ask her to help you stop drinking."

Patty was already on his knees by the bed, and he lowered his head and clasped his hands. He made a silent prayer to St. Anne. Mama pushed her rosary beads into his hands and smiled.

Patty then got up and kissed his mother on the forehead. "I have to go to work now Mama," he said. I'll stop by when I get off and check in with you.

For a few days, at least, Patty seemed to kick his habit. One night, though, as Isabella lay awake in bed next to Patty, unable to sleep, she heard Patty mumbling something. She turned and saw that he was fast asleep, but he was most definitely talking. She could not make out what he was saying, and it sounded as if he was perhaps speaking Chinese.

Patty repeated this for many nights in a row. Isabella brought it to the attention of his mother and father, knowing full well that she would not get any answers from Patty.

"I'll tell you what we'll do," Frank advised. "I have a tape recorder that you can borrow. When he does it again, just record what he says, and then I will take it to Charlie, the Chinese man that does our shirts. Maybe he could shed some light on what Patty's saying."

Isabella agreed to the plan, and the next time she was awakened by Patty's mumbling, she clicked on the recorder. The next day under the guise of bringing a cake to Mama Anna, Isabella went over to the DiMarco's and dropped off the tape. That same day Frank brought the tape to Charlie and explained the situation.

"None of us speak Chinese," he said, "and we're very concerned for Patty. Please could you help us?"

Charlie was a little hesitant. "Suppose he's saying something personal. I don't want to get into the middle of anything personal. You know Patty's been coming in here since he was a youngster, to practice his Chinese with me. He speaks it nearly as well as I do now. I wouldn't want to do anything to hurt him now."

"Charlie," Frank said, his eyes taking on a strong authority, "I would keep this just between you and me. I'm just trying to help Patty. You know he's having a tough time."

"I know," Charlie said. "I'll see what I can do."

Charlie listened to the recording twice and wrote down what Patty said. Patty talked a lot about his best friend Bobby McGee and seemed to be reenacting the moment when Bobby died in his arms. Patty kept crying that he was sorry, so sorry, that he had tried all that he could.

Also, the name of a Chinese woman kept coming up. Her name was Mei Feng, and it was obvious that Patty was very much in love with her. Charlie had seen that name tattooed on Patty's arm, but he never asked who she was. Now he understood. Charlie did not know what to do. He did not want to reveal anything that would hurt Patty, but at the same time he saw the desperation in Frank's face. He explained his predicament to Frank.

"My word is my bond," Frank assured him. "I will keep this just between you and me. Charlie, I know there was a Chinese girl and her name was Mei Feng." Frank pulled a piece of paper from his pocket. On it was written in Chinese characters Mei Feng . "You see Charlie," he went on, "I want to see if I can help Patty without telling him anything you tell me. I already know about this woman, and I'm afraid she is the reason Patty's been drinking so much, and the reason for his nightmares. Tell me the truth, is this what this is all about?"

Charlie could not deny him. "Yes it is. Also, Patty talks a lot about a friend that died in his arms."

"Thank you Charlie," Frank said. "I really needed to know this. I won't mention anything to Patty. I want to see if I can do anything to help him." Frank then walked out the door.

When Frank arrived home, Isabella and her two small children were waiting for him. She stood up as he stepped into the kitchen.

"Well," she asked anxiously, "did you find out what he said?"

"He talked a lot about being in the prisoner of war camp, and of his best friend who died in his arms. I'm going to hold onto this tape, because I have a doctor friend whom I want to listen to it. Maybe I can get Patty to go in and see him."

Isabella hugged Frank, tears streaming down her face. "Thank you," was all she managed to say.

That afternoon, when Frank returned to the job site, he took Patty aside for a talk. "Look, Patty," he said bluntly, "I know you've been through a lot and I know of a doctor who could try to help you deal with your memories of the war."

"What is he, a shrink? Well I'm not crazy and I don't need to talk to a shrink." Patty stormed off. He jumped in his truck and headed straight for the Rainbow Lounge. He did not get home that night until two in the morning. Isabella was waiting up for him when he walked in the door.

"Where have you been," she demanded.

"Nowhere," Patty mumbled and went off to bed.

Meanwhile, Frank got in touch with his friend, Doctor Sinclair, the psychiatrist. Frank explained the situation he was in with Patty. The doctor nodded his head in understanding and asked Frank if he would like for him to go and see Patty. Frank explained that Patty had refused to talk to a doctor even when he told Patty about his sleep-talking in another language and that the doctor might help him get rid of his nightmares.

"I don't want to talk about it to anyone, because I don't have a problem," was all Patty had said.

There was nothing Frank could say to persuade Patty otherwise. Patty's' nightmares continued and worsened, often causing him to wake up in a cold sweat. Other nights, Patty would not return home at all. One week he stayed out for three nights in a row. He was skipping work almost everyday and the days he did show up, he was not in much condition to work anyways. No matter what Isabella said to him, no matter how hard she tried to help, there was nothing she could do.

"What's wrong Patty?" she asked. "are you happy with our children? Or is it me that's the problem?"

"I'm very happy with our children," Patty answered, "so don't bring them into this anymore! And there's nothing wrong with you."

"Well, what's wrong them?"

"Nothing's wrong!" and Patty stormed out of the house.

Isabella took her two children and went to see Patty's mother and father. "Patty has not come home in two weeks," she told them, "and he was drinking more than ever before he left."

"He hasn't been showing up for work either," Frank told her. "Isabella, what have you been doing for money?"

"I receive Patty's disability check. Things are tight, but I've decided to go back to work just as soon as I find a good babysitter for the kids."

"You just bring my grandchildren here and I'll watch them for you." Mama Anna told Isabella.

Frank told the women he'd be right back and left towards the back of the house. Isabella turned to Anna with an inquisitive expression on her face, but Anna just shook her head to say that she had no idea what Frank was up to.

A few minutes later Frank returned with a large wad of cash in his hand. He shoved it into Isabella's palm

"Oh, I can't take this," Isabella gasped, slightly embarrassed and uncomfortable.

"It's just a loan," Frank assured her. "You can pay me back once you're working." Frank was merely letting Isabella take the money without losing her pride. He would never really allow her to pay him back.

The weeks passed without any word from Patty. He had dropped completely out of sight. Isabella did not know how to reach him, and neither did any of his friends. She finally mustered up the courage to admit that she did not know where her husband was. After many sleepless nights spent worrying about Patty, Isabella finally came up with a plan. She would do some detective work and take a ride down to Scarborough Beach and Julian's High Tide, to see if Patty was hanging out there. She arranged for her sister to watch over her kids, and the following Saturday night Isabella made the drive.

As she pulled into the parking lot of The High Tide, Isabella's stomach dropped. The parking lot was nearly empty; a depressing contrast to the overflowing lots from the summer nights when she had come to see Patty sing. *That seems like another lifetime,* Isabella thought to herself. She parked the car, took a deep breath and got out. She did not know which would be worse, finding Patty at the bar drunk, or not finding him at all.

Isabella opened the swollen wood door of The High Tide, and walked into the bar. It was darker and smokier than she had ever remembered, and the smell of beer was overwhelming. Dave Julian spotted her immediately, so different was she from his regulars, and ran over to greet her.

"Hi, Isabella," he exclaimed, "what brings you here?" Dave Julian smiled widely, and gestured that Isabella should take a seat.

"Hi, Mr. Julian," Isabella replied modestly. "If you don't mind, I came here because I want to ask you some questions." She was embarrassed, but determined to get the information she needed.

"Sure thing, darling. I hope I can help you out."

"Well this is strictly confidential…" Isabella paused for a moment, unsure of how to phrase her request.

"Oh, you can trust me, Isabella," Dave earnestly replied. He then looked around the bar to make sure they were out of everyone's earshot. "What is it?"

"Has Patty been coming around here lately," Isabella asked, flinching before she heard any reply.

"No, I haven't seen him in a long time," Dave answered, "and I would have seen him too, if he'd been in here. I'm here seven days a week, and if I was in my office, one of my staff would come and notify me if Patty walked in. Everyone knows Patty he's got a big name here."

Isabella looked distressed. She was thinking hard. "I just want to ask you one more thing. Last time I came in here Patty was sitting at the bar talking with a girl. Her name was Nicole. Has she been in here?"

"Nicole? No, I haven't seen her either. Is there something wrong Isabella?"

"No, nothing's wrong. Thank you Mr. Julian." Isabella got up and left the bar. It was not until she was sitting in the car that she let the tears come.

13 HENRY READS THE RIOT ACT

Five months later, Henry DiMarco was sitting in his office, looking over a newspaper, when an overweight man, unshaven and unsteady on his feet, walked in through his door. Behind him, the frantic secretary exclaimed that she had told him not to come in, but Henry cut her off.

"It's okay, Edna," Henry said, "He's my brother." He motioned for his secretary to close the door behind her as she left, wide-eyed and baffled. Henry remained seated at his desk. His face remained expressionless as he assessed the state of his brother, Patty.

"Looks like you've been sleeping in the woods," Henry finally said. Patty's clothes were wrinkled and soiled. He had gained at least 25 pounds since his disappearance, and his shirt scarcely stretched over his protruding belly.

Patty was silent.

"Don't you know Mama and Pop are worried sick about you." Henry continued, his voice getting louder. "And Isabella's been searching all over the state for you. Where in God's name have you been, Patty?"

Patty kept his eyes on the floor. "I've been to see a friend of mine in Connecticut." He mumbled, then slid into a chair, as if trying not to make a sound.

Henry flashed his brother with a look of disgust. "Was it a woman friend?" he asked.

"No, not a woman," Patty apathetically replied.

"And you've been drinking." Henry declared. "Don't tell me you haven't, I can smell it. Are you going to go see Mama and Pop? What about Isabella and your kids?"

"I don't think I'll be going to see anybody today," said Patty, his voice getting quieter until the last word was barely audible.

"Why not?"

"Some other day, not today."

Henry was losing patience. "You know it's been six months since you've seen your family, the least you could do is stop by and let them know you're alive."

"Not today," Patty said again.

Henry sighed and realizing that this conversation was a dead end, he decided to change the topic. "So why did you come to see me Patty?"

"I came to ask you a favor."

Henry lifted his eyebrows. "What kind of favor?"

"I need to borrow some money."

"Why, so you can buy more booze?" Henry's entire face and neck went red. He could not believe the gall of his brother.

"I'm sorry I asked," Patty said, and he began to get out of his chair. "I'll see you later."

"No wait." Henry did not want Patty disappearing again. "Wait a minute. I'll let you borrow some money on the condition that you take a shower and shave here in my private bathroom. Then I'm going to take you to buy a new suit, because Aunt Josephine is getting married. You two were always so close, Patty, and it would mean the world to her if you came."

"When's she getting married?" Patty asked.

"In two weeks. She's getting married at the same place you did Patty."

"I'll be there," Patty agreed. "But I don't want you to mention this to anyone."

"It's a deal," Henry said. He got up from his chair and walked around to the other side of the desk. "I'm sorry I was so short with you at first," and he gave Patty a big hug. "There's just one thing," Henry continued. "Look, I'm your brother, Patty. Tell me, what's bothering you. What's making you want to drink so much and throw your life away?"

"You wouldn't understand. We're brothers, and I love you, but I just can't go down that road with you. Not just yet."

Though Henry wanted to press further, he knew it would be best to let it go for now. "So how are you going to get to the wedding? You want me to pick you up?"

"No, I'll get there."

When Patty finished showering, Henry took him out and bought him an entire new wardrobe. The two brothers stood side by side on the sidewalk in front of the tailors, and for a moment, it was as if Patty had never gone. "Where are you going from here?" Henry asked. "Do you want to stay at my house?"

"No, I'll be okay. I just need to make a phone call."

The two went back to Henry's office where Patty placed a phone call to Danny Boyle. Danny knew not to ask any questions, and when Patty requested that he pick him up at his brother's office, Danny immediately replied, "I'll be right there."

"Well, I'll be going now," Patty said to Henry after hanging up the phone. "I'll see you in two weeks."

"You make sure you're there," Henry replied. Then he reached into his desk drawer, and pulled out a thousand dollars. He handed to Patty.

I'll pay every cent back, Henry," Patty said, looking appreciatively into his brother's eyes.

"Forget about it. I don't want anything back, I just want you to straighten out!"

When Patty got into his car, the first thing Danny asked was, "Where in the world have you been?" I've been worried. Nobody's heard from you in months!"

"I've been around," was all Patty said.

When they arrived at Danny's house, Danny's wife Alice was overjoyed to see Patty. She was already cooking up a meal for him. Patty sat down at the kitchen table, and cut straight to the chase. "I need to ask you two for a favor," he said.

"Whatever it is, Patty, you've got it," Danny replied.

"I need a place to stay for two weeks."

"We'd be delighted," Alice jumped in.

"You can stay as long as you need to," Danny added.

"I don't want anyone to know that I'm staying here, and after Josephine's wedding, I'll be out of here."

The day of the wedding rolled around, and that morning Patty asked Danny if he would mind giving him a ride to the church.

"No problem. Do you want me to come in with you?" Danny offered.

"No, that's okay," Patty replied. "I don't want them to know I've been staying with you. I will call you to pick me up."

At the wedding reception, the entire DiMarco family, including all of Patty's brothers and sisters as well as Isabella, sat together at a large round table. Isabella was sitting next to Mama Anna and Big Frank, and they all talked in hushed voices.

"I've decided that I am going to divorce Patty," she told them. "He hasn't been home in months. He doesn't work, he doesn't want to stop drinking. I just can't take it anymore. I'm going out of my mind worrying about him, and for what reason? What does he do for this family?"

Mama Anna and Big Frank did not say a word. They just listened, knowing the decision was Isabella's to make.

Suddenly they heard a commotion up front by the buffet. A large group of people had gathered around someone, and Frank stood up to see if he could get a better view of what was going on. Finally, someone shouted for all to hear, "It's Patty. Patty's here!"

Henry thought to himself, "Well at least he kept his promise," and he went over to greet his brother.

Patty did not waste any time greeting all of his old friends and relatives. Instead, he went straight through the crowd and up to his Aunt. "Congratulations Josephine," he bellowed, and gave her a huge bear hug. She nearly drowned in Patty's chest, and finally he let her out for air.

"Where have you been Patty?" she exclaimed. It was the only thing she could think to say.

"Oh, nowhere important," he replied. "And besides, I wouldn't have missed your wedding for all the tea in China!" Patty gave his aunt a kiss on the cheek, shook her husband's hand then went over to see his mother and father.

Anna was on the verge of tears. Patty picked her up in his arms and gave her a sloppy kiss on the forehead. "No matter what, Mama, I'll always love you."

"Are you still drinking?" Anna asked once her feet were back on the ground.

"A little," he said, not fully looking her in the eye.

"You know, I pray everyday to St. Anne to make you stop drinking."

Patty then went over to his father and shook his hand. "Nice to see you Pop."

Big Frank just smiled and nodded his head. Patty went up to his brothers and shook all of their hands, then gave each one of his sisters a hug. Everyone was so surprised at his presence they did not know what to say. It was only Patty's sister, Anna Marie, who actually said anything other than hello.

"What a nice suit you're wearing Patty," she exclaimed.

Finally Patty made it around the table to Isabella. She was looking towards her feet, and fiddled nervously with her young daughter's hair. Patty kissed and hugged the children first. Then he stood straight and soberly said hello to Isabella. "How you doing?" he asked.

"Okay, I guess," her voice shaking. "Would you like to have a seat next to me?"

"No thanks," Patty said, "I think I am going to sing a song."

Patty walked confidently up to the stage to talk to the band. They could not come up with any reason not to let Patty sing – they had nothing to lose – and within moments Patty was on the microphone. Everyone at the reception was already looking Patty's way, still surprised at his attendance, and unsure of what would happen next.

"Hey, what's your name?" the man on lead guitar asked.

"Patty DiMarco."

"Hey, I've heard of you. Didn't you used to sing at The High Tide down in Scarborough?"

"Sure did," Patty gave him a big smile and asked if he could borrow his guitar.

When Patty leaned into the microphone, the entire party went silent. "Today, I am going to sing a song I wrote," he said. "This song is about my best friend. He died in my arms in Korea, and today is the anniversary of his death, I will never forget him."

Patty strummed a minor chord, and began to sing a solemn ballad. He was so engrossed in the song that everything in the world seemed to disappear but his voice. Even the guitar melted into the background, and everyone became captivated by the sadness and beauty of his song.

When he finished, everyone was quiet for a moment, and then they broke into applause. They asked to hear more, but Patty just waved and said, "Not today." He stepped down from the stage and went to find a phone, to call his ride.

Meanwhile Isabella had begun to cry. Once she started she could not stop and everyone was startled by her incessant sobs. She cried to Mama Anna that she could not divorce Patty that she could not bring herself to do it. Anna comforted her and tried to calm her down, and by the time the commotion had settled, Patty had left the wedding.

The promise to his brother now fulfilled, Patty hung his suit in Danny's hall closet and said it was time for him to go. He shook Danny's hand, gave Alice a hug, and thanked them for all their help. Danny followed him to the front door, and just before Patty stepped outside he stopped him, shook his hand again, and handed Patty some money. "Call me if you need anything," was all he said.

14 NEW YORK

Patty's small duffel bag contained toiletries and a change of clothes. He planned to thumb his way to a truck stop in Connecticut, where he hoped to hitch a ride on an 18-wheeler to New York City. Before hitting the road, though, Patty stopped at a package store to buy a couple bottles of whiskey.

Luck was on his side and Patty easily found a ride all the way from Providence to Connecticut. He was dropped off at the truck stop where he went into a diner to talk to the truckers that had stopped for a rest. Patty sat up at the counter and ordered himself a burger. He struck up a conversation with a man sitting next to him, telling him that he was looking for a ride to New York. The trucker pointed to a woman driver who was sitting in a nearby booth.

"She's scheduled for a drop off in the city tonight," he informed Patty. "Why don't you go and ask her?"

Patty looked over at the woman skeptically. "Nah, I'll wait for someone else," Patty said. He did not feel like riding along with a woman.

Patty hung around the diner for three more hours, drinking coffee and chatting with the waitress. After hearing that Patty was looking for a ride to New York, the waitress offered to ask the drivers as they came in. It was not long before she pointed out to Patty a driver sitting at the end of the counter.

"That there is Harry," she said. "He's driving to New York. Why don't you go ask him?"

Patty went over to Harry and extended his hand. "Hi, my name's Patty. I heard you're going to New York. Would you like some company?"

The trucker scanned Patty up and down, slowly chewing his grilled cheese sandwich. He took a sip of Coke to wash it down, then said to Patty, "Sure, why not."

"Great!" Patty replied, "I really need to get myself to the city." He sat down on the open stool next to Harry.

"Where are you coming from?" Harry asked.

"Providence, Rhode Island."

"I just passed through there on my way up. Didn't stop though." Harry left the conversation at that and finished his sandwich in silence. When he was done eating, he told Patty that he was going to wash his face then he'd be ready to leave. Patty went over to the waitress and thanked her for her help.

"Good luck," she said.

Harry came out of the restroom and nodded to Patty to go.

As they were pulling out of the truck stop Patty asked, "Are we going straight through?"

"Straight through." Harry affirmed.

About half an hour down the road, Harry shifted in his seat, and asked Patty, "So what are you going to New York for?"

"I don't know," Patty answered.

"Is it a woman?" Harry smiled slyly, wanting some details.

"You see I recently got discharged from the Marines," Patty explained.

"Really, my son was a Marine. He was in Korea."

"Is he out now?"

"Yeah, but he was wounded pretty bad. He was riding in a Jeep when an elderly woman walked into the road and threw a grenade straight at him. He's lucky to be alive, but he sure isn't of any use to the Marines anymore." Harry then paused for a moment, and turned to look at Patty. "Say Patty," he asked, "are you married?"

"Yes I am," Patty replied.

"And you left your wife?"

"I guess you could say that."

"Is she a good wife?"

"She's the best in the world. She'd do anything for me."

"Do you have a family?"

"I have a very large family. We're really close."

Harry was confused. "Now why in the world would you want to leave all of that?" he asked.

"You asked me if there was a woman. Well there is a woman in a way. I met her in the war and I just can't get her out of my mind. There's also something else that's been killing me…" Patty drifted off, unsure if he should continue.

"Well, if talking about it makes you feel better," Harry offered, "you go right ahead and talk. I'm a good listener."

Patty was silent for about five minutes, just staring at the yellow line of the highway disappearing under the wheels of the truck. Then abruptly, he began.

"I was captured by the North Koreans and given to the Chinese to be questioned. They thought that I was an officer, but they couldn't get anything out of me because I didn't know anything. I speak Chinese, but they didn't know it."

"You speak Chinese?" Harry interrupted.

"Yeah, pretty fluently. I started studying it back in junior high."

"Let me hear you say something."

Patty spoke a short sentence, just to satisfy the driver's curiosity.

"Wow, that's unbelievable," Harry exclaimed. "I never heard Chinese before! But please, continue with your story."

Patty opened his mouth to speak, but Harry interrupted him again. "Oh, and by the way Patty, if you feel like having a drink, it's all right with me. I can see a bottle sticking out of your pack."

"Do you mind?" Patty asked. He was feeling the need for a drink.

"Not at all. Just as long as I'm the one driving."

Patty took out the bottle of whiskey, uncapped it, and had a long swig. He wiped his mouth, and continued on. "Well the Chinese officer told two other soldiers to take me across a sway bridge into North Korea and to kill me there. He told them to make sure they didn't kill or bury me on the Chinese side of the river. Because I knew what they said, I was prepared, and when we reached the bridge, I made my escape."

"How'd you do it?" Harry asked, fully intrigued.

"I'd rather not say," Patty said quietly. Then he went on. "I hid in the weeds and bushes for four days then I made my way down the Yulu River. Later I found out I was in Dan Dong China. I don't want to go into the details, but I ended up on a farm and because of my knowledge of Chinese, I was able to communicate with the woman who lived there. I was in bad shape, and she nursed me back to health. Before I knew what had happened, I was in love with her. I guess I'm still in love with her." Patty looked out the window. "And another thing…my best friend died in my arms when we were prisoners of war. There's not a day that goes by that I don't think of him."

"Is all of this why you drink?" Harry asked, once he was sure Patty was done talking.

"Well, it helps me forget," Patty replied.

"What are you looking for in New York?"

"I don't' know. I don't know where I'm going to end up. I just needed to go somewhere."

"Don't you miss your wife?"

"You know Harry, I'm feeling very guilty about that. She's a nice girl, and I didn't want to hurt her. After all, she really loves me, and she waited for me when everyone else thought I was dead. She wanted to get married, and I didn't want to tell her that I was in love with somebody else. My mother knows about this other woman, and she said that maybe in time I would forget her, and I honestly hoped I would. Don't get me wrong, it's not that I'm a coward, I just didn't think Isabella could bare it if I told her I didn't love her."

"Isabella, that's your wife's name?"

"Yeah."

Harry sighed. "Well Patty, it sounds like you have a full plate. Maybe if you give it more time, you will forget about that other woman." Then he shook his head. "Man, that's one heck of a story you got there. Listen, there's another truck stop in a couple of miles. Why don't we stop and take a break. We can get another cup of coffee and quickly refresh ourselves. We'll be in New York in no time.

When the 18-wheeler arrived in New York, the sky was black and the city was orange. Harry said goodbye to Patty, and Patty thanked him for the ride. "Good luck forgetting," Harry called after him, as Patty walked down the road, not knowing where he was going. Patty just kept walking. Soon it started to rain. Patty looked at his watch, and found that it was two o'clock in the morning. As he went around a corner, Patty ran straight into two men mugging an older man with a large duffel bag. Patty went towards them, and easily disengaged the muggers from the man. The thieves went running off, leaving the older man behind, scared and shaking. He thanked Patty profusely, almost clinging to him as he shook his hand. "They could have really hurt me!" the man cried to Patty. "Thank you, thank you."

"What are you doing out at this time of night?" Patty asked.

"I'm a janitor at Mount St. Charles Academy, and I had to work overtime because we were short two men today. I was waiting for a bus and I didn't see them two guys come up behind me. I don't know how to thank you enough. If you didn't come around that corner when you did…"

"How are you feeling now?" Patty interrupted.

"I'm still a little shook up, I guess."

"Well, let's get a bus and I'll give you an escort home."

Soon a bus came by, and Patty waved it down. When they got on the bus, and the rain was no longer getting them wet, Patty asked the man what his name was.

"Frank," he said. "What's yours?"

"Patty."

"I normally don't take the bus, you see," Frank attempted to explain himself, "It's just that my car is in the shop. My wife must be very worried, I should have been home hours ago." He was still on edge from the whole experience.

Patty got off the bus at Frank's stop, and accompanied him two blocks more to his house.

"Well this is as far as I go," Patty said when they reached Frank's door.

"Oh, no you don't," Frank exclaimed. "You come inside and meet my wife."

Patty had nowhere else to go, so he agreed.

Frank's wife made coffee and they all sat down together at the kitchen table. Frank dramatically recounted the events of the night to his wife. She teared up as he told his tale, and when he finished, she gave Patty a huge hug and thanked him with all her heart.. After things had calmed down a bit, Frank asked Patty where he was going and if he had a place to stay for the night.

"I don't have a place to stay yet," Patty told him, "but I'll find one, don't worry."

"Not at this time of night you won't," Frank's wife said. "You stay here. We have an extra room; it used to be our daughter's before she got married. You can sleep in there, and you're welcome to stay until you find your own place."

Frank was the night foreman for the cleaning crew; he went into work at 3 p.m. and got off at 11. Patty decided that he would go into work with him, and wait until he got off so he could walk with him to the bus until Frank got his car back from the shop. Frank told him that it was unnecessary, that the mugging was just a freak occurrence, but Patty insisted.

Frank offered to find out if the two workers who had been absent were coming back, and if they were not, he would give Patty a job. Patty thought that was an excellent offer. That night when Frank got off his shift, he told Patty that the job was his if he wanted it.

"I'll take it," Patty immediately replied.

Frank told Patty to follow him, so he could show him around and explain his duties. He took Patty down to the boiler room and showed him a cot where he could sleep. The boiler room could be entered from the back of the building and Frank gave Patty the key so he could come and go as he pleased.

"And don't worry about being disturbed, I'm the only one who comes in here," Frank assured him. "Is this okay for you Patty?"

"It's just fine," Patty told him. "It's more than fine."

The arrangement worked out well for about two weeks. Having his days free gave Patty plenty of time to drink, and then in the afternoon and into the night he would help with the cleaning. Soon, however, his drinking caused him to miss work and eventually he stopped working altogether. Frank had a talk with Patty and explained that his absenteeism could not continue.

"You either straighten out, or I will have to let you go." Frank laid out the ultimatum, and it was up to Patty to decide what was more important. Frank, however, did not still feel indebted to Patty, so he tried to explain his situation. "You know Patty," he said, "this is coming from higher up, and I can't jeopardize my job. Why don't you try to stop drinking."

Patty nodded that he understood, but in his head he was thinking, "How am I going to forget if I don't drink?"

The next day Patty made it to work, but that was the last time. The following day, he was back into his old habits and did not show up for work for the rest of the entire week. Frank had no other choice but to let him go. Patty did not argue or even attempt to explain himself. He simply nodded his head, took his small bag and went looking for a place to bed down.

Patty finally found a flophouse on the lower side of the city where he could stay, under the condition that he paid on a daily basis or in advance if he wanted to stay the whole week. Patty agreed to the terms and the flophouse became his new home. There were plenty of bars in the neighborhood, and Patty started to make his rounds. He would go into a bar, have a few drinks, then strike up a conversation with the manager and ask if they would like to have their floors swept and washed daily. Many agreed, and soon enough, Patty had a handful of customers. He was able to afford both the rent and his drinking habit – which was all he was looking for.

Things went on like this for a few months. Patty had a nice routine for himself, and though he was not able to save any money, he always managed to pay his rent before spending the rest on booze. One night on his way home from the last bar, Patty stopped at his usual package store to buy two bottles of whiskey. Little did he know that two derelicts were watching him and had been watching him for the past two weeks. They knew which way he would be heading home, and they waited for Patty in an alley, half way down the street. As Patty passed the alley, the two derelicts jumped out of the dark with steel pipes in their hands. They struck Patty from behind, hitting his head, back and neck. Then they grabbed his whiskey and ran.

Patty was left lying unconscious on the sidewalk, his legs dangling limply out into the street. Anyone who might have witnessed the scene was long gone, knowing full well- to mind their own business while in that part of town. Three hours later, a police car drove by and noticed the body half-lying in the street. Two officers got out of the car and walked over to Patty, poking him with their batons to see if he was a sleeping bum. Patty grumbled and moved slightly at their touch.

"He's drunk," one of the officers said, smelling alcohol.

The other officer looked a little closer. "I think this man's been jumped," and he pointed to the blood on the sidewalk. "Let's call for an ambulance and get him to St. Elizabeth's.

It was Sister Sandra who was on duty that night in the emergency room of St. Elizabeth's Hospital. Along with a male orderly, she rolled Patty into an examination room and began to check him out. The male orderly commented, "He's just a drunken bum, why bother," but Sister Sandra had noticed something else.

"You see that," she said, pointing to a tattoo on Patty's left arm. "That's the insignia of the U.S. Marine Corps. Were you in the armed forces?"

"No."

"Well, this man here probably fought for us, so help me get his shirt off."

That was enough to silence the orderly, and he dutifully helped the sister with the examination. Upon taking off Patty's shirt, the two noticed another tattoo.

"That looks like Chinese," Sister Sandra commented. "Why don't you go and see if Doctor Ming is busy. I think I hear him talking in the hallway."

The orderly went and fetched Doctor Ming and he came in to have a look at the tattoo. He informed Sister Sandra that the writing was the name of a Chinese woman. Sister Sandra wanted to know specifically what the name was, so Doctor Ming told her "Mei Feng."

Patty had a concussion and was severely bruised all over his body. His injuries were not life threatening, but he would need to stay in the hospital for at least a week, so the beginning stages of his recovery process could be monitored for complications. Sister Sandra had smelled liquor on Patty's breath as she checked him out of the emergency room and into the recuperating ward. She had asked Patty his name, but he did not respond. Sister Sandra felt that there was something different about this patient, something special, but she just could not put her finger on it.

"Okay, bring him upstairs. He must have complete rest." She relayed to a nurse then went on to continue her rounds.

Throughout the rest of her shift, Sister Sandra could not get the thought that there was something else to that "bum" patient. It was standard procedure to file a report directly to the Mother Superior for all unidentified patients treated in the emergency room that had to stay on longer in the hospital. The next morning Sister Sandra decided to deliver that report in person. She asked the Mother Superior for permission to treat this specific patient, and when asked for her reason, she replied that she wanted to see if she could help him with his alcohol problem.

"And how many have you helped with a similar problem before?" the Mother Superior asked.

"Only six, Mother," Sister Sandra replied.

"Go ahead then, you have my permission."

The following day, Sister Sandra went in to check on Patty. She still could not shake the feeling that there was something more to this man than met the eye, but still she did not have a clue as to where that feeling was coming from. Patty was resting when she came into his room, and from what his chart read, it appeared that everything was going well. She instructed Patty's nurse to have someone check on him often until he improved. She would check on him personally the following day when she did her rounds, but if there were any sudden changes in his condition, she was to be paged immediately.

By the end of the week Patty was sitting up in bed and feeding himself. When Sister Sandra saw that he was now doing better, she came in and informed Patty to prepare himself, because she was going to take him somewhere the next morning. She then instructed the nurse to have Patty in the wheelchair by eight o'clock, because she was taking him for a ride.

St. Elizabeth's had a large conference room in the basement, in which Alcoholics Anonymous would have a meeting everyday on the hour, between eight and twelve. Anyone from the street was welcome to attend, and people turned up from all over New York City. Next to the conference room was a workout center, where members of the public were welcome for a minimal fee.

Sister Sandra wheeled Patty into the Alcoholic's Anonymous' meeting, and put him right in the front row so he would be sure to listen, then went to the back row to keep an eye on things. She did the same thing every morning from then on, putting Patty in the front row for two weeks. Patty never once complained or refused to go and as the days passed, she felt as if the meetings had been doing him good. Furthermore, Patty had not had access to alcohol since he received his injuries, and she could already notice an improvement in his demeanor.

Finally, Patty was able to stand up and walk, but still a bit hesitant, on his own. Sister Sandra was very pleased to see his progress and she told him that now he could start walking to his meetings alone.

"You know Sister," Patty said, "they told me that when I get off my wheels, they want me to speak in front of the group."

"That's great, maybe you'll tell us your name then," Sister Sandra replied. Though her tone remained light, she sincerely hoped he would.

"When I start to speak, I only have to give my first name," Patty told her. "Are you coming tomorrow?"

"I wouldn't miss it," Sister Sandra promised. "Oh, and now that you're walking, don't forget to take a peek at the exercise room. After your meetings you can start using the gym." Sister Sandra then said goodbye to Patty and left him to rest. As she went out into the corridor she ran into Mother Superior, who just happened to be passing by.

"How's he doing, Sister?" Mother Superior asked.

"He's making good progress," Sister Sandra replied.

"Well you keep at him."

The following day when Patty went to his meeting, everyone came up to shake his hand and congratulate him on being able to walk again. They asked him if he was ready to speak.

"Why not?" Patty said optimistically.

Sister Sandra had come in and seated herself in the back of the room to listen.

It was announced from the stage that a first time speaker was ready to speak. Everyone clapped and Patty was beckoned to the podium. He cleared his throat once before talking into the microphone.

"Before I speak, I want to thank a wonderful person who really helped me stay away from that poison I was drinking. That person is Sister Sandra." The group applauded. Then Patty began. "My name is Patty."

"Hello Patty," everyone chimed in.

Their open voices gave him the support he needed to continue: he had never really talked about this so bluntly before. "I started drinking after the war. I drank to forget a woman I met in China whom I loved but was forced to leave, and I drank to forget my best friend who died in my arms. But this program has made me realize that I don't need to drink to forget my past. My father once said to me, 'When the bottle is empty and you still got the problem, the real problem is the bottle.' Today, when I look in the mirror, I won't have to call myself the wanderer. I want to thank all of you for helping me change. I know everyone here prays to their own higher power, well, my higher power is St. Anne."

With that Patty looked up and threw a kiss to St. Anne. He whispered thank you to her, and walked off the stage. Everyone applauded and congratulated Patty. Sister Sandra walked up to him and shook his hand. She asked him, "Are you through here Patty," smiling as she said his name for the first time.

"Yes, I'm through," he told her.

"Then come with me," she said, still smiling.

Sister Sandra took Patty into the workout room. She began to give him a tour of the facilities, but as soon as Patty spotted the punching bags, he went straight for them.

"You know how to use those?" Sister Sandra asked intrigued.

"Watch me," Patty said, and began to punch the bag so hard that he drew an audience. One person walked up to him and asked Patty if he would teach him how to punch like that. "Sure thing," Patty told the man, and started to teach him the proper form.

Patty began working out everyday after his AA meeting. Before long, four more members had asked Patty to teach them how to punch the bag. Then a heavy man in his twenties asked Patty to help him learn how to box because he wanted to lose some weight.

"Well you just follow me," Patty told the man. "Let's start on the treadmill. Just walk for now, and I'll pick it up later. I'll start you on a complete program, and that weight will be off in no time."

Then a young woman tentatively went up to Patty and told him that she wanted to lose some weight off of her lower body. "Do you know how I can do that?" she asked.

"No problem," Patty told her. "Follow me," and Patty showed her the correct exercises.

Word spread quickly about Patty's expertise, and soon he had a throng of people following him around in the gym asking him about what exercises to do, and how to do them. Sister Sandra had been watching Patty daily, seeing his status in the gym rise. One day she went over and talked to him.

"So you going to be here for a while, Patty?" she asked.

"I'll be here for the rest of the day. I was going to use the treadmill next. You know Sister, I've lost 30 pounds already."

Patty had enthusiasm and determination radiating from his deep brown eyes.

"How much more do you plan to lose?" Sister Sandra asked.

"A lot more. I plan to get back to what I used to be."

"Well I know you can do it Patty," the Sister said. Then she told Patty that she had to leave because she needed to meet with the Mother Superior.

When Sister Sandra walked into the Mother Superior's office, her face was all lit up. "I have some good news Mother!" she said. "Well you know how we were looking for someone to run the exercise room? I found someone who is perfect for the job."

The Mother Superior raised an eyebrow. "And who might that be?"

"Patty!" Sister Sandra exclaimed.

"Can he do the job?" the Mother asked, still quite skeptical.

"He sure can. Everyone is already asking him how to do certain exercises and he really knows his stuff. Also, have you seen him lately? He almost looks like a professional athlete."

"Well, I'll take your word on it," the Mother Superior agreed. "He will have to fill out an application, though. Explain what it pays. It will be the same as we discussed before, and you can offer him room and board if he is interested. Also explain to him the conditions. Like everyone else that we hire, he will have a sixty day trial period."

"Oh, thank you Mother. He'll be so happy to hear the news," and Sister Sandra ran downstairs to find Patty.

When Patty heard that not only would he now have a job, but also a permanent place to stay, he was thankful beyond words. Sister Sandra had really turned his life around, and now because of her, he would not have to worry about being back on the streets.

"There's just one thing I want you to do Sister before I accept the job."

"What's that?"

"I want you to tell the Mother Superior to take out a portion of my pay check each week to repay what I owe for being treated while I was recuperating from my injuries."

"I'm sure the Mother will think that's a fine idea," Sister Sandra replied.

Sister Sandra then showed Patty to his office, which had a phone and a computer. "Do you know how to use a computer, Patty?" she asked.

"Of course I do," he laughed, as if the question were absurd.

"How much schooling do you have?"

"I graduated from Providence College," he told her. "I was planning to go to law school, but then the war happened, you know."

"Well, I think you are very qualified for this job. I've seen how good you are with all of the members; I think you'll be happy here. Do you have any questions, Patty?"

"Just one. Do I get a secretary?"

Sister Sandra laughed," Are you serious? Well, I guess if you get stuck, I can come and give you some help."

"Thank you Sister," he said, then Patty went off to talk to some members that were lined up to ask him questions.

In between answering questions from the members, Patty would run on the treadmill then work out. Every time he would punch the bag, he would draw an audience. Everyone wanted to be able to punch the bag like Patty, and he promised to teach them all. He would show them how to start slow then pick up the pace little by little. Patty broke the members down into three groups: those who wanted to lose weight, those who wanted to tone their muscles, and those who wanted both. He then said that he would have group weight training sessions, where he would demonstrate how to use each of the weight machines and also he would be starting a cardiovascular group workout to music. Everyone was quick to sign up for the classes.

The same afternoon that he announced the cardiovascular class, Patty went out to a music store and picked up tapes with the instrumental versions of popular rock and roll songs. When he got back to the hospital he went to the storeroom and found a microphone and a tape player, so he could sing along with the music during the cardiovascular class.

By the time Patty made it back to the gym, so many people had signed up for his class that he had to break it down into two time periods – one in the morning and one in the afternoon. Sister Sandra had heard the buzz about the new classes, so she decided to come down into the gym to check on Patty and see what was going on. Patty explained to her about the immense interest in his class and also about how he had set up the microphone so he could sing.

"You sing too?" Sister Sandra asked surprised.

"Yes, I do. I used to sing at a bar and I even did a concert for over 200,000 troops when I was in the Marines."

Sister Sandra shook her head. "You know Patty, you seem to have something different up your sleeve everyday. Is the class open to everyone?"

"Sure is."

"Well how about myself?"

"Of course."

"Well, I also go jogging everyday. Perhaps I will use the class as a warm up for my run."

"Where do you go jogging?" Patty asked.

"I always go to Central Park. I love running under the trees there. You jog too?"

"I used to jog eight miles, then rest and jog eight back."

"You've got to be kidding."

"I kid you not."

Then Sister Sandra laughed. "See what I mean, something else up your sleeve. Well you do look good Patty, you've lost even more weight."

"I want to get back to my original weight." Just then Patty realized that over ten members were waiting to ask him questions. Sister Sandra was quite impressed at his popularity and gave him a smile. Patty turned to the members and told everyone that he had papers hanging next to his office and he wanted everyone to write down their names and fitness goals. There was also a sign-up sheet for the aerobics class that would be starting the following morning. One of the lists was already full, but there was still some room left in the earlier class. Sister Sandra walked over to the list and signed herself up.

"I look forward to hearing you sing Patty," she said. "See you tomorrow."

The following morning, the gym was jam packed with people. The Sister showed up in a red jogging suit, waving at Patty over all the heads as she walked in the door.

"You're going to be hot in that Sister," Patty told her. "You should have worn shorts."

"I'll just take my jacket off. I want to sweat anyway."

Patty stood in front of the class in his shorts and T-shirt, with his broad shoulders and toned muscles. Patty went through a dry run of the exercises that the class would be doing. He demonstrated the proper form and explained the exact purpose of each movement.

"Okay everyone, are we ready to begin?"

"Yeah!" the class called back.

Patty hit the tape player and began singing "Reeling and Rocking." Everyone was startled at the quality of his voice, especially Sister Sandra.

"What is this, Elvis aerobics?" someone in the back of the class joked. By the end of the class a crowd of listeners had gathered by the door and before anyone knew what had happened, they had all signed up for the class.

Patty finished the class with a cool down and some stretches, then told everyone he would see them tomorrow. Many of the members went up to him and thanked him, expressing that they had never realized exercise could be so much fun. Sister Sandra was one of the last to come up to him.

"You have a beautiful voice Patty, I never would have guessed."

"Thank you Sister."

As the days passed the exercise room grew more and more popular. New members were joining every day and it soon became apparent that Patty could not handle everything by himself. Sister Sandra told Patty that he could hire some more instructors and that the hospital was extremely pleased with all he had done so far.

"We're in the black, Patty, so put an ad in the *Times* for both a male and a female trainer. You can pay them whatever is the average pay scale for this type of work, though we can't offer anymore room and board." Someone then interrupted, to ask Patty if he could show him how to punch the bag. Patty excused himself, and went to help the man.

Other members saw that Patty was approaching the bag and a crowd quickly formed. Everyone wanted to learn, so Patty said that he would give them group lessons. After explaining the basics to the group, and showing them a few punches, everyone wanted to see Patty really hit the bag.

"Okay, I'll give you a demonstration, but remember make sure you always wear gloves. Starting tomorrow, I will be selling them right here. We don't want any injuries." Then Patty started hitting the bag. No one could believe how hard he was hitting. The pounding was vibrating throughout the room.

Looking at him from a distance, with his broad shoulders, large muscles, and his six foot five frame, Patty looked like the Jolly Green Giant. Sister Sandra stood in awe thinking that this man must have had quite a life. With that strength he must have been a great heavyweight fighter. "Maybe someday he'll tell me all about it," she thought.

Sister Sandra excused herself and told Patty she was going jogging because she had to be back early to work in the Emergency Room that night. "By the way," she asked, "are you still going to the AA meeting?"

"Everyday," Patty told her.

"But I see you here everyday. When do you go?"

"I go at six in the morning."

"I thought they started at eight. How do you go at six?"

"I got them to start having a six o'clock meeting so everyone could come in before they had to go to work."

"And how are the meetings going?"

"They're standing room only. We pass the basket around and collect money. Now we're self-sufficient and the hospital doesn't have to supply any coffee or anything else. All the extra money that we raise will be turned over to the hospital."

"Are you running those meeting now, too?"

"No, but I definitely have a say in things."

"You see Patty, without you drinking, you could be governor."

"Shey Shey," Patty said with a smile.

"What does that mean," Sister Sandra asked.

"It means thank you in Chinese.

The Sister laughed. "See you later Patty. I'm going for my jog."

Patty thought to himself, *One of these days, I'm going to go with her.*

That afternoon, Patty had his assistant take over for a while and he went to purchase a used car that he had been looking at. He explained that he also had to go get the vehicle registered and get a new license for himself. He just had to show his old Rhode Island license and the Department of Motor Vehicles would transfer it to a New York one.

Patty was really happy now; things were really looking up. He was now going to own his own car, he hadn't had a drop of alcohol in over six months and he had a great job that he enjoyed. Patty paused for a moment, looked up, and said thank you to St. Anne. When he returned to the gym his assistants told Patty that everything had gone smoothly in his absence.

Sunday was Patty's day off, and he called up his friend Frank and told him that he would be coming over that Sunday to pay him a visit.

"We'd love to see you," Frank told him.

When Frank answered the door, he wasn't sure who the person standing in the doorway was. He looked at Patty with a puzzled expression. "Are you Patty?" he asked.

"I sure am."

"Wow! You've lost so much weight. You look amazing! I never realized how handsome you are." Frank called to his wife to come and see Patty. She could not believe it.

"Do you notice anything else different about me?" Patty asked.

"What is it?"

"I quit drinking. I don't drink at all anymore."

"That's wonderful Patty! You seem to really have turned yourself around."

"And I have a job and a car now."

"What kind of job do you have?"

"I'm in charge of the exercise room at St. Elizabeth's Hospital."

Frank invited Patty in to have a cup of coffee and chat, but Patty said he wanted to get back to the hospital because he had a lot of paperwork to get done in his office.

"Well, you're welcome to visit anytime," Frank told him.

The following morning when Patty and his assistants were preparing the gym for opening, Sister Sandra came in. She was wearing her red warm-up suit, and asked if she could leave her jacket in the gym while she went jogging, because it was too warm outside and she did not want to go all the way back upstairs to leave it in her room.

"Of course," Patty told her. The Sister smiled, and was on her way.

Just as she left, Patty decided to go himself. He was already dressed for working out, so he quickly told his assistants where he was going and went out. Patty knew Sister Sandra's usual route because they had talked about it many times before and he decided to follow it in the hopes that he would catch up to her and they would be able to jog together for a while.

Patty entered Central Park and could see Sister Sandra running about 300 yards in front of him. The jogging path then went into the tress, and the Sister rounded a bend and went out of Patty's view. When Patty went around the corner himself, Sister Sandra was nowhere to be seen. Patty thought it was very strange, so he started to walk and look to see where she could have gone.

All of a sudden, a scream came out of the thick brush. Patty quickly ran towards the sound. He saw three men attacking someone on the ground. He spotted red jogging pants. One man was pulling them off, while the other two were forcefully holding the woman down, hitting her when she moved. Patty immediately charged the men, shouting, "Get off of her!" The three men stood up and pulled out long bladed knives. Little did they know that this was right up Patty's alley. This was what he had been trained for. The men did not have a chance to think. Patty grabbed the first guy and threw him into the other two so that all three were knocked to the ground. Then he picked one of them up, and intentionally broke his arm. He grabbed a second one, and did the same thing. Then Patty went after the third one and said, "I've got a nice surprise for you." This was the man that had been pulling the Sister's pants off. Patty proceeded to break both of his arms.

Sister Sandra was lying on the ground, sobbing. Patty went over to her, comforted her and checked her for injuries. She did not have any broken bones, though she was severely bruised all over her upper body and had two black eyes. She told Patty that her leg hurt and she was not sure if she could get up. Patty told her not to worry and picked her up in his arms and brought her back to a bench.

"Thank you Patty, thank you so much. If you hadn't come by when you did, I don't know what would have happened." Sister Sandra was still shaking in fear.

"Oh, don't you worry about anything, now. Just concentrate on your breathing and try to calm yourself down."

He then held Sister Sandra up on her good leg and told her to get on his back with her arms around his neck.

"Can you hold on?" Patty asked.

"I'll try," she told him, though it was obvious she was having trouble.

Patty supported her legs with his hands to take the weight off of her body.

"Let's get out of here before the police arrive."

After a short while, the Sister was getting tired, so Patty stood her up on her good leg, then picked her up and carried her in his arms.

"I must be too heavy," she said.

"No, this is nothing," Patty assured her.

Soon they reached the hospital and Sister Sandra told Patty to go through the rear entrance and not to use the elevator. She did not want to create a scene. Her room was on the top floor with all of the other nuns. She shared her room with Sister Janice. As they reached the top floor, they met Sister Janice in the hallway. She wanted to know what had happened.

"We'll explain later," Patty told her. "Let's just get her in her room quickly."

Sister Janice unlocked the door and Patty took Sister Sandra in and placed her on the bed. He checked her again to see if she had any broken bones. He asked Sister Janice to get some ice packs and a first aid kit.

"Do you have a pair of shorts, Sister Sandra?" Patty asked.

The Sister nodded.

"Janice will you fetch the shorts for me and put them on Sister Sandra?"

Then Patty turned his back until Sandra was fully changed.

Sister Janice went down to the emergency room to get a first aid kit, leaving Patty and Sister Sandra alone for a moment.

"Patty," Sister Sandra said, tears beginning to form in her eyes. "I'll forever be grateful to you."

"Forget it," Patty said. "Don't worry about anything."

"We must inform the Mother Superior as soon as possible," Sister Sandra said, suddenly concerned.

"You just rest and don't worry about a thing. When Sister Janice returns, we'll send her to notify the Mother Superior."

Moments later, Sister Janice returned and handed Patty the medical supplies. She then began to apply ice packs to Sister Sandra's injuries. Sister Sandra said her leg was still very sore, and Patty guessed that was where the men had kicked her.

"Maybe we should go down and get it x-rayed," Sister Janice suggested.

"That can wait until later," Patty said. "Let's just let her rest for now."

At that moment, Mother Superior walked into the room. She had heard a man's voice and was coming to see what was going on. She nearly dropped the book that was in her hand on the floor, when she saw the state that Sister Sandra was in.

"Oh my poor dear! How did this happen?" the Mother asked. "I did not see them coming and they dragged me into the thick bushes. It's a good thing Patty came along and heard me scream or I might have received a much more severe beating or worse."

The Mother Superior turned to Patty. "Well, we are grateful to you. Can you come to my office later this afternoon? I would like to speak to you."

"Of course, Mother," Patty replied. "I'd be happy to."

"Sister Janice, you stay here and take care of Sister Sandra, I'll get a nurse from downstairs to come up and help you. Patty, you can go back to the gym." Then the Mother Superior squeezed

Sister Sandra's hand. "I thank the Lord that you are safe," she said, then exited the room.

Later that afternoon, Patty went into the Mother Superior's office.

"Have a seat, Patty," she said. "I want to ask you a question."

"What is it Mother?" Patty asked as he lowered himself into the chair.

"Do you go jogging with Sister Sandra often?"

"No. I never went jogging with her before. Why do you ask?"

"Well it's a little strange you being there on the one day she is attacked,

"Yes, I guess you're right. I didn't even think about that," Patty said.

The Mother Superior leaned a little closer and looked Patty in the eye. "I think of it as God's graciousness," she said.

"If I left at the same time as Sister Sandra and not later, maybe I would have been attacked from behind as well."

"I guess you're right," the Mother Superior agreed. "Patty, I want to thank you again. What you did for Sister Sandra was wonderful."

"Oh, it was nothing," Patty said modestly.

"You can return to the gym now, Patty."

"Thank you Mother."

The following morning Patty went to check on Sister Sandra to see if she needed anything and to make sure she was comfortable.

"See, you looked after me and now it's my turn to repay you for all you've done for me," Patty said. He asked how she was feeling.

"Sore," she replied.

Meanwhile, the Mother Superior had read in the newspaper that three men in Central Park had attacked a young lady. When the police arrived they found two of the attackers with one broken arm each and the third with two broken arms. They also found three knives with twelve-inch blades in the bushes nearby. Mother Superior thought to herself that it could have been much worse if Patty had not come by when he did. She shuddered, not wanting to imagine what could have happened.

Patty stopped in everyday to see how Sister Sandra was doing. One day, she told Patty that she was going to return home to Buffalo, New York to recuperate. She had already received permission from the Mother Superior to go. The only problem was her elderly grandparents, with whom she lived in Buffalo, were not able to come and pick her up and she was in no condition to ride the train.

"Don't you worry about it," Patty told her. "I will take you home."

"Oh no Patty, you're busy and that would be too much driving for you."

"I don't mind. I'm used to staying up. I went many nights in Korea without sleep, so I'm sure I'll be fine. If I do get tired, I'll load up on coffee."

"Are you sure?"

"Positive."

"Well thank you, very much. I really appreciate it. When we get to my grandparents' house you can rest there a while before heading back. There is a guest bed for you to take a nap in."

"It's a plan," said Patty.

Sister Sandra and Patty talked for the entire drive up to Buffalo. Although she said she was going to sleep in the car, Sister Sandra did not close her eyes once. Patty did have to stop for coffee repeatedly to keep his mind sharp for the road. Before they knew it, they had reached the Sister's grandparents' house. Her grandparents were waiting up for them. They could not thank Patty enough, both for driving their granddaughter all the way up there, but also for saving her that day in the park.

Sister Sandra explained to them that Patty had driven all the way up without sleeping, and that he would have to rest a while before heading back.

"We'll have a nice, hot meal waiting for him when he awakes," her grandmother said.

Sister Sandra went to her bedroom and immediately fell asleep. Patty was directed to the guest bedroom where he slept for six hours. He awoke to the smell of a roast cooking. Patty ate heartily then said he had to be on his way before the Mother Superior started looking for him. Sister Sandra told Patty that she would be staying in Buffalo for at least two weeks.

"Make sure you call me and I'll come and pick you up," Patty told her. He said goodbye to her grandmother and grandfather. They thanked him again for everything he had done and told him to came visit again soon. Patty waved goodbye to them and headed back.

There was a note waiting for Patty in his office when he returned, telling him that Mother Superior wanted to see him. *What in the world does she want now?* Patty thought to himself, but he dutifully went right up to see her.

"When did you get back?" the Mother Superior asked as Patty walked in the door.

"Just a few minutes ago. I came right up as soon as I saw your note."

"How was Sister Sandra?"

"She was sore, but she seemed to have a lot of energy. Neither of us slept the whole way, but when I got there they let me sleep in the guest room for six hours."

"Did she mention when she would be back?"

"No. She said a few weeks maybe. I'm sure she will call you to let you know exactly when."

"Okay. Thanks Patty."

Patty went straight back to work. The gym was full as ever and there were plenty of questions to be answered. Patty soon got a tap on the shoulder from a beautiful, young girl. She asked him if he would teach her how to punch the bag.

"Of course I will. What's your name?"

"Beth Chamberlain."

"I've never seen you in here before. Where do you work Beth?"

"I work for an investment company."

"What do you do there?"

"I'm a private secretary."

"Do you have any good stock tips?"

"I could connect you with one of our sales people," she replied.

"How about side tracking the sales department and going through you," Patty said giving her a wink.

She laughed. "Oh, no. You wouldn't want that. I can't even pick a good head of lettuce when I go grocery shopping."

Patty laughed. "Okay, let's go get you started. The first thing you need to know is that you always wear gloves when you punch the bag. If you don't have any, we sell them here." Patty then demonstrated mildly how to hit the bag. As soon as he started punching he drew a crowd.

"I heard you can hit the bag real hard," Beth said. "That's what I want to see. I don't want to see you hit it lightly."

"Okay," Patty said and proceeded to give her a full demonstration. "You could be hitting the bag like this in no time at all, as long as you practice," Patty told her.

"And all you other people, you pay attention if you want to learn how to punch the bag too. Now why don't you try Beth."

Beth started to punch the bag, but Patty stopped her almost immediately. "Hold on a minute," he said. "Let me show you something." Patty stood behind her and held up her hands in the proper stance. "Here, like this." Beth felt like she was being held in a vice, Patty's hands were so strong. She turned her head and looked up at Patty, her eyes shining like a Christmas tree.

The words of an old Italian saying came to Patty's mind, *Watch the eyes, and they will tell you everything.* It was like reading a book.

"Do you have to go to work tomorrow," Patty asked.

"No, it's my day off," Beth replied.

"Well there's an aerobics class in the morning that I run. Why don't you come over and give it a try? I don't only run the class, if you can stand it, I'll be singing too."

Beth gave Patty a big, white smile, her eyes twinkling. "I'll be there."

The next morning, there was a full house waiting for the aerobics class. Beth was very surprised that so many people wanted to workout that early in the morning. Patty greeted Beth as he saw her walk in, and guided her to the front row, so she could be sure to see how to do all of the exercises. Patty then instructed the class to follow Ariana, his aerobics instructor, and he would sing along with the music to keep everyone lively.

When the aerobics class was over, everyone applauded Patty and thanked him for his beautiful singing. Beth came up to Patty and told him that she was quite surprised and impressed that he had such a beautiful voice. Just then, Ariana called to Patty, telling him he had a phone call in his office. He excused himself, telling Beth that he would be seeing her soon.

It was Sister Sandra on the phone. She asked Patty how he was doing and he told her that everything was going great.

"We just finished aerobics class and pretty soon we'll be starting another one."

"Did Mother Superior ask you any questions when you got back?"

"Yeah, she gave me the third degree made me go up to her office and everything. How are you feeling? When will you be coming back?' Patty realized that he already missed her very much.

"It won't be long. I've been getting a lot of rest and I'm feeling better every day."

"Well you just call me when you're ready to come home, and I'll come and pick you up."

"Patty I don't know how to thank you enough. When I get back I'm going to buy you a cup of coffee." She then gave him her grandparents' number and told him to call her whenever he felt like it. "I told my grandparents everything, how you saved me from a serious beating and how those men were all carrying knives and how they attempted to attack you. Lying there helplessly, I saw how you thwarted their attack on you. And you were a real gentleman to put my jogging pants back on me, then carry me all the way back to the hospital and up those stairs. You are very strong Patty. My grandparents want to thank you."

"When I come to pick you up, I'll give them a big hug. How about that!"

Sister Sandra laughed.

"Well, I have to go to another aerobics class. I'll talk to you soon."

The aerobics classes were so popular, that Patty decided he would try to start a karate class and see how it went. He had been trained by one of the best karate masters when he was a Marine, so it would be easy for him to teach beginners the techniques. All of the other classes were running at full capacity and Patty had to hire two more people, one instructor and one administrator to handle the books and collect whatever money was due. In turn Patty would bring all the monies collected to Mother Superior.

Mother Superior began to ask questions, when all of a sudden the money coming in doubled. "I'm not angry Patty," she said, "I just want to know how you do it."

"Well, I've added on karate classes and right now we're running at full capacity. We don't have any more room for new customers. We have a waiting list just to get in, but nobody's dropping out to open up the spaces."

"I don't like the idea of turning people away," the Mother Superior said, "I don't want to lose any business."

"Oh, we're not losing any business. It's just that we only have so much room, Mother."

"Okay, we'll talk about this again soon. I'll see what I can do."

Patty had to hurry back to the gym because the members were waiting for him. When he walked in the door, the entire aerobics class was already assembled and ready to go. Patty hollered to Nancy that he was sorry he was late, and to get started right away. Beth was right up in the front row, and she waved to Patty enthusiastically. Patty gave her a wink.

After the class was over Beth approached Patty.

"I could listen to you sing all day," she said dreamily.

"All day without stopping?" Patty asked skeptically. "Surely you'd get sick of it."

"Oh, no. I'd never get sick of it," she replied. "Have you ever considered making a recording?"

"Not really, I guess I never really thought about it. And besides, right now I'm so busy with the gym, I don't have enough time to do anything," but there was something in the back of Patty's eyes that suggested the idea of making a recording thrilled him. He changed the subject. "Hey did you know we're doing karate classes now? We have one that specifically teaches self-defense techniques. Do you think you'd be interested in it?"

"I might," Beth said, disappointed that she couldn't go on talking about Patty's voice.

"There's one starting in 15 minutes. Why don't you come over and see what it is all about?"

"I will," Beth said.

After the karate class was over, Patty made a point to go over to Beth and ask her what she thought.

"I liked it very much," she told him. "I would love to join it. I think it would make me feel safer on the streets."

"Well the class is technically full," Patty explained, "but I think I can squeeze you in."

"That would be great. I'd really appreciate it." Then Beth paused for a moment, "Patty would you let me buy you a drink?"

"I can't leave the gym now, I'm too busy," Patty quickly replied.

"Well how about later, when you're through with everything here?"

"I don't drink. I wouldn't want to waste your time." Patty really did not want to go out for a drink, but at the same time he did not want to hurt Beth's feelings. "I'll tell you what," he said, "Let's go get something to eat instead. It will be my treat."

"Oh, no you don't," Beth said, "I'm the one who asked you out, so the dinner will be on me."

"I have a better idea," Patty said, "why don't we just go Dutch?"

Beth did not want to blow her chance with Patty, so she agreed. She told Patty that she was going home to shower and change, then she would come back and meet him when he got off work.

Half an hour before closing time, Beth returned to the gym, but Patty was not there. He had gone to clean up and change clothes. Beth waited in his office. Soon everyone left for the night and she was all alone. For a moment she wondered if Patty would be coming back down at all, but soon enough he arrived, wearing a nice sports coat and smelling fresh.

"You ready?" he asked.

Beth could not get over how handsome he looked; she had never seen him out of his workout clothes. "Let's go," she said, giving Patty a huge smile.

There was a nice restaurant, which was only five blocks from the hospital. The two got a nice quiet table in the back and sat down across from one another.

"Are you hungry?" Patty asked Beth.

"A little," she said.

"Well how about a glass of wine first?"

"If you don't mind," Beth said. "If you're not comfortable with me drinking, I really don't have to."

"No, don't worry about it. I don't mind at all."

Beth ordered a glass of wine, and Patty asked for soda water with lime. The two talked for a while about trivial things, about their work, about living in the city, and then the conversation started to take a more personal turn. Beth started to ask Patty some questions about his past, but Patty interrupted her.

Beth, do you want to be friends?" he asked.

"Of course I do, Patty,"

"Well, then don't ask me any personal questions."

"Okay, I won't ask any personal questions," she agreed, though this hurt her feelings a bit.

"All right. Now we understand each other, and we'll get along fine. But I do want to ask you a question, Beth."

"What is it?" she asked.

"Where did you get those beautiful blue eyes from?"

Beth laughed. She had been expecting something much more serious. "My mother has blue eyes."

The rest of the dinner went on smoothly, the two joking and talking up a storm. After they received the check, both paying their own share as planned, Beth asked Patty if he would like to come back to her place for a cup of coffee.

"Maybe some other night," he told her. "I've had a tough day at work, and I'm pretty beat."

The following day, Patty received a call from Sister Sandra. She told Patty that she was feeling much better. The two weeks of rest had done her a lot of good and she was now ready to come back to St. Elizabeth's.

"Would you mind driving down here to pick me up?" she asked. "If it's too much trouble, I might be able to take the train."

Patty did not let her finish the sentence. "Of course I'll come pick you up," he said. "I'll leave first thing tomorrow morning, you just be ready."

"Thank you Patty. I'll see you tomorrow then."

When Patty reached Sister Sandra's house in Buffalo, her grandmother and grandfather greeted him whole-heartedly. They were extremely happy to see Patty, and they thanked him again for everything that he had done for their granddaughter. Patty told them that he was only repaying a favor, for Sister Sandra had saved him once too. Then Patty loaded up the suitcases in the car and said goodbye. They told him to come again soon.

While riding back, Patty asked Sister Sandra if she would like to enroll in a complete exercise program.

"You can do the aerobic class and we now have a karate class specializing in self-defense that will help you get over your fears and get some confidence back. Also, you can do your jogging on the treadmill until you get your full strength back and feel ready to go outside again. What do you think?"

"I think I would like that," Sister Sandra said slightly unsure of herself, but determined.

"Why don't we stop for a bite to eat," Patty then suggested.

He pulled the car over into the next rest stop that had a diner. The two sat together in a booth and talked for a bit.

"Don't forget," Sister Sandra told him, "I owe you a cup of coffee."

"That's all right," Patty said. "Don't worry about it for now, but one of these days I'll be sure to take you up on it."

"What I want to do when we get back," Sister said, "is I want to walk on the treadmill slowly and take my time progressing up to a jog. The karate class sounds great for defensive purposes and I think I'll do the aerobic as well because in that class I can just keep my own pace."

"I'll tell you what I'll do for you Sister. I'll work out an entire personalized program for you, complete with specific exercises that will help you recover faster."

"That sounds great Patty. I don't know what I'd do without you."

"I got a present for you," Patty said. "It's nothing big, just something I picked up on my drive out here." Patty then pulled a small can of pepper spray from his pocket. "You take this with you when you go out," he said. "It will make you feel safer and if anyone tries to harm you, just give them a spray, right in the eyes."

"And that will stop them?"

"It sure will."

Sister Sandra slept for the rest of the drive home. After that, he did not see her for two days, but she finally did show up in the gym. Beth showed up also, and she kept following Patty around, asking him more questions than were perhaps necessary. Sister Sandra noticed this, and started to wonder if Patty was dating her.

When the time for the karate class rolled around, Patty called for Sister Sandra to follow him into the class. Patty began to give Sister Sandra some instructions and Beth decided that was a good time to walk up to them and ask Patty yet another question. The two women stood face to face. Patty hesitated for a fraction of a second then introduced them to one another. The two women shook hands then Patty informed them that after they got through in here, they would do aerobics.

When Ariana started the aerobics class, Patty put Sister Sandra right up front. Beth put herself right next to Sister Sandra. When the class was over, Sister Sandra told Ariana that she enjoyed the aerobics class very much and would be looking forward to the next class. Patty asked her how she felt, and Sister Sandra told him that she felt much stronger than she had expected.

Beth kept following Patty around, trying to get his attention to ask him a question. When she finally got the opportunity to talk to him she asked Patty if he wanted to do a repeat of the dinner they had had the other night.

"Why not?" Patty replied.

"How about tonight?" she asked.

"Tonight's fine with me. I might even be able to get out of here a little early, I'll ask Ariana if she'll take over."

"Do you think she'll mind?"

"I doubt it. I've covered her shifts before, so she owes me anyway. Come back at eight and I'll be waiting for you."

Beth arrived at the hospital promptly at eight. Patty was outside waiting for her, looking sharper than ever.

"So where are we headed?" she asked.

"I know a nice little Italian place not far from here where we can get something to eat. Then afterwards they have dancing. Do you like to dance?"

"I love to dance, especially if I like the person I'm dancing with."

Patty looked at her with a sparkle in his eye. "And do you like this person?"

"I sure do."

"Well, we should have a good time then!" And Patty took her by the arm.

When they got to the restaurant Patty ordered Beth a glass of wine. The wine was followed by a first class dinner and Patty explained to her all of the ingredients and about how the meal was prepared. Beth was very impressed and Patty explained to her that his mother was an excellent cook and taught him everything.

After they were through eating, Patty asked Beth if she would like to dance. She accepted the offer and Patty pulled her close to him. Beth rested her head on his strong chest, loving every bit of it. Finally, Beth asked Patty if he would like to come to her place after they had finished dancing.

"Okay," Patty agreed.

Beth gave him a mischievous smile. "You want to go right now?"

"Right now is good for me," Patty replied.

Beth was thrilled that Patty was coming up to her apartment, even if it was just for a cup of coffee. She had been spinning over him for a while, and she was hoping that this would be the start of something more between them. Beth put on soft music and brought out a bottle of wine. Patty declined the wine, but said he would love a cup of coffee. Beth apologized, and said that she forgot that he did not drink.

"Did you ever have a problem with alcohol?" she asked, trying to sound as casual as possible.

"I told you before, no questions," Patty said. "And I won't tell you again."

"I'm sorry Patty, there won't be any more questions, I swear. Will you accept my apology?"

"Just forget about it, and come give me another dance," he said.

Beth obliged and Patty held her body close to his again. Her breathing started to get heavier and Patty kissed her deeply on the mouth. His hands were moving all over her body and Beth could not resist him. Patty picked her up and brought her into the bedroom. He passionately undressed her and she helped to undress him. He started to make love to her body with an intensity she had never experienced before.

Trying to catch her breath, Beth said, "Patty, you're a man – a real man."

They laid there for a while talking when she asked Patty, "Would you want to spend the night with me?"

"No, I have to get back since I have to get up early tomorrow. As a matter of fact, I should leave right now."

"Do you want to do this again?"

"We'll see."

"They're having a party at my company. What do you say, you want to go?"

"I don't want to make a commitment. I'll see you at the gym."

Beth was trying hard to see Patty again.

When Patty went to the gym the following day, Ariana was already there ahead of Patty. "What did you do, sleep here last night?"

Patty kidded with her, "I couldn't sleep so I decided to come in early."

Around nine that morning, Sister Sandra showed up early also, wanting to get in a long workout. "How are you feeling?" Patty asked.

"Much, much better."

"Go ahead then, get started. If you need me, call me."

She started all of her exercises. She punched the bag, attended karate class and aerobics and then ran up to Patty and said, "I have to run, I've got a very busy day ahead of me," and she gave Patty a kiss on the cheek. "Now don't forget, I owe you a cup of coffee. One of these days, we'll go for that cup of coffee."

Patty was quite surprised she gave him a kiss on the cheek. He never expected that. Three days went by before he saw Sister Sandra again. When he did see her, he asked, "Where you been?"

"I've been very busy"

"What's the matter? Is Mother Superior pushing you?"

"No she's not. Listen," she said to Patty, "Saturday night I'm off. How about I pay my debt then, okay Patty?"

Patty said, "Well, you pick the place."

"And of course I will have my civilian clothes on."

Patty was looking forward to Saturday night. Later that day, Beth came to the gym to workout. She went right up to Patty to say hi to him. Patty couldn't talk too much to her because he had a first time member who he had to spend time with. But she did get in that she had a wonderful time last night. She asked him how about a repeat this Saturday night.

"I'm sorry, but I have somewhere to go. How about some other time? I'll let you know."

Just then Sister Sandra walked in and went straight up to Patty and asked, "Am I interrupting anything?"

"No, not really."

Beth started working out and Sister Sandra said to Patty, "Leave your car unlocked Saturday night and I will be waiting inside exactly at eight o'clock."

"Will do," Patty said.

"Then I'll see you then.

As soon as Sister left, Beth went up to Patty and asked him is that your girlfriend?

"No, that is Sister Sandra and she is a good friend of mine."

Saturday night came. Patty went straight to his car and Sister was there waiting for him. Patty asked, "How about a kiss on my left cheek?"

"What's that for?"

"Well you kissed me on my right cheek. Now my left cheek feels empty and I haven't washed my right side yet."

"How come she asked?"

"Because it felt so good."

"Remember Patty, we are just friends. Let's keep it that way. Don't spoil a good thing."

"Well, if you don't want to give me a friendship kiss, there's only one thing to do." And he kissed her on her cheek and he said to her, "That's just a friendship kiss. Where are we going for a cup of coffee? I know a nice place not too far from here where we could have something to eat too."

"Didn't you eat tonight?"

"No, I haven't."

"Well, I'm only buying you a cup of coffee."

"Don't worry about anything tonight. We are going to celebrate tonight."

"Celebrate for what?"

"You helped me since I stepped in St. Elizabeth's. You helped me in the accident room. You were instrumental in me putting the drink down and you got me the job in the gym and now I'm in charge there."

"Let's face it Patty, if you didn't put the drink down you wouldn't have gone anywhere and remember Patty, if a person doesn't have the material, they'll only go so far and if it wasn't for you maybe I wouldn't be here today." She smiled and said, "We're even."

"That's why we should call this night a celebration," Patty said. With that Patty called the waiter and asked for a glass of the best Italian wine in the house. "I hope you like wine."

"Occasionally, I have a drink and I do like a glass of wine."

"How do you like this place?"

"It's nice – the food is good and they even have a band."

The waiter brought the wine. She tried it and said, "It's good."

They finished their meal and she also finished her wine. That's when Patty took her hand and said, "Come with me."

"Where are we going?" Patty took her straight to the dance floor. "What are you doing?"

"We're celebrating, aren't we? Now don't give me a hard time. Let's have a dance to strengthen our friendship."

"Just remember Patty, please respect that I am a nun and that I took certain vows. Now, let's have a dance."

Patty held her tight, but out of respect, he kept his distance. He didn't give her his famous Patty closeness dance. He asked her, "How am I doing so far?"

"Fine."

Just then the band started to play a much faster song. "Do you want to sit this one out?" Patty asked. He did not want to press his luck with her.

"No, I'll dance this one." Patty was surprised. She could really dance and she was enjoying the dancing very much.

Now they started playing a slow song called *Love Me Tender*. Patty started to sing it to her softly and as he did, he pulled her in close to him and thought again of the Italian saying and looked into her eyes. They were lit up like a Christmas tree. That's when he pulled her in real close. She was staring into his eyes. He said to himself, "I'm going to go for broke. It either goes further or it ends right now." He held her tight and gave her a kiss and it wasn't a peck. It was loaded with passion. She did not pull away either. She did not get mad at Patty but said, "Let's sit down after this dance."

When they returned back to their table Patty asked her if she was having a good time.

She said, "Yes. Now are you going to tell me what state you're from?"

"I'm from one of the New England states. For now, that is all I'm going to say." She was satisfied with that because it was more than he would say before. "Patty, tomorrow is Sunday. Do you want to go jogging together at Central Park because I'm not ready to go alone yet."

"Sure," Patty said.

"I'll meet you downstairs at the rear entrance at eight o'clock sharp – okay?" Sister Sandra said. "Now take me back. It's getting late."

As they were riding back she told Patty, "When nobody is around and we're alone you can call me Sandra. Now when all your girlfriends are around, then you can call me Sister."

"What girlfriends?"

"Oh, come on Patty. Don't you think that I don't notice every woman there has her eyes on you? You should have a new exercise and call it Patty's Special Eye Exercise. I especially notice that girl Beth."

Patty met her the next morning at eight o'clock and they went straight to Central Park. She mentioned to Patty that she is not ready to jog alone. "I do feel safe with you here with me. Suppose they're here again and they see us?"

"I don't think that they will be around for a while. I promise you, Sandra. If they ever tried anything again with us, they would be found in a morgue. Stop worrying about it and let's jog." She smiled at Patty and said, "Let's go."

After they had jogged a while she said, "Let's sit down at the next bench. I want to tell you something." They soon came upon a park bench. She said, "Let's sit for a while. You know I haven't slept all night."

"How come?"

"You kissed me and an unbelievable feeling has been going through my body that has never happened in my life before."

"Is it a bad feeling?"

"No, it's a good feeling."

"Has it gone away?"

"No, it hasn't."

"Let's see if it hasn't." He stood Sandra up, embraced her and kissed her pulling her close to him with her breasts pressing against his body. She did not pull away.

"Patty, people going by us are staring at us. Let's start jogging again."

As they were jogging her eyes never left Patty and her smile couldn't leave her face. She was happy. She said to Patty, "Let's stop for a while. I've got a stone in my sneaker." So they pulled off the path. He told her to sit down on the grass. He took her sneaker off and removed the stone.

"Does that feel better?"

"Yes, it does."

While they were both sitting, Patty leaned her back on the grass and proceeded to kiss her and then he put his hand on her breast. She pushed him off, but her eyes were tearing.

"We'd better be going Patty." So they jogged back to his car.

"Want to jog again tomorrow?"

"Sure. I'll meet you again at the same time tomorrow morning."

When Patty got back to the gym, Ariana was already there and anyone who needed help, she was able to assist them. Patty gave her a high five and said to her, "You are my assistant and if I'm not here in the morning, just get everything started like you did today. You are now in complete charge. I'm going to see if I can get you a raise."

Later that day, Patty went to see Mother Superior to see if he could get Ariana a rise. When he got to her office she asked, "What brings you here today? Let's hear it."

"You know Mother, we are extremely busy at the gym and I made Ariana Verducci my assistant because I need some help. I can't do it by myself."

"So make her your assistant. Why do you have to ask me?"

"Well I think we should give her more money because she is worth it and if anything happened to me, you will have someone to take over."

"Why, where are you going?"

"In case you throw me out, you could move her in my place."

"What are you considering for a raise?"

"I think one dollar an hour more and one and a half more for overtime."

"And you really think she deserves that?"

"Yes, I do."

"Well then, give it to her then."

"Thank you, Mother."

When Patty returned to the gym, he told Ariana the good news. She was all excited.

The next morning, Sister Sandra was at Patty's car at eight o'clock sharp. Patty was there waiting. Unknown to both of them, Mother Superior was observing both of them from the stairway window. The only thing she could think was she knew Sister Sandra liked to jog and was taking Patty along for protection. She thought it better not to approach her on this matter.

"Did you have a good night's sleep last night?"

"Yes, if you call twisting and turning all night a good night's sleep."

When they reached Central Park, Patty couldn't resist the temptation to kiss her again and he held her tight in his arms. "Let's get started Patty."

Patty said, "Let me know if you get a stone in your shoe and I'll help you remove it."

This time they did not stop but when they got to his car Patty did not waste any time and put his arms around her and started kissing her. Now his hands went from her breasts to rubbing her legs. She just held him while he was doing that.

"We'd better leave now Patty."

It became a regular thing to meet everyday. If they didn't go jogging, they would go for breakfast. Now it became seeing each other everyday and every Saturday night. This went on for at least two months.

One Saturday night, they decided that they would go for a quick jog before they would go dancing. They were there a short while when they got caught in a rainstorm with thunder and lightning. They decided to turn back. It was raining very hard. Patty knew enough not to go under a tree for cover. "Let's just keep going. We are wet anyway."

They finally made it to the car, laughing all the way. They were soaked from the rain. She was shivering so Patty went to his trunk and got a blanket and put it around Sandra to help keep her warm. He drove to a restaurant with a drive-thru and ordered two coffees and they parked in the parking lot, both of them laughing. "Okay, let's go."

When they got back to the hospital, Patty took her up to his room making sure no one was around. He started removing her jogging suit and drying her off at the same time when suddenly he brought her close to him and started kissing her and started to undress her. He soon had her top off and her breasts were completely exposed. The kissing was getting heavier and at that he started removing her shorts.

"Patty what are you doing? He picked her up and placed her on the bed and made love to her. They spent a good part of the night together.

"Now what do you think of me now?" Sister Sandra asked.

"Why do you ask me that question?"

"Usually afterwards in making love, it's all over."

"Where do you get that from?"

"Well, I haven't been a nun all my life. I did go to school before I became a nun."

"I would say this is the beginning, not the end. Let's see each other Sunday and we can talk about it. It's late now and I have to go."

"Okay, I'll see you in the morning."

After Sunday morning mass, she went to see Patty in his office. "Let's talk Patty. I want to let you know that I am going to get out of the sisterhood."

"How come you want to do that?"

"Because I have sinned."

"That doesn't make you a bad person."

"But I broke the vows I gave to God."

"But God even forgave Mary Magdalene."

As the weeks went by, Patty did not see Sister Sandra too much at all. Patty felt something might be happening, so he started to groom Ariana more and more, about his job so she would be able to take over his job completely. Patty always had a sixth sense. He could go into his own business and open up his own gym. He had some wealthy customers that would put up the money for him, but he couldn't do that to St. Elizabeth's who were very good to him.

It had been three months since he had last seen Sister Sandra. He ran into Sister Janice, Sister Sandra's friend and asked her about Sister Sandra. She told Patty that Sister Sandra wasn't feeling well.

"That's too bad," Patty said. One day during the week, Patty received a message saying that after the gym closes tonight Mother Superior wants to see Patty in her office.

When nighttime came Patty went up to see her and entered her office. It was dimly lit. He approached her desk and she stopped him. "That's as far as you go," she said with a loud voice. "Do you know what happened to Sister Sandra?"

"No, I don't know."

"Well she had a miscarriage. Do you know the shame you will bring to St. Elizabeth's, you dirty bastard!"

Patty did not know there were about 30 more nuns in the dimly lit room and they all started to swing the straps they were holding, striking Patty from all angles.

Just then, a nun came running into the room and told Mother Superior that the Bishop was downstairs and wanted to see her. She said, "Quick put him into that storage closet and lock the door. We'll finish with him when the Bishop leaves.

They all left Mother Superior's office. Patty was alone in the closet. He felt around for a light and looked around to see if there was anything in there to help him escape. He looked through the keyhole but he couldn't see any light. Patty surmised that the key was still in the door. He put a piece of paper under the door and he took a pen he had found in the storeroom and pushed it through the keyhole. The key dropped onto the paper, which Patty pulled through under the door and was able to open the door from the inside. He went directly to his room and packed whatever he could take with him. He made three trips through the back door. He even took the gun that he had a permit for. He always carried it with him for protection when he went to the bank at night to make a deposit. He then went down to his office. He had two paychecks coming so he took them out from the cash drawer and explained it all to Mother Superior in writing.

Then he wrote her another note:

Dear Mother Superior:

I'm sorry for what happened. I didn't mean for this to happen this way, but it did. Sister Sandra is a good person. She loves God and her church. She wants to leave the sisterhood. Don't let her leave. I'll leave it in your hands to do the right thing.

There was a person who was crucified that we all know and love and we found out it was a mistake. Don't let another mistake happen. I will be praying to my patron saint, St. Anne to pray for you and Sister Sandra.

May God bless you and Sister Sandra,
Patty DiMarco

15 ALABAMA

Before Patty left the gym, he called Beth and asked her if he could come over. She said to come right over.

When he arrived at her apartment, she greeted him wholeheartedly and asked him what was wrong. He showed her the black and blue marks on his arms and other parts of his body. He said, "I hope you don't mind. I called you to come here, but I won't stay here long."

"You can stay forever if you want to," she said. "I will take tomorrow off to take care of you."

"I don't want you to take any time off from work. I don't want you to get into any trouble, after all, you need that job."

"I can take a sick day."

"I'd rather you didn't do that. Do you have an office?"

"Yes I have."

"Well, we can call each other. It would be better that way."

"Okay," she said, "if you feel more comfortable, I'll do it your way. I'll just keep calling you to make sure you're all right."

"I'll be fine. I'll keep putting ice on my arms. It's time you get some sleep now. You have to go to work tomorrow. We'll talk when you get back from work." Patty gave her a kiss and said good night.

The following morning, Beth got up early. She first checked in on Patty then made him a big breakfast. It woke Patty up with the smell of bacon and eggs cooking. He got right up and joined her in the kitchen. "Something smells good!"

"Are you hungry?"

"Yes, I am."

"Good, I made plenty. Sit down and eat. I'm going to take a shower. When break time comes, I'll get something at work."

When she came out of the shower, she told Patty she put towels out for him so he could take his shower. Before she left she reminded him to keep using ice.

"Would you mind if I make a phone call?"

"Of course not. I'll see you after work and I'll call you later."

Later in the day, Patty called his friend Bubba Johnson in Tuscaloosa, Alabama.

Bubba could not believe it was Patty calling. "I think of you a lot Patty. Where are you now?"

"I'm in New York."

"Are you still fighting?"

"Not in the ring."

"Well, what are you doing?"

"I'm getting ready to come to Alabama. I want to see you and your family."

"When will you be here?"

"I'll leave in about a week. I'm going to be driving down by myself."

"How's business going?"

"Very good – thanks to you. I will never forget you Patty."

"I'll call you when I get close to your home."

"We'll be waiting for you."

Patty iced himself, and Beth had called him three times already and asked him if he

likes Chinese food.

"I sure do."

"I'll bring some home for supper."

"Only on one condition," Patty said.

"What is it?"

"I pay."

"No," she said, "you are my guest."

"Well then, we'll go out to eat and it will be on me."

"Okay, I'll buy that," she said.

As they were eating she said, "Can I ask you a question, which I wanted to ask you when I first met you in the gym?"

"Well, seeing you've been so good to me I'll allow you one question."

"What does that Chinese writing say on your arm?"

"It's the name of a very, very good friend of mine."

"What does the name say?"

"That's as far as I go on that one. I'm very grateful for you letting me stay here. I'm just staying here one more week and then I'll be leaving."

"Where will you be going?"

"I'm not sure yet."

"You could stay here forever. My house will always be welcome to you."

Patty promised he would take her out to eat Saturday night. Beth was all excited about going out with Patty Saturday night.

Saturday night came. They both dressed up. She asked, "Where are we going?"

"We'll go where we went last time. Did you enjoy the food there last time?"

"Yes I did and we could dance too."

Patty had made reservations. She asked Patty to request the same table they had before which he did. When they arrived, their table was ready for them with a bottle of champagne on ice, waiting for them. She was very impressed with what she had seen and was full of smiles. She said, "You really know how to make a woman happy."

"Is that what you refer to yourself as – a woman? Well I say you are a lady."

They had the same waiter as before and he welcomed them back again. Patty said something to him in Italian.

Beth asked, "What did you say to him?"

"I thanked him."

"That was a long thank you."

Soon the waiter was back with two dozen roses – half red and half yellow. Beth could not believe it and said she never was treated with such royalty. The waiter said, "I'll put them in the fridge till you're ready to leave."

"Patty you know how to make someone happy. This is surely a wonderful night for me, one that I'll never forget."

"Well, when you're with the right lady, it's easy to do nice things."

"Patty, are you leaving tomorrow?"

"I planned to."

"Can you stay just another week? I want to make sure you're feeling better. Those bruises you have are not one hundred percent healed."

"I'll think about it. For now let's eat and dance."

When they finished eating, Beth made a toast with her champagne and asked, "You still don't drink Patty?"

"No, I don't intend to drink anymore, but I will make a toast with my ginger ale. I want to make this toast to a lasting friendship." With that she gave Patty a kiss on the lips. Patty said, "Let's dance." Then he held her real close to him. He then gave her a big kiss. You could see she was really happy. Patty looked into her eyes and smiled because he knew what her eyes were saying. They kept dancing till the band took their break.

As soon as they sat down she asked, "Have you thought about staying another week?"

"Do you really want me to stay another week?"

"Yes I do."

"Okay then, I will. But I want to ask you a favor."

"What is it?"

"When I leave, can I use your address as mine? What I mean is if I need an address to refer to can I use yours?"

"You can use my address forever. Where are you planning to go Patty?"

"I'm not sure yet."

Patty knew where he was going but he didn't want to let anyone know where he was going for the time being.

"Are you still going to go to the gym?" asked Patty.

"Yes, I plan to."

"You should because it's doing you a lot of good."

"In which way is it doing me a lot of good?"

"You want to keep up that beautiful shape you have."

"You're full of compliments Patty."

"Let's face it Beth, you are beautiful."

"I bet you tell that to all the girls."

"Remember Beth, liars can figure, but figures don't lie. And you have the figure."

"Come on Patty. Let's go dance."

The band started to play a fast song. Patty noticed she could really move and she looked good. He asked Beth "What are you trying to do, get me all excited."

"No, I'm just trying to get even with you because you excite me and I'm going to excite you even more tonight."

"I'll be waiting."

They were having a real good time but it was soon time to leave for they were closing now.

When they got to Beth's house she told Patty, "You are not sleeping on the couch. You will be sleeping with me in my bed from now on." When they got into bed, Patty reminded her to start exciting him. She did and they made love for a good part of the night.

Patty awoke to the smell of bacon and eggs and the smell of coffee. She wanted Patty to know she could cook and she would always do it for him and take care of him. She was getting ready to go to work and left Patty instructions that she left cold cuts in the fridge so he could make lunch and she would be home to make supper for the both of them. "I just want you to rest and relax," Beth said. "I'll take care of everything else."

"I might go say goodbye to some friends."

"Where do these friends live?"

"They live in Buffalo."

"That's quite a way."

"I'll be back."

Patty left that morning and went straight to Buffalo not stopping except for a cup of coffee. He finally reached Grandma and Grandpa's house. They were happy to see him and wanted to know how Sister Sandra was.

"She's okay."

"What's happening?" they asked Patty.

"Well, I'm leaving New York and I wanted to say goodbye to two wonderful people.

Just then the phone rang. Of all people, it was Sister Sandra not knowing that Patty was there. Grandpa told Sister Sandra that Patty was here saying goodbye to them.

"Let me speak to him," she said.

He handed the phone to Patty, unknown to him that Sister Sandra was on the phone. A familiar voice said, "Hi Patty, what are you doing there?"

"I just came here to say goodbye to them, that's all. I'll be leaving soon."

"May I ask where you're going?"

"I'd rather not disclose where I'm going. Listen, I'm going to say goodbye Sandra and lots of luck." Patty also said goodbye to Grandma and Grandpa and headed back to New York City.

When he got back to Beth's apartment, it was two in the morning. She was so glad to see Patty back again and gave him a big hug and kiss. She told him, "I was afraid you might not be back."

"I wouldn't do that to you, but I am going to be leaving early tomorrow morning so I can miss some of the traffic."

"Will you take me with you?"

"No, it's best you stay here."

Beth said, "Let's get some sleep—you look tired."

"I am."

"Why don't you leave the day after and you will be fully rested and I'll help you pack too."

"That sounds good."

When morning came Beth tiptoed out of the room making sure not to awaken Patty. She wanted him to sleep.

When she came home from work, she helped him pack and put everything in his car. It was still early yet but he told Beth he would leave at three o'clock. She made supper then told Patty to get some sleep.

The alarm was set at three o'clock, when it went off. Patty jumped out of bed dressed and said to Beth, "I'll be seeing you."

"I'll walk you downstairs," and she kissed him. "Please call me."

"I will. Thanks for everything."

He drove straight towards I-95 heading for Alabama. He would sleep in the car at rest areas and in hotel parking lots with his pistol on the passenger seat covered with his jacket just in case. According to his directions he would stay on I-95 to Florence, South Carolina then pick up Route 20 and straight to Tuscaloosa, Alabama.

While he was on Route 20, he was getting tired so he turned into a hotel parking lot in the rear of the hotel. He drove to the end so he couldn't be seen, so if someone seen him he wouldn't look conspicuous. He was very tired and he fell asleep right away.

Patty was soon awakened by the sound of someone trying to open his door. They shouted to Patty to open his door. It was two men who both had guns in their hands. Patty lied to them and said that his side door was broke and it wouldn't open. They shouted to him to get out the passenger side. Patty opened the window and said I'll give you whatever you want.

"It's you we want, now get out or we're going to waste you right where you are."

"I'm getting out," he shouted.

It was dimly lit as he was opening the door. He grabbed his pistol and pushed the door open hard and hit the first guy so hard that he went into the other guy with his gun in his hand. He fired into his leg and immediately fired into the other one's leg as they were lying there withering in pain. Now their guns were on the ground, as they lay there helplessly. Patty said to them, "Now what are you guys going to do now, you cowardly bastards? I'm going to even them up," and he shot both of them again in the other leg. "Now they're even," he said. He got in his car and took off down Route 20 to Tuscaloosa, Alabama.

He stopped at a restaurant and bought a newspaper. On the front page it talked about the two men found shot in their knees lying on the ground in the parking lot, of the hotel. Evidently the police discovered that the guns they found were used in robberies and the gruesome murder of two young women whose car broke down on Route 20. They believed that they had the Route 20 bandits in custody. The article read, "The person who done this to them is a hero because it led to their capture. If he would come forward and identify himself, no charge would be placed against him. There would also be a $20,000 reward for him."

As Patty was reading the newspaper he was impressed, but he was not going to claim the reward money. He did not want any publicity.

He finally reached Tuscaloosa. He was driving by a place called The Golden Lantern advertising food and music nightly and weekends. What attracted him most was a help wanted sign in the window. When he inquired about the help wanted sign he was told he had to see either Michelle Jean or Betty Ann in the office in the back room. Patty went in and asked for Michelle Jean.

"That's me – what can I do for you?"

"I'm inquiring about the help wanted sign. I'd like to know what the job consists of."

"We need someone for all around work: you'll work in the kitchen, you'll bring product into the kitchen from the storeroom, you'll stock the storeroom shelves, you'll place dishes in the dishwasher and load the coolers with beer and ice cold drinks. Are you a Yankee?" she asked.

"No."

"What are you then? I'm an American."

"What else do you know how to do?"

"I can build houses. I can do brick laying, I sing and I can play the guitar."

"What brings you down here?"

"I'm going to see a friend."

"You are the sixth person to apply for this job."

"Well, you won't have trouble finding someone."

"Great, you can start tomorrow."

"How about Monday morning?"

She thought to herself, *There's something about this guy that I like.*

"Okay, I'll see you Monday morning."

Patty left and drove straight to Bubba Johnson's house. He called and said, "I'm on my way."

"We're waiting for you."

As soon as Patty entered the grocery store, Bubba and his family came out to greet him. He shook hands with all the men and gave all the girls a kiss. Then he said to Bubba, "I have to see you in private."

"Of course. Let's go in my office. What's up?"

"Take a look at this newspaper. I'm the one who shot them."

"That's okay, you're a hero. You shot those two animals. That's what the police are saying. Let me call Chief Williams and I could explain everything to him. We know each other. We went to school together."

"Okay, go ahead."

"The chief said to bring you to the station. He wants to talk to you. If you got a clean record, you've got nothing to worry about."

He asked Bubba, "Let me speak to this guy."

He said to Patty, "Before you get here, let me have your complete name and social security number and I'll see you in my office."

When they reached the police station, the chief was waiting for them. He extended his hand out to Patty and said to him, "Thanks for a job well done. I've already checked you out. You're from Rhode Island and you don't even have a parking ticket on your name, and the report came back that you're a war hero. You have two purple hearts and two other medals also. You were captured twice and escaped once, is that true?"

"Yes it is."

On hearing that, Bubba was beaming with excitement.

"The only thing I need from you is your fingerprints." His fingerprints came back without a thing on him.

"One more thing Patty," the Chief said, "Here is a check for twenty thousand dollars. It's the reward money. And just so you know, to escape the death penalty, they both pleaded guilty to the murders of them two girls. And everything else they had done they confessed that they planned to kill you too – so you done the right thing. Do you plan to stay around here Patty?"

"I don't know. Why do you ask?"

"Well, we need another deputy and I would like to hire you if you do plan to stay."

"I will get back to you. One more thing I would like to ask you Chief."

"What is it?"

"Can we keep this out of the papers?"

"I can't because the press is waiting outside my office. They picked it up on the police radio."

The reporters interviewed Patty and even took his picture.

The next day, the newspaper had Patty's picture on the front page saying "War Hero Patty DiMarco Captures Route Twenty Bandit."

On the way back to Bubba's place of business, Patty said to Bubba, "Take half of this reward and hold the other half for me."

"I can't do that Patty, after all that belongs to you."

"We're going to split it and you don't have a say."

"My wife and I were planning to give you some money."

"I don't want anything, I just want your friendship."

"You got that Patty. As a matter of fact, you got our friendship for the rest of our lives."

Patty stayed there until Monday morning then he left early so he could report for work early and wanted to be on time. When he got to the Golden Lantern, he went straight to the kitchen and told the chef he was starting work today and he was supposed to meet Michelle Jean or Betty Ann today. "It's still early for them, but I can get you started till they arrive which will be around ten o'clock. Soon they both arrived and asked Patty to come to the office. Michelle Jean said, "So you're a war hero."

"Where did you get that from?"

"It's been in all the papers, on the radio and TV. Aren't you excited about it?"

"Not really."

"We've never had a war hero working here before. I'll show you what your job consists of. You will be responsible to see what the kitchen needs as far as supplies. It will be your responsibility to keep the kitchen well supplied."

"Where is the storeroom?"

"I'll show you. You have to be careful of this ladder. We use it to stock supplies on the top shelves. It sometimes get stuck." She climbed the ladder to show Patty when suddenly her foot slipped and she started to fall. Immediately, Patty grabbed her and picked her up and put her down gently on the floor. As he did that he couldn't help but notice that she rubbed against his body and he looked into her eyes. He saw those Christmas eyes all lit up. She didn't plan it that way, but she couldn't believe what a strong grip he had on her and with her body pressing against solid muscle. She felt like some kind of sensation going through her body. She quickly regained her composure. "Come into my office and we can discuss more of your duties," Michelle Jean asked Patty, "Where are you going to stay?"

"I'm going to have to find a place."

"Well let me show you a place that you can use."

"Where's that?"

"It's in the rear and it has everything including a bath and shower and appliances."

Patty liked it and asked how much.

"To you?"

"Yes to me."

"Well seeing it's you, it goes with the job."

"Whose room is this?"

"I use it when I'm staying real late."

"What does your husband say when you sleep here for the night?"

"Oh, he's a salesman and he travels around the country. Are you married Patty?"

"I don't answer personal questions."

"All right then, you can ask the chef what he needs for supplies and also ask the bartender what he needs and always make sure the tables have plenty of napkins and whatever else the table needs."

Patty had been there for a month. All the employees liked him, especially the women. Michelle Jean was always calling him in the office for something or another. One day she said to him, "Be careful of the ladder in the storeroom."

"You don't have to worry about that ladder in the storeroom anymore."

"Why not?"

"Because I fixed it."

"Let me see that. I don't believe it"

When they went into the storeroom she climbed the ladder and was inspecting it when Patty put his hands on her waist and picked her up and brought her down, rubbing her body against his this time. He turned her around to face him. He held her tight and kissed her and she didn't try to pull away. Patty kept kissing her and he started rubbing her breasts.

"Patty, someone's liable to come in here and see us."

"Why not come down to my apartment?"

"No, not now. Maybe some other time."

She hurried out and went into her office. She was trembling all over. She kept thinking, *Did he really do this to me?* She couldn't believe that this was happening to her. She was hoping that she didn't make a mistake. I'm not going with him to his room.

Soon temptation got the best of her and she went straight to his room and knocked on the door. Patty opened the door and was surprised to see Michelle Jean standing in the doorway. "Did you forget something?" he asked.

"Yes," she replied. "You can finish what you started," which he did. He brought her close to him and started kissing and undressing her. She did likewise. Patty placed her on the bed and started making love to her body. No one had ever made love to her like that before. She put her arms around him and would not let go. Finally, she said to Patty, "We can't stay too long. They might be looking for me but we will get together again."

"How long have you been working here Patty?"

"Four months."

"That went by fast didn't it?"

"Yes it did."

"I'll see you later on," and she left.

Patty thought, *Here's another one.*

Later on that day, she called Patty in her office and her sister Betty Ann happened to be in her office with her. She greeted Patty with a "Hi, Patty." Michelle Jean didn't quite like the look Betty Ann gave to Patty, but she didn't' mention anything to her. Michelle Jean said to Patty, "You told me that you built houses and you've done brick laying, is that correct?"

"Yes it is. Why do you ask?"

"My husband called me last night and said he wants to have a barbecue grill built, as a matter of fact a large one, because we do a lot of entertaining. Can you do something like that?"

"That's no problem. You get some prices, and then I'll submit mine. I'll draw you a diagram of the barbecue pit I will build? You say your husband wants a huge one built?"

"Draw me what it will look like." Patty drew a huge barbecue pit that had three grills: one huge grill in the center with a spit so you could roast whole prime ribs or even a pig and a smaller grill on each side and connected to the main grill. He gave it to Michelle Jean and Dennis, her husband, to see. They fell in love with it and they didn't want any other bids. They wanted him to start right away. Dennis wanted to know how much.

"Just pay me what you're paying me now to work at the Golden Lantern and when the job is completed, you give me two hundred dollars extra. You order the supplies and I'll give you a list and you pay for them." Patty also included the tools he needed. Michelle Jean told Patty when everything would be delivered so he could be there to inspect what was being delivered to make sure everything was there that he ordered. When Patty got there, Michelle Jean was there too waiting with Patty. She asked him, "When are you going to start?"

"I'm going to start right now."

"I'll go inside to change. I want to help you."

"You sure you're going to help or can I do it myself?"

"Yes, I really want to help, but if you want to play around, that's for after work."

"What does your husband do?"

"He's a sales manager for a very large Dutch company and he's in charge of the United States division. Right now he'll be in Europe for two weeks.

They were almost through for the day when Michelle Jean said she was going inside to prepare some supper and she reminded him, "Come in when you're through."

When Patty finished he went inside. She was waiting and told him everything was prepared for him in the shower. Michelle Jean made him a beautiful T-bone steak. Just then the phone rang and it was Dennis calling from Europe wanting to know how Patty was doing.

"I guess he's doing all right. I'll go check when he leaves."

"Okay, I'll call you again. I love you Michelle Jean."

"I love you too."

She went back to be with Patty when he put his arms around her and kissed her. "I couldn't wait for you to kiss me again. You don't know what you're doing to me Patty."

"What am I doing to you?"

"When I see you, I get goose pimples. Don't you get any kind of feelings when you kiss me?"

"Yes I do. I get goose pimples just to hear you talk like that. Let's go to the bedroom. I want to hear you moan. I'll make you moan with a punch."

Michelle Jean asked Patty, "You coming back to the lounge? The weekend is going to be big. We have a new singer starting tonight and I want to be there when he arrives."

"I'll be there."

When Michelle Jean arrived at the Golden Lantern, she was informed that the singer called and said that the singer's plane has been grounded because of a terrible storm. Now she started thinking, "we've got problems. Now we don't have anyone to take his place."

Her father was getting ready to announce to the crowd that their guest singer wouldn't be singing tonight. He was hard of hearing. Michelle Jean didn't know what to do. Just then Patty bumped into her and asked what was going on. She explained to him what was going on and a lot of people would be disappointed because they wanted to listen to a singer. Patty said, "That's no problem. I can fill in."

"You know how to sing?"

"I sure can."

She hollered out to her father that she had a replacement, he couldn't hear her too well and asked his name. As she was trying to shout his name, he kept saying who. She said Pat the Yankee and he mistook it for Pat Yonker and Michelle Jean figured I'm not going to be here all night telling his name so she said to him that's right. And he announced to the crowd that we have a new singer from back east. His name is Pat Yonker.

Patty had a new stage name. With his guitar in hand he walked over to the mike and said to the crowd, "I'm from back east but my heart has always been in the south." He knew how to calm the crowd. "I would like to pick up with a song called *I Can't Stop Loving You*." Patty belted out that song. Everyone was on the floor dancing and enjoying his singing. Michelle Jean couldn't believe the voice he had. When he got through singing the first song, the crowd went wild and they wouldn't stop clapping. Pat Yonker was an instant success and was also going to be the new singer at the Golden Lantern. That's what Michelle Jean said to him when she went on stage out of earshot of everyone.

"You shocked me Pat Yonker. You're coming home with me tonight. Listen," she said, "the crowd likes fast music but put a slow one in now and then take a break."

"The next song I'm going to sing will be *For the Good Times*." After he sang that song he took a break. As he was walking across the dance floor a bunch of girls called him over to their table and asked him, "What is it, Patty DiMarco or Patty Yonker?"

"Well Patty replied Pat Yonker is my name when I'm singing."

When he reached Michelle Jean who was standing there waiting for him, her sister Betty Ann was with her also. Michelle Jean was beaming from ear to ear. She kissed him on the cheek and so did Betty Ann.

"Come to my office so we can discuss your future singing here." She shouted to Betty Ann to take over. He followed her in her office. She started kissing him and telling him when she gets him tonight, she's going to make love to his body.

"I can hardly wait."

Soon it was time to close. Customers were buying tickets for Saturday night's performance in advance making sure not to miss Patty Yonker singing Saturday night.

When Michelle Jean left, Patty didn't want to leave yet because Betty Ann was still there. Betty Ann said to Patty, "You were wonderful" and gave him a kiss on the lips. He watched her leave and then he left. Her father locked up the lounge.

When Patty arrived at Michelle Jean's house, she was waiting for him as usual. He went straight to the shower and then they retreated to the bedroom. She said to Patty, "I have something to tell you."

"What is it?"

"I'm going to divorce Dennis."

"Why are you going to do that?"

"Because I don't love Dennis."

"You must have loved him if you married him."

"I thought I did."

"Am I the cause of that?"

"Not really, but you convinced me of the fact that I don't love him."

With her talking like that the red flag went up because he didn't want any part of that. He started to think his stay in Alabama wouldn't be long.

The following morning, Patty got up early to finish the barbecue pit.

When Saturday night came, Patty finished his first set of songs. Michelle Jean approached Patty and said to him, "I hope we don't have trouble tonight."

"Why?" asked Patty.

"Trouble is starting at one of the tables."

"What's the trouble?"

"It's Freight Train."

"Who's that?"

"He's the Alabama bully. He's 400 pounds and he's got his gang with him and they're all drunk."

"Where is he?"

"Don't go near him. We'll call the cops."

"He doesn't scare me any!" Patty approached Freight Train and asked him what the problem was while everybody watched in fear. They knew what a bully he was.

"My problem is you, pretty face!" and he started to charge Patty like a freight train. That's why people called him that. At the last second, Patty stood aside and shoved him forward sending him crashing through tables and chairs. He laid on the floor shaking his head in disbelief. The crowd was cheering in what was happening.

Patty said, "If you want to finish this, step outside," which he did. He did not want to lose his image as the great Freight Train. But he better be careful because he finally met up with someone that was solid muscle and was once called Mr. Universe. If this fight were held in a ring, it would be called the Great Freight Train vs. Mr. Universe.

Freight Train went into his usual stance by charging Patty straight on. Patty hit him full force in his jaw and stopped him in his tracks. If you could see it, Train went walking in a circle on his tiptoes and down he went sitting in the parking lot looking like a giant teddy bear. The people that followed him out couldn't believe the Great Freight Train was half-unconscious from one punch thrown by Patty DiMarco.

Michelle Jean followed the crowd outside with a baseball bat in her hands. Freight Train's men ran for their truck and came back with two-by-fours in their hands. Just then, Michelle Jean threw Patty her baseball bat. Patty shouted, "Step aside everyone. I'll take care of this and he went into them swinging his bat into their two by fours knocking the first one's two by four out of his hands with such force it sounded like Babe Ruth hit a grand slam.

The other three started to run away. Patty grabbed the first one and said, "You're coming with me." He took him inside and told him to clean up this mess inside and he kept telling Patty he wouldn't make any trouble. Just then, the police arrived and saw Freight Train lying on the ground, out cold. "Well he finally met his match. Let's get him in the car and take him to the station. Let's go inside – I want to meet the person who done this."

When they went inside they asked Michelle Jean who was the one who done this. She said, "Do you know Patty DiMarco."

"I don't know him, but I heard a lot about him. Where is he?"

"That's him singing."

"He must be some tough cookie. Well, we'll be seeing you Michelle Jean. By the way, you don't need a bouncer. You got one singing right now."

A couple of days went by when Freight Train went to the Golden Lantern to see Patty,. Michelle Jean did not want to see him in her place.

Patty said, "Let me see what he has to say."

"Well, I'm going to keep my eye on him."

Patty went up to him and said, "What can I do for you?"

"I want to tell you I'm sorry for the other night and I want you to know I'm not drinking anymore."

"That's good Train."

He called Michelle Jean over and asked, "how much do I owe you for the damage I done the other night?"

"You broke two chairs and a table. That's all right for now."

"Patty, I want you to know I was never hit as hard as I was from you in my whole life. Can you teach me how to fight like that?"

"I will as long as you don't drink anymore. Do you know of a gym around here?"

"Yes I do."

"Tell me where it is and I will meet you there."

Train said, "I'll do one better. I'll come to pick you up tomorrow morning."

"See you then."

Michelle Jean on hearing that, wasn't happy and asked Patty, "What are you doing that for? He's nothing but a trouble maker."

"Maybe I could change him. His problem might be alcohol and now we might be able to see the real Train."

"I think he's a waste and don't say I didn't warn you."

Patty was thinking about himself if Sister Sandra didn't help me, only God knows what could have happened to me.

"Do you mind if I come along with you. I want to see what type of place that is?"

"I'd rather you went by yourself, after all, I can't tell you where to go."

When Patty reached the gym with Train, he introduced him to the owner as Patty DiMarco.

"Are you the Patty DiMarco from back East I've been reading about who caught them two bandits? I also read that you were some heavyweight fighter and quite a war hero." He extended his hand. "I'm sure pleased to meet you."

Patty explained to Train what he wanted him to do and we're going to take some weight off you. And I want you to get into AA and I'm going to get you to start jogging.

Train asked Patty if he could punch the bag. "I sure can."

"Will you show me how?"

"I sure will."

Patty started to punch the bag then he picked up the pace. Patty would hit the bag so hard that the sound would echo through the whole gym and also drew a crowd to watch Patty punch the bag.

"Come here Train. Always wear gloves."

Michelle Jean was with the rest of the crowd watching Patty give lessons. She was stymied seeing how hard Patty would hit the bag saying to herself, "What a man!"

He was instructing Train to start slow. "I'll tell you when to pick up the speed."

"Can I try?" Michelle Jean asked.

"As soon as Train is through." When he was through, Patty took him to the big punching bag and then through a series of exercises and then got on the treadmill. "Start slow, I'll tell you when to pick up the speed."

Patty went back to Michelle Jean and showed her how to punch the bag. Jim, the owner was watching Patty and asked him how come he knew so much about exercising.

"I ran a gym in New York. Can I ask you a question, Jim?"

"Sure."

"How's business?"

"Could be a lot better."

"You want to give me a job and if I don't pick up your business, I'll leave – no hard feelings."

"Sounds good to me," Jim said. "When do you want to start?"

"Tomorrow."

As soon as Patty started, he started an aerobic class, karate and a boxing class. Word spread fast. New customers were joining. Even Michelle Jean joined and brought in six waitresses. Also, Jim was all excited that new customers were joining everyday.

Now, they heard Patty singing at the aerobic class. Jim made a comment that Patty even sings and that he didn't know he sang. He would run the aerobics and then go over and run the karate class and in between help whoever needed it with the exercises.

As the weeks went by, he was bringing in new customers. Train was doing fabulous. He took off 100 pounds. Already, he was going to AA faithfully and he was very happy with what Patty was doing for him. He was becoming a new man. As a matter of fact, even Michelle Jean made a comment about how well he was doing. She said to him when she saw him, "You look like a new person."

"That's all because of Patty and I owe him a lot," said Train.

Later that same day, Michelle Jean told Patty that her husband Dennis was on the way home and that she would be picking him up at the airport. "There is something I want to talk to you about."

"What is it?"

"Well, you know we have a jam-packed crowd on Friday, Saturday and Sunday nights and while I'm singing, I need someone else walking around to make sure we have no unruly drunks causing any problems."

"Do you have anyone special in mind?"

"Yes, I do."

"Who is he?"

"Train."

"Well he is a different person now. I'll go along with that. It's all up to you who you want to bring in."

The next day when Patty saw Train, he told him he had a job for him.

"Where?" he asked.

"At The Golden Lantern."

"Doing what?"

"You'll be the bouncer because the place is jam-packed on the weekends. What do you think?"

"Yes, I would love it Patty. You don't know what you've done for me."

"I don't want you to be too tough on the customers but just keep them under control and if you need any help, I'll be right there with you."

When the waitresses heard about it, they liked it very much knowing that with Patty and Train around they would be able to keep the drunks under control.

Michelle Jean wasn't there the next day when Patty went to the gym, because she had to pick up her husband. Betty Ann was there instead, and she asked Patty if he would show her how to punch the bag.

"Of course, I would."

As he was teaching her, you could see she liked Patty. Her eyes were all over him. You know Patty, you've done a lot for the Golden Lantern. We've never done so much business since we've been open. You've done a lot for Train and you've tripled the business over here. I was talking with Jim and he still can't believe it. What are your plans for the future? Do you plan to stay around here?

Just them Jim interrupted them saying that the new girls that he advertised for are here to be interviewed.

"Listen, let's go for a coffee later and we could talk."

Betty Ann was pleased about that. Patty went to interview the girls. Six in all showed up for the job. Right now, he needed one for physical therapy and one for the aerobic dancing. They all had to be interviewed wearing shorts and they also had to have a good shape, after all, this is how the women customers would look like if they worked out at Jim's Gym.

He decided to go with one called Lynda Lee and the other's name was Barbara Jean, two beauties, for he knew how to pick them. He took Train with him showing the girls what their job would consist of. He took Train with him because he would like to see Train take over when he left. He told the girls that he could use them as soon as possible, just in case. He didn't want to leave Jim flat and he didn't want to hurt him any. Patty went up to Betty Ann and said, "Let's go for coffee."

When they got to the restaurant, Patty was quick to ask her, "What do you mean by asking me if I was going to stay around here?"

Betty Ann answered, "If you're honest with me, I'll be honest with you."

"Why should I lie? I might not want to answer certain questions, but I'm not going to lie.

"My sister told me she was going to ask for a divorce and all this happened since you arrived. Do you have anything to do with that?"

"I didn't plan anything nor do I want to see that happen. I think I told you too much and I don't want to lie. Tell me, why are you so interested in what my plans are?"

"Because I want to go with you."

"Why do you want to go with me?"

"Because I like being with you and I will admit I do like you too."

"I usually don't want anyone traveling with me, but I'm not sure yet. Maybe I could use a rider. How much time can you take off?"

"Whatever I want."

"Would Michelle Jean allow you to take time off?"

"There is something you might not know, but my father gave half of the business to each of us, so I own the same amount as she does."

Patty replied," I'm not sure yet, but I should know shortly. Let's get back Betty Ann because I've got a lot of work to do." Actually Patty wanted to cut it short. He had a feeling she might start asking questions between him and Michelle Jean. Betty Ann brought it to Patty's attention there was more she wanted to talk about. Patty was quick to respond, "We'll do it at the next cup of coffee."

Patty went back to the gym and asked Train, "How's everything going?"

"Going good."

When Patty returned to the Golden Lantern he went straight to his apartment. He wasn't there long when there was a knock on the door. It was Michelle Jean. "What are you doing here?"

"Why?" she asked.

"Your husband is home, isn't he?"

"Yes he is but he's home resting."

"I don't think you should come here when he's home."

"Are you trying to shake me off?"

"No, but I'm not going to get caught with you in my apartment."

"He saw the barbecue pit and he loves it. He wants to run a party and barbecue. Are you coming?"

"I don't think so."

"Why not?"

"Because it won't be long before he figures things out. You know Michelle Jean, there's an old Italian saying, when something's going on watch their eyes. Without saying a word, their eyes will tell you a lot."

That Friday night, Dennis went to the Golden Lantern and Patty was singing at the time. Dennis was quite surprised at Patty's singing. He mentioned to Michelle Jean what a beautiful voice Patty had.

When Patty came off his break, Dennis went up to him and said, "what a nice job you've done with the barbecue pit and by the way, you've got a nice voice. We're going to have quite a large barbecue party over our house. Why don't you come over and you can sing a couple of songs?"

"I'll be singing here and I won't be able to come."

"You don't start singing 'til nine here. You could leave in plenty of time to get here to sing."

"I'll think about it." Michelle Jean wasn't saying anything at all. "And we'll pay you for singing. There's going to be quite a few important people there and I'm even going to hire the same band that you sing with."

Patty finally agreed to sing at the barbecue.

The following day, Michelle Jean went to see Patty at his apartment. Patty said, "What are you doing here?"

"Why do you say that?"

"I need to say some thing to you. We're not involved so please get out."

"Don't do that to me, Patty."

With that he opened the door and said again, "Out!"

"I thought you were in love with me."

"Well you thought wrong."

"Did I ever tell you I assumed so?"

"Well you assumed wrong. I don't get involved with married women or if women have a boyfriend. For the last time, get out!"

"But I don't love my husband."

"That's your business, not mine. Goodbye!" and he closed the door. Patty started thinking it was time to get out of there.

He called his friend Inu in Nome, Alaska whose life he had saved in Korea. He always told Patty that after the war, make sure you come up to Alaska. My parents want to meet my hero. So he called him at the Nome post office where Inu's father was the postmaster and Inu was the assistant postmaster. Inu couldn't believe he was talking to Patty. He was so excited.

"What's up my main man?"

"I'm in Alabama and I want to get out of here and get as far away as I can."

"Well, is Nome far enough?"
"I guess so."
"Well come on up."
Patty then called Bubba Johnson and told him his plans.
"You stop here first. I have your money."
"How much?"
"Twenty thousand dollars."
"I only want ten thousand and you keep the rest."
"No, we want you to have the whole twenty thousand."
"Just give me the ten and if I get into trouble I'll send for it. I'll see you soon."

It was now time for the barbecue and Patty went there. He sang some songs and then mingled in with the crowd and ran into Betty Ann and they went to sit in the shade. Patty said, "Want to talk?"
"Sure."
"First of all, are you married?"
"Of course not."
"Well, I'm going to leave here."
"Where are you going?"
"Far away. You want to drive me?"
"Of course."
"It's quite a way."
"That's okay, you're worth it."
"I've got a better idea."
"What is it?"
"Take me with you."
"I want to get settled first then I'll take it from there."
"When are you planning to leave?"
"This coming Monday."
"Where will we be going?"

"Up to Washington."

"That's fine with me."

When that Monday came, Patty went to Michelle Jean's office to tell her he was leaving. She was not there, so he wrote her a note and also explained to her that Betty Ann was driving him to where he was going. Betty Ann followed him with her car and then went straight to Bubba's place.

"You can stay here forever Patty."

"Thanks but I already made plans. Look I'm leaving you my car because I won't have any use for it anymore.

16 ALASKA

Patty said goodbye to Bubba, his wife and children. As they were driving away, Bubba said to his wife, "There goes the best guy in the world."

"Okay," Patty said to Betty Ann, "let's get started."

"Where are we going to?"

"Jackson, Mississippi – our first stop."

"What's going on over there?"

"That's where one of my best friends lived and I want to see his family if I could."

Patty directed her on which way to go and after getting more directions from different people, he finally found the house he was looking for. He could see a bunch of people sitting at a picnic table and children playing. They pulled into the driveway with everyone staring at them wondering who they were. Patty and Betty Ann both got out of the car. Everyone went quiet as if on signal. The eldest person stood up wondering who this tall muscular young man was and slowly approaching the picnic table.

"Can I help you?" he asked drawing stares from the rest of the people.

"I hope you can. I am looking for Mr. and Mrs. Bobby McGee."

"Who are you?" the elderly man asked.

"I'm Patty DiMarco."

Just then, upon hearing the name Patty DiMarco, a scream went out from the gathering. Apparently it was Eva McGee, mother of young Bobby McGee. Everyone sitting at the table all got up at once for Patty DiMarco was a well-known name in their household. Bobby McGee had written home many times mentioning his best friend Patty DiMarco. Eva McGee went up to Patty and hugged him, and she wouldn't let go of him. She felt a part of her son was back.

"Patty, please do me a favor?"

"What is it?"

"Were you with Bobby when he died?"

"Yes, Mrs. McGee. He died in my arms."

"Please Patty, tell me everything."

"I don't want to hurt you with details."

"You won't, but I must know. It seems you're the only one who knows. I was told they didn't know where the body was. Is it true?"

"I know where he's buried."

"You do? How come you know?"

"Because I helped bury him. I made a cross for him and I engraved on the cross, 'I know you're up there Bobby.' He's buried in Hamhung, North Korea. My suggestion to you is to get in touch with your state senator and see what he can do for you."

"You two were in a prisoner of war camp together?"

"Yes, we were captured together. Bobby got very sick and he couldn't pull out of it. I have something for you that belonged to

Bobby and I thought you might like to have them." He handed her his dog tags. Patty had them silver plated with a sterling silver chain and he placed them around her neck. She hugged him again.

Patty said, "Did he ever tell you that we used to sing together?"

"Yes, he did."

"Well, I have something else for you."

"What is it?"

"We used to write songs together and I wrote this song for him after he died."

"Bobby mentioned to me that you had a beautiful voice. Will you do me one more favor?"

"If you want me to sing, of course I will."

Upon hearing that, the rest of the family gave Patty a big applause. "It just so happens I have my guitar in the car."

Betty Ann ran to the car and got his guitar. Patty said to them, "I'll be playing *Me and Bobby McGee*."

When he got through singing, there were a lot of teary eyes. Bobby's mother and father invited Patty and Betty Ann to have something to eat and wouldn't take no for an answer. So they accepted the invitation.

Eva asked Patty, "Where are you heading?"

"Did Bobby ever mention our friend Inu to you?"

"Yes, he did. He said that you three would do everything together."

"Well, I'm on my way to see him."

"And where is he at?"

"He lives in Alaska."

"But that's far away."

"I know it is."

They stayed two or three hours at Bobby's family home then decided to leave. Patty shook everyone's hand and gave Eva a hug. She said, "Now don't forget to write us or even call us."

Patty told Betty Ann, "You drive for now. When it gets dark, we'll pull into a hotel or motel and we could shower and get some sleep. We'll get a room with two beds."

"We will like hell. I didn't come all this way to sleep in separate beds. We are going to sleep in one bed"

"Have it your way," Patty said. "There's a hotel at the next exit. Take it—we might as well stop there for the night."

The hotel clerk asked single or double bed. Betty Ann replied single. Patty didn't say too much. He was doing a lot of thinking.

When they got to their room, Betty Ann went straight to the shower while Patty checked the map. When Betty Ann was through with her shower, Patty went in. She jumped in bed waiting for Patty. When he was through showering, he wasted no time getting into bed with Betty Ann. She started kissing Patty right away. They made serious love. She was waiting for Patty and couldn't get enough of him. When they finished, she asked Patty, "Please take me with you. You won't be sorry, I'll do everything for you and I will love you like you've never been loved before."

"I planned to make this trip alone, but I can't predict the future. Who knows, but if I change my plans I'll call you. Now let's get some sleep. We've got a lot of driving to do tomorrow."

After they had breakfast the following morning, Patty said, "I'll drive, you rest then you can drive and I'll rest." As they were driving Betty Ann was trying to start a conversation and she asked Patty, "What do you like me to call you: Patty Yonker or Patty DiMarco?"

"Whatever you like to call me is fine."

"I like Patty best."

"Then call me Patty. Now let me ask you a question. How long can you stay away from work without getting in trouble?"

"I can stay forever if I want."

"What will Michelle Jean say when she finds out?"

"Let's put it this way, Michelle Jean is my older sister, but she's not the boss. I own half of the Golden Lantern. It's the same amount that she owns. Besides, I told my father that I was driving you to Seattle. He told me it was all right with him. He's the one I answer to. Besides, he'll inform Michelle Jean that I drove you to Seattle."

"She will be upset, that I know for a fact."

"Why do you say that? I might be younger than her, but I am not a baby nor am I blind to the fact what's been going on between you and her."

Patty was quick to respond, "She told me she was divorcing her husband. She completely fooled me and this is the reason that I'm leaving Alabama. I asked you if you were married and you told me you were not."

"If I were married I would not be driving you to Seattle. You might as well know Patty, from the first day that I saw you, I liked you and when you kissed me last night, I couldn't sleep all night."

"Well then get some sleep. Later on we'll stop for some lunch."

Much later, they stopped for lunch and then headed straight out. It was getting dark and they pulled into another hotel.

"You want the same arrangements?"

"Yes the same arrangements. As soon as they got into the room, Betty Ann headed for the shower first. Then they dressed and decided to eat in the hotel. She noticed on the itinerary that there was dancing to live music in the ballroom. She asked Patty, "What do you say – you want to dance later?"

"Sure, why not?"

"You want a bottle of wine?"

"No just a glass is fine."

They did a lot of talking. Betty Ann was thrilled being with Patty. She couldn't take her eyes off him. "What are your plans for tomorrow?" she asked Patty.

"We're going to drive straight to Seattle."

"Do you mind if I ask you once again, are you going to take me with you?"

"No, I'm not. I don't know what I'm going to find when I get there. Once I know for sure, then I will decide my next direction.

Betty Ann thought to herself that she had better let that subject go for now.

As soon as they were through with dinner, Betty Ann asked Patty, "You ready to dance?"

"Let's go."

When they started dancing, Betty felt like she was in heaven being in Patty's arms. She commented to Patty about what a nice dancer he was.

"You don't do too bad yourself."

Before they knew it, it was two in the morning and Patty said, "We'd better go, it's getting late. Check out is at eleven and we still have a long way to go."

"I could dance all night with you Patty, but let's go."

As soon as they got back to the room, Patty started checking the map to see how they were doing. Betty Ann was calling to him to come to bed.

"I'm trying to make sure we're going in the right direction."

Betty Ann asked him, "How are we doing?"

"Okay, we're now in Missouri. One more day of traveling and we'll be in Colorado then straight through to Seattle. Okay, let's get some sleep."

But Betty Ann started to kiss him for she had other things on her mind and said to Patty, "You don't know what you do to me."

The following day during breakfast Patty said to Betty Anne, "We are going to drive as much as we can without stopping. You drive first and I'll rest, then you rest and I'll drive. Stay on Route 70 until you come to Route 25 and then Route 90 straight into Seattle.

Soon Betty Ann told Patty that she was getting tired. Patty said there was a fast food restaurant at the next exit. Go down there and we'll get something fast and I'll take over."

As they were eating Patty asked her, "Do you miss being home?"

"Not really?"

"Who do you miss?"

"I'll tell you who I'm going to miss."

"Who's that?"

"I'm going to miss you something terribly."

Betty Ann did not realize that Patty was not trying to get any women. He didn't mind dating them, but then there were problems that would follow and he was tired of all of this.

When he spoke to Inu he explained all of this to him and Inu said his father had land deep into Alaska. As a matter of fact, he had thousands of acres that he would let him have free of charge. Inu explained to Patty if he wanted to be alone, he could be, over there.

As soon Patty and Betty Ann finished eating, they took off. Patty said, "No stopping until we get to Seattle, then we'll sleep over and I'll leave in the morning.

They finally reached Seattle and registered in a hotel. Patty called to see what time the boat would be leaving for Nome, Alaska. He told Beth that he would be leaving at ten in the morning.

She said to Patty, "Don't remind me."

"How about we get some sleep. We'll get up in plenty of time to have breakfast and then I'll leave."

The next day Betty Ann asked Patty one more time, "You sure you don't want to take me?"

"Not this time Betty Ann. If I decide to come back, I'll call you, I promise."

He gave her a hug and kiss. She didn't want to let him go and she started to cry. Just then, the boat blew its horn, which meant they were getting ready to leave.

"I've got to leave now."

He was on the boat starting to leave waving goodbye to Betty Ann.

Patty reached Nome, Alaska. The post office was closed for the day so he called Inu at his father's house. They knew that Patty was coming so they were waiting for him. Inu drove straight to the post office to pick up Patty.

When he first met Patty he hugged him and said, "I am so glad to see you Patty. You are my man."

On the way back Inu asked Patty, "The women getting too much for you?"

"Not really, it's just that they all want to get married. I would just like to be alone for a while."

"Well my Dad has something for you. Maybe you will like it."

"What is it?"

"I'll let him tell you."

When they arrived at Inu's father's house, his father, mother and sister were there waiting for Patty. He didn't have a chance to enter the house before they all hugged Patty. Inu's father was the first to speak.

"Our house is your house. We are so happy to meet the guy who saved our only son's life in Korea by risking his own life. You know that's all Inu talks about is what a great guy that Patty is."

Then Inu's mother got a hold of Patty and said to him, "We love you Patty. You want to take a shower first? I also made you a beautiful supper."

Inu said, "She made your favorite."

"What's that?"

"Polar bear!"

"I thought she might have made roast seal," and they both laughed like old times.

Inu showed him where the bathroom was. After the shower, Patty put on a clean T-shirt that really exposed a picture perfect body. When he walked into the dining room there was now about twenty relatives there for they wanted to meet the person who Inu called the "Great Patty." He went around the room shaking everyone's hand. Their eyes turned to stare, admiring his good looks and his muscular body and commenting that they didn't know that he was so tall.

Inu sat next to Patty at the dinner table. As they were eating, Patty said to him softly, "Do you remember when you were shot?"

"I'll never forget that day."

"Well after you were shot twice, I went after that bastard. You were out cold and I thought you were dead. I brought you back to safety dodging bullets all the way. I went back in the building from the back. Our company was firing everything we had to distract them. I climbed the stairs and there were two of them firing away with a machine gun. I threw in a hand grenade and that was the end of the two of them. I grabbed a souvenir for you."

"What is it?"

"I'll tell you after dinner."

Inu couldn't wait for dinner to be over for he wanted to see what Patty had for him. As soon as dinner was over Patty went over to his suitcase to get his souvenir for Inu. He took out a plastic bag.

Inu asked, "What is it?"

"I took it from the one who shot you. I cut it from the hair of the woman who was firing the machine gun at you from the window. I've carried it with me quite a while since that day.

"This is really something Patty. Every time I see that I'll always remember she was the one that wounded me but you were the one that carried me out of there under live fire and that is something I will be grateful for the rest of my life."

Inu had a glass showcase in the den and inside he had momentos and medals he had received in Korea. He put what Patty gave him right in the middle of the showcase.

His father came into the den and asked Inu, "What did Patty have for you?" and he showed him.

"This is from the girl's hair that shot me."

His reaction was, "Patty's quite a guy. That's why I want to talk to him."

"Patty," said Inu's father, "Inu told me you want to be alone for a while. If you're interested, I've got just the place for you and you have to get there by boat."

"Where is it?"

"It's in the middle of nowhere. I own a few thousand acres and if you think that you would be comfortable there I will give you two thousand acres to start off with. I'll have Inu show you the place tomorrow. I'll tell you this Patty--the place is beautiful. It has fresh water on one side and the ocean on the other side. It also has a cabin there. We don't use it anymore. I want you to know Patty, we are so grateful for what you have done, you will be like a son to us."

The next day Patty and Inu went to see the land that Inu's father promised Patty. They rented a motorboat and had taken provisions to stay for a few days, including two of Inu's rifles, and a chain saw.

As they were driving there, Inu told Patty there was a mountain there that was part of the land.

"What would I do with a mountain?"

"You could go skiing."

"I doubt it." Then Patty commented that the lake was beautiful.

"You could go ice fishing here too."

They pulled up to a dock which they built when Inu was a kid.

Patty said, "It's really quiet here. Are there any animals around?"

"Plenty. We have a shed in the back of the cabin where we keep a snowmobile and lots of tools and equipment. What we'll do is start the snowmobile and take a ride around."

When they went behind the shed, Patty noticed a stream there coming down from the mountain. Inside the shed he noticed some mining pans and asked Inu about them.

"When you got nothing to do, you can go look for gold."

"Did you ever try?"

"I sure did, but I never found enough that was worthwhile. You can try your luck. If you find any, there is an assayer's office in town. Maybe you can find enough to meet expenses. But I doubt it."

They got the snowmobile started and took a ride around the land they wanted to give Patty. It was all staked out with cement markers. They drove up to the ocean.

"Did you ever see polar bears?"

"I sure did, but I always stood clear of them."

"How come?"

"If I needed to kill them it would be different."

"How much land is your father giving me?"

"I think it's two thousand acres."

"When am I taking you back."

"I'm going to stay with you until you're settled in. When we get back to the cabin, we're going to cut some trees down because you're going to need plenty of firewood. It gets pretty cold up here and firewood will keep you alive. What do you think Patty? Do you think you can survive out here?"

"I think so. I will have to make a few trips with plenty of supplies and plenty of food and I will buy a good sized boat."

"We have a two-way radio and phone at the cabin. You can call me anytime. If you need me in a hurry and everything is frozen in, I can fly in on the water or on ice. Let's get back to the cabin. We've got a lot of work there. So let's get started. I just thought of an idea. We checked everything out. What do you think, could you handle this kind of a life?"

"Piece of cake."

"I was thinking we could hire some help in town so we could gather plenty of firewood. That is very important on our list."

"Okay, that sounds fine with me."

They returned to Inu's home and made a list of everything they would need including plenty of food. They would make plenty of trips back and forth stocking the cabin to capacity. Patty made sure he had extra rifles. He was planning to do a lot of hunting.

Inu decided to hire three helpers to start cutting down trees. While the three hired hands were cutting wood and stacking it, they were also doing other chores in and around the cabin. Inu connected the two-way radio so that Patty could contact Inu any time he wanted or needed him. He reminded Patty, "If the lake was frozen I could put skis on the plane and be here in no time. Before we are ready to leave here you will only need the boat to go fishing or if we've forgotten something from town, you could run down and pick it up in Nome."

Inu showed Patty by connecting a rope to the boat and to this tree at the edge of the dock. "There is a winch in the shed that you could use to pull the boat out of the water for the winter," said Inu.

The hired hands stayed there for a week to make sure everything was finished and all set for Patty.

"When we get back to Nome tonight, my father is going to come back here with us to make sure everything is all set for you Patty.

The following day, Inu's father returned with Patty and Inu to make sure that they did not forget anything. He even looked in the cellar of the cabin to double check the food supply, which he said was more than adequate. He shook Patty's hand and said "Lots of luck. You'll have all the peace in the world here. I could guarantee that you won't see a soul here and if that's what you want, this is the place to find it."

"When we get back to Nome I want you to tell me what I owe you for this land."

"You owe me nothing. As a matter of fact, the papers are all drawn up by my attorney and they are waiting for you at my house."

When they returned home, Inu's mother had supper ready for them and informed then their attorney would be over shortly to explain everything. When their attorney arrived he said to Patty, "The land is all yours. The only condition there is if you don't want the land anymore, it will go back to the original owners. Do you agree to that?"

"I do. I feel like I'm getting married."

Inu asked Patty "You want to shoot some pool?"

"Why not."

"I'll call a couple of friends over and you and I can challenge them Patty."

They came right over, especially when they heard that Patty DiMarco was there. They had heard so much about him. When they arrived at Inu's house, they weren't surprised at the impression Patty had made on them, for he was all Inu had explained to them. When they shook hands it felt like a vice was closing on their hand. They admired his muscular body, his good looks and how tall he was. One of them made a comment that he felt he was meeting Mr. America.

"I wish," Patty said.

Just then, Inu's mother and father came downstairs to watch them play. Her eyes started to tear. She saw how happy her son was with Patty and if it weren't for Patty saving his life, Inu would never be here. She meant it when she said to Patty, "You are like a son to me and you will always be. I want to ask you what time are you leaving tomorrow morning?"

"I'm going to get up early."

"The reason I ask is because I will get up early to make you breakfast. Inu will get up with me. He wants to drive me to the dock."

Patty told Inu's father and mother that he would be back now and then to see them.

The following morning came fast and Patty was all ready to go. He wanted to check out the stream coming down from the mountain. Patty said his good-byes and headed for the dock where his boat was docked. He checked to see if the name of the boat had been painted on. He named the boat *Mama Anna*. Patty told Inu he would call him.

Inu asked Patty "What will you be doing?" Like I said before, "I'm going to check out the stream coming down from the mountain. I'm going to see if I can get lucky. See you later."

Patty liked the feel of the boat and headed for the cabin that he named *The Hideaway*.

When night came the only sounds that he could hear were animal sounds. "Maybe I'll get a dog or two to keep me company," he thought to himself. He could feel the temperature dropping, so he started a fire, turned the radio on and listened to some music. He got the fire going good and decided to turn in for the night. He wanted an early start in the morning.

The next morning he got up early and made himself a large breakfast. Then he made a lunch, put his knife and pistol on his belt and also took plenty of matches. He thought, *You never know what I'll run into.*

It was about an hour's walk to the stream. He started to survey the stream and the area around as far as he could make out. It looked like the stream was coming from the mountain. From the point of where he started, it was about a mile to where he stopped. He still thought the stream was coming somewhere from the mountain. It would have to take further research. Patty thought he had done enough checking for today but more will have to be done later.

He was anxious to start panning for gold. He carved his initials in a tree so he would remember where he stopped walking. Patty started to pan for gold and he planned to work back from where he started. An hour went by when Patty realized that he found small pieces of gold. He thought, *Maybe I should go towards the* mountain and maybe I would find the 'mother load' but I will do that some other day.

Patty was finding more and more gold. Before dusk set in he decided to head back to the cabin realizing that he should have a tent so he could sleep there.

"Oh well, I'll put that on my shopping list."

He put the gold nuggets he had found in a sock he had hanging from his belt. If he were going to find more gold he would need something different to carry the gold in. He headed back to *The Hideaway*.

When he got back he laid the gold nuggets on the table and was quite impressed with the first day panning for gold.

Later that night, Inu called and wanted to know how the first day went. "What did you do the first day being alone?"

"I went panning for gold and I looked around a little."

"Did you find any?"

"I found a little."

"Well that's not bad."

"I'm going to go there again every day while it's still warm. Then I'll go to the assayers office to see how much it's worth."

"Call me on the two-way radio if you need anything."

"I will."

Patty put the nuggets that he panned in a canvas bag that he had made and tonight he would make a strap that he could carry it around his shoulder.

The next morning, he got up early and went down to the stream and started panning again. He made sure he always wore his pistol. He even took his rifle along. "I know I'm in the middle of nowhere but you never know what will happen," He said aloud.

As the weeks went by, Patty was starting to realize that he was panning a lot of gold nuggets and he was thinking that maybe he hit something big. Winter was now starting to set in so Patty took his boat into town figuring that this might be the last time he would get supplies till the lake thawed.

When he got into town he went right over to Inu's house. The family was glad to see him. He told them that he needed some supplies before the lake froze up. He was going to the assayer's office to see what his nuggets were worth.

"If I don't see you again, I'll call you."

He went straight to the assayer's office. Of course he did not take all the nuggets that he found, fearing a stampede. The assayer told him it was worth one thousand dollars.

"How long did it take you to pan this?"

"All summer."

"Are you going to go back for more?"

"I don't think so."

"How come?"

"I'm not going to spend six months panning and only make one thousand dollars. That's like making ten cents an hour." Patty didn't want to let on that if what he had here was worth one thousand dollars, then the canvas bag he had at home must be worth at least a half a million dollars. And if it ever got out, there would be a stampede out there if there was that much gold. The assayer seemed to believe him because as far as he knew, there never was much gold there.

Patty came up with an idea. It was now time to call Danny Boyle, his best friend in Rhode Island and explain to him the situation and ask him if he would make a trip up here and take some nuggets to an assayer's office in California. As far as they're concerned, it might have been found there. He wouldn't give them all the nuggets, maybe $100,000 worth. When the time was right, he would then announce that gold had been discovered.

He would also give to Inu and his family 50 percent of whatever the mine would be worth. He would call it the Alaskan Mine Corporation.

He made plans with Danny to get ready to leave and gave him full instructions where he would meet him. He also told him to bring an extra suitcase half full but he would go back with that same suitcase so that it would not arouse any suspicion.

Danny finally arrived as planned. Patty met him at the boat landing in Nome. He instructed Danny to check in at the Holiday Inn. He had a room already registered in his name. What Patty was trying to do was not to let on that gold was found, not yet anyway. Patty wanted to make sure it would be protected until he let the discovery out.

"After you get the money, keep $10,000 for your expenses"

"I don't want anything Patty. I'm not working anyway."

"No, I want you to have it. You are now on the payroll. I'll call you at your house so you can return here with the money."

Danny returned in no time at all. "What's next?" Danny asked Patty.

"Well I heard the manager at State Bank is a very smart person and a clever businessman and those are the type of people I like doing business with.

They went straight to the bank to see the bank manager. Patty had set up an appointment with John Delaney, the branch manager and an officer of the bank. John immediately asked Patty for his name and where he was from. "Now what brings you to my bank?"

"I want to deposit $100,000 in your bank for starters and I'm hoping to bring much more than that if we could make an agreement between us--just for a short while, that's all."

"Well, I believe I've struck gold and a lot of it. I don't want the news to get out until I'm able to handle it and to protect my interest in the mine."

"Who owns the land?"

"I do and I brought documents to prove it. Now here's the deal: if you can keep it quiet till we are ready to announce the discovery, I'll do all the banking here and when it goes the way I expect, I'll buy the bank and you will be the number one person in the bank. I understand you have 20 branches."

"How about a share in the mine?"

"I'll go one better than that. I have an idea with what's up there, I could buy this whole bank and present it to you lock, stock and barrel."

John liked that business deal and said to Patty, "I have to check you out first."

Patty gave him all the information he needed. "Now when are you going to get back?"

"Before the ground freezes."

"I'm going to call the attorney general's office in Rhode Island right now so just wait around a few minutes. He reached the attorney's office in Rhode Island and inquired about Patty DiMarco and if they could check him out for him. He explained who he was. They said they knew who he was because they had to do a report on him for the police department in Alabama. "I can tell you now, he came up clean, not even a parking ticket violation. As a matter of fact, he's a war hero. I'll check him out again and fax it to you right away."

John said to Patty, "Let's have a cup of coffee. He's going to fax it to me as soon as possible."

It wasn't long and the fax came in from Alabama. John was anxious to read and was very comfortable to read that report about

Patty. As far as he was concerned, it was a triple A report. Patty then asked John, "Is it a deal?"

"It sure is and you can trust me. What do you want me to do next?"

"I want you to open a checking account with this check and give my friend $10,000. After all he made that trip to California."

"Well he won't have to go anymore because I have an assayer's license. We could do it right here and I will deposit it for you."

Patty decided to buy a scale so that he could weigh the gold himself before he gave it to John.

"I'm going to get started. I've got a lot to do and I'll be back with more nuggets."

"See you then."

"Come on Danny, we've got a lot to do and then I'll take you to my cabin."

They first went to the grocery store and stocked up on plenty of food.

"What are you going to do, feed an army?" Danny asked.

"I don't want to run out."

They went to a sporting store. They bought two more rifles, more ammunition and more clothes. They then went to a dealership and Patty ordered a four-wheel drive truck so he wouldn't have to borrow one anymore. He informed the dealership he would be back the following day to pay him the balance and pick up the truck.

Patty and Danny left to go back to the cabin. They made it back just before dusk and they carried everything back to the cabin. Danny asked, "Why do you have a lock on the door?"

Patty replied, "You never know. Come on, I'll cook you a T-bone. We'll get up early tomorrow and I'll show you where I'm panning for gold. Then I'll take you back."

"Patty you don't have to give me all that money. That seems like too much money."

"Don't worry about it. I think there's a lot more in that mountain."

The next day, they got up early and headed down to the stream. "This is where I stopped panning. I'm going to show you something." Patty picked up his pan and started panning. "Danny, look, here's some nuggets. I thought I'd cleaned this spot out. Now look here's more. I tell you Danny, I think the mother load is in that mountain and I'm going to find out. Let's start going back, I want to pick up my truck and take some more gold to the bank."

Patty weighed some more gold to see if what he weighed matched what John said.

His truck was waiting for him. Everything was fine. "Seems like old times," Danny was quick to say.

"Let's go to the bank."

Patty had John weigh the gold and he was happy that the weight matched what he had. Patty felt better knowing that John also told him he had around $200,000 in gold. "You deposit it in my account and take $10,000 for you and $10,000 for Danny." They both didn't want to hear of it, but Patty insisted.

"John, I still want to pan some more before it starts to freeze and then next spring I'm going to start digging into the mountain."

Patty took Danny to the dock. Before Danny left they had a last minute talk.

"Tell no one where I am."

"I won't Patty, and thanks for everything."

Patty left his truck at the dock where his boat was. He had made arrangements with the owner to keep his truck in the back of his store. Patty noticed that there were a lot of seaplanes in the water and a sign saying driving lessons and planes for sale. He went inside to get more information and he was told with the purchase of a new plane, he would throw in lessons for half price.

"How much for parking my truck?"

"Are you going to buy your supplies here?"

"Yes I am."

"Well it will be free parking. When do you want the lessons?"

"Today."

"Okay, I'll call my instructor."

Patty spent the whole week taking lessons. He ordered his plane. He also ordered skis for the plane. When it was ready to put them on he would show him how to do it.

Patty was now flying around the lake and he even landed at his dock. He would now travel back and forth by plane and boat.

The first thing he did was to take another $200,000 to the bank. The first comment that John said was, "You might be right Patty, about the mother load. I want you to know that I didn't take the $10,000 you wanted me to take. You already made a deal with me and I think it's a darn good one."

"I bought an airplane and I'm already flying it. When the lake freezes I'm going to have skis put on. I'm going to head back now because I want to do as much panning as I can."

This time, Patty bought a tent so he could sleep at the stream. When Patty retired at night, he would lay in bed thinking, "Come on spring!"

He was going to have to move in some heavy equipment to start digging into the mountain. He was certain that the mother load was in there somewhere. His plan was to follow the stream into the mountain. But he felt he must first get in touch with Inu and his family and explain to then that he wanted to make them a partner in the Alaskan Mine Corporation. After all, they didn't realize how much gold was in there.

The following morning, Patty called Inu and told him he had to have a meeting with him and his parents because it was very important. "I'm going to fly in tomorrow."

"You'd better hurry because the lake is going to freeze."

"Good because I'll have skis put on."

Patty went straight to the house. Inu's father said, "What's going on? Inu told us that it was important."

"It sure is. I'll get right to the point. I've discovered gold and I think there's a lot of it up there on our land. I'm making you a partner because I'm sure if you knew about the gold being there, you wouldn't have given me the land."

"Patty, are you sure?"

"Of course I'm sure and I'm not a dishonest person. Whatever we dig out of there, you own half. There is one thing you must do. You cannot tell anyone about this because there will be a stampede up there. We will announce it when we feel we're fully protected."

"But Patty, you are like a son to us. My son is here today because of you. Patty we are so happy he's alive, we want you to have that land and whatever is on it. No amount of gold or diamonds could bring Inu into our arms again. You've made us so happy."

"I want the papers drawn up this way: I will own 60% and your family own 40% of whatever we take out of there. Make an appointment for me with your lawyer and Inu and I could get it started. One more thing, we have a million dollars in the bank. Four hundred thousand is your share. I say we don't touch any of that because we're going to need much more than that to get started. Is everything all set now because I'm going to head back."

"You must be tired. Why not stay and get some sleep and leave tomorrow?"

"I'm going hunting tomorrow. I want to get an early start. Let me know when the lawyer is coming and I'll come over to sign the papers."

Patty went straight to the dock to pick up some more supplies before heading back to the Hideaway. He went inside and spoke to Hank, the owner of the dock.

"How are you doing Patty?"

"I'm doing all right. Are you going to take care of my plane and put skis on when it's time to do so?"

"We sure will."

"How much do I owe you?" Patty asked.

"You owe me your life," Hank said jokingly.

Patty was excited to go hunting the next day. That's what was on his mind. He wanted to clean his rifle and start his snowmobile and have everything ready for tomorrow morning.

When morning came Patty was already making breakfast. He wore his pistol and took some extra food just in case. He got the snowmobile going and he was on his way. When he got a little way out, he saw a lot of deer tracks. He stopped the snowmobile and started walking. He could swear something was following him. He thought that maybe it was some kind of animal, maybe a wolf. Just then he saw a deer. He got one shot off and as he did he heard some kind of a scream. It was kind of eerie. He looked around with his rifle, ready to fire again at the direction where he thought the scream came from. He still could not see anything. He started to walk towards the deer that he shot. As Patty was advancing slowly, he started getting that feeling that someone or something was following him. So he spun around fast and fired two more shots in quick succession and again he heard that eerie scream. But he couldn't see anything. He went over to see the deer that he shot. He still didn't see anything. So he gutted the deer and left everything he cut out right there. He put the deer on the snowmobile and headed back to the Hideaway.

While driving back, he was scanning the territory to see if he could see anything but he saw nothing. Patty decided to hang the deer from a tree and cut it up in the morning.

When he went back to the cabin, he called Inu and explained to him what happened and the strange scream he kept hearing. Inu couldn't figure it out.

"It must be some kind of animal because there're no people around there for thousands of miles. You want me to come up and we'll check it out together?"

"No, I don't think that would be necessary."

After supper, Patty decided to turn in for he had a lot to do in the morning.

When he awoke the next morning he looked out that window to check on his deer and to his astonishment, he discovered the deer gone. He quickly dressed and went outside and looked around but could not find any clues on where it went.

"Now what?" he thought, "I'm going to take the plane to Hank's dockside to buy some bait. I'm going to catch that bastard," he thought to himself.

When he got to the dock he asked Hank what he had in mind. Hang suggested a large pork ham hock. "Whatever it is will love this. Let it stay hanging around in the cabin so it will smell a little. That will attract whatever it is."

"I hope it's a polar bear."

"How come, Patty?"

"Because I need a coat to keep me warm. You got a stronger rifle than a thirty-o-six?

"I sure do."

"Let me see it." He examined it and said, "I like it. I'll take it and give me plenty of ammunition."

After about a week Patty hung the ham hock from a tree close to his cabin so he could see. The following morning he went to check the bait and it was gone.

"That son of a bitch!"

He went right to his plane to start it and warm it up for he was going to buy more bait right away.

He spoke to Hank about his situation. "I'll take two hocks this time because I'm going to catch whoever it is that's doing this and give me some chain because I'm going to catch that thief. The only thing that I feel sad about is that it must be hungry.

When he got back, he set his trap right away and went back in the cabin to wait. It didn't take long when he heard that eerie sound again. He went out with his rifle and he could see something strange but he couldn't quite make out what it was. Yet it looked like big foot. He was tall like Patty. He had a large beard. Patty approached him closer. He now took out his pistol. As soon as he saw the pistol, he started screaming. It was the same scream as when Patty shot the deer. That's when he figured it was the gun that he was afraid of. So he fired the pistol and the thing went crazy with fear. Patty figured out that that's what he was afraid of, so he pointed to him to get on his knees, which he seemed to understand. He then cut a slice off the pork hock under the close stare from the thing and handed it to him to eat, which he did, and then he went inside and came out with a cup of black coffee and handed it to him.

"One thing I have to say to you is that you stink. Don't you ever take a bath?" The thing didn't know what he was saying but he had an idea. Patty said, "You smell like a cesspool and that's what I will call you – Cessy." Patty then went even closer to him and said, "You are Cessy," and he kept saying it to him over and over and then pointed to himself and said, "I am Patty. You are Cessy and I am Patty." After about a half a day of that, Patty cut the pork hock down and handed it to Cessy, unchained him and waved him off, which he did and everything went smooth – better than Patty thought.

After a short while had gone by, Patty realized that he missed him.

The following morning there was a knock on the door. Patty opened the door and there was Cessy standing there pointing to himself saying, "Cessy come in." Patty was cooking breakfast of bacon and eggs with beans and homemade bread. He told Cessy to sit down and he fed him. Cessy loved every bit of it and wanted more.

For the rest of the day, Patty taught him plenty of words. He taught him the difference between yes and no. Patty showed him to bring in more firewood and then he made chicken for supper and gave him plenty to take with him.

Weeks had gone by and Cessy was there everyday learning more each day. Patty even gave him a bath and shaved his face clean and he even gave him all fresh clothes. Now he looked like a brand new person. Now they would spend everyday together. They would even go fishing, which Cessy loved to do. Patty took him on his plane and they went to see Hank and got more supplies and plenty more food.

As time went by Cessy was speaking more and more English. Patty really liked having him around. Cessy told Patty that he had to leave. Patty gave him a sack full of food and he gave him a pork hock, which he loved.

The following day he did not see Cessy and was hoping that nothing was wrong. Three days had gone by and in the middle of the night while a fierce snowstorm was coming down, Patty heard Cessy calling for him. He opened the door and there stood

Cessy with a woman and a little baby about two years old.

Patty asked, "Are these new boarders?"

Cessy told Patty that his son was very sick and nothing was working that they kept trying on him. Patty took his temperature. It was 103°. He had all kinds of medicine. He called the situation into the hospital and they gave him instructions on what to do.

The following day, the fever started to go down. Patty looked at Cessy's wife and said, "What a stink, you smell like a septic tank and that's what we will call you Cepty." Between Patty and Cessy, they got her to understand what her name was. "But first she must take a bath and you help her Cessy."

She wouldn't take her eyes off Patty and her eyes would follow Patty around the cabin like some animal waiting to pounce on him. As the weeks went by, Cepty was speaking more and more English and would follow Patty and Cessy everywhere with Little Junior right behind them. Patty told them that they were going to go on a plane. They were going to go to town and do some shopping. Patty wanted to buy them more clothes. Cepty was all excited for she never was on a plane. Patty told her what they were going to do. He asked her, "You like?"

"I like Party," she answered. She never called him Patty. It was always "Party."

When they got airborne, Patty asked her, "What do you think – you feel like a bird?"

When they reached the town they were walking through when suddenly Cessy decided to run across the street. Patty yelled to him to stop but it was too late. Cessy was hit by a truck. When Patty and Cepty reached him, Patty kneeled down beside him to see if

there was anything he could do for him but he could see that he was dead. Cepty just stood there looking down on him. She looked at Patty and said, "Cessy no more."

Patty made all the arrangements with the local funeral director. He also put Junior in a private school and also contacted a private school for Cepty to learn to read and speak English. He put her in a boarding house and instructed her, "This is where you will live and I will come around to make sure everything is all right. He bought her all new clothes and sent her to a beauty salon to do her hair and nails and whatever, and then he went back to the cabin where he restocked the cabin with more food.

A month had gone by when Patty decided to go checking on Cepty and Junior to see how they were doing. When he arrived at the boarding house, he knocked on Cepty's door and Cepty answered the door and Patty was the most surprised person on earth. He wanted to say "Is Cepty here?" but that *was* Cepty, the most beautiful woman he ever met. He just couldn't believe it. Her hair was all done differently. She even had on lipstick.

She said, "Party you like?"

"I like very much."

Patty took her out for dinner and he explained everything to her. He would still send her and Junior to school.

Just then Inu came in. Patty had called him to meet at the restaurant. He was quite surprised to see that Patty had a woman. He introduced them to each other. Inu said to Patty that he knew how to pick 'em.

Patty explained to Cepty, "Inu and I are best friends and Inu and his family were half owners of the Alaskan mine."

"What we're going to do Inu, is come this spring, we're going to bring in some heavy digging equipment to go into the mountain and we're going to have to hire some help.

Inu said, "Why don't we try and do it ourselves, so we can keep it secret for a while so we don't get a stampede up there?"

Patty said, "We'll manage with us three till we get it started."

Patty noticed Cepty watching people dancing. Patty asked her, "What are you watching?"

She said, "I've never seen people do that before."

"They are dancing. I'll teach you how to do that. Come on, I'll show you."

He took her in a corner and started showing her how to dance and she said, "Me like."

Soon Inu gave Patty a tap on the shoulder. "I'm going to be going. I'll see you later."

"I'll call you," and they both waved goodbye.

"You want to stop?" Patty asked her.

"No, I don't want to stop." She was determined to learn to dance.

It was soon time to leave so they had to stop. "I'll come to town next weekend and we'll go dancing again, you like?"

"I like."

The following week, Patty returned to take her dancing again. But first he went to see her teacher to ask how she was doing.

She said, "She is doing fine, as a matter of fact, very good. By the way, there will be no school all next week because they have a week off."

"Good, I'll be taking Cepty back home and bring her back here again."

Patty said to Cepty, "Let's get going, I want to get back before it gets dark." Patty felt comfortable having Cepty with him especially since she could speak better English.

Patty said to her, "I just checked our food department and we could use some meat. What do you say we go hunting tomorrow?"

"Whatever you say Party. You're my boss now."

"We'll go early in the morning. You pack some food and I'll pack everything else. Cepty started to get ready for bed. She even brushed her teeth.

Patty said, "She even taught you that too?" Patty couldn't help staring at her noticing what a beauty she was and admiring her beautiful shape.

She asked Patty, "Where do I sleep?"

"We sleep together all the time."

When they got into bed, they did a lot of laughing. Patty said to himself, "I guess I won't be cold at night anymore." With that he gave her a kiss and that night was the first night they made love.

That night Patty had a hard time falling asleep. That's all he could think about was that he had made love to plenty of women in the past, but this was the first time he felt that he was a tiger.

Patty was awakened by the smell of bacon and eggs. Cepty had everything cooked. Even the coffee was ready. She had also put wood on the fire. Then she put everything on

the snowmobile that they had to take with them and then she hooked a trailer to the snowmobile and put his rifle in the trailer. Patty wore his pistol. They even brought extra blankets. Both of them dressed warmly.

After they had traveled quite a distance, Cepty said to Patty, "A snowstorm is coming."

"How do you know?" Patty asked.

"I could feel it," she said.

Let's stop a while and we'll make coffee. They had brought their portable stove. When they finished their coffee, Patty tried to start the snowmobile but for some reason it would not start. Patty covered the snowmobile with a canvas He carried in the trailer. Now it started snowing, She told Patty to gather as much firewood that he could and bring it here. "What are you going to do?"

"I'm going to start to build an igloo so we could have some cover. She started to hack out blocks of snow. Then she started to put them together and it was really shaping up.

When Patty returned with the firewood, he was quite surprised at the progress she was making. "You don't waste any time, do you?"

"We don't have much time. It's really starting to snow. Now you give me a hand so we can get this done."

She taught Patty how to cut the blocks and to place them on the igloo. "This is like laying bricks like I did back home."

After a while, with the snow coming down even harder now, the igloo was ready for occupancy. "All done Party. Let's bring everything inside and I'll light a fire so we can keep warm." They huddled together so they could keep warm during the night.

When morning came it was snowing harder and Patty said to her, "The igloo was a life saver."

Cepty made breakfast for them. Patty said, "As soon as snow stops, we'll go hunting for deer."

She pointed in the direction that the deer were. "How do you know that?" he asked.

"I can hear them."

When the snow stopped, that's the direction they took and sure enough Patty spotted one and he brought it down with one shot.

"I told you Party, they were here."

"You're pretty good."

Cepty said, "We bring it back and I'll cut it up."

"You can even do that when we get back to the igloo. I'll work on the snowmobile."

Patty worked on the snowmobile for quite a while but he couldn't get it started. He did find out that there was ice in the carburetor so he took it off and brought it inside hoping that the fire they had going would thaw the ice out. Patty had forgotten to put de-icer in the fuel tank but he had some in his toolbox. He explained to Cepty, "We'll keep it inside for the night and tomorrow I will install it in the snowmobile.

When the morning came, Patty tried starting the snowmobile and it started right up. He made sure he put the dry gas into the gas tank and he kept it running while Cepty made coffee. She had the deer all cut up and wrapped and ready to take back with them. They finished and they loaded the trailer.

"Are you ready to leave?" and she shook her head no. "Why?" he asked. She pointed to the ocean and she wanted to go that way. "Why?" Patty asked again.

"Bear over there. Big bear. I want bear to make a blanket for Party. Okay Party?"

"Let's go see first."

When they got to the ocean, Patty took out his binoculars and scanned the distance low and behold, he spotted one and made Cepty see for herself. She was all excited.

"Is that what you want?"

"Yes."

"Okay, let's go."

They drove as close as they could then approached the bear slowly and being cautious, walked very slowly. Then they both stopped for the bear spotted them coming and was getting ready to charge them when Patty fired and the bear dropped. They went to examine the bear and to make sure it was dead, which it was. All they had to do was get it on the trailer but Cepty said, "No, I will skin it here and then it will be easier to lift."

"What do we do with the rest of the bear?"

"We leave it. Other bears will eat it."

It took her no time at all to do it and they left right away because it would be too dangerous to stay around with the smell of the dead bear. As they were heading back to the cabin Cepty told Patty that there was another snowstorm coming and that they should hurry so they wouldn't get caught in this one. If they did, they could just build another igloo.

They were almost back at *The Hideaway* when it started to snow. Cepty was right again. Immediately, Cepty hung the bear fur out to dry. Patty reminded Cepty that she should get ready to leave tomorrow to go back to school.

"I will come back to see you. It won't be long and spring will be here. Then you will be back for the summer because I will need you to get more gold and I will be installing more machinery to go into the mountain. Inu is coming up also to help out and we will hire more help as well.

The next morning, Patty took Cepty back to school. He gave her a hug and a kiss, which she enjoyed. She waved and said, "Goodbye Party."

Patty went back to the dock and picked up more food supplies and plenty of it for he would need it for the extra people that they would have there. He just had to have the weather break. He contacted the dock and made arrangements to convert his plane into a seaplane. They asked Patty to come to the dock and they would fly him back and when his plane was finished, he could take his boat back to pick it up.

As the weeks went by, the ice started to break up and the weather was getting warmer. Patty called Cepty that he would be there to pick her up and also called Inu to hire the three guys who came up there before. Patty wanted those men to start building living quarters for about thirty people with separate rooms. He ordered all the materials that he would need. He wanted to start that project right away.

It didn't take long before everything was built. He also received all the equipment to start the digging into the mountain. He had Cepty in charge of the stream where they were still panning for gold and Inu in charge of the mountain digging and Patty would do the supervising. He even taught Cepty how to shoot and carry a pistol

If they found the mother load, he would have to hire plenty of security because once the word of the gold discovery was out there would be a stampede.

Patty asked Inu if he could stay with them in the cabin but he said that he would stay in the house that they had built. He said there was plenty of room there, and it was warm there. The mining was going right on schedule and it was just as Patty figured. They were taking a lot of gold out of the mountain. They hired more workers and plenty of security. They were patrolling the lake and guarding the rest of the property. They also had radar to see if people were coming in from the ocean. Patty, Inu and Cepty would have daily meetings. They paid their help triple than what they would make elsewhere. They were attracting college people who wanted to work at the mine.

Cepty told Patty that Junior was coming home for the summer and she would go pick him up with the plane. Patty had her take flying lessons and she was flying very well. They were having a house built in Nome. The house would have everything in it. It would even have an indoor swimming pool.

While it was being built, they would stay in the cabin and they would have to build another house near the mine.

They were now mining millions of dollars every single day of the week. Inu managed that part. Patty made good on his promise to John, the bank manager, and he purchased the bank and made John the CEO of the bank. He also gave him plenty of shares and a million dollars for being honest.

Everyone in Nome was happy about the Alaskan Mine Corporation. It was bringing plenty of work into the area. The mine was paying plenty of taxes. Patty and Inu were now millionaires. Cepty was very happy with Patty and she was in love with him, and they were always together. Junior was with them for the summer and he was speaking English very well.

One day the three of them went to town to go to a fancy restaurant and to check on the building of their house. Patty met with the contractor. Everything was on schedule. He told the contractor that he wanted a statue of St. Anne to be put in front of the house. He wanted a fountain put there too with beautiful flowers all around the statue of St. Anne. He didn't want to spare any expense.

A few years had gone by when Patty was asked to run for Senator. He said he would think about it and would let them know.

When they asked him if he had decided, he said, "I will not be able to run because I am too busy at the mine, but I will support the candidate who is running and I will donate a million dollars towards his campaign.

Patty and Cepty were planning a kickoff party at their new home for their candidate who was running for Senator. They had it all catered with plenty of food and champagne. A lot of important people would be there. Patty was friends with people from both parties and donated generously to both.

Patty was called to another room to meet someone when he heard a commotion coming from the room where he just came from and where he left Cepty. When he reached that room, he saw a crowd of people gathered around someone laying on the floor and he spotted Cepty there also. Patty asked her what happened and she said, "He grabbed my bum so I knocked him out."

"Good, I'm glad you did."

Inu was there and he said that he saw it all and that's exactly how it happened. Come to find out, it was the one who was running for Senator.

Right away, the members had a meeting and threw him out and said they would need someone else. Patty said, "I have someone who I would like to nominate."

"Who is that?" they asked.

"My good friend Inu." He was surprised to hear his name nominated and he did accept the nomination. Everyone congratulated him and made a toast to their next Senator.

Now, Patty would have a good friend in the Senate if he got in. Patty was sure he would because he would donate millions, if he had to, to make sure he got in. Inu's parents were very excited that their son had an opportunity to become a US Senator. They said, "Since Patty came here, he's made us wealthy and now he's got something to do with Inu becoming a U.S. Senator.

Three months had gone by and it was now election time. After they counted the votes, Inu won by a large margin. It wasn't even a contest.

"I told you so," Patty said to Inu. They rented a large hall and everyone was invited to an open buffet. Patty introduced Senator Inu to the crowd. After all, he was Inu's campaign manager. He gave a speech and explained to the crowd, "If you need me for anything, feel free to call me anytime."

Inu's parents were very proud of their son. Patty was happy about Inu being a U.S. Senator for if there were any changes by the bureau of mines, Inu would be on top of it.

They had hired a band for anyone who wanted to dance.

Inu said, "Patty, you have to do me a favor."

"Of course, what is it?"

"I haven't heard you sing in a long time. What do you say, could you fill that request?"

"For you, I could never say no."

So Inu announced that Patty would sing a song. Cepty was surprised that Patty could sing. "You sing?" she asked Patty.

"Just a little."

"Well, I'm going to listen to you."

Patty went on the stage and he announced that he would sing just one song and the title was *Never Been to Spain*. When the crowd heard him sing, they were surprised to hear the beautiful voice he had.

When he was finished, he received a big hand from the crowd, especially from Cepty who was clapping and jumping up and down. She ran up to Patty and gave him a hug and a kiss. "You my Party," she said.

Soon it was time to go home. Inu's parents went to say goodnight to their adoptive son.

The years had gone by and Junior was graduating high school. They were deciding which college he should attend. They finally decided to send him stateside. Patty said to

Cepty, "I know of a good college."

She asked "Which college?"

"Brown University in Providence, Rhode Island."

She said to Patty, "You are the boss. If you say it's good, that's good enough for me."

Patty told Junior, "We would like to see you go to Brown University in Providence, Rhode Island."

"That's fine with me."

So they applied at Brown and in a few weeks he was informed that he was accepted. So it was settled, Junior would enroll at Brown.

While Junior was at Brown, Patty and Cepty ran the mine and kept depositing the gold nuggets at the bank. Patty had the land cleared up the mountain for he was putting in a ski trail with a tram. He also hired a ski instructor to teach anyone how to ski including Cepty. The lessons would be free to the employees and the price to ski would be free also.

Patty would go skiing quite often with Cepty. One night he said to Cepty, "You know what I would like to do?"

"What?" she said.

"I would like to go hunting again with you."

"Okay."

"How about if we go during another snowstorm. I had a wonderful time with you last time."

"If you want to go in another snowstorm, there is a very big one coming."

"Let's leave tomorrow and I'll know we'll run into it."

The following day, they left early, this time they each had a snowmobile. They headed straight for their igloo. They wanted to get there before it started snowing. When they reached the igloo, the last time they had blocked the entrance with logs. This time Patty brought along his chain saw so he could cut more firewood. He said to Cepty, "What do you say we go for deer before we do anything else?"

"Okay," she said.

"Which way should we go?"

She pointed to a direction and sure enough they spotted some deer. He told her to shoot a deer, which she did. She wanted to cut up the deer where they were and they could take it back in the trailer.

The snow was coming down very hard now so they headed back to the igloo. Patty had some wood cut from last time and cut even more with the chain saw. It didn't take long at all to cut. He took a lot inside where Cepty had a fire going. She took all the cut up deer inside and they covered their snowmobiles with canvas that they brought along.

Cepty was making something to eat when she grabbed her pistol and went to the entrance. Patty didn't know what was happening and grabbed his rifle. He asked her what was happening,. She said, "Wolves are out there. They can smell the deer. I think you should build a fire to block the entrance to make sure that they can't get inside."

Patty cut a block of snow out because it was still light. He wanted to see if he could see anything. Sure enough he could see at least four of them. He said to Cepty, "I'm going to fire my rifle Maybe it would scare them away."

The sound of the rifle scared them away. Cepty said, "We keep the fire going in front of the entrance in case they come back and if the snow stops tomorrow, we'll leave."

The following morning, they decided to leave because the weather started to clear. Patty reminded Cepty to wear her pistol because if they run into the wolves and if they had to use their weapons, they would be there.

Patty had his rifle slung beside him on the snowmobile and he would lead, pulling the trailer. He said to Cepty, "I don't want to kill the wolves, but if they become a threat then we will have to."

They drove all the way back to their house and they did not run into the wolves. Waiting there for them were the hired hands. Patty instructed them to put the snowmobiles away and to take the deer meat inside. They informed Patty that Inu was inside waiting for them. Patty was glad to see Inu and asked him, "What's up?"

"I want to ask you something."

Patty had the cook make dinner for them. "Sure, we can discuss whatever's on your mind."

After dinner, Patty asked Inu, "What do you want to talk about, Senator?"

"To you, I'm Inu. How much money do we have in the bank right now?"

"Let's go into my office," and he took out the ledger book and showed it to Inu and it showed that they had about three hundred million dollars in cash. Patty reminded him, "Don't forget, half of it is yours. We are partners on everything. What's on your mind?"

"How would you like to build the biggest shopping mall in Nome?"

"I would like it very much. We don't even have to touch the money in the bank. We'll just increase production at the mine."

Inu said, "I can handle the purchase of the land and we can start everything else right away."

Patty gave Inu 20 blank checks to use as he needed. "Just tell me what you spend so we can balance the books. Are you getting your pay every week?"

"Yes I am."

They each receive $20,000 a week, not bad for two ex-Marines.

While Junior was at Brown University, Patty paid all of his college expenses. He sent him money as he needed and also bought him a brand new car.

After a while, Junior wrote home to tell them he had met a girl at school and that they liked each other very much. Cepty was happy to hear that.

The four years at college flew by very fast and it was almost graduation time. Junior called home asking Patty and Cepty if they would attend his graduation.

His mother said, "Of course we'll be there."

They made plans to fly to Brown and stay at a hotel in Providence. On graduation day, they went to see Junior. He wanted to introduce his girlfriend to Patty and Cepty.

When they met, she was a beautiful girl. Junior said, "This is my girlfriend, Anna DiMarco."

Patty had a stunned look on his face. He asked, "Who is your mother?"

"Isabella DiMarco."

"And where do you grandparents live?"

"They live on Branch Avenue and my other grandparents live on Luna Street."

Patty was shocked because unbeknownst to her, she was speaking to her own father. He hadn't seen his daughter in 20 years. He embraced her and she looked into his eyes, not knowing why he done that.

She noticed a tear in his eyes. She asked him, "What's wrong?"

"You are my daughter."

"But, I've never met you before."

"No, you haven't."

Anna couldn't believe it. Just then, her mother noticed someone hugging her daughter so she came over with her son to see what was going on. She immediately recognized Patty and said, "Patty where have you been?"

"Mother," Anna said, "he said that he is my father."

"Yes he is."

Now Patty gave her another hug. He looked at the boy next to his mother and Patty said, "You must be Patty."

"Yes, I am."

He was the spitting image of his father. Patty shook his hand. Isabella explained to her children that he was their father. She asked Patty again, "Where have you been for the past twenty years?"

"I'm living in Alaska right now."

"Who is this girl you're with?"

"This is my girlfriend, Cepty."

Cepty called Patty aside and said I'm going back to the hotel so you can be with your family and she left.

Isabella said to Patty, "Your father and sister are here. Why don't you go say hello?" She pointed where they were sitting. Patty walked over to his father and said to him, "Hi Pop."

Frank turned around and said, "Patty, I don't believe it!"

Anna Marie jumped up and gave him a hug. "Where have you been?"

"After graduation, we are having a party at my house. Make sure you're there."

"Can you give me a ride?"

"Of course. Wait for me when this is over."

"I'm not sitting here. I'm sitting on the other side."

When graduation was over, Patty went over to where his father and sister were and rode back to Patty's father's house.

When he arrived, everybody was happy to see Patty again, but all were asking the same question, "Where have you been?"

"All over, but I'm glad to be back with my family."

Patty asked his father where Mama was.

"Since you left, she hasn't been well. She stays in bed all the time."

Patty went to her room and stood in the doorway and said, "Hi, Mama."

She sat up and she was smiling.

He said, "Mama, I don't drink anymore." He walked towards her and got on his knees and gave her a hug.

"I know."

"How did you know that I quit drinking?"

"I saw St. Anne standing in the doorway with you. Help me out of bed, Patty."

"Do you think you can Mama?"

"Yes I can."

They walked together into the kitchen. Everyone was commenting on Mama walking again and the huge smile on her face.

Frank said to Patty, "You see what you've done. You've made your mother so happy to see you that she is walking again."

She couldn't take her eyes off of Patty. His brothers and sisters started to ask him questions and wanted to know where he has been living.

"I live in Alaska."

"Why way up there?"

"Because I now own one of the largest gold mines in the world."

His brother Tom said, "They had a large gold mind strike there!"

"I'm the one who discovered the gold mine."

Just then the phone rang and someone asked for Patty. It was a private detective Patty had contacted from Alaska. Patty had wanted him to check out St. Elizabeth's Church in New York. He informed Patty that the parish was doing very bad financially and being Christmas time, they were on the verge of being closed and only a miracle could save them.

Patty said, "Pop, can I use your office?"

"Go ahead."

He called St. Elizabeth's and asked for Mother Superior.

"Who's calling please?"

"I want to surprise Mother, is that all right?"

"Okay," she said.

Mother Superior got on the phone. "Who is this?"

"I will tell you Mother. Will you promise me you won't hang up until I'm finished?"

"I promise that I won't hang up."

"This is Patty DiMarco. I'm sorry for what I've done. I also understand the church isn't doing well financially. Well, I want to make a Christmas donation of five million dollars."

"Are you kidding me?"

"No, I'm not. You once told me that you wanted to have a soup kitchen. Get it started right away and I will send you money every month. Give me your address and I will send you a check right now. The name of the bank is on the check and the bank is in Nome, Alaska. You call there, Mother and ask for John Delaney. He's the CEO of the bank. Tell him I told you to call. Don't be afraid to call because I own the bank and I'll call you when I get back to Alaska."

"Thank you Patty and May God bless you."

Patty then called Isabella and his children in the office and had a talk with them first. He said, "I'm sorry how I treated you kids. That's all behind me now."

"Isabella, it must have been hard bringing up the kids alone. Again, I want to say I'm sorry." He took out his checkbook and wrote a check for one million dollars to each of them.

"That's a lot of money."

"I can afford it. If the kids need cars, I'll pay for them and I'll pay for a car for you too. I have to write more checks. Will you tell my father to come in his office?"

His father went right in the office. "What is it Patty?"

"I'm going to give you, my uncles and aunts, and my brothers and sisters a million dollars a piece."

"Patty, that's a lot of money. Where are you going to get that money?"

"I'm a multi-millionaire now and I want to give some to my family. Why don't you come to visit me in Alaska and I'll show you around." I sure will.

Patty wrote out all the checks to his family and went out in the kitchen and gave each one of his relatives a check.

"How can you afford this?"

"I just can. I'm going to leave now. I have to go see my girlfriend."

Henry asked, "Are we going to meet her?"

"Yes, I'll bring her here tomorrow. See you all later," and he left. He went back to the hotel. Cepty was lying on the bed. Patty tiptoed in the bedroom and he could hear Cepty crying. He went up to her. She looked up to him and said, "Party gone. Party no more. Why you come back?"

"I want to ask you something."

"What?"

"Will you marry me?"

She jumped out of bed and put her arms around Patty and said, "Yes, I marry you."

They embraced and kissed.

The End

Printed in the United States
73426LV00005B/30